FROM ANGELS TO ASHES

CONTENTS

PROLOGUE

The God's City blazed around her. She hid her face against the glare of the bronze buildings and sprinted ahead, away from the promise of safety. Away from *her*. The cobblestone streets scorched her bare feet as she knocked elbows with the townspeople, pushing them aside only when there wasn't a gap big enough to squeeze through. She glanced behind her only once, but the swollen crowd obscured anyone who might have followed.

The gate stood wide open. Merchants covered in sweat carried large crates on their backs and cursed at her in strained voices as she weaved between them. There, just on the other side, a little boy with wide brown eyes and freckles stood watching them intently. He hadn't seen her. Not yet. Her long dress caught under her feet. She was almost there.

High above her, the God watched from the top of his spire and grimaced. The hours that had been spent to make her look perfect were wasted. The hood fell as she quickened her pace, and long brown curls spilled out.

They would be dull and lifeless when the time came for the ceremony. He tilted his head back and let the dry liquor slide down. He enjoyed the hot bite of it against his tongue, the burning trek to where it coiled in his stomach. The glass clinked against the tray as he set it back down.

"Viero." His voice was sharp.

"Yes, Lord?"

"It was your daughter who was assigned to guard the angel. Have I been mistaken?"

"No—no, sir. You are correct. Has there been a problem?"

He turned in time to witness the warring expressions settle into one. Viero had a head of thick hair that covered an even thicker skull. The lines on his forehead and around his mouth had started to deepen with age, and they were full now with a concentrated tension. The God beckoned him closer and looked out the window. There was nowhere for her to go, even if she did make it past the gate. He wasn't worried. He was proving a point.

Viero scrambled away from the window, knocking over a pile of papers, and nearly breaking the opal owl that perched, lifelike, on the edge of the God's desk. He caught it in both hands.

"I'll have the watchmen called immediately," he said in a rush. "This was my fault. I'll take full responsibility—"

"See to it that you do."

Viero looked as if he wanted to say more but stopped himself. The owl scraped the desk as he hoisted its weight back up and rushed from the room. The top of the spire was made up of glass walls, so the wide spiral staircase in the middle of the floor was the only way in or out. The God placed his hand against the hidden pocket in his robe, feeling the book's familiar edge, and listened to Viero's receding footsteps before following him down. And down. And down.

When he finally reached the bottom, someone—he didn't pay attention to who—handed him a wet towel. He mopped it across the back of his neck before stepping out into the sweltering sun and looking around. The streets were congested with his people. The watchmen not guarding the clearing were ushering merchants back to their posts, where they would wait until the events of the evening were past and people were inspired to spend their coin.

His pace quickened as he passed into the circle of watchmen. The stake had been set up in the heart of the small clearing. The familiar excitement stirred in his stomach as he took his place beside it, scanning the crowd. They saw each other at the same time, and just as his lips arched into a smile, the angel's shaped to a scream. Her feet were tied together with rope, and she bucked wildly, swinging her weight between the two watchmen. One stuffed a rag into her mouth.

He had been right. Her auburn dress was tattered at the hem and ripped on the sleeves. It billowed out in front as her hands were forced behind her back and knotted around the stake. Her screams had stopped. Instead, a well of tears glistened from her eyes and dripped from her jaw. She was scanning the congregation with intensity, pulling against the rope.

The God raised his arms, and the congregation cheered. Babies resting on their mothers' hips smiled gummily up at them. Men with lean muscles and dark skin watched, enraptured, as he pulled the book from his robes.

"Today we honor our home and our futures. We know the histories." His voice boomed over the crowd, proud and commanding. "When an angel falls, they've been stripped of their wings. Our soil offers redemption. Will we give her redemption?"

The roar was deafening. He smiled through his mask of mercy and turned to her.

"You should be thanking me," he murmured.

Her forehead was slick with sweat as he laid his palm against it and pushed, forcing her head against the stake. Ice flooded his veins and with it came the familiar tingling that wrapped him like a cocoon. Her eyes, once full and dark, faded to the whites and basked him in heavenly light as her mind broke.

He could see. A million memories that were not his and a thousand faces he had never known flashed in front of him. The book burned in his hand, and he knew that what he could not commit to memory now, the book would absorb for him. He would come back to it later, hungry for what was not food, and fill his mind. The faces faded to flashes of green and blue, but it was only when the heat singed his whiskers that he turned away, cupping his hand against his chest. The rag must have fallen, because she screamed, long and terrible, before it choked off and was gone.

In her place was a pile of ashes. He turned to the congregation that seemed to him a lifetime away and lifted the Black Book in his good hand. Feeling their eyes on him, he began to read.

His flock listened.

I

PARTY

S yron took the turn too sharp. Her old '98 Toyota Corolla veered to the side, spilling the contents of her hastily packed bag across the passenger seat. She had buried her phone under a mound of clothes and toiletries. Now, it buzzed loudly and incessantly on top of the pile. She looked pointedly in the rearview mirror and wiped at her smudged mascara with a shaking hand.

The apartment complex was new and expensive looking. She followed the glare of the streetlights across the wet road to a parking space in the back. The pool and basketball court were off to her right. To her left was Will's building. A staircase dominated its center, separating the rooms across from one another with thick white plastic railings.

Taking a deep breath, she scooped up what had spilled and piled it back in the bag, tossed her keys on top, and slung it over her shoulder. She slammed the car door shut behind her and followed the whisper of music up the steps, eyeing the numbers on the doors. From this height, she could see the dog park high up on the hill, reserved for members of the complex, and rolled her eyes. Whatever he was paying for this place, it was probably way too much. Will didn't even have a dog.

Mr. Vermilion stood by the railing on the top floor. Will had warned her about his neighbor earlier that day, saying he was the reason they had to keep the music low and the parties indoors. She nodded politely and, finding Will's apartment number, rapped on the door.

"Tell them to mind their manners in there. And there's a limit to how many can stay overnight." Mr. Vermilion's voice was cracked with age, one wiry eyebrow shooting up as she glanced over at him and knocked louder, trying the handle.

"That boy is nothing but trouble if you ask me. Nothing but people coming and going. You ought to see more sense."

Will was mid-laugh when he opened the door. A rush of familiarity coursed through Syron as he leaned in for a hug, blond curls spilling across his forehead. He paused when he saw Mr. Vermilion and nodded at him, but the old man only grunted and tapped the ashes of his cigarette over the railing.

Syron pushed him back inside, following close at his heels.

"I was worried you wouldn't be able to make it," Will said, closing the door behind them. He took the bag from her shoulder and set it next to a pile of shoes. "We were waiting for you to play beer pong. I'm out a champion."

"I don't know if I'd call myself a champion," she said, looking up at him. "Maybe slightly above par."

Will rolled his eyes playfully and led her through the small hallway and into the kitchen and living room. It was one room, separated by only the couch back and carpet. Alice in Chains played on one of the two TVs, and in the kitchen Hayden and Zepplin were grabbing cups out of a plastic bag and arranging them on the beer pong table.

"Syron!" Zepplin squealed. She ran over with outstretched arms, her choppy black hair tickling Syron's nose as she hugged her.

"I thought you were going to stand us up!"

Syron blushed. "I promised I'd come, asshole. Where's Matt?"

"He canceled on us." Will had moved to the fridge and was holding a pitcher packed with floating fruit. He looked over his shoulder at her. "Guess he had better things to do."

Zepplin gasped and pelted Will in the back with one of the cups. It bounced off harmlessly, but he jerked to the side anyway, dotting the counter with jungle juice.

"It was his first day!" Zepplin protested.

"I was only joking!" He raised his hands in mock surrender and cast a conspiratorial look at Syron. "He started night shift at some bigwig company."

"At least someone has better things to do than hang out with you all day." Zepplin snatched up the bag of cups and started toward Will, who dodged the next throw and barreled through Hayden to the living room, barely missing the wires that lay in tangles across the floor. Syron caught the edge of the tattoo peeking over Will's shirt as Zepplin cornered him.

Syron's hands still shook as she picked a cup at random off the table and poured herself a drink. She preferred this to straight liquor, and she gulped it down quickly, relishing the sour tang it left in her mouth. She looked toward the hall without thinking. Her phone was undoubtedly still ringing. Whatever waited for her when she went home, she had no idea. She wasn't sure she wanted to know.

Hayden had walked over and leaned against the

counter beside her. He had graduated from college this past year and still wore the old university logo. "I'm glad you came. Will's been talking about you incessantly. It's actually getting kind of annoying."

Syron rolled her eyes. "That's some bullshit and a half."

"Swear to God," Hayden said, but his words were slurring. "He was going to call but didn't want to cause trouble. Can't say I disagree. Last time…"

He didn't have to finish. The last party she had gone to, Evyn was with her. He had seemed fine at first. It was only after he got some drinks in him that things started getting bad. It was one of the reasons Will had moved, and why he was so polite to Mr. Vermilion.

Syron poured herself another cup. "Evyn doesn't know where this place is. It's fine." It was, wasn't it? The location was off on her phone. She'd pulled off the side of the road to check. There was no way he'd find her.

"Syron!" Will yelled. She looked up. Zepplin's assault was over. Will perched on the couch, waving her over.

"Don't think about him," Hayden said. "His type doesn't know a good girl from a pile of shit on the ground." He tapped his cup to hers as Zepplin came up behind him and hugged his back.

Syron nodded awkwardly and went to Will. When she plopped next to him, he leaned forward, all blue eyes and toned muscles. She'd lost count of how many years they'd known each other, but it was still weird seeing him all grown up, and weirder still to think that if she hadn't known him before, he would be the type of guy she'd probably try to avoid. He looked almost too perfect.

He handed her his phone. "It's peeling, or I'd show you in person."

Syron looked down. The last time she had seen his tattoo, it was only the line work. The ointment on his chest made the demonic ocean glimmer in the photo. The artist had accentuated the rise and fall of his chest to make the waves swell, and inside was a clash between angels and demons. In the forefront, an angel that looked as if he were chiseled from stone raised his sword. The wings on his back were clipped and covered in blackish blood as he fought off the tide, but it was a losing battle. Mutilated body parts floated around him. In front of the angel, another stone head lolled on a swell, its forked tongue tasting the macabre waves.

She held the phone closer. Inside the waves were the tortured faces of the devil's advocates. They wound their way up the angel's chest, searing into him. Every detail was perfect, right down to the fighting in the distance.

"It hurt like a bitch," Will said under his breath. "Especially the sternum."

She touched his chest where she knew the angel's head would be.

"That's amazing, Will. Seriously. What made up your mind?"

He shrugged, but a smile played on the edges of his lips. "I didn't want it to just be the angels winning, you know? They're fighting over a man who doesn't want either of them. It makes more sense that they destroy each other."

She raised her eyebrows. She was *not* drunk enough for that.

"Is that what you're going to tell people when they ask?"

"Probably not," he said, laughing. "But I'm sure I'll figure something out."

She dipped her head to hide her smile. It was nice to hear his laugh again. Somehow, it made it seem as if everything were going to be okay. But that little voice in the back of her head still nagged at her. It had been months since they'd last spoken. Every time she had tried to reach out, the guilt would come back stronger than before, reminding her that she was the problem, the burden.

She itched for her phone.

Hayden toppled over the back of the couch, scattering her thoughts.

"I'll be right back." She left them like that, with Hayden's feet still in the air and Will trying to roll him to the side, and nearly ran past the kitchen. Zepplin was pouring shots from a particularly nasty-looking bottle of whiskey as she passed, only pausing long enough to scoop up her bag before shutting the bathroom door tight.

The space was small and cramped. She riffled through her bag and pulled out her phone. The screen was black—Evyn had stopped calling. She hesitated with her thumb over the screen and pressed her back against the door. Took a deep breath. When she opened her eyes, her reflection stared back. Long ebony hair fell in waves down her back. Large brown eyes made her look like a deer in the headlights, bridged by a nose that was too proud for the angles of her face.

She closed her eyes against the flush in her cheeks. She didn't have to call him, right? Whatever he wanted to say could wait until tomorrow. It wasn't a big deal anyway, not really. He knew Will and Zepplin and Hayden. It wasn't as if she were doing anything wrong.

There was a rap on the door.

"Almost done," Syron croaked. She tossed her phone in the bag and leaned closer to the mirror, wiping the wet from her eyes, when the door burst open and Zepplin stumbled in, beelining for the toilet.

"Sorry, Sy," Hayden said, rushing in after her. "She thought she could go shot for shot."

Syron gave a terse nod and scooted past him to the door.

"If she needs anything, just yell," she added as an afterthought, but he was already crouched by Zepplin's side and holding her hair back. Zepplin's back convulsed as Syron slid the door shut and took a shaky breath.

It didn't matter what Evyn thought. She had come here to have fun.

The song changed as she rounded the corner. Will was still on the couch, his head bobbing along with the music. She turned instead to the counter and poured two shots from the half-empty bottle. She held her breath for the first one and swung her head back. It was stronger than anything she was used to, but that was good. The other shot she carried to the living room. Will jumped when she touched his cheek and he grabbed her hand, but he must have realized who she was because he let her tilt his head back. A set of ocean eyes stared up at her, and when she tapped her lips, he understood.

He squeezed his eyes shut as she poured the shot. The dark liquor arched in the air and hit his chin before going in his open mouth. She suppressed a smile and ran to the hall, pausing only to set the glasses on the table, and slid on her shoes.

The night air was chilly against her bare skin. Mr. Vermilion was gone, and it took Will until the second set of stairs to catch up with her.

"Are you running away?" he asked, thrusting a jacket into her arms.

Syron ran her fingers over the rough leather before pulling it on. "Kind of. I needed some fresh air."

"So giving me a shot and leaving is how you ask me to come with you?"

She could hear the smile in his voice and shrugged, glancing over. He hadn't grabbed a jacket for himself, and his arms were pressed tight to his sides, hands buried deep in his pockets. "You didn't have to come."

He smirked from beneath his curls. "Like I had a choice."

She rolled her eyes and ran ahead. It was the first time she'd been here, but it was easy enough to cut across the parking lot to the path that led to the pool. She hopped the low fence in a single stride.

"There's a camera in the corner," Will said, landing hard behind her. "If we stay on this side, we should be fine."

She nodded absently and plopped down at the closest table, looking around. The apartments were situated next to the interstate on one side and the edge of the forest on the other. They were far enough away from the city lights that the buildings didn't obscure the night sky. Millions of stars shone brightly above them, and what was most likely a satellite blinked up to their left.

The thick scrape of the tarp drew her eyes away. Will had pulled it away from the water's edge, and the lights in the pool made the water glow blue.

"Aren't they supposed to turn those off?" she asked.

"Guess not." He rolled up the edge of his pant legs and slipped off his shoes. The chair squeaked under her weight as she got up to join him. The cool water lapped gently at her ankles, slipping up to her calves as she settled in.

She leaned her head against his arm. "How long has it been since it's just been us?"

"Hmph. Probably when we drove up to Centralia. Do you remember that guy—"

"The homeless one?"

"—that chased us off with a hammer?" He laughed and shook his head. "I thought we were going to bite the dust."

"Who even says that?" Syron giggled.

"Me." He nudged her. "*I* like it."

"Of course *you* do" She laughed. Their feet created wrinkles in the water's surface, disappearing beneath the tarp as the seconds stretched. She could sense something in the silence between the chirping of the crickets and Will's steady breathing. She took a deep breath.

"Just say it," she whispered, and looked up at him.

His lips parted and closed again. Instead, he took her hand. The bruises had faded from purple to green, but they were still there. His fingers brushed them gently.

"I hate him," he whispered back.

She thought about it. "I think I do too."

"Then why—" He broke off as Syron lightly touched his arm. Something was moving in the forest behind him. Syron leaned back, following what looked to be a flash of blue past the tree line. It looked distinctly…human.

"Will? Something's out there."

He turned, but whatever it was had disappeared. "Listen, if you don't want to talk about Evyn, you can tell me. I just want you to know I'm worried…"

His voice faded into the background as she spotted it again, closer this time. She grabbed his arm and pointed, holding her breath as it retraced its steps and darted out of view.

"It was probably just the groundskeeper or something," Will said, but he didn't sound certain.

Syron shook her head. She was itching to find a way

out of the conversation about Evyn, and besides, something about the figure seemed to draw her to it. "It's too late to be the groundskeeper, and it's off the property. Come on." She tugged at him.

He rolled his eyes but let her pull him up. As soon as he grabbed his shoes, she ran for the fence and propelled herself over it, landing in a strip of freshly mowed grass.

"Did you see which direction it went?" Will called, jogging to catch up.

"I think so."

As soon as he reached her and took out his phone, she started forward, with Will close at her heels.

The forest was loud around them. The bob of Will's phone light distorted her shadow against the thickening trees. She tried to follow the direction of where she had seen the light, but everything looked the same. She quickened her pace, barely avoiding the gnarled roots.

"This isn't just to avoid what I was saying, is it?"

The hoot of an owl startled her. A distant part of her mind screamed that she should turn back, that no good could come of running headfirst into the forest after dark, but something intangible urged her forward, drowning out the voice of reason.

"I promise we can talk about it later, okay?" Heat rushed to her cheeks. They were deeper now. She couldn't see the apartments anymore. "I know what you think about him, but he has a good side too."

Will muttered something unintelligible and grabbed her arm. She whipped her head to him, but his face was hidden in shadow.

"Sy," he said, his voice strained. "Look."

She spun where he pointed the light. Just ahead, a little girl peeked from behind the base of a tree. A halo of frizzy hair framed her face. She chuckled.

Syron gasped and took a step back. She could see the darkness through her, as if she were barely there. The bluish-white glow that surrounded her illuminated the forest floor as she glanced behind her and back at them, questioningly, and ran deeper into the forest.

Syron didn't realize she was clutching Will's arm until she let go. She swallowed.

"You don't have to come with me if you don't want to."

Will had turned off his phone light. Her own voice sounded too loud in the darkness. Logically, she knew they should turn back, but a burning curiosity urged her forward. The little girl was already far ahead of them, her dress flying behind her.

His hand slipped into hers and led the way. They were running now, trying to keep up. Every rustle of the leaves sent a little thrill through her, and when the treetops thickened so they couldn't see the stars, she tried to remember how big the forest was, where it led out to, but she couldn't remember. Hell, even if they turned around now, she doubted they would be able to find their way out.

The girl's light was gone. Syron kept her eyes strained forward as Will stepped high on top of a thicket of brambles. They scraped against her jacket as she clambered up behind him and down the other side. In front of them, the forest opened into a small meadow. Leaves sprouted from the surface of a pond that reflected the silver moonlight. The little girl stood waist deep in its center, cupping a purple lotus flower to her chest. The tangled roots that draped across her dress stretched easily as she held it out to them.

A part of Syron wanted to run. If she turned away, she doubted the girl would follow. They would find their way out, sooner or later, and be back safe and sound in Will's apartment. Maybe take a nice shower. But a larger part of her wanted to *know*. She took a step closer.

"Syron," Will hissed.

"Come with me." She let go of his hand. Whether he did or not was his decision. The freezing water reached her knees as she waded in with her. The girl's radiant skin soaked in the moonlight as she smiled, and Syron thought vaguely that it was a curious smile filled with innocence and knowing before she placed the flower in Syron's outstretched hands. The girl's fingertips, where they brushed hers, were cold.

Syron looked back at Will, who had taken off his shoes and was dipping a foot in the water. The sultry, floral aroma wafted up, and she held the flower closer to breathe in its scent. The ends of the petals curled delicately around its center as her hands started tingling. The electricity traced its way up her arms, spreading to the crown of her head and soles of her feet. The sounds of the forest grew until they were almost deafening, and behind it all was the slow, steady pull of the water.

She looked up at the strange, glowing girl. Panic clutched at her chest and she tried to shove the flower back at her, to drop it into the vibrating cool of the pond, but her body wouldn't listen. The world started to blur. She felt herself falling, twisting, rising, and she closed her eyes against it.

When she opened them again, the tingling was gone. Treetops grazed the soles of her shoes. She looked down at her body, suspended in air, and ran her hands over her chest, her legs. Her heartbeat thudded wildly. Around her, the forest stretched for miles in every direction. Far to her left was the apartment building. One light still shone in the upstairs window.

She looked below her. Another girl that looked just like

her but was not her—it couldn't be her—handed the flower to Will, and next to them the little girl was staring up at the night sky. The light in her eyes waxed and waned before she looked away.

Above the treetops, something cold and infinite yanked her backward.

2

SAHIIT

L ike a giant hand had gripped her midsection and tugged, the air whooshed from her lungs. Syron glimpsed the city, the soft curve of night around the towering buildings that shone like beacons, and felt the numbing cold of altitude that ate through her clothes. Her breaths, when they came, were pale plumes of smoke.

The cold faded to nothingness as the pressure on her stomach ceased. She cradled her throbbing head in her hands and counted her breaths to steady herself.

The empty expanse of space had swallowed her whole. Faraway stars burned steadily, but their light did nothing to break up the inky blackness. It was so thick and full that when she lifted her arms, she half expected them to come away stained.

I'm dreaming, she resolved. *That's the only way this makes any sense.*

Somewhere along the way she had lost her shoes. After all, who needed shoes in a dream? Slowly, tentatively, she wiggled her toes. She tried to walk, to run, but if she moved at all, she couldn't tell.

She pinched herself. It certainly didn't *feel* like a dream.

Then the pressure was back, propelling her forward. Wisps of hair tickled her face and neck. She angled her body with it, letting it guide her. A lick of light, bizarre next to the faraway stars, appeared in the distance.

She recognized the slope and curve of the brick building as she got closer. Old, grated windows looked out to the streetlight, which illuminated the solitary figure that marched up the sidewalk. Bangs hid his eyes as the bag slid off his shoulder. He stumbled and caught himself against the door, fumbling with the lock.

Syron's chest tightened. She landed on the solid pavement and followed him inside, narrowly dodging the door when he swung it shut behind him.

He hadn't seen her.

Their apartment was just as she'd left it. Dishes were piled high in the sink, waiting to be scrubbed. Two full garbage bags lay propped against the kitchen wall, and through the doorway to the living room, old Chinese takeout littered the coffee table. She grimaced. Even in a dream, he couldn't be bothered.

Evyn ran a hand through his hair and disappeared into the bathroom. Her eyes skirted from the door to the bag. She remembered how long it had taken to sew the patches on just right, how giddy he had been when she'd given it to him. Now, something wet and reeking soaked through the bottom. It made streaks on the carpet as she pulled it closer to peer inside. A bottle of absinthe was tilted sideways, its cap missing. She riffled through, oblivious to the wet, but there was nothing besides soaked clothes and ruined cords. His phone must have been with him.

She pursed her lips. He hadn't told her he was going anywhere. *He might have,* a voice in her head whispered, *if you had just picked up the phone.* Almost as an afterthought, she unzipped the front pocket of the bag. It was wide and deep, and she'd almost convinced herself she was just curious when she pulled out a handful of condoms.

She let the slippery foil fall through her fingers and pushed the bag away. How long had it been since they'd used condoms? The splinter of something deep inside her chest made her eyes burn. She gritted her teeth, fighting back tears, and kicked the bag.

The bathroom door swung open and cracked against the wall. She whirled toward it. Evyn had stripped down to his socks. His cock was hard and swung to the side as he rounded the corner. She covered her face reflexively, hunkering down. She knew how this would go. Rough hands would grip her wrists and pull them back painfully, trapping them over her head. Evyn would scream at her, crocodile tears dripping on her cheeks from where he'd climb on top of her, and just like when he'd lost his job, or thought she was flirting with the waiter, or anything else, there would be more bruises. Always by accident, always swollen and purple until they healed, and it would end with her apologizing.

But nothing happened. She looked up through splayed fingers. He wasn't looking at her. He was focused instead on the condoms, strewn across the floor like a sick joke. He spit in his hand. Disgust and, she hated to admit it, fear forced her eyes to follow his clumsy walk to the window. His shoulder pumped.

She tore her eyes away, but she couldn't stop his ragged breathing. She cupped her shaking hands around her ears and hummed to drown it out, rocking back and forth on the cold tile.

She didn't know how much time had passed, but when she found the strength to open her eyes again, Evyn was gone. A woman sat cross-legged on the floor across from her. Her wrinkles were deep and full, and the bright orange fabric of her dress made her dark skin look darker. A worn shawl covered her shoulders.

Syron heard a faraway whisper that quickly grew to an echo.

"This is your home?" It came from the woman, she was sure, but her mouth hadn't moved. She met Syron's wide eyes with her knowing ones.

Syron shook her head. Whatever this place had been to her once, it wasn't anymore.

The woman offered a soft smile, and with it came the whisper of memory.

"Have we met before?" Syron asked. She was confident they hadn't…but something about her was strangely familiar.

The woman's smile widened to show gaps in her yellowed teeth.

"Many do not remember me." There was no echo this time.

Syron opened her mouth to ask who she was, how she knew her, when the ceiling lifted soundlessly and toppled to the side. The walls reared backward like a stage set and fell away into the star-speckled sky. The floor shrank and re-formed so instead of tile, they sat on an ancient Persian rug, the metal feet of a cauldron leaving indentations in the center. A ladle lay next to it.

The woman raised her hand, and everything exploded. Streaks of luminescence shot down like lightning and flavored the blackness with pinks and purples and blues, mingling with other colors Syron didn't have a name for. Clusters of pure, white light conjoined with some and bounced off others. It happened so fast, and it was so chaotic and beautiful, that she shot to her feet, turning in a circle to sear it into her memory.

When she looked down at herself, her skin was like a mirror.

"Are you controlling this?" Syron asked.

The woman's laugh brushed against Syron's mind like a breeze. Syron sat back opposite her, the light doing somersaults in the woman's eyes.

"Me?" she asked aloud in a voice like cracked pepper. "I am only the Watcher. Everything you see here is our reality."

"I thought I was dreaming."

The Watcher smiled again, almost sadly. She picked up the ladle and dipped it into the cauldron. At first, Syron thought it was a piece of the sky held inside, but the surface wrinkled when she drew it out.

"Do you know why I brought you here?" She handed the ladle to her.

Syron accepted, careful not to let it spill, and shook her head.

"I showed you what was happening at present. Evyn couldn't see you, of course, but I wanted you to understand the danger before we met face to face. He's waiting for you now. The moment you walked through that door, well…every star burns brighter before it dies. Yours was blinding.

"I decided to give you a choice." She nodded to the ladle in Syron's hands. "If you refuse, everything will go back to the way it was. You'll walk through that door the same as before, but you won't walk out again."

Syron's thoughts twisted and warped around themselves, dizzying in the eclectic light. She cleared her throat. "And what if I drink?"

"You will have a second chance."

She didn't offer anything more, and Syron didn't ask. She stared down into the water. If her future was truly written in black and white—if Evyn would really hurt her so badly she couldn't recover—then was it really even an option?

"And Will? He was in the water with me."

When she didn't answer, Syron looked back up. The Watcher's lips were parted as if she wanted to speak but held herself back. Syron thought for a moment, picturing Will mid-laugh, how his nose had scrunched up when she'd poured the drink in his mouth, his hand in hers. The cold metal brushed her bottom lip. If he couldn't be with her, at least he would be safe.

"What about you?" Syron whispered. "Will I forget again?"

The wrinkles around her eyes deepened. The Watcher leaned forward and eased the ladle higher, pouring freezing water over Syron's tongue. She gulped it down.

"You never forgot," she whispered back. "There was just no reason to remember."

Syron opened her eyes to darkness and sat up groggily, wiping at the grass stuck to her face. The full moon was half-hidden by clouds, but enough of its light peeked through to illuminate the blue lake. The water was clear enough to see through to the thin roots that stretched like vines to the bottom. At their tips, the petals of lotus flowers were shut tight.

She scooted her bare feet away from its edge and looked around. Forested hills rose on either side, and behind her a dirt road led to a cluster of houses not too far away. They were old and leaning, and as she climbed to her feet and walked close enough to see the layers of chipped paint and boarded-up windows, she paused.

Wherever she was, it wasn't anywhere she was familiar with. Will's jacket slapped against the back of her thighs and she shrugged it off, tying it around her waist. She tried not to think about Will or Evyn as she climbed the warped steps, or about the woman in the sky as she peered through the window. A layer of dust covered it from the inside, too thick to see through.

The front door swung open easily. She scrunched her nose against the smell of mildew and stepped inside the small living room, empty except for a couch and coffee table. Blackened flowers drooped out of a vase in its center.

The kitchen was across from her, and a small hall to the left led to the bedrooms and bathroom. She peeked in each one and circled back to the kitchen, hoisting up the windows to let in the warm night air.

She was reaching for the kitchen window when something thumped beneath her feet.

Syron froze, her hand still outstretched. Her eyes went automatically to the front door. It was still wide open, looking out to the houses across the street. Another thump, followed by rough voices. A muffled scream.

Right under her feet, a man was laughing.

Had the floor creaked when she'd walked through? She couldn't remember. Slowly, carefully, she got to her hands and knees and pressed her ear against the floor. The voices were gruff and deep, but she couldn't make out what they said.

Something slammed behind her. She jumped to her feet and peered through the little window just above the sink.

"Fucking sahiit bit me!"

The doors of a hatch in the backyard were wide open.

Two hulking bald men stalked out, one gripping his forearm.

"Careful there, brother. You're bound to get rabies."

"They…don't have rabies, do they?"

The one without the bite turned and Syron ducked, holding her breath. The doors slammed shut.

She counted to thirty and poked her head up. They were walking in the opposite direction from the lake, heading farther into the open. She watched them until she couldn't tell their shapes from the dark and leaned back. She had been stupid, and lucky. So incredibly lucky. She stared at her hands where they clutched the kitchen sink and unlatched them by an act of will.

She should run. She had seen the direction they went; she could just go the other way, far away. Whatever was in the cellar wasn't her concern. No one would ever know.

But she had heard the scream.

She crossed to the front door, keeping her hands in fists by her side. Everything was dark and quiet. She hugged the side of the house, listening for anything that might give someone away, but there was nothing. Whoever those two were, they must have come alone.

There was no lock on the cellar door. The hinges squealed as she pulled it open and looked back the way they had gone, checking for…what? They're gone, she scolded herself. You *watched* them leave.

A dim light came from below. She kept her eyes forward as she followed it down, her bare feet tapping against the concrete steps. It opened to a rectangular room fashioned from concrete blocks. A table and chairs had been pushed into a corner, and against one wall was a wire rack full of rags and purple vials.

In the center, six sets of eyes glared at her. Their wrists had all been chained to a single post connecting the floor and ceiling, and their mouths had been stuffed with rags. They looked nearly identical: tall, slender bodies, wide eyes, and pointed, downturned ears. Their light gray skin was mottled with delicate patterns.

Syron took an involuntary step back. Whatever the Watcher had meant by a "second chance," this was definitely not what Syron had expected. Her head buzzed with the enormity of the choice she had made, especially given how unclear the implications had been.

A man in the back rattled his chains and strained toward her. A collection of dark gray markings gathered on his forehead over fiery eyes and thinned to a line along the bridge of his nose. Syron maneuvered closer to him, pulled out the rag, and backed away.

He spit off to the side and spoke. His voice was honey soaked in salt, curving beautifully in a language she didn't know. He sneered at her and looked over his shoulder, toward a woman with long dark hair and golden eyes. It took Syron a moment to realize he hadn't been speaking to her. They were staring hard at each other, the rest watching, before the woman lifted her manacled wrists and beckoned her closer.

Syron made a wide berth before pulling out her gag too. It landed sopping at her feet.

"What Briar meant to say," she said in perfect English, "was thank you. My name is Naveen. Judging by your expression, I'd wager it's your first time seeing one of us?"

Syron hesitated. "The man outside said a sahiit bit him."

Someone chuckled through their gag, but Naveen's mouth thinned to a line. "They'll get much worse than that when we get our hands on them. But that's better left for a different day."

She raised her manacled wrists to point to the wire

rack on the wall. "Those vials can melt the chains. It's a finicky poison the temporals are quite fond of. If you would."

Syron was back in seconds and unlatching the top. It reeked of ammonia and metal. She held it away from her, eyeing them warily.

"Why were they after you? Why bother to chain you up and leave?"

The man with fiery eyes, Briar, yelled something in that strange language, and Naveen bared her teeth at him. He backed down, but still stood up as far as the chain would let him. Even half-crouched, he was almost as tall as her.

"They were looking for someone, and we got in their way. It's a miracle they hadn't found her, really. All you need is to pour one drop," she continued, moving her hands as far to the edges of the manacles as she could, "and I'll do the rest. Put it directly in the middle, but be mindful not to touch it.

"They won't leave us here for long," she said when Syron hesitated. "If they find you, you'll be tied up with us."

Syron searched her golden eyes. Carefully hovering the vial over her wrists, she let one drop fall. The shackle sizzled and crumbled into dust.

The hand she extended to Syron was twice the size of her own with long, slender fingers. She placed the vial in them. Naveen was quick to free the others, saving Briar for last. He rubbed his wrists as Naveen let the bottle fly. It shattered against the table, eating away at the wood until only a few black shavings remained.

Out of all of them, there was only one sahiit who stood out. He was shorter than the others, only a head taller than herself, with a paler complexion and a crop of shocking white hair. She looked away sheepishly when he glanced up.

"Now then," Naveen said after all the gags were out, "you've met my brother, Briar. This is Calais, Zariah, and Yira. Leon's off in his own world again." She nodded to each of them in turn. The boy she had been watching, Leon, appeared deep in thought.

Yira moved forward and took her hands, guiding her to the floor. Impressionist leaves colored her left temple and cheekbone. The others formed a tight circle around them. She looked back up at Naveen, who only nodded politely.

"We owe you a debt equal to your kindness. What is your name, fallen?" she asked, still holding Syron's hands.

She gave it, albeit in a whisper.

Yira seemed to decide something, and flipped her hands so their palms were touching. She closed her eyes. "Syron, whatever you do, don't pull away."

Before Syron could object, the tingling started in her hands and spread outward, sending a chill up her spine before coiling at the base of her neck and rising to the crown of her head. She remembered the little glowing girl with the lotus flower almost by instinct and shied away from it, scared to be whisked back to the place with no name, the place where her skin shone like glass.

"Does it hurt?" Yira whispered.

"No," she whispered back.

"Good, I did it right this time," she said, chuckling. "But it's easier if your eyes are closed."

How she knew they were open, Syron couldn't tell. Yira's consciousness was a light pressure in her skull as she squeezed them shut, and behind her eyelids something flickered. The image materialized into a vast wilderness in the cloak of night. In the star-speckled sky streaked a single meteor. She felt Yira's focus shift, and together they watched as it plummeted down to the soft earth, toward a lake. At the lake's edge lay a girl with alabaster skin and long black hair fanned over the grass.

The image faded as Yira pulled away. When Syron opened her eyes, the room was empty except for them and Naveen.

"This is her first night," Naveen said. It wasn't a question.

Yira got to her feet in one lithe motion and nodded. "If she'd gotten here minutes before, the watchmen would've seen her."

"Who are the watchmen?" Syron asked, only half paying attention. Her head was spinning. None of it made sense. None of it should have been *possible*.

"When a meteor falls, it marks the passage of an angel. Those men were the watchmen sent to collect you. They were so close." Naveen said, then laughed, almost to herself. "I wonder how disappointed the God will be when they come back empty-handed."

"An angel?" Syron croaked. She cleared her throat. "I'm not—"

"I know it's a lot to take in, but we have to leave. They'll be back any minute, and trust me, they'll do worse than chain you to a post."

In a haze, Syron allowed herself to be pulled to her feet and followed them back up the steps and out of the cellar. The group of sahiit waited at the entrance, skimming the dark for any signs of danger. At Naveen's arrival, they gathered behind her and let her lead them back across the meadow toward the lake, avoiding the road.

She had to jog to match their long strides, every few steps glancing over her shoulder to make sure they weren't being followed. Despite Briar, who was glaring at her from the side, she had to admit she was glad she wasn't alone.

Wandering around in the middle of the night by herself would lead her to trouble sooner rather than later, and it didn't sound as if the God were someone she wanted to meet.

Her arm swung into someone by her side.

"Sorry," she mumbled.

"It happens." The boy with white hair slipped something into his pocket. "I heard them say it's your first night here. What do you think so far?"

She watched the dark heads bob in front of her. "I think," she said slowly, "that you guys don't have rabies."

She cracked a smile at his quizzical expression and waved it off. "I think it's nothing like where I came from. It's not all buildings and people, for one thing. And it doesn't smell like piss."

He laughed under his breath. "That sounds terrible."

"It was pretty gross."

She dipped her head to hide her smile and watched him from her peripheral vision. He seemed content to match her pace, glancing up periodically at Briar.

"It's Leon, right?" When he nodded, she continued. "Do you mind me asking what happened back there?"

"You mean us getting chained up, or what Yira did?"

She hesitated. Questions converged on the tip of her tongue, but she bit them back. Hopefully, there would be time for that later.

"I meant more like…how did you guys end up there?"

He grimaced and kicked at the ground. "We were scouting. A contact in the God's City told us an angel would be falling soon. We were trying to get to you before they did, but either he withheld information or didn't know they'd send as many as they did. Either way, the intel we got was bad."

"So, they ambushed you?"

"There were a lot more when it happened, but yeah. They're still out there, somewhere. Looking for you."

He said it all so matter-of-factly, she didn't notice the group had stopped until she ran into someone. The girl's face was awash with freckles, her scarlet hair fanning around her waist in tight ringlets as she turned, but Syron's eyes slid past her. Three black silhouettes stood knee-deep in the lake, their hands resting on its surface. A fish splashed to their right, breaking it into a thousand gleaming ripples. Their hands traced the rise and fall perfectly.

"What are they doing?" Syron whispered.

The girl she had bumped into, Calais, leaned over. "They're opening it," she said, and plopped on the ground.

"Opening…the water?"

Calais rolled her eyes and patted the space next to her. She waited until Syron sat to speak again.

"You don't understand our world yet, but you will. It's too dangerous to walk all the way home with temporals on our land, so they're making a doorway."

Syron blanched.

Calais pulled her knees to her chest and stared out at the lake. "Most everything can be made into a doorway," she continued. "Water is the hardest, but it's a lot faster."

"Why water?"

"Because it was here before the world was created," Leon answered, taking a seat beside her so they formed a half circle. "It has memory. Controlling something with memory is like controlling a person. It takes a lot of practice."

The clouds over the moon parted, revealing the outline of fragmented diamond markings that gleamed on one side of his face before Calais leaned over and punched him.

"Stop it! You're going to freak her out."

His eyes crinkled when he laughed. "You expect me to baby an angel?"

The sudden clash of waves turned their attention back to the three in the lake. The water dipped and surged in perfect synchronicity with their circling arms, rushing up past their waists until their arms swung again and the water was sucked back into the center. With each pass the water rose higher and higher until it reached their necks. When it crashed to the center again, they thrust their arms forward, palms out, and the lake thinned and stretched to a sheet of silver that touched the sky.

"Hurry!" Yira panted. "We can't hold it!"

Before she could move, a rough hand grabbed Syron and yanked her to her feet, pushing, then almost carrying her through mud that felt like quicksand and pulled her down with every step. She risked a glance behind her. Naveen, Briar, and Yira were running to catch up, their faces a mask of concentration and fear.

"Faster," Leon gasped in her ear, throwing up chunks of mud as he let her go and raced ahead. She barreled after him, barely noticing her distorted reflection before the cold swallowed her whole.

3

THIRD EYE

Syron narrowly avoided landing on her face when three bodies piled on top of her, pushing her deeper into the tall grass. They cursed and untangled themselves while she was still trying to catch her breath.

When she managed to sit up, someone was whimpering. The water had brought them to the edge of a forest in front of a wide field that stretched for miles. A single light shone in the distance. She turned away from it, scanning the dark for the source of the noise and found Naveen cradling her arm against one of the enormous trunks. Even in the darker shade of the trees, her shoulder stuck out painfully. Zariah was crouched next to her, her hands hovering just above it. Naveen said something through clenched teeth and leaned her head back, breathing hard. As soon as she closed her eyes, Zariah grabbed hold of her wrist and pulled her arm forward and straight. Syron flinched as it popped back into place and Naveen hissed.

"We'll get you some ice for it at home," Zariah said. When Naveen didn't answer, Zariah nudged her with her foot. "It's your arm that's fucked up, not your legs. We need to keep moving."

When she turned, it was to glare directly at Syron. Zariah's hair had been pushed back from her face, allowing Syron to see the scars where before they had been hidden. Half her face was smooth and beautiful with a dimpled chin and pouty lips. The other half, the half that made Syron want to run away to avoid her fury, was pockmarked with patches of skin that had been burned and healed over. A crescent-shaped scar curved over them to her jaw, just missing her eye.

"When we get there," she growled, "keep your mouth shut. I'll do all the talking."

She stormed past, knocking hard into Syron's shoulder and rocking her off balance. Syron clenched her jaw and stared after her, struggling to control the sudden wash of anger that threatened to spill to her lips. Beside her, Calais sighed.

"Just ignore her. That's what we all do."

"Does she talk to everyone like that?"

"Like shit? Pretty much." Calais pulled her shirt tighter around her. "Come on, I'm freezing."

The light Syron had seen earlier ended up being a lamppost next to a shoddy little shed. The wood was gapped and uneven, with rusted metal hinges where the door should've been. There was no way they would all fit inside, much less whoever Zariah had expected to be there.

Leon ducked through first, followed by Naveen. Syron hung back as the others trailed in, watching curiously, when a hand wrapped itself around her arm. She tried to jerk away, but Zariah's grip was firm as she pulled her, stumbling, through the doorway.

She squinted against the sudden light and drew her free hand up against it. The shed was gone. In its place was a large room lined with bookshelves and rows of tables. Zariah pushed her into the nearest chair and leaned on the table in front of her, blocking the view of the doorway. The rest of the sahiit were already seated. Syron rubbed at her arm and looked back the way they had come, but where the shed should have been was only a plain wall.

She squeezed her eyes shut to fight off the wave of nausea and laid her head on the cool table, focusing on her breathing. With every second that passed, she understood less and less of what was happening around her.

An overwhelming smell of perfume permeated the air, followed by the clack of approaching heels and a rush of voices. Syron clasped her hands tightly in her lap and prayed she wouldn't throw up. The table shifted and creaked, and when she raised her head, three identical women in long white dresses sat across from her. Syron closed her eyes. When she opened them again, there was only one. From the folds of her dress, the woman brought out a hardtack candy and slid it across the table.

"I was taught not to take candy from strangers," Syron said, but her voice sounded weak even to herself.

The woman raised one perfect eyebrow. "Candy, maybe. Consider it medicine."

Syron eyed the rest of the sahiit as she unwrapped it. It was ginger, and after a moment or two, the room stopped spinning.

"Thank you," she whispered.

The woman nodded and clasped her hands under her chin. Her dark eyes seemed to look at her and through her, gauging her value. Syron shifted in her seat.

"Yira tells me you're an angel."

Syron's eyes flitted to where Yira sat perched on a table. Not once had she heard her speak.

"I'm sorry," Syron said. "I don't know what that means."

The woman chuckled. "I wouldn't expect you to. My name is Idris. I'm the leader of our faction." She waved a hand behind her, not moving her eyes. They were beady, curious things, and Syron had to fight not to look away.

"I sent them to rescue you. Funny thing it was you who saved them. You have my thanks."

"She hid until they left," Zariah said with a sneer. Her hair had fallen back over her scars. "I'd hardly call that saving us."

"I avoided them," Syron corrected. "And if I hadn't, you'd still be chained in a cellar. You're welcome." Maybe it was too much, but the shock on Zariah's face made it worth it.

Idris smiled almost imperceptibly and stood, swiping her dress out behind her. "You must be exhausted. I'll have a room made up for you."

"There's an extra bed in mine," Calais offered. "I could use a roommate."

Idris nodded thoughtfully. "It's settled, then. Until tomorrow." Her dress billowed behind her in soft waves as she turned for the door. Zariah was quick at her heels, glancing back resentfully.

Syron had only a moment before Calais pulled her to her feet, leading her silently out the door and into the dim hall. They took a sharp turn into a long corridor, leaving the thick scent of flowers and pine behind. A giant mural decorated the wall at the far end, so colorful and curious that when Calais stopped at her door, Syron brushed past to get a better view.

A sprawling landscape had been painted in a soft hand, with a woman so high above the earth that even the towering pines looked shrunken and nondescript. A trail of feathers fell from her battered wings, too weak and broken to keep her naked body from plummeting to the world below.

"Her name was Dye," Calais said, coming up behind her. "She was the first angel. That we know of anyway."

Syron peered up at the pleading angel's face, at the glimmering tear on her cheekbone, and shivered.

"Did she really have wings?"

"Did you?"

Syron shook her head, wondering, and followed her back to her room. It was small and cluttered, with a large dresser crammed against one wall and two huge beds that left enough room for only a side table between them and room to walk around. She stood awkwardly in the doorway as Calais riffled under her bed, pulling out a wad of blankets.

Syron caught them midair and got to work stretching the thin cotton over the mattress, chewing on her bottom lip.

"Is that why everyone keeps calling me an angel? They think I had wings?"

She glanced over her shoulder. Calais was sprawled on the bed. She hadn't bothered to change her clothes, and they left dirt marks on the sheet when she moved.

"They call you an angel because you fell from the sky. Everything else is superstitious bullshit, including that painting." Her mouth thinned to a line. "But people will believe whatever they want to if they like the sound of it."

Syron wanted to ask more, but the hard look on Calais's face made her think twice. She climbed up on her own bed, leaving the blanket knotted at her feet.

"Thanks for sharing your room," she said instead.

Calais untied her fiery hair and flipped off the lamp. "Don't mention it."

~

Syron didn't remember falling asleep. Calais snored softly as Syron slipped out into the empty corridor and quietly retraced their steps back to the library. Anything was better than lying in a dark room with only her thoughts for company. She needed a distraction.

Artificial light spilled out into the hall. She stepped into its halo and through the door, her eyes scanning the rows of bookshelves. She ran her hand along the embossed titles, pulling one out at random.

"I thought I'd find you here."

Syron pivoted. It was no wonder she hadn't seen her—trying to look at her was like looking through water. Her edges were blurry and indistinct, the book she flipped through perched on her phantom legs.

"Do you remember me?"

How could she not? Syron clutched the leather-bound book tightly to her chest, glad for the sturdy weight of it. She saw again the little glowing girl who had run fast and far, her feet kicking up dirt and dead leaves as she and Will struggled to keep up.

"You accepted the flower," the girl said. "But if your third eye had been closed, you couldn't have come."

"What about Will? Was his open too?"

She shrugged. "It's hard to tell. Everything has moving parts. You're the only one I was sure of."

She couldn't have been older than twelve, probably younger, but she spoke like an adult. Her actions were smooth and decisive, her tone absolute. If she knew he were here, Syron thought, would she even tell her?

The book she had been holding skidded across the table. It wasn't so much a book, Syron noted, as a journal.

Its spine was cracked open to a drawing of an eye, its lashes thick and looped to form long, pointed petals.

"This is one of the journals from the first philosophers that came here. The rest of them are probably in this library somewhere. Everything inside of them is important." The girl paused, her eyes darting to the door. "The Nightman…he's biding his time right now, waiting to see what the next move will be. In the meantime, be careful who you trust. And if you see anyone like me," she said, rising to her feet, "you *run*. Understand?"

Syron absolutely did not understand. She wanted to demand that the girl stop being so cryptic, to ask who the Nightman was and why she should care, when footsteps sounded in the hall. The girl was already backing away.

"I didn't look like this before," she whispered. "With your help, I won't have to anymore." She whirled and dashed to the wall, the same one Syron had come through hours before, and was gone. She hadn't even gotten her name.

Syron's eyes snapped to the journal, as if that one detail could be enough to prove she hadn't imagined it. She slid into a seat quickly, listening to the metronome of steps echoing in the hall.

"I thought I was the only one who couldn't sleep."

Disheveled white hair dusted across Leon's forehead. He leaned against the doorframe, hands in his pockets, and smirked at her.

"I didn't know I was joining a club," Syron said.

"It's quite exclusive, actually. Only two members so far." He plucked a book from the shelf and sat at the far end of the table, thumbing through. Syron raised the journal to hide the flush in her cheeks and flipped to the first page. Meticulously neat cursive spelled out a single word: "Evangentine." She turned the page and tried to follow the tight script, but it was so congested and long that her eyes kept skipping ahead, and besides, she couldn't focus when she felt Leon watching her. She let the book fall slack.

"What you said before…about the watchmen looking for me. Naveen said the God sent them."

Whatever Leon had expected her to say, it wasn't that. His face changed to a mask of hard edges as he started to speak and stopped himself. "I'm sure Idris will explain everything in the morning."

She grimaced. The idea of being around Idris again was unnerving, even more so if she would be the one answering her questions.

"I'm happy for it," she lied, "but you were there. Did they say anything about me? I mean, besides looking for an…angel?"

Leon placed his own book on the table. "They didn't have to. They're pawns in a bigger game. What's important to keep in mind is that the God isn't some all-powerful being. He's just a man who likes the title and keeps tricks up his sleeve."

"Tricks like the Nightman?" It was a gamble, of course, but Leon only let out a chuckle and leaned back in his chair.

"Did Calais tell you about him? He's a bedtime story for naughty children, Syron. Nothing more." The curve of her name on his lips drew her up short. His voice was soft and mysterious, and she found that she liked the way he almost whispered it. She ducked her head to hide the blush in her cheeks as a group of sahiit still dressed for bed padded through the hall.

"Breakfast already," he said, and deposited his book back on the shelf. "It's fine to leave that here if you aren't finished. Most people here prefer to look at books instead of reading them."

"That's a shame," she said, sliding her book next to his.

The night before, she had followed Calais down the rightmost hall to her room. An identical hall stretched on the left, but Leon walked beside her down the centermost aisle, past arched doorways that looked into rooms filled with gear, weapons, and sheets of metal pinned to racks before the aisle opened into a cafeteria.

Syron breathed in the savory sweet aroma and let him guide her past rows of tables to the circular kitchen. Berry-filled tarts, sweet bread, and strips of steak cut thick and juicy over a bed of roasted peppers were arranged on metal trays. She picked a tray up for herself, poking at the small orb dusted in flour, and followed him to a table in the back.

The room was filling quickly. She peered past Leon to the line of people that stretched out the door, thankful he had sat in front of her. It was enough that not *everyone* was staring, at least.

She swallowed the last bite of the tart. It was rich and flaky, and her stomach thanked her for it.

"Am I the first angel who's been here?"

Leon nodded, stabbing at the peppers with a fork. "The first angel, yeah. But there have been others that aren't like us. Viero, of course, but he's a faction leader."

"Is Viero not…?"

"A sahiit?" Leon's pointed ears quirked up when he laughed. "He's a temporal, like the rest of them. He's—"

"I thought temporals were bad."

His face fell. "We don't discriminate like they do. The ones who were hunting you were temporals too, but Viero is on our side, and there are a whole lot more outside the border who wouldn't care one way or the other. Some of them…"

His voice was drowned out by someone yelling her name. She perked up, scanning the room, and found Calais bursting through the line toward them. Her red hair was tied in a braid down one shoulder.

"Everyone's talking about you," she said, sliding into the seat next to Leon. "Apparently you faked the fall, and you're actually an evil spy who wants to murder us in our sleep."

Calais scooped an orb from Leon's tray and rolled it in her fingers. "But of course, I'd be dead already."

"What?" Syron nearly shouted.

Leon smirked. "Don't be rash. Espionage is too subtle to murder everyone right away. Besides, they'd be more interested in araasi."

Calais choked back a laugh, but Syron wasn't paying attention to her retort. A group had sat at the far end of the table. A girl with pinned hair was staring daggers at them, whispering something to the boy beside her. He wasn't very old—Syron guessed maybe sixteen or seventeen—and he met her eyes warily before looking away.

Syron swiped her hair out from behind her ear so it formed a veil between them and tried to concentrate on the rest of her food. She picked up the strange flour-coated orb and bit into it.

A well of cold water spouted from her mouth and poured down her chin. She let out a surprised yelp and cast it aside, grimacing down at her soaked shirt.

Harsh laughter erupted down the table, and in front of her Calais was red-faced and chortling. Leon hid his smile behind his palm, trying to control his expression.

"So that's um…water," he managed.

"How was I supposed to know that?" she demanded, and Leon's smile widened.

"Here," he said, picking an orb up from her tray and turning it in his palms. It flexed but held its shape. "It's called maang. The cooks use rice and cane sugar to hold in the purified water. The powder is just so it isn't sticky."

This time she was more careful. The maang reminded her of a dumpling until she nibbled the bottom and crisp, cool water flooded out, right into her open mouth. She grinned at him.

"It's crafted to keep us hydrated for hours at a time, and the outside gets us through scouting without having to hunt. Depending on how long we're out, of course."

"Of course," Calais grumbled next to him. "I could've gone with more than that when we found the watchmen, though."

"Do you have to complain about everything?"

"One of us has to." She shrugged and pushed the loose hairs from her face, turning her attention back to Syron. "Naveen's looking for you, by the way. She said to meet her outside after breakfast."

Syron nodded, half to herself, and stood to leave. Calais caught her arm.

"But you're not going anywhere dressed like *that*. What are those pants even made of?" She made an expression of mock horror, and Syron looked down at her jeans, half expecting to have grown a third leg. "I mean, how do you train in those? You have zero range of motion."

"They're just pants. And what do you mean train?"

Calais rolled her eyes and swiped a tart from Leon's tray.

"Come on, we'll find you something."

Syron cast a pleading glance at Leon before skirting the edge of the table, keeping her head down until they were out of the cafeteria. Their bare feet tapped along the cool linoleum all the way back down the long corridor and to the room.

Syron collapsed on her bed, watching Calais dig through overstuffed drawers and toss clothes over her shoulder. She mumbled something under her breath, but it was too low to hear.

"What did you mean," Syron asked again, "about training? Is that what you do here?"

"Mostly," Calais admitted, pulling out a copper-colored dress and pulling at the hem. "Our faction is the closest to the God's City, so we're in charge of keeping them on their side, and vice versa. We have a contact that gives us information from inside the wall. It's how we knew they'd be looking for you, plus some extra help."

She stood and handed her the dress. It was made from rough cotton, decorated with golden chains that dangled off the shoulders and waist.

"So, you train to keep them away? Why?"

"We're in the middle of a war, Syron. I know it may not seem that way at first, but," she paused, shaking her head, "I'm sure that's what Naveen wants to talk to you about. Even the biggest building falls if you take away its supports. The God wants you, so we want you, you know?"

"But why does the God want me?"

Calais only nodded to the dress in her arms. "The only way in or out is through the library. Just walk through when you're ready. I'm sure Naveen will be there."

Syron watched her leave, fighting the tidal wave of questions that hovered just on the tip of her tongue. She turned her attention, reluctantly, to the dress. It was pretty, she admitted to herself, in a fierce kind of way. The neckline was high and plummeted before the shoulders, and two slits had been cut for both legs, probably for "range of motion." She undressed quickly and slipped it over her head, pulling up the shorts that were sewn inside with a sense of relief. There was no mirror, but she grabbed a hairbrush that lay half-hidden on the dresser and raked it through her tangles.

The decorative chains tickled her arms as she followed the curving hall back to the library, half expecting the little girl to be there waiting, maybe this time with another book, another vague warning, but it was empty. *Of course,* Syron thought as she walked to the far wall, *she wouldn't want anyone else to see her.* The worry in her face when she'd heard Leon and ran, mid-conversation, was evidence enough. Whatever her plan was, she had trusted Syron to keep her presence here a secret, and she would keep it, for now. At least until she had a reason not to.

She squeezed her eyes shut to walk through the wall and opened them when a light breeze caught at the hem of her dress and sent it rising. She yanked it back down, looking out of the ramshackle shed to the field beyond. Virgin light landed on dozens of sahiit in loose groups. Some held long poles and were vaulting at one another, the clack of wood against wood splitting the air, while others dug their poles in the soft earth and launched themselves skyward, turning effortlessly before landing in a defensive stance behind their opponent.

The grass was soft and wet with early morning dew. More sahiit sat cross-legged on the ground, and to the left, picnic tables that had before been lost to darkness were crowded with bodies. No one paid her any mind as she weaved between the groups toward them. She had almost reached the tables when she spotted Naveen. Her shoulder was only a little swollen from last night, and she stood in the middle of a network of bodies fanned across the grass. One of the boys had started to spasm.

His back arched and fell violently. His fingers clawed up chunks of dirt at his sides as he wheezed, but Naveen only watched. Syron raced forward, reaching out to help, when he jerked up and stumbled to his feet.

"Goddamn it!" he yelled. "I can't do this anymore. I won't."

"You have to," Naveen said, calmly. "You have to learn to control it."

"I can't control it," he hissed, red-faced. "Every time I think I'm getting somewhere, something happens that pulls me back out."

"It's all that temporal blood in him," Syron heard someone snicker. "Makes him weak."

"None of that." Naveen glared at the girl who spoke, who squared her shoulders but said nothing more.

"Atlas," she tried again. "What good is your third eye if you don't know how to use it?"

He shook with rage and spun on his heels, either too angry or too ashamed to look up as he barreled past.

"Not good enough," he hissed, so low that only Syron could hear.

Syron stared after him, at the tight set of his shoulders, the bowed head, before turning back. Naveen was watching after him too. Her golden eyes shifted to Syron, and her lips drew up in a half-hearted smile. The black dress she wore was a similar cut to her own, and her bare legs showed through the slits as she sidestepped out of the circle.

Syron fell into step beside her. Once they were away from the groups, Naveen let out a gust of air.

"Don't mind Atlas. His third eye struggles to stay open. We're trying to rectify that."

"What was he doing?"

"The same thing you did to come here. The sixth sense

is a big part of opening your eye, but trying to explain it is like telling someone how to breathe or how to think. It's instinctual, but some people struggle with it more than others."

"Because of his blood?"

Naveen grimaced. "There's mixed blood here that shows more promise than some would like to think. No, the block on his mind is his own doing. But enough about him." Naveen dropped to the earth, stretching out her long legs, and looked up at Syron.

"I suppose we should start with the basics. Mom was supposed to be the one to talk to you, but she had a last-minute meeting." Naveen rolled her eyes and patted the spot next to her.

The cool grass tickled Syron's thighs as she joined her. She plucked a blade of grass and pried it apart absently.

"Your mom is Idris?"

"Yeah. She's…very excited you're here. Evangentine has been a confusing place since the war, and angels," she said, nodding to Syron, "are the biggest prize. You're the first one whose fallen since the uprising—when we broke out of the God's City."

Syron pictured the flowing script of the journal. She knotted the remains of the blade of grass around her finger.

"Calais mentioned something about the war too, but I thought Evangentine was a philosopher. I found his journal."

Naveen smiled at her. "So, you've been reading the journals? Good. This land was named after him. He lived next to one of the lakes, like the one you landed beside. He was a temporal, so his third eye wasn't open, but he was smart enough to know that the lotus flowers weren't only for their looks. He was chronicling them, recording what they did and when, especially when they started blooming at night too. The night the first angel fell, they had been in bloom for three whole days."

"The girl in the mural."

Naveen nodded. "Dye was the one that led to his breakthrough, and the God's new religion. Evangentine believed she had been stripped of her wings and our soil offered redemption. The flowers are supposed to be some kind of gateway." She moved her hair behind her shoulders and stared out at the sahiit. Her features softened, almost as if she were reliving a memory.

"It wasn't always like this, you know. The sahiit used to live in the God's City too. But after more angels started falling, things got complicated. It was his city, it had always been his city, but…things started changing. He saw the angels as a chance to become something greater. Things only got ugly after that."

Syron stared across the field, trying to imagine the world Naveen described.

"But if Evangentine said they were angels," Syron asked, "why would the God want to hurt them?"

Naveen sucked in a breath. "He preached that it was his responsibility to give the angels the redemption they deserved. But later, he found a way for their deaths to open his third eye. Temporals *can't* do that, Syron. Somehow, he was able to see into their world before he murdered them. When he described it to the congregation, it was enough to convince even the skeptical temporals that he was a god."

"But not you."

"Not the sahiit. When he touched them…it was as if we could feel what the angels felt. The defilement, the hopelessness. And we were forced to watch like the rest of them." She wrinkled her nose. "That kind of pain has a way of sticking with you, like a layer beneath the skin."

Above them, the sun shone high over scattered clouds. Syron pulled her knees tight to her chest. If the watchmen found her, it meant she would just be another sacrifice for the God.

"How many?" she whispered, silently praying Naveen understood her question.

"Countless," Naveen whispered back. "There were other things…experiments the God was doing with the lotus flowers, mostly on us. He wanted to understand how the angels fell, and he thought the answer was a part of the third eye. In that I suppose, he was right.

"When we finally managed to escape the city, it was chaotic. Most of us got out okay, but the watchmen kept some lives for themselves. Yira's mom was one of them."

The air grew thick around them, and for a long time neither of them spoke. Finally, Naveen stood and dusted the grass from her dress, holding out a hand to Syron. It swallowed her own as Naveen pulled her to her feet. They walked side by side back across the field. The sounds of the forest made a peaceful hum in the background, filled with the cadence of sparrows and scraping leaves, but inside Syron was reeling. She imagined the little girl peeking out from the base of one of the tall pines, her not-so-young eyes watching them, studying them, and shivered.

They were almost to the groups now.

"Naveen?" she asked, before anyone could overhear. "Are there spirits here?"

<h1 style="text-align:center">4</h1>

<h2 style="text-align:center">INITIATION</h2>

Atlas was at their table. Somehow, Calais had found him after he'd stormed off and dragged him back here. They whispered in hushed voices, but Syron wasn't really paying attention. She poked at her steak absently, staring down at her tray as if the spices could mimic tea leaves and give her some semblance of stability in a tilting world. Just one certainty she could hold on to. But it was just spices with probably oil or butter, and she wouldn't know how to read them anyway.

Naveen hadn't answered her, not really, but the look in her eyes had said enough. How she avoided the question said more, and how she was suddenly anxious not to miss lunch was louder than if she'd screamed. Syron huffed and dug the fork in the meat until the prongs hit metal. Every time a question got answered, more filled its place.

Something wet hit her arm. She ignored it and concentrated harder. Maybe there was something right in front of her she was missing. If she could just put her finger on it…it hit her arm again. She looked up, exasperated, and found Leon smiling at her from down the table. He was in the middle of a group she only vaguely recognized from walking past, but they weren't staring at her as if she were a spy, so that was an improvement.

"Is it a habit for angels to tune everyone out?" he asked. He was wearing all black. It leached what little color he had out of his skin, so he looked even paler next to the others, his tousled hair even more like snow.

She picked up the grape he had thrown and popped it in her mouth.

"That depends," she said. "Is it a habit for sahiit to throw food when they want attention?"

The guy next to him snorted. "She's sassy. Bet she's smart too. Smart enough not to have a breakdown in the middle of a lesson."

Across the table, Atlas tensed.

"I mean, how hard is it just to lie there? If a little mixed blood takes away what's good about you, maybe you shouldn't even be here."

He moved to face Atlas the same time Leon cast him a warning look. Syron sat straighter and tucked her hands between her thighs.

"You hear me, Atlas? I'm talking to you."

The people at the tables nearest them had turned to stare. Across from her, Calais placed a hand on Atlas's shoulder.

"Are you really going to let your girl tell you what you do? Guess you're just as much of a pussy as I thought."

Syron's chest tightened. She closed her eyes, but she could still hear the chair scraping as it was forced back, Calais whispering, "He's not worth it," and then another chair toppling over.

She snapped her eyes open. Atlas was broad and well built, with close-cropped brown hair and a strong jaw. The other guy was smaller but bulkier, with an ugly grin and eyes that were too innocent for his face.

"Mind your own fucking business, Elias. He's one of us." It was Calais, moving to stand between them. "It's not like your own blood is so pure."

His eyes flashed. Behind him, Leon was all lean, tense muscle. He sat on the edge of his chair with his leg extended, waiting.

Out the corner of her eye, she saw Naveen with her arms crossed, ready to break something up if it started. It would happen fast, as fights always did. Just one move, however slight, and it would take more than just Naveen and Leon to pry them apart.

But Elias saw her too, and when his eyes flicked back to Atlas, he only laughed.

"Be careful how close you get, Calais. You wouldn't want the mutt to rub off on you." He winked and turned away. After a beat, the rest of the group slid from their chairs and followed, leaving their trays scattered across the table.

Naveen nodded in her absent way and disappeared into the hall, leaving Atlas still standing, red-faced, staring after Elias.

He jerked away when Calais tried to take his hand, and his angry eyes flashed to Syron. The pain behind them hit her like a smack in the face. His mouth parted slightly, as if there were so many things he wanted to say and couldn't.

"I never asked for any of this," he said instead, and turned on his heels. Calais's hard eyes found hers before running after him, but whatever she was mad about would have to wait—because Syron had understood the undercurrent of his words almost as if he had said them plainly, and they were rich with the flavor of blame. It was somehow an angel's fault that he was like this, unable to do what the sahiit could or be who the faction needed him to be. And since the blame was on an angel, it fell on Syron's shoulders too. The realization that someone she'd never met, had never even spoken with, had taken to hating her so intensely was jarring.

She dumped her tray numbly and took her time going back to the room. The main hall was filled with sahiit coming and going, but they ignored her for the most part as she glanced into the arched rooms beside the cafeteria and wandered down the stretch on the other side of the library. It was the same as her own except for the smell of sandalwood and shouts of men, and then she was standing at her cracked bedroom door, avoiding looking at the mural. She took a deep breath and pushed it open.

Calais lay in a ball at the foot of her bed, hugging a pillow. The door clicked shut behind Syron and she collapsed on her own bed, staring up at the ceiling. There were no windows, and the shadows of the lamp danced in the corners.

Finally, she heard Calais sniffle and flip around.

"He's leaving."

Syron turned on her side. Calais's face was red and puffy. "I tried to make him stay, but he wouldn't listen. So, I thought," her breath caught, and she said the rest in a whisper, "maybe he'd want me to come." Fresh tears welled in her eyes.

The only thing she could think was the worst thing she could say. "I'm sorry."

Calais's mouth twisted as if she'd tasted something sour. "Elias wasn't the only one harassing him. He was just the loudest. But then you came and…"

"And?"

Calais looked up at her, still wrapped around the pillow.

"You're a threat, you know. Being here. If you hadn't come, Atlas wouldn't be leaving."

"I don't have anything to do with Atlas." Syron's voice was barely above a whisper.

"You'd like to think that, wouldn't you? That nothing you do affects anyone." Calais leaned up and wiped her face, sending tears glistening across her forehead. "Why didn't you do anything when Elias was yelling at him? Or before? He told me how you just stood there when Naveen was harassing him."

"Naveen wasn't harassing him—"

She let out a harsh laugh. "An angel's word over mine? What's next, you're going to use your third eye to convince me you're right?"

"Calais, I didn't do anything wrong! If Atlas wants to leave—"

"He can't leave!" Calais yelled, jumping to her feet. "He's the closest thing to home I have. And now a fucking angel is ruining it just like everything else."

Syron's heart beat fast and loud in her chest. Heat tinged her cheeks and ears as she shot to her feet too, mirroring Calais's stance, when there was a knock at the door.

Neither of them moved. Syron matched Calais's fiery gaze with her own. She'd find a different room, even if it meant sleeping in the library, anything to be away from the whirlpool of emotion that filled the room with a tension as thick and suffocating as smoke.

"Bad timing?"

Calais's eyes slipped to Leon. He stood awkwardly in the doorway with his hands raised in mock surrender. Syron expected her to yell at him to get out, but in the blink of an eye, she was the girl wrapped around the pillow again. Her chest deflated, and she pushed past him out the door, taking the smoke with her.

Leon's eyebrows knitted together as his gaze swept from Calais's retreating figure to Syron, but she only shook her head once and crawled on the bed, pulling the covers up to her chin.

She put her head against the cool wall and waited for him to leave. Instead, the bed lurched to the side, and she heard the faint sound of buzzing beneath the rapid pulse of her heart. He sat with her in silence as she feigned sleep, too overwhelmed to move and too angry to speak, and tried to turn off her mind. She had almost succeeded when Leon whispered her name. He said it gingerly, as if he were worried about bothering her.

Syron let the seconds stretch, unsure whether she should bother. Leon and Calais had been friends long before she had fallen—so of course he would side with her. Eventually, though, Syron rolled on her back, looking up at the ceiling so she wouldn't see the look of disappointment that was surely on his face.

"If you want me to apologize to her, you're wasting your time. I didn't do anything wrong."

When Leon didn't answer, the little ball of anger in her gut flared. She tried to hold it back, but it spilled out anyway, like floodgates bursting under the pressure. "I didn't do anything to Atlas, Leon. I just—I keep catching myself looking around, expecting to see the city I grew up in. I can't help thinking if I walk far enough, there will be a paved road with guardrails and signs, and it'll be like none of this ever happened…like it's all an elaborate dream, even though I know it's not. I don't know how to handle everything that's happened, so sometimes it's better if I just try to ignore it."

Heat prickled behind her eyelids, and she blinked

rapidly to ward it away. "If I pretend everything is normal, then maybe eventually it will be. But that's the thing. This place—me falling—it's the farthest thing from normal, and there's not a single thing I can do about it." *Why am I even bothering? It's not as if he'll understand. If Will were here with me though…* But the fire in her gut swelled, and the next words burned through before she could stop them. "I just want to belong. But I can't even do that."

The silence that followed was deafening. Her words seemed to echo around the room, turning her cheeks to what must have been bright scarlet by the time Leon finally spoke.

"You're not normal, Syron."

Her thoughts splintered. She shouldn't have said a word. Should have let the anger wash over her until it dulled and faded. Should have pretended she was okay. Pretended it didn't bother her. Pretended she wasn't freaking out on the inside.

"And since you fell here, I'm willing to bet you didn't fit in before either." He paused, and when she looked over at him, the scarlet had spread to his cheeks too. "But that's not a bad thing. Normal people are just the ones who got too good at pretending."

"Which are you?" she whispered, but was answered instead by a quick rap on the door.

Maybe it's Calais coming back to yell some more. She watched silently as Leon got up to answer it. She couldn't see from this angle, but whoever it was spoke in hushed tones, and Leon nodded before clicking the door shut.

"Your initiation starts soon," he said, coming back and sitting on the edge of the bed.

Confusion must have been written clearly on her face. His lips quirked up in a sideways smile. "I thought Naveen would have told you. Your initiation to the faction? It's not usually a big deal, but it's also usually not an angel."

She grimaced. "I wish everyone would stop calling me that."

He ducked his head to hide his breathy laugh and pulled away. "When you're ready, I'll be in the library."

He paused with his hand on the door and turned to her, all traces of humor gone. He was looking at her, *really* looking at her, as if he were thinking hard about something.

"You asked me whether I'm normal. The thing is, I got tired of pretending a long time ago. After your initiation, don't come back inside. This is important, okay? There's a tree out by the picnic tables. Climb up and stay there. There's…something you need to hear."

His eyes searched hers, beseeching, and Syron stared back in shock. What did she need to hear that he couldn't tell her himself? But on the outside, she only nodded.

He left her then with only the shadows for company. She climbed out of bed and tried to pull the wrinkles from her dress, ran her hands through her hair, and fixed the golden pendants that dangled on her arms and waist. Thoughts racing, she followed the silent hall back to the library where Leon waited, as promised.

He had dressed quickly in an all-black suit with white accents. The ends of the cuffs and hems were folded over and decorated with abstract patterns. It even had a little cape. She looked down at herself despairingly—maybe she *should* have looked through Calais's drawers for something a little fancier—but he only tucked something back in his pocket and held out his arm.

"Don't worry. There will be plenty of people there that aren't dressed up."

She rolled her eyes even as she slipped her arm through his. "And here I was fishing for a compliment."

Outside, the night sky was clear and lit with a million stars. Crickets chirped proudly as he led her across the open field. Even far away, she could spot the group of shadowy figures on a rise, disappearing one by one.

She hadn't realized she'd gripped his arm harder until he pulled free. *Of course.* She let her arms fall to her sides and kept her face forward when his arm looped around her shoulders, draping her in his cape.

"Is this okay?" he whispered in her ear.

She shivered, whether from the chill or something else, and nodded mutely.

By the time they reached the small hill, everyone was gone. Leon knelt against the cool grass, bringing her with him, and craned his neck up. She followed his line of sight until she saw it. A quiver of opalescent light hung suspended in the air, so faint that if he hadn't shown her, she never would've known it was there.

"What is it?"

"A glamour." His voice was warm and soft. "Similar to the one in the shed. Are you ready?"

Despite the heat coming off him, goose bumps rose on her arms and legs. She nodded, and Leon pulled her forward into the glamour…

…and onto a well-lit stone pathway. Fairy lights hung like a blanket over the clusters of trees that framed the path. A stone archway stood at its end, and past it must have been at least a hundred sahiit all dressed in fine clothing and gripping wineglasses. She turned to look behind them, but the smooth stone only formed a circle with a railing tall enough to lean on and look out at the empty field. Past the railing, the air rippled like water.

"Don't forget what I told you," he whispered before

lifting his arm and fixing his jacket. "And don't worry, you'll do great."

Her throat was dry. The razor-edged wings of butterflies cut at her stomach as he moved to the side of the archway. People were already turning to look at her.

She didn't want to be here. Being the underdressed center of attention wasn't her idea of a good time, but she took a deep breath and plastered on a fake smile, keeping her head high as she walked down the center.

Everywhere was beautiful. The giant courtyard was lined with evenly spaced trees covered in the same lights, and every free inch besides the path was taken up by long stone benches that spanned nearly the length of the courtyard itself. The sahiit themselves were beautiful and strange against the backdrop. It was almost exciting. Almost terrifying. But she kept her eyes focused on the clearing ahead. A hulking statue took up its center, its details so warped with weather and time that she could only just tell it was supposed to be a person, and in front of it sat a solitary chair.

When she reached the last bench, someone grabbed her hand. Idris's blond hair was done up in waterfall curls, the top sections held up with a silver circlet that glistened in the light and matched her dress. She nodded to the seat beside her, and Syron sat. Briar—God, she hadn't seen him at all since the first night—was to her right. The glass that dangled from his hand was stained red, but he wasn't paying attention to her.

I suppose, Syron thought, *there are such things as miracles.*

Something deep reverberated in the crowd, and the last of the talking died down as everyone still standing took their seats. Syron scanned the courtyard, not knowing what she was looking for, when the noise sounded again. It came like a bass drum, like a sleeping giant taking in its first breath, when she found her.

A woman—a normal, human woman—stood under the archway. She was old and unmemorable, with thin hair in tangles over a baggy black dress that flared at the neck and feet. She balanced a mallet and a large, awkwardly shaped hunk of wood littered with holes. As soon as the beat faded to almost nothing, she struck it again, all the while walking down the path. By the time she reached the chair and hoisted it into her lap, the crowd was hers.

"She used to be a temporal, like the rest of them," Idris whispered, leaning over. "Now, she's one of the Faces of Fortune."

"Why that name?" Syron whispered back.

Idris looked over at her, for once her dark eyes not quite so penetrating, and smiled. "Just watch."

This time when she struck the instrument, she sang. Her voice was deep and smooth and harmonized with the beat instantly and passionately. She hit it harder, and her voice arched and fell, faster, until she was chanting without words. Some primordial part of Syron woke up, and it was as if everything was want and need and rain and storm, and she felt it in her bones. She stared, amazed, feeling the bass in the soles of her bare feet and in the tingles on her neck. And as the woman sang, she changed.

At first, Syron thought she imagined it. The woman's hair was a little thicker. The wrinkles that deepened her forehead were a little less severe. Then her hair grew to her waist in tight ringlets and deepened to black. The thick fingers that held up the instrument were now thin and delicate. The air quivered as if she were a fire, and every time she stopped to breathe and began again, the face would change too. One was a blond girl with fair skin, another a brunette with a splattering of freckles. A handful of faces became a hundred, each one flitting by so fast Syron was scared to blink, and all the while came the steady beat of the mallet off the wood and the deep chanting that could reach out, surely, and touch the end of the world.

The temporal closed her lips and her waist widened, the auburn hair fading to tangled gray, and with the last beat still echoing, the old woman got to her feet and walked back the way she had come. Syron stared at where she had sat, still feeling the rush of adrenaline coursing through her veins, begging her to cheer or yell or chant or scream.

Then Idris was pulling her to her feet and placing her in the chair that was not hers. The crowd shot to its feet as one and cheered. It was harsh and chaotic in comparison, and Syron tried to look past the mass of bodies to see the temporal walking away, or maybe looking back at where Syron now sat, but Idris's hand dug into her shoulder and forced her to stay in place.

When Idris held up her glass, the cheering turned to a dull roar. Syron looked up at her dazzling smile against the framework of stars and back to the crowd, keeping her eyes strained on the top of the stone archway at the other end. Everything was so intensely peculiar that she would have thought it all a dream if not for the steady pressure of Idris's hand.

When she spoke, it was in the swirling language Syron did not know. She recognized her own name swathed in a blanket of pride, but everything else was lost. Once she finished, those in the crowd raised their glasses, and in the front row, Briar picked up an extra glass from under the bench and walked with smug confidence to her other side. His black hair formed a spiral over his right temple, and his eyes had the same knife's edge she recognized from the cellar as he handed it to her.

"Tonight, we celebrate our first angel," Idris sang. "The tongue we use is not to harm, but to ensure our future. Will you welcome her to our factions?"

The crowd erupted in a tumult of cheers and whistles. Syron found herself staring into the sea of strangers, unable to look away. Her eyes flitted across the courtyard under the open night sky and found Yira almost by accident. She stood off to the side against the stone wall, covering her mouth with her hand. Her eyes met Syron's with a look of barely concealed horror before the crowd moved to block her view.

"Araasi welcomes you."

Syron ripped her eyes away. Idris raised the glass to her lips and drank. Syron followed suit, forcing down the thick, bitter wine that reminded her of blood before wiping her mouth.

"Araasi welcomes you," Syron whispered back, but the words came out lilted and wrong. Idris tucked a curl behind one of her downturned ears and beamed at her.

Briar was close enough she could smell the warm sandalwood of his cologne.

"The angel speaks," he purred, and the crowd went wild.

Bark broke off under her fingertips. She whispered a curse and shifted her weight, trying to keep her balance from where she sat in the crevice of a branch. The initiation had ended an hour ago, and still no one had shown. She looped her ankles together and watched the black shapes of the leaves rustle in the breeze.

Leon's request had slipped her mind until she was nearly to the shed. After sneaking around the back, she had waited for the stream of people to pass before dashing for the tree beside the picnic tables and scrambling up. It had rained while they'd been gone, so by the time she had found a branch that was strong enough to hold her weight and high enough to hide her from view, she was wet and irritated. Specks of bark still tickled at her arms and chin from where she had almost fallen, and her ass was sore from sitting so long.

Whatever Leon had wanted her to hear, if there ever had been anything, obviously was not happening. She grabbed hold of the trunk and started to shimmy to a lower branch.

"...safer to go through a glamour—"

"No." She recognized Briar's confident voice and froze. "You know we both need to be here when Idris shows up."

"So it's true, then? Idris is with the contact now?"

As quietly as she could, Syron put her weight on the top branch to push herself back up—

and slipped. The next branch sagged under her weight, and she grabbed at the width of the tree with both hands to stop her fall and sucked in a breath. Heart hammering, she craned her neck in the direction of the voices, but she couldn't see anything through the thick branches.

After a pause, Briar grunted. "You heard it from Yira?"

"Yes, but she's not a rat. I wouldn't worry about her."

"I know you guys have a history together, but if she becomes a problem..."

"She won't."

Syron recognized the hard edge to her voice and saw again the half-beautiful, half-mutilated face pockmarked with burns and the single long scar. She squeezed the tree tighter.

"There's a lot that can go wrong with this," Zariah said. "If anyone finds out—"

"No one will."

"But if they do," Zariah continued, "we'll need to take precautions. I've already taken the liberty of holding off faction transfers, and the supplies we have stocked up will last us a few months at least. Long enough for this whole thing to blow over."

"And how long do you think that will be?" Briar asked, laughing. "If we get the go-ahead tonight, it may be only a handful of days at most. What are you so worried about?"

"You know as well as I do the God isn't exactly keen on following through with his word," Zariah snapped. "Even if he does say yes, it's better to be prepared for the worst."

Briar only chuckled to himself. "He won't hesitate to get his hands on her. Besides, you should focus on more important things. Who did you say she's friends with?"

She imagined Zariah rolling her eyes. "I have better things to do than babysit, Briar. Calais offered her room. If you want more, ask your sister."

"Why would I? Naveen thinks this is a game. If Idris hasn't told her what's going on, I trust her judgment."

Silence. Then, "You really think handing her over will stop the war?"

"Is there anything else that could? Even if the others disagree, we're saving our people in the long run."

"Yes, but by sacrificing a life. I thought I was done with this angel business."

"We're never done," Briar said, from farther away. "The way we do it changes sometimes, that's all."

The table creaked as someone leaned against it, but she didn't dare try to look. She barely dared to breathe.

Zariah spoke next in a hushed voice, not quite a whisper. "The code of araasi is so the temporals can't understand us. Why bother giving her an initiation at all if she'll be in the God's City soon?"

Syron wet her parched lips. In the direction of the shed came a peal of boyish laughter.

"What's the harm in it? We're following protocol, and the more she thinks she's one of us, the less likely she'll be to suspect anything. Besides," Briar added with a hint of humor, "shouldn't all sahiit speak in code?"

Zariah grunted but, as far as Syron could tell, didn't make a move to follow.

Syron's muscles protested with a dull, persistent ache. But she kept her arms wrapped tightly around the trunk and took long, shallow breaths even though it felt as if she were suffocating. Even though no matter where she went, somehow, she was always meant to die.

The revelation came quickly and without warning. Naveen was right—it was just a game. Whatever the Watcher had tried to do, it had only changed the hands on the board. I'm still the pawn, Syron realized, and pawns are always the first to fall.

She heard the almost indistinct brush of footsteps on grass. Gathering her courage, she found her footing and scooted to a lower, sturdier branch. She was more careful this time, and even though the foliage wasn't thick enough to hide her entirely, it also meant she could see through it. A dark silhouette walked away from the tables. The deep slope of the dress showed off Zariah's lower back, but if there were scars there too, Syron couldn't tell.

Her eyes were used to the dark by now, and she watched silently from her perch as Zariah turned into the shed. The chirping of the crickets had long faded into a deep silence, only broken occasionally by some far-off scuffling. With aching fingers, she climbed her way back to the lowest branch and jumped, landing on the balls of her feet with her knees bent.

She stayed crouched by the tree long enough to be sure

Zariah wasn't waiting for her before following. She peered into the black corners of the shed just to be sure, and slipped through the glamour into the library, squinting her eyes against the light.

It had been stupid to take the faction for face value. On the outside it was perfect. Only once she got in the thick of it did the ugly truth start to seep out: no one cared what happened to her, so long as they got what they wanted. She had believed the lies without hesitation, and now look where it had gotten her. Even Naveen, who she thought had been honest and kind, had kept the darker details to herself. There was no way, Syron decided, that Naveen didn't at least have suspicions. What was it she had said in the field? Oh, right. *A last-minute meeting.*

She swiped at the tear that burned a path down her cheek and cracked open the bedroom door. Calais was snoring softly on the other side of the room, a mound of blankets piled high on top of her. Syron stripped off the wet clothes and grabbed one of the oversize shirts that lay in a ball on the floor. She slipped it on quickly and tugged her pillow to the other side of the bed, keeping her eyes on the door as she slipped under the blankets and pulled them up to her chin.

The door didn't have a lock. The weight of sleep pulled at her eyelids, but she strained them open. If what they had said was true, and she didn't doubt it, one night soon the handle would twist. Briar, or more possibly Zariah, would ease in and creep up to her sleeping body, limp in the blankets. One cold, firm hand would cover her mouth while the other arm looped around her.

It wouldn't matter how much she fought back.

5

STRATEGY

weat dripped from the stubble of his beard. He gripped the hammer tighter and pressed it against his side, trying to make himself as small as possible. He was in one of the many abandoned stores that lined the main road, crouched behind a filing cabinet that still had the peeling 7.99 sticker on the corner. Across the room, the watchmen were hunting him.

He peeked through the crack between the cabinet and the wall. There were four of them, each one twice his size with a shining sword in their belt. The building was old and leaning, the contents left inside mostly infested and stinking, but they swung out at everything in their path, demolishing anything within reach.

He was supposed to be dead already. If he'd stopped for just a moment, he would have been. His hand not gripping the hammer played with the edge of the blood-soaked cloth wrapped around his stomach. He'd been lucky it was just a graze, and luckier still he had pulled away fast enough. They wouldn't stop, he knew. Once the God gave an order, they never did.

Something crashed above his head. He hid his face against the shards of glass that cut at his bare back and arms, and ground his teeth together. He risked another peek.

Past the dirt and grime that caked on their clothes and exposed skin was the symbol he had learned to dread. The inverted triangle was tattooed in thick ink on the center of their foreheads, the point ending just between their eyebrows. The symbol of the God.

Adrenaline and fear coursed through him like a wash of acid. He knew the clean, smooth rush of it as surely as he knew the back of his hand. The barren shelves he had hidden behind before had been reduced to splinters. Even if he tried to smash the window and make a run for it, they were close enough to grab him before he would even hit the ground.

Something scuttled through the rubble next to him. He held his breath and listened to the crunch of glass and wood under thick-soled boots. He'd never been much of a fighter, but maybe if he could surprise them...

He raised his hammer and readied to leap out when a booming voice shouted outside. One of the watchmen let out a dissatisfied grunt and kicked a barrel hard enough to send it crashing to the other side of the store. He ducked back down and listened to their muffled footsteps under the shriek of dented metal and waited.

As soon as he was sure they were gone, he stood and stretched his sore legs, hunching slightly to avoid pulling at the gash.

The hinges on the back door had been busted. He pushed it out of the way and peered outside, holding his breath. There was no sign of the watchmen, but in the half-light between sunset and nightfall he spotted a woman in rags down the street, sweeping off her porch. She didn't seem to notice him.

Looping his hammer through his belt buckle, he slipped outside, keeping his pace slow, even though everything in him screamed at him to run. He strained to hear past the wild thud of his heartbeat and took deep, desperate gulps of air as if at any moment his breath would be ripped from his lungs, and he'd be left unmoving, unbreathing, unremembered.

Somewhere far away, a dog was barking.

Syron woke in a cold sweat, grasping at her stomach. She remembered the sharp pain of the blade, fast and quick, how she had wrapped the gash with whatever she could find to stop the bleeding. She pushed back the covers and stared at the smooth skin of her stomach, at her soft hands that had been rough and calloused just moments before.

A dream, she thought. *But it had felt so real.*

"Are you okay?"

Syron's head snapped up. Leon was sitting on the floor with his back against the end table, looking up at her with a worried expression. Calais was awake too, watching her eagerly.

"You were rolling around in your sleep, muttering something."

"I don't…I mean I didn't." She grimaced and sat up, wiping the grime from her eyes. "What did I say?"

"Gibberish, mostly," Calais said. "For the past hour."

Syron gaped at her. She hadn't been able to see the face of the man in her dream—it was as if she had experienced it with him instead of just watching it happen—but she didn't want to talk about that now, especially with Calais.

"I thought," Syron said finally, letting some acid seep into her voice, "that you were still mad at me."

"Oh, trust me, I am." She nodded to the foot of Syron's bed. "But Leon said it was important I stayed, so here I am. I took the liberty of getting you a change of clothes too, since you ruined the last ones."

Syron rolled her eyes, but something she said clicked into place. The initiation rushed back to her all at once, and after. She could still hear Briar's boyish laughter cutting through the night and imagined what he must have looked like—debonair in his suit, the darkness blurring the edges of him until it was only his gleeful face looking back at Zariah. She rubbed at where the scar should be as the familiar pressure settled back between her shoulders.

Leon got up to peek out the bedroom door and pressed it firmly shut behind him. His black shirt hugged his shoulders and accentuated the lines in his arms. His eyes met hers, and he clenched his jaw.

"I didn't find out myself. Yira told me yesterday, right before I came to find you. I didn't want you to think I was making anything up. I thought if you heard it for yourself…"

Syron swallowed. If he had told her, would she have believed him even when everyone else said otherwise? She wasn't sure.

"Did they say how they'd do it?" Calais's eyes darted between the two. "What? If we know what they're planning, we'll know how to avoid it."

Syron clasped her hands in her lap and ran her thumb over the jagged edge of a nail. She didn't want to say it out loud, as if maybe it wouldn't be real if she didn't voice the words. But it wasn't something she could hide from either.

"They only said Idris was meeting with the contact. Once the God agrees, it will probably be only a couple of days." She bit her lip, deciding. "They wanted to know who I'm friends with…I don't know why. But maybe it's better if you guys steer clear of me. You know, with everything going on."

She waited for them to agree, or maybe rush to her defense, but after a beat, Calais only said, "It must be Julian. Even if he botched the last one, he wasn't *wrong* about Syron being there. Do you think Yira can figure out what they agreed to?"

Leon nodded. "I'm sure she will. But Syron," he said,

drawing in a sharp breath, "I don't know what Naveen told you out there, but everything we did to get out of the God's City wasn't just so one rash faction leader could play into his hands now."

"Hold on," Calais objected. "I hate the God as much as the next guy, but Idris isn't coming from a bad place." Leon started to object, but she cut him off. "You know their houses go out way past the gate now. They're not scared of us anymore, or anyone else, for that matter. And the fucking poison they have?" She crushed Syron with her gaze. "Why do you think we have maang? It's because all our food and water—everything—comes from other factions. It's not safe to drink the water in the stream right beside our fucking house. The last time we went hunting, what happened?" Her gaze swept to Leon. "The only animal we managed to find was a bear that was already half-dead, and by the time we realized its fur was brushed with poison, we were already covered in blisters. Idris is not evil. She's just desperate."

Leon glowered at her. "But that doesn't make it right."

"I never said it did, but—"

"Just for fun, let's say she has a point," Leon continued in a voice that was too calm, "and handing Syron over really does stop the war. What then? It's our land, so why would he send the watchmen for the next angel when he can just have us do it? If we say no," he said, shrugging, "then the war is back on. Before long, we'll be working for him all over again. The only difference is we'll be getting our hands dirty."

Syron had brought her knees to her chest. She dipped her head between them to control her erratic breathing. There were so many moving pieces, she couldn't tell whether she belonged on the board at all. *Maybe Calais is right, and it would be better for everyone if I'm gone.*

A sob ripped through her. She pressed her lips tightly together to stifle the scream building in her chest, but the well of tears didn't go away. She'd thought…what had she thought? That the sahiit would protect her? That they cared, at least, whether she lived or died? At the initiation, it had almost been easy to believe.

An arm wrapped around her shoulders, and Syron jerked away. Calais must have moved to sit beside her; she let her arm fall but stayed where she was, watching Syron curiously. The anger was gone, and in its place was something quieter. Determination, maybe.

"What I was going to say is that because Idris thinks she's right, there's no way to change her mind unless the God declines, which he obviously won't do. But she confides in Yira. Maybe she can persuade Idris to hold off a little longer, at least until we can figure something out."

"If it would make you feel better, you could sleep in a different room. Somewhere they wouldn't find you as easily," Leon added. His hands were in fists in his pockets, the veins in his arms vibrant blue against the white of his skin.

"Like where?" Calais scoffed. "There are no empty rooms left, and anyone else she bunks with would rat her out in minutes."

Leon shifted uncomfortably.

"He means move in with him," Syron murmured. "But you're a guy. Wouldn't it be obvious if I…"

His lips quirked up at the edge. "That's why they wouldn't expect it. If you still pretended to sleep here and came after everyone was already in bed, no one would know. And on the off chance someone did see you, well, girls stay the night in our corridor all the time. Right, Calais?"

A flare of something strange shot through Syron. Calais's face flared beet red under her freckles, but it wasn't until she muttered something about him not having to worry anymore that Syron recognized it as jealousy. Of course, he had meant with Atlas. Syron scolded herself and reached past Calais to grab the pile of clothes.

"I'll think about it," she said, working hard to keep her voice even.

Leon nodded and slipped out the door. Syron turned away from Calais and dressed quickly in the black dress. It was the same cut and material as the one before, with silver chains instead of gold ending in small, circular pendants. She turned to see the back when she caught Calais's appraising look.

"I suppose it could be a good idea. You'd have to stay away from him outside of nights, though, if you don't want people getting suspicious." She flicked her hair back from where it coiled in the gap of her collarbone and crossed to the dresser. "You'll get to train with us today. It's already started, but there isn't really a set time anyone has to be there."

"Where is it?"

"Behind the shed, close to the forest. I'd grab something to eat before we go, though, you slept past—"

But Syron was already out the door, heading for the library. She needed some fresh air and a space to think. One thing was abundantly clear: she couldn't be here for much longer. She needed a plan, and whatever Yira's role in all this was, it might be best to talk with her first. If Leon trusted her, maybe she should too.

Hot midday rays scorched her shoulders as she rounded the shed and stopped at the crest of a small hill. At least half the faction stood in a scattered group by the edge of the forest, gripping the long wooden poles she'd seen them practicing with before. A handful were clustered to one side trying to find an opening. She recognized Leon in the mix, and across from him, deftly blocking thrusts and jabs, was Zariah.

Syron's breath caught, but she kept her face blank as she followed the downward slope. The grass was sparse at the bottom, and what remained was hot and rough under her feet. No one seemed to notice as she navigated around the poles pressed into the ground and leaned against one of the slimmer trees, watching them fight. They left enough space between them to avoid hitting one another, and each movement was calculated, swift, and sure. One of the girls, a blonde with faded spirals marking her cheeks, leaped at Zariah's back.

Right before she struck, Zariah whirled around. At the same time, one of the poles landed squarely in Syron's lap and she jumped, jerking her head away. Calais smirked and plucked one out for herself, running her hand along the beveled end to brush off the dirt.

"Angels don't get to just sit and watch," Calais shouted over the clack of wood. "If this were a real fight, it would either be for you or because of you. The least you can do is help."

Heat rushed to Syron's cheeks, and she got to her feet, gripping the swaying pole awkwardly in both hands. Calais was already lost in the horde of swaying, dodging, spinning bodies when a series of sharp clacks sounded from the other end.

Two poles were raised to form an X, but even on her tiptoes, Syron couldn't spot Leon and Atlas until the fighting turned to a dull clamor and most of the others had turned with her.

They stood in a spot of shadow under an overhanging tree. Like the rest of the boys, Atlas wore a thin T-shirt tucked into baggy linen pants, and the muscles in his arms bulged from where he gripped the staff. He was twice as wide as Leon and nearly three heads taller, but he still looked down at him, as if waiting. Leon glanced up and nodded, circling around Zariah to the right side while Atlas came up on the left. He stopped midway through and motioned everyone nearer.

Maybe Calais had been wrong, and Atlas had decided to stay after all. Syron scanned the group for Calais's shock of red hair, but she only managed to catch Zariah's eye, standing patiently in the middle with her pole behind her back. Syron looked away quickly and slipped through the gaps between the packed bodies.

"…targeting each side at the same time." Atlas spoke in a hushed tone, barely loud enough for Syron to hear. She pushed closer, keeping her staff tight to her side.

"She can't block all of us, especially if we time it right. Follow my lead, but if you see an opening, don't hesitate. Remember, all we have to do is touch her and the lesson is over." His gaze scanned the knot of people before landing on Syron. "Once it's done," he continued, "we can all go back to normal."

His gaze lingered a second longer before turning away. The muscles in his back bulged through his shirt so obviously it must have been at least two sizes too small, but he twirled the staff expertly and took his place in front of the group, to the right of Zariah. The sahiit filtered obediently to his sides, joining with Leon's group to form a tight circle. Zariah was trapped.

He might not be great at using his third eye, Syron thought, *but he makes up for it with a weapon in his hand.*

The air was thick with sweat and rich with the smell of rain. Syron took a great gulp of it and mimicked the stance of everyone around her, holding the staff diagonally to her chest.

They lunged. The force carried her forward, and the

sharp smack of wood formed a chorus that sent her body thrumming in anticipation. Zariah was a blur of motion, dodging, kicking, blocking, actually grabbing staffs and throwing them back with incredible speed. A crack of thunder shook the sky as Syron slipped under an outstretched arm. Here it was: her opening. She repositioned the staff with clumsy fingers and held it up to strike.

When suddenly she was yanked backward. One second Zariah was in her sights, the next everything was a whirl of green and blue, a flash of red, and Syron was flying. Something hard slammed into her back, the side of her head, and she opened her eyes to a filter of light streaming through neon leaves. She lay sideways against the base of a tall oak, trying to suck in a breath that wouldn't come. Pain blossomed through her head, and the neon jumped and spun above her, impossibly vivid.

"You shouldn't be here."

Syron jerked to the sound of the voice over the clash of fighting. Atlas stalked toward her under the windblown leaves, his staff gone. His eyes met hers and held her in place, and suddenly it wasn't Atlas anymore. Evyn's dark hair blew sideways in the gust of wind, and she could feel his hands around her throat, the press of his thumbs in the soft divot of her collarbone.

The memory was gone as quickly as it had come, and she scrambled to her feet. It didn't matter that her body ached like one giant bruise, or that every breath might as well have been a punch to the stomach. She couldn't show him it hurt.

"Don't touch me," she growled. But he was tall and fast and strong, and her voice quivered without permission.

A smile crept up his face like a hidden thing. An ugly thing. He was close enough for her to see the sweat on his black shirt. She stumbled back, snapping twigs beneath her bare feet.

"They won't let you hurt me." The words rushed out before she could stop them. They were in the language she did not know, her tongue curling and lisping of its own volition.

But Atlas only rolled his shoulders. "You think that's true, don't you? That you're special?" His eyes narrowed. "If that were true, they would have noticed you were gone by now."

Her eyes flicked over his shoulder. The darker shapes of the sahiit were still visible past the foliage, but barely. She wet her lips.

"Idris made a deal with the God, Atlas. It'll be any day now."

His smile wavered. "You're lying." Then, "How stupid do you think I am?"

She shook her head. "Why would I lie? Besides, I'm doing you a favor. What do you think Idris would do if she found out you damaged the only thing she has to trade?"

Another crack of thunder sounded overhead. Atlas's expression turned bitter as the first drizzle of rain broke through the leaves and trailed down his face. Syron ignored the chill of it against her own skin. If he tried to grab her, at least it would make it easier to slip out of his grasp.

"Calais—"

"Calais isn't a part of this," he snapped. "She doesn't understand."

"She understands as much as I do, maybe more. If you still think I'm lying, just ask her."

His eyes flashed, and Syron remembered what Zariah had said. Somewhere between planning Syron's death and asking about the initiation, she had mentioned Atlas.

"That's why you want me gone," Syron realized. "They won't let you leave with me here."

His gaze didn't waver. He took a step toward her, calmly. Syron tensed.

"I want you gone because you're not one of us. We aren't meant to cater to anyone outside of our own, and I know a lot of people who feel just as strongly as I do."

Behind him, someone shouted. Cheers broke out over the patter of rain, replacing the

chorus of fighting. His mouth twitched. "For your sake, I hope you're right about Idris."

He turned on his heels, sending beads of water flying from his hair. Syron waited until he was gone to let out the breath she had been holding. She knew how lucky she was, how quickly he could've overpowered her if he had tried.

The rain soaked through her dress and slid like icy fingers down her back. She recognized Leon's voice calling her name, and a part of her was glad. But another, larger part hoped he wouldn't find her. There wasn't enough energy left to be relieved or ashamed. She let herself collapse back against the base of the tree and squeezed her eyes shut.

If there were any tears, the sky washed them away.

6

ONOCALCUM

"Okay," Calais said when Syron walked into the room. "If you were an intruder, would this," she motioned to the stack of pillows under the blankets, "look like you?"

Syron raised her eyebrows. The hot shower had gotten rid of the constant chill and helped to calm her nerves, but the thought of someone creeping into her room made all the thoughts she'd managed to suppress come rushing back. She fought back a shiver and shoved her hands deep into the pockets of her borrowed linen pants.

"I don't know why you're bothering. It's not like it'll convince anyone for long."

Calais pressed down on where Syron's waist would be and ran her hands over the blanket before stepping back to admire her handiwork.

"Maybe not, but it will make them think you snuck out by yourself. At least then I can get a chance to warn you before they find out where you actually are."

"What makes you think you'll wake up?" Syron glanced out the open door. The hall was empty. There was no way anyone would hear them, but she lowered her voice anyway. "Did Atlas say anything to you?"

Calais froze for a fraction of a second and continued stuffing a little tote full of clothes.

"I thought he was leaving," Syron continued, watching the curve of Calais's jaw since she couldn't see her face. "I guess something must have changed his mind."

"Isn't it great?" There was a smile in Calais's voice. "He apologized for being such a dick, said he lost control for a minute there. But he's better now, I think." She glanced up with a glint in her eye. "He did good at the lesson, though, right? Taking control like that? I always told him things would work out if he just showed some initiative.

"We have this lame thing we tell each other," Calais continued when Syron was about to speak, drawing her up short. "That it's us against the world. In this case, I guess the world would be our faction."

Syron cocked her head. "You and Atlas against the world doesn't make much sense if he wasn't willing to bring you with him."

"He didn't leave, though, did he?" Calais frowned at her. "Not that it's any of your business. I just wanted to say I'm sorry for yelling at you like that. You didn't deserve it."

"But you still think it's true."

"It doesn't matter. I shouldn't have said it." Calais scooted the overstuffed tote next to Syron's bed and turned to the dresser, fanned the pages of a journal, and pulled out a thick square of paper. She pushed her own sheets to the side and opened the paper on the bed, running her hands along the wrinkles to smooth it out.

Syron moved to hover beside her. The map was old and hand drawn, with large portions scribbled out, smaller portions circled, and notes scribbled in the margins. The araasi shivered delicately and switched to English, but the words were too sloppy to make out.

Calais pointed to the largest piece of land, circled in red ink. "This is Evangentine. And this," she said, tracing the old lines of cities and rivers, "is us. We live right on the border of the God's territory. His city is in the center, right over here." She drew a line to the east. "When you leave, your best bet is to go up north. I've never been there, but I know others who have. It's a hodgepodge of temporals and umbriels. Just don't tell *anyone* you're an angel. Pick a new name and make up a backstory. Angels are welcome outside of Evangentine, but there's plenty of people that will sell you out to the God to make a quick buck."

Syron's eyes darted over the shaky green, blue, and gray lines. She'd never had to read a map before. Hell, even in her car the GPS had read the directions out loud. What was she going to do in the middle of the forest when she couldn't even figure out which direction she was supposed to go? She knotted her fingers together. The watchmen had been hunting the man in her dream. If she left and Idris told the God, did that mean both the temporals and sahiit would be looking for her?

She watched the scrunch of Calais's eyebrows as she leaned down to better see the names to the west. *It doesn't matter,* Syron thought. There are no other options, and even being lost in the forest is better than the alternative.

Calais leaned up, and without thinking, Syron wrapped her in a hug. After an awkward moment, Calais squeezed back.

"Apology accepted," Syron said, pulling away. Maybe Calais wasn't so bad after all. She was going out of her way to help her, at least. Atlas, on the other hand…

"Calais, I think you should know—"

"It's late," Calais said. "The others should be in their

rooms by now." She folded the map and handed it to Syron before looping her arm through the tote. Syron started to follow and doubled back, snatching Will's old leather jacket from where it hung on the bedpost and shrugged it over her shoulders.

Someone had come through with a mop since she'd showered, and the trail of mud that had led from the library down the main hall was gone. They only ran into one person, a girl sahiit with a barely concealed smile coming out of the guy corridor. Syron nodded as they passed, but the girl only averted her eyes.

Calais led them confidently down the corridor and rapped on a door halfway through. Too loud. Syron hit her arm, but Calais only winked and grabbed the handle.

"Alright," she shouted. "You *have* to stop masturbating now."

She threw open the door, and at the same time Syron felt the heat color her nose and cheeks, Leon looked up from his spot on the bed. He lay stretched out facing the door, one hand supporting his head and a book open in front of him. His skin was offset by the black shirt and linen pants, his white hair in a wispy disarray.

He didn't miss a beat. "At least give me time to zip my pants."

Syron ducked her head to hide her smile and squeezed in behind Calais, pressing her back against the closed door.

His room, unlike Calais's, was spotless. A lamp and neat stacks of books covered the top of the dresser, and on the wall next to it, in place of where the extra bed should have been, was a simple wooden desk covered in thick rolls of paper, paperweights, and charcoal pencils. She followed the trail of canvas paper up the wall and shifted to the other side of Calais to see better.

The drawings spanned the length of the wall and

switched from sketches of antique pocket watches and fractured necklaces to different angles of a hand or a shoulder. Scattered between them were profiles of girls they had seen only seconds of, but it had been long enough to remember. The Faces of Fortune stared off to the sides, as if posing for a photograph.

Calais nudged her with her elbow, breaking Syron's reverie.

"What?"

"There's another glamour," Leon repeated, "in the spare room by the cafeteria. Every faction has a back door. It's supposed to be a fail-safe so we can get out if we're overrun, but in this case, it works just as well." He leaned forward on the bed, the book forgotten in front of him. "If someone does come to Calais's room—"

"I'll pretend to be asleep until I'm sure they're gone and make a diversion. They'll be watching the library glamour for sure, but I can get them away from the other one long enough for you to get out."

Syron shifted. "How will we know when you make the diversion?"

"Trust me, you'll know."

"This is just a backup plan, though," Leon said. "Once Yira finds out what Idris is planning, we can stay one step ahead of her. We should be gone before it comes to that."

"What if it's not at night, though?" Syron asked. "What if it's during a lesson or something and I just never come back?" Atlas appeared in her thoughts again, rainwater trailing down the sides of his face. "We don't really know, do we?"

"That's why you always stay where people can see you."

Calais made a noise under her breath, half grunt and half laugh, and inched toward the door.

"Here," she said, pushing the tote into Syron's hands. "You know where to find me if you need me. If anything changes, let me know as soon as you can."

Syron looked down at the overstuffed tote and back at Calais. "Are you going to tell Atlas what's going on?"

She rolled her eyes. "The fewer people who know, the better. Speaking of," Calais added in a whisper and leaned in close, "I did pack something special. It's in the bottom." She winked and was out the door faster than Syron could object. It clicked shut behind her, and Syron stayed resolutely where she was, keeping her eyes strained on the floor.

She had been too busy thinking about everything that could go wrong, that was going wrong, that she hadn't considered the very real possibility of how awkward it would be to stay in Leon's room. She remembered how he had wrapped his arm around her on the way to initiation and the warmth that had spread through her chest as he pulled her in close, the absolute rightness of it. It's awkward now, she thought, because they hadn't been in his room. With only one bed. She held up the tote distastefully. Whatever Calais had hidden in there, she wasn't sure she wanted to know.

"I know what you're thinking," he said, chuckling. "The bed is yours. I swear I didn't invite you to stay over with indecent intentions."

She tucked a loose strand of hair behind her ear. "I don't mind sleeping on the floor. It *is* your bed, after all."

"Exactly, and I'm the one who offered it." He raised his eyebrows and leaned up and off the bed, taking the tote from her.

"Do all guys have rooms to themselves? It hardly seems fair."

"It mostly boils down to luck. Most of the others

don't." He opened the empty top drawer of the dresser and set the tote inside. "I wasn't sure whether you'd be bringing anything, but I cleared some room just in case. You know, to make sure no one gets suspicious if they come in and see dresses everywhere."

"Would they, though? I think they'd suit you."

Leon chuckled as she came up beside him. She shrugged off the jacket and started grabbing and refolding clothes at random, mindful of anything promiscuous Calais may have packed. Whatever Calais thought they'd be doing was definitely *not* going to happen. But being in his room, this close to him, the earthy, soapy smell of him was everywhere. It would've been calming if it weren't so intoxicating. It was enough that she avoided looking at him directly and instead watched him lean back against the dresser from the corner of her eye and rest his hands on the edge, pushing against a stack of books.

"Have you read the journals?" she asked suddenly, remembering the little glowing girl's strange request. "From the first philosophers that came to Evangentine?"

She glanced up at him fleetingly and saw the spark of something in his purple eyes. Had they always been purple? Or had it just been too dark any time she'd been close enough to tell? She refolded the shirt in her hands.

"Is that what you were reading the other day?" Leon asked. "It didn't seem like you enjoyed it very much."

"I mean, it's hard to get invested when I can't read the handwriting, but the best place to start understanding the present is by studying the past, right?"

He nodded and looked over her head to the piles of books, then glanced at the door. "They should all be in the library. I need to get more blankets anyway." He pushed himself off the dresser at the same time Syron's fingers scraped against hard, padded lace. She folded the bag hastily, crammed it into the back of the drawer for good measure, and followed him out into the hall.

"Where is everyone?"

She stayed close to Leon's side and glanced into some of the empty rooms where the doors had been left ajar. She was almost sure they'd been closed when she had come through with Calais.

"There's a party outside. I guess they made too much wine for your initiation and the rest was sent back to us."

"Is that allowed? What if the watchmen come?"

Leon shrugged. "They don't know where the factions are, at least not yet. But it also means we don't have to worry about running into anyone…probably."

The library was dim when they walked in, and the row of tables closest to the back wall were covered with large plastic jars full of the thick red wine. She scrunched her nose, remembering the bitter punch to it, and picked up Evangentine's journal from where she'd slid it next to Leon's book before. He'd been right about people not bothering to read anything; no one had touched it since she had put it back on the shelf.

Leon had crouched on the other end of the row of bookcases, trailing his finger down a row of forlorn-looking volumes wrapped with cords of leather. He pulled one out from the middle, unwrapped it, and took out a folded sheet of paper.

"There are four journals altogether. They used different terms from what we do now, but I found the translated definitions and copied them down." He handed her the journals with the paper on top before getting to his feet. "Evangentine and Alaman's are the interesting ones. The other two were either drawing graphs or complaining they didn't have a proper bed to sleep in."

Syron opened the sheet of paper. The araasi shivered and re-formed into cursive.

"So, you studied them?"

He nodded. "You're right about studying the past. It's a shame there isn't more material to go off."

From across the room came a bout of laughter. Syron jumped as a group of sahiit stumbled through the wall and snatched up a couple of the plastic jars. A guy with long blond hair pulled back in a bun fumbled and caught it at the last second. He looked up with a wide grin and glazed eyes.

"Leon! We've got a race going if you want to join. I called winner."

"Thank you, but we were just leaving." Leon gave him an amused smile and caught Syron's elbow. The guy shrugged and wrapped his arm around the girl next to him, who swatted him away. He laughed again and grabbed another jar as Leon angled Syron to the door.

"You don't have to say no for me," Syron said when they were far enough away. "It might seem less suspicious if you did, actually."

"Are you saying you want me to leave you alone?"

"No, I'm saying I don't want to hold you back if it's something you wanted to do." She gave him a soft smile, hoping he wouldn't see the sadness in it. "Racing sounds like fun."

"You are trying to ditch me!" He feigned shock and nudged her, and she bit back a smile.

"I'm exactly where I want to be," he said, more seriously. "Racing through the treetops is pretty amazing, but it'll be harder to do with an angel on my back."

"Wait, *through the treetops*? What else do you do for fun?"

He reached for the door handle when his face fell. "Shit. Make yourself at home. I'll be right back." He turned on his heel. Syron watched him jog away, the stark contrast of black and white against the beige corridor, before pushing the door open.

She tossed the journals on the bed and ran her fingers through her tangled hair, tying it in a knot on the top of her head. She avoided looking at the portraits on the walls as she readjusted the loose extra layer of fabric that was supposed to work as a bra but definitely did not, and just reached for the worn cover of Evangentine's journal when one of the drawings caught her eye. Unlike the ones on the wall, the portrait on Leon's desk looked at her head-on. A scattering of freckles covered the woman's nose and cheeks, a lone one on the center of her chin. Her lips were pursed between different-sized dimples, almost as if she were trying to hold back a smile.

Syron crossed the space to it and sat in the chair amid the rolls of paper and utensils. She started to reach out before thinking better of it and pulling her hand back. It could've been a photograph. It was real enough that at any moment she expected the woman to break out in laughter, or the wind to push her hair back, or her eyes to flick around the room. It was obvious in the soft shadows of her face and the darker strokes of her hairline that whoever she was, Leon had loved her. Still loved her.

The whisper of bedsheets landing on the floor drew her away, and she glanced behind her. The humor in Leon's face was gone, replaced with an age-old sadness that reached out as surely as his hand settled on the back of the chair, or the warmth of him as he reached across and pointed to the woman's mouth, her forehead.

"There should be smile lines here, and here. Just a little bit. I haven't had time to add them yet."

"She's perfect," Syron whispered and cleared her throat. "It goes without saying, you're an amazing artist. I don't mean to pry, but do you mind me asking who she was?"

He drew back, taking the warmth with him. "You're a little unnerving sometimes, you know?"

"Am I wrong?"

"Not usually."

But instead of answering, he went back to the pile of sheets and spread them on the floor next to the bed, doubling them over and putting an extra pillow against the bed frame. Syron waited until he settled against it to move to the end of the bed, angling herself so the light from the lamp landed on the pages of the journal.

No one spoke for a long time. Syron let herself get lost in the journal, pulling out the page of translations here and there, until Leon snapped his book shut.

"What was your first impression of me?"

Syron's head jerked up. "Excuse me?"

"The first thing that came to mind when you saw me, good or bad." Confusion must have been written plainly on her face, because he added hastily, "If you'd rather, I'll go first."

Syron guffawed. "You probably thought I was a little idiot."

His eyes caught hers and held her in place. Slowly, he shook his head. "The opposite, actually. You were scared, yes, but also incredibly brave. Anyone else would have run away as soon as they knew the watchmen were there."

"I thought about it."

"But you didn't," he said, pressing. "When I saw you, and how you helped us even after Briar freaked out, I wanted to take you away from this. All of this. I couldn't look at you when Naveen introduced us, because I was thinking about what would happen if I stole you away. With the factions, but also what you would think of me if I did. The choice I would have taken from you. And I decided I didn't want to be that person." He ripped his eyes away, leaving a purple stain in her vision. "If I had known then what Idris was planning, I would've done it regardless."

She drew in a sharp breath and looked down at her hands still holding the journal. She looped the leather cord around her finger, again and again. Trying to pin down her emotions when she had met not just him, but all the sahiit, was like asking her to find a single blade of grass in a field, or more likely, how to spot a glamour when she didn't even know where to look.

"My instincts aren't the most reliable," she said finally. "I know you made me curious. I…wanted a chance to get to know you if you'd let me. I didn't get the impression you would try to abduct me, if that's what you were worried about," she added, trying to lighten the mood.

It worked. Leon smirked, and when he looked at her, the purple of his eyes lightened ever so slightly.

"The woman in my drawing? Her name was Astrophe. I used to look like her. I had the same dark brown hair and eyes. I even had freckles." He laughed without humor.

"She was your mom," Syron realized. "What happened to her?"

"The same thing that happens to all the angels here. The God sent his watchmen after her, and before long she was just another pile of ash." He swallowed hard and looked down at his hands from where he'd grabbed fistfuls of the blanket. He unclenched them slowly and stared at the wall, as if he were forcing himself to keep talking. "I had heard enough by that point to know the lotus flowers weren't a crazy idea. A lot of the scientists were doing experiments with them, trying to figure out how they were involved with angels being able to come here. If you open your third eye, they had a theory you could use them to see into other worlds. If you were strong enough, that is. I figured I'd be able to see her world easier than a stranger would, you know?

"I locked myself away for a long time. I did see… things. Sparks of something in empty space. But I never got anywhere, and by the time I realized what the flowers had done, it was too late." He picked up one of the journals next to Syron and opened it to a bookmarked page before handing it to her. She accepted, looking down at the circled passage.

The temporals and sahiit ate the flowers without thought. Almost immediately, the temporals reported "splitting headaches" and "vulgar bowel movements." The symptoms lasted two days, during which I chose to monitor the sahiit more closely. Their bodies underwent physical changes: lightening of hair and skin, eye-color deviation, lighter markings. Their mental states too, became troubling. Most sahiit rambled incoherently. Worth noting, however, was a female sahiit of undetermined age, who took to writing "Watcher" on the walls. When prompted, she only smiled. Needless to say, the sahiit were incapable of transitioning back into society . . . . . . .History keep the rest.

Leon moved to sit beside her on the bed, reading over her shoulder. When she let the journal sag, he brushed his fingers through his hair and leaned back, the edge of his shirt coming up just enough to reveal the point of his hip bone.

"I stopped before my mind was affected, but nothing could be done for my appearance. When I came out, no one recognized me. It was like every proof I had that she existed at all, even me, was just…gone."

His mom, Astrophe, watched from her perch on the desk as Syron put her hand on his. She waited for him to recoil in disgust—she was another doomed angel, after all. But he squeezed it instead.

"That's why you wanted to steal me away?"

"I meant what I said, Sy. If I had any idea—"

"You're doing more than I could ever ask for. If it weren't for you and Yira, I wouldn't even know I was in danger here."

If she had ever imagined herself to be right here with him, watching his eyes flick down to her lips, she had pushed it down so far, she had forgotten it had been a thought at all. Her breath caught. He was so close, all she needed to do was lean forward…

Leon's back went rigid. She followed his gaze to where Will's jacket lay in a pile on the floor, forgotten, and felt his hand slide out from under hers. He cleared his throat.

"There's something you should know. That dream you had in Calais's room…did it feel like you were there? I mean, as if you were physically in someone else's body?"

The question was so out of place that she pulled away. Whatever she had been thinking the second before vanished as surely as though it had never happened.

"There was a gash," Syron said, "on his stomach. I woke up thinking I would bleed out because I fell asleep and forgot to keep pressure on it."

Leon didn't meet her eyes as he cracked the spine of another journal and flipped to the end. Their fingers brushed when he handed it to her, but it only sparked the anxiety coiling in her stomach.

The paper of translations lay between them, but she didn't reach for it. Halfway down the page in the same tight, elegant script, an indented passage caught her eye. She tilted the journal toward the light, watching the shadow melt away.

…Our experiments also point to the existence of the onocalcum. Some angels have experienced a beautiful and unpredictable tethering of the minds, in regard to their third-eye capabilities. This occurrence

is believed to be caused by an extreme emotional provocation that links the two parties by altering the dream state of the angel, causing them to experience the life of another. Be aware, these dreams are disrupted from time and are not in this moment believed to be linked by familiarity or a shared history...

The words started to blur together. She blinked, and the ghost of pain sliced across her stomach, fresh and hot. She pushed the journal away with pinpricks of glass falling over her back and arms. She stumbled to her feet as the rush of adrenaline flooded her veins like ice and begged her to run, but the knowledge of what would happen if she did kept her frozen in place. She had experienced it all with him, but the scars weren't hers to bear. Excitement and fear rose to bile in the back of her throat. It could mean only one thing.

Will is in Evangentine.

7

DÉJÀ VU

he stolen jacket flapped around him like a flock of crazed birds pecking at his neck and back. He wrapped it tighter around him, but if it did anything for the cold, he didn't notice.

The God's City stretched for miles in either direction, protected from the rest of the world by the giant bronze wall that surrounded it. Storefronts glowing with neon signs offered enough light to see the deserted streets, but not enough to even touch the base of the spire tower that reached up past the wall and seemed to touch the sky.

He craned his neck to the circle of glass that made up the walls of the top floor, ignoring the sting of the wind against his cheeks. The light was still on, but this time a dark silhouette stood motionless. Whether the God faced away from him or toward him, he couldn't tell.

A shiver raced up his spine, and he shrank back into the protection of the overhanging trees, looking back the way he had come. The berries he had collected along the way had ravaged his stomach, and the water from the stream he'd found had tasted sweet and chalky. He rubbed the palms of his hands down his cheeks, gave himself a light slap, and did his best to pick his way down the steep hill. The world tilted dangerously, and he paused more than once, squeezing his eyes shut, before continuing.

It had been pure luck the watchmen hadn't been able to find him again. More than likely, they hadn't suspected he would be stupid enough to come back. Not that he'd had a choice. It had been clear from the moment he had finally stopped to rest and found himself too weak to even set a snare that he wouldn't make it out of Evangentine. If he had any sense, it would have been clear from the beginning. There was only one truth he was sure of: he couldn't run anymore.

By the time he reached the wall, his breath came in shallow rasps that left him lightheaded and nauseated. He wasn't at the gate, not yet, but two watchmen stepped out from the swath of shadow next to where he knew the giant metal hinges would be. Their blades glinted dangerously in the moon's glow as they neared him.

He swallowed back his fear. Whatever happened next, at least it would be on his terms. The weight of the hammer made his arm shake, but he willed himself to grip it tighter and took another clumsy step forward.

"What do we have here?" The one on the left gave him an ugly, unnatural smile that was too wide for his face. The second one spit off to the side and nudged the first, the armor clanking together, and gestured to the hammer.

They could have been twins. All the watchmen had the same huge, muscular bodies, bald heads, and lidded eyes. Even without the inverted triangle stamped on their foreheads, they could've been swapped for each other, and no one would be the wiser. But he tried anyway.

"You're Alistair and Fennec. The two watchmen the God would prefer to stay out of the way. If you let me in, I'm sure he'll make it worth your while."

The one on the right, Fennec, snorted. "You know our names, so what? There's no open call for traders, and it's past curfew." He glanced at Alistair. "You're lucky we're not in a very giving mood. Get you and your lousy metal out of my sight before Lady here changes her mind." He twirled his sword expertly and slipped it back into his baldric.

Alistair grimaced at Fennec, the skin scrunching together where his eyebrows should be, and brought his weapon higher. "Who's to say," he said in a drawl, "that we can't have a little fun? It's been awhile since we've had anyone dance for us."

"With good reason, so I hear." His voice cracked coming out. He was glad he couldn't see the flash of malice that surely crossed Alistair's face, because as soon as he spoke, Fennec grabbed the bronze plate on Alistair's shoulder to hold him in place. Alistair jerked from his grasp and whirled forward. There was just enough time to see the glint of metal before the butt of the sword slammed into him.

His vision went black, but the pain was still there. It pulsed like an aura, overshadowing the tiny rocks that needled into the side of his face as he slid and the cheap material of the jacket scraping across the ground.

Alistair snapped an order at Fennec before he was hauled up by the armpits. He blinked, and one of their faces swam across his vision, but he couldn't tell which.

"Give me one reason," the watchman said, "why I shouldn't cut you down here and now."

He surprised even himself by laughing. The watchman at his back let him go, and he fell in a heap on the ground. Every part of him was screaming. He heard them whispering as his laughter turned to violent coughs that squeezed at his chest and tried to suffocate him. He smiled through it, even when his mouth tasted like iron.

When the bout ended, he sucked in a ragged breath. Beneath him, little black dots were painted like gothic art on the stones. He rolled to his side.

"One reason?" he rasped. He pulled aside the jacket and lifted the hem of his shirt. The cool air brushed against his scar. It had healed, but badly. "Angels aren't meant to be murdered by your hands."

Their faces melted into shock. One of them—it had to be Fennec —looked as if he were about to be sick.

Alistair muttered a curse and attempted to tuck his sword away. He missed twice before giving up and throwing it to the side. It clattered against the ground as he turned his attention back to the massive gate.

"Open it up!" he shouted at the top of his lungs. "We found the angel!"

∾

Syron didn't move for a long time. She lay silently, listening to Leon's soft snores on the floor next to her and staring at the ceiling. Finally, when the throbbing of her head dulled to an ache, she kicked off the blankets.

She'd stacked the journals with the rest of the books on the dresser the night before. They hadn't bothered to turn off the lamp, and she avoided looking at them as she maneuvered around Leon's sprawled body and dug through the top drawer. Half of her wanted to wake him, but the other half thought better of it. There was no way to tell how early or late it was, and besides, whatever had happened between them the night before made her want to bury her head in her hands and forget it ever happened.

But it had led to another dream. Another instance of the *onocalcum*.

She shook her head warily. Will, because it had been him, she was sure now, had gone back. He had seen no other option. The way the watchmen had looked at him after he said he was an angel…

She glanced back to make sure Leon was still asleep and turned away, hastily pulling off her shirt and slipping the dress over her head. When she was sure she was covered, she slipped the pants off too and pulled up the tight shorts sewn into the fabric.

She slipped into the hall. Everything was quiet—the

faction was still asleep. She angled her feet as she walked to make as little noise as possible and trailed her fingertips along the wall, deep in thought. Trying to find another passage about the onocalcum had been a waste of time. It was mentioned only the once, in passing. Leon had pulled into himself after that, leaving her alone to get lost in the text. But even though she'd read every passage, studied every picture, and skimmed every graph, there had been nothing.

She was so consumed by her winding thoughts that she didn't hear the voices until she was nearly to the library. There were two of them, both female, their voices slipping in and out of araasi as if it were second nature. Her racing thoughts slowed to a halt. She ducked into the library without thinking, pressing her back against the wall, and let out a string of internal curses. Because right where the little glowing girl had sat before was Idris.

"There's our angel." She smiled. "We were just talking about you."

Yira sat by her side, her short, straight black hair parted in the center, hiding all but the edges of the abstract markings in the shape of leaves and the points of her ears. Syron noted they were shorter than those of the other sahiit—except for maybe Leon's and Atlas's. Yira's expression was perfectly flat as Syron regarded her, so different from the initiation that Syron thought she may have imagined it.

"Calais was very talkative last night," Idris continued. "Not at all like usual. It was the wine, I'm guessing. It has a rather…potent effect."

"The wine," Syron repeated. Every detail of Idris's appearance was perfect, but the soft wave of her blond hair didn't hide the hollowness in her cheeks, or the cold calculation of her almond eyes. Her markings were a shade lighter than her skin—Syron hadn't noticed before—spreading like frayed symbols across her shoulders.

Idris crossed her legs delicately. "It's stronger than most people give it credit for. Of course, I'm sure word would have gotten out that you're sleeping with Leon eventually. It is a small faction, after all."

Blood rushed to Syron's cheeks, her neck, without her consent.

"That's—" she stopped herself. "Nothing is going on between Leon and me. We're just friends."

"Of course. But if you were," she waved her hand, "there's no shame in it. We all have needs. Leon is a solid candidate, though, if you don't mind the baggage. I'm just happy you're finding your place here is all. As I'm sure Yira is." She glanced next to her, but Yira's focus was on the top of the doorway. Syron tried, and failed, to read her expression.

"I think I know perfectly well what my place is here."

"Good, I'm glad for it." Idris gave her a dazzling smile. "You're welcome to join us if you'd like. Breakfast won't be for another hour or so."

"Thank you," Syron clipped. "But I was just heading out."

She kept her chin high and her pace even as she walked past them down the aisle. When she reached the last bookcase, the table creaked behind her.

"Oh, and Syron?" Idris said. "I wouldn't worry about Calais. Poor girl begged over Atlas nearly half the night before she said anything about you. She was probably just jealous."

Syron's mouth thinned to a line. "Probably," she agreed, and stepped through the wall, out the shed, and into the dull gray of early morning. The clouds hung low and full, and the grass was wet under her bare feet, but it wasn't still raining, and that was something.

The picnic table next to the tree was empty like the rest of the field. She climbed on top and lay with her back against the splintered wood, wrapping her hands around the table's edges, and stared up at the lilting leaves.

Maybe, she thought, I should have stayed with Evyn. It would've been better, surely, than the constant upheaval that had her second guessing every little thought, regretting every action. And at least then, the only person she would have hurt was herself.

The hollow gap in her chest throbbed at the edges. She leaned forward to catch her breath and pulled out the map Calais had given her. The mess of lines covering Evangentine was no clearer than before, but she did her best to trace them to the east, where a smudge of pen marked the center of the God's City—exactly where Will had been in her dream.

The sun had broken through the clouds and beat down fresh and hot, but she shivered despite its warmth and drew her arms tight to her chest. She remembered everything Naveen had said about what the God did to angels and the experiments he did on the sahiit. She remembered her dream too, and felt again how the fear written plainly on the watchmen's faces only layered with her own. She didn't want to think about what they would do to him—to *her* Will, who had such a clear future in front of him before she had gone and ruined it.

Her breath hitched. All that time he had spent trying to save her, now it was her turn to save him.

She had just picked up the edge of the map when someone shouted her name. She jerked her head to the hill behind the shed and found Atlas and Calais side by side, flanked by a swath of sahiit all dressed in black gear with clasps down the chest. Calais slid her arm from his and started to run over. Her hair was down, but it didn't hide the purple blotch on her neck that peeked out just above her collar. Her eyes fell on the map. "I wouldn't have that open out here. You're the last person Idris would want to have it."

Syron clenched her jaw and folded it back up. As if that wasn't what she had been doing already. "What do you want?" she snapped.

Calais startled. "Well, I *was* going to ask whether you wanted to help scout for watchmen, but since you're obviously not in the mood, I won't waste my breath."

Syron barked a laugh and climbed off the table. "You're right. Sorry if I'm not interested in talking to the person that told the *whole faction* I had sex with Leon." Her cheeks burned, but she kept her voice low and even.

Calais's eyes rounded. "I didn't—" She faltered and looked at her hands. The gear extended over her palms, cutting off at the joints of her fingers. "I didn't mean to. It just came out."

Syron clenched her jaw. "Yeah, trying to get the attention of your boyfriend must be pretty hard without screwing over everyone else. Even if you couldn't care less about me, you know that puts Leon in danger too." Her fingers twitched around the fold of paper, and she flung it at her. Calais caught it reflexively. Over her shoulder, Atlas was already heading their way. "Oh," Syron added, before she could interrupt, "and next time you lie to someone's face, the least you can do is look them in the eye."

She turned her back before Calais could say anything else and beelined for the shed, not caring about the stares that stacked like burning coals between her shoulders. Across the field, Syron just caught a glimpse of something disappearing into the bushes before she was in the shed, through the glamour, and walking down the stretch of hall past the crowded gossip of the cafeteria.

She let her pace slow as she reached the guys' corridor, not making eye contact with the sahiit she passed, and keeping her head high as she counted down the doors. She stopped at the fourth on the right and twisted it open.

"Leon?"

The bedsheets he had slept on were folded neatly at the bottom of his bed. He perched beside them and stared at the corner of the room, not moving his eyes as Syron slipped inside. "I was just going to ask whether you heard what everyone's talking about…Is everything okay?"

She followed his gaze to the corner of the room…and froze. The ghost of a girl with tangled, frizzy hair and a wrinkled nightdress looked up at her from the gap between his desk and dresser. In the low lamplight, she was just as blurry as she had been in the library.

"It's about time you came back. This one nearly had a heart attack," the girl said. She flashed a smile at Leon, who cringed. "Apparently, your little talk got Idris all hot and bothered. She moved up the trade to tonight. Yira and I want you as far from here as possible before they think to miss you."

"You and Yira," Syron repeated, after a beat.

She nodded. "The sooner we leave, the better. The glamour next to the cafeteria will take us to the forest behind the shed. We'll circle around the right side to meet up with Yira. She's probably already there."

Syron gaped at her. "Even if I wanted to go with you, what makes you think we could get out without being seen?"

"I got in, didn't I?" She clasped her hands in front of her and rocked side to side, looking up through her doll-like eyelashes. Syron took an involuntary step back.

"She's lying." Leon jerked upright and took a step closer to Syron. "Yira would have told me if she made a deal with one of the nightchildren."

The girl cocked her head. "I have a name, by the by. It's Adaline. And you mean like how Syron would have told you if she had already met one?"

His eyes flicked to her briefly, and back to Adaline. "I'm sure she has her reasons."

"Just as I'm sure Yira has hers."

A sudden patter of footsteps in the hall sent a thrill through Syron, and she clicked the door shut, pressing her ear against the cool wood. There were muffled voices, and then more footsteps passing again before they faded into silence. The room seemed to let out a collective breath.

"How do you expect me to trust you," Syron asked as she turned around, "when every time I've seen you, you've either turned my life upside down or made demands and left? And now you're wanting me to disappear again with *the woman who acts like she's Idris's bodyguard*. I don't know what you're expecting from me." Her voice cracked, and she cleared it. "But I'm not who you think I am. And I'm not going to follow you blindly."

The portrait of Leon's mom was visible through Adaline, just over her heart. It was warped and blurry as Adaline turned to face her. "I'm not pretending I know how everything works. You think I knew what I was doing when I found you? No, I got lucky as shit. But here I am and here you are, and the only way you're going to get out of this mess is if you *listen to me*. If you stay here, your time's up. That's that. And Leon here," she jerked her thumb at him, "may not have seen as many angels burn as Yira, but he's seen enough not to want that to happen to you. Am I right?" She whipped her head in his direction.

Leon clenched his jaw and nodded.

"So even if you decide you want nothing to do with me, at least if you come with me, you'll get to make that choice."

She walked right up to the door beside Syron and grabbed the handle. "Are you coming or not?"

No, Syron thought.

"Yes," Leon said. He crossed the few feet to stand next to Syron, so close that when he spoke next, his breath fanned her face. "If you're telling the truth and Yira is out there, that means it's too dangerous for her to come get us out herself. But if she's not waiting like you say," he looked down at Syron, "then we turn Adaline in to the faction. It should distract them long enough we can get a head start on our own."

Syron swallowed the lump in her throat. Never in a million years would she have expected him to drop everything to help her. It made her hopeful, even if it were also because of Yira.

Her thoughts soured. "I saw Yira this morning with Idris, in the library. She acted as if she couldn't care less."

"That's a good thing. It means she doesn't want Idris to know she's invested in you. She was protecting you, Sy." He glanced around the room, pausing at Will's jacket that was hung up on one of the dresser knobs. "Did you want to bring anything with you?"

"There's no time," Adaline hissed. "The way you two go on, we could've already been outside." She cracked open the door and peeked out.

"Keep up," she whispered, and darted into the hall.

A second later, Leon's warm, calloused hand grabbed Syron's. She had to jog to keep up with his long strides, and then they were through the arched doorway to the left of the cafeteria, looking up at the half-empty racks of gear the sahiit had worn to scout in. The sheets of metal were gone, replaced by more of the metal staffs she had only glimpsed before. In the corner, a child's hand vanished from view.

Adaline would be in the forest now. Waiting for them.

Syron let go of Leon's hand. He jerked to a stop and turned around, his eyes shifting from her to the doorway, as if at any moment he expected someone to barge in. Syron didn't blame him. She expected it too.

"Leon, I—" Damn it. She sucked in a breath and tried again. "This faction is your home. I don't want to be the one responsible for taking that away from you. I know you want to help," she continued, *but you can't possibly understand what that means. I won't be the reason you lose your home, your family, your friends. I don't want you giving everything up for me just to discover that I'm not worth it.* "But I don't want you to risk everything when you have a life here. No one knows you've helped me so far. If you stay here, no one has to."

She didn't wait to hear what he had to say. She pushed past him to the corner where Adaline had disappeared and started to walk through when he caught her hand again, sending a jolt of electricity up her arm.

"I don't care what other people think," he said. "What matters is making sure you're as far away from this place as possible. Yira has a plan to tell the other factions what Idris is doing, and I can't sit here wondering whether you're okay when I know there is something I can do to help."

Syron raised her eyebrows in mock offense. "What makes you think I need your help?"

Leon smirked, and she felt a little fire start in the pit of her stomach. "You probably won't. But at least this way if you need me, I'll be with you." He moved to stand beside her in the glamour. When Syron looked down, half their bodies were just…gone. She looked up dizzily and met his eyes. "If you don't want me to come because you don't want to be near me," he said, squeezing her hand tighter, "then tell me. But if it's because you're worried about me, just know that the risk of leaving together is well worth the regret of staying alone."

Behind him, a murmur of voices came from the hall. The crease between his eyebrows deepened, but he didn't look back. His eyes were locked on hers, depthless and overflowing with one question.

She should say no. That it was too dangerous, that she was the reason everything always went wrong, and she didn't want him stuck in the middle of something with no way out. But the answer formed itself around her tongue and slipped between her lips before she could stop it.

"It's not because I don't want you."

"Then I'm yours for as long as you'll have me," he said simply, and pushed them through the glamour. The fluorescent light morphed into warm sunlight under a canopy of leaves. Leon helped to steady her as she regained her footing and looked around. She recognized the spot where Atlas had threatened her, and farther away, the swath of foliage that would hide them from view if anyone were training. But there was no clack of wood this time, and Syron suspected anyone in training would be in the scouting party anyway.

"Wait," Syron said. "This morning—"

"Don't worry." Adaline stepped forward from where she had been standing, unseen, against the base of a tree. "The scouts went to the houses by the lake to check whether the watchmen ever showed up. They should be on their way back now, but they won't find us if we hurry."

Adaline whipped around and quickened her pace. Syron hesitated before running after her. Even though this was a completely different forest and Leon was decidedly not Will, the sense of déjà vu that warped around her still brought goose bumps to her arms and had her scanning their surroundings for anything out of the ordinary.

She avoided a thicket of brambles and looked up in time to see the hem of Adaline's dress disappear behind another. She pumped her legs harder and jumped over a stream framed by a scattering of ripe berry bushes. She glanced over her shoulder at Leon, who looked from her to the bushes and shook his head once.

Sweat tickled her neck and back when Adaline finally started to slow. The forest spread out evenly in every direction, unchanging. Leon's steps slowed to a crawl. He must have had the same idea.

"Adaline—" Leon started to say.

"She should be here." Adaline turned in a slow circle. "The only way she would have left is if—"

"If what?"

Syron followed the voice up the tree on their left. Yira must have been perfectly still for them not to notice her before. Now, she swung her legs over the side of the thick branch and jumped down effortlessly.

"I suppose I should have expected you would want to come." She nodded to Leon and swiped at the pants of her gear.

"Am I that predictable?"

"Sometimes," Yira said, giving him an amused smile before turning her full attention to Syron. The bored expression she had worn in the library was gone, replaced with a mixture of intrigue and worry. Behind her, pressed into the tree where a strip of bark was missing, hung a quiver of opal light.

"Syron, I know I haven't given you a reason to trust me, but I hope you know I have your best intentions at heart. Yours and the factions. If we can get to Viero, he can help us get word to the other factions and stop what

Idris is doing here. She's dug herself deep enough that even if she weasels her way out, she'll have a lot of explaining to do.

"This glamour," she said, glancing behind her, "is bigger than the ones we usually use. The last time you crossed a large distance was with water, but even though it was faster to form, that method is extremely risky and won't get us as close as we need. Not to mention we don't have a body of water big enough nearby. This one won't be as pleasant, but you'll come out the other side unscathed, I promise."

"So, Viero had someone form a glamour on his side too?" Leon asked.

Yira nodded. "We'll come out inside his faction. It's the safest way."

"How long until it fades?"

Yira grimaced. "Hours, maybe, or days. We just have to hope they don't notice it. But if no one saw you leave, they shouldn't know where to look. They didn't, did they?"

Syron shook her head. The voices she'd heard in the hall should have been far enough away that they wouldn't have seen them. And even if they hadn't been, everyone walked past those doors without a second thought anyway.

Adaline's girlish chuckle broke through Syron's reverie and sent a chill racing down her back. "Do you hear it too? They're not far now."

Syron shook her head at the same time Yira lurched forward and took hold of her shoulders. Her grip wasn't like Zariah's—she could duck away if she wanted—but then she did hear it. Faintly. The scrape of old leaves and the snap of twigs. The low voices. She tensed but let Yira position her in front of the tree.

"Glamours use living organisms to make them stronger," Yira whispered in her ear. "The tree itself is part of the glamour now, so you need more force to make it activate. You have to *run*."

"We'll be right behind you," Leon offered, but she didn't look at him. She was staring at the glamour, shimmering and alive. She took a deep breath.

To their right, someone started laughing.

"Now!" Yira hissed and pushed her. Syron used it to propel herself forward, keeping her eyes focused on the glamour and *not* on the hulking tree she was about to run into. The damp soil stuck to the soles of her feet as she closed the distance and squeezed her eyes shut.

Then she was falling.

8

ADALINE

Icy breath fanned up from somewhere far below and wrapped around her ankles. The biting cold sank into her skin like the pinpricks of a thousand needles and whooshed higher, digging into her pores. She opened her mouth to scream and tasted the white pain of it pouring inside her, carving her from the inside out.

When she landed, it was in an underground tunnel. Syron choked on the sudden air and fell to her knees, clutching at her chest to make sure she could still feel the rapid pulse of her heart. White spots dotted her vision, but it wasn't until Leon blinked into the tunnel with her that she realized they were only fairy lights.

He caught himself against the wall and grabbed at his stomach, grimacing down at the dirt floor. Yira appeared where he had stood just a moment before, followed by Adaline. They both looked as if they were about to be sick.

"Never again," Yira said, grunting. "Is everyone okay?"

Syron glared at her. "Barely. What *was* that?"

"A necessary evil." Yira squared her shoulders and looked to her right. A warm, white light marked the exit.

"Come on. They'll be expecting us, and I think some introductions are in order."

Syron bit back her retort and climbed unsteadily to her feet. Leon stayed close behind Yira as they started forward, and after a few shaky steps, Syron followed along behind them. The tunnel wasn't very long, and within minutes they came out on a platform overlooking an underground city. Her breath caught.

Whatever she'd been expecting, it hadn't been this. The whole faction was a giant dome fashioned from the earth. Wooden steps and platforms crossed the sloped walls, leading up to circles of light pressed into the dome's face in rows. In the center, a giant willow tree woven through with light brushed against the constraints of the ceiling, as if its being there is what held the whole faction together.

Soft music played from somewhere far below. In a daze, Syron walked right up to the railing and peered down.

"It feels good to be back," Leon said beside her. "I'm glad you're here to see it too."

She looked away from the thick, snaking roots that wove in and out of the earthen floor.

"I can't believe this is a faction. It's so…"

"Down to earth?" Leon asked. He smiled at his own joke and nudged her before looking back over the faction. "I used to live here before Yira decided to go to Idris's faction. She thought she could make more of a difference there."

"You miss it." It wasn't a question.

"Who wouldn't? This whole place is alive," Leon said. "It's nothing like the old-world buildings Idris copied hers from." He pointed down to a sahiit pushing a wheelbarrow along one of the winding paths. On another, a group of them sat in a loose circle with their heads dipped low and cocked to the side, studying one of the sections of flowers that grew in an open spot between the roots. "No one will look at you differently because of what you are. It's who you are that matters here."

"Are you sure about that?"

Behind them, Adaline stood with her arms crossed and her eyebrows raised. "From what I remember, you were pretty quick to write me off."

Leon frowned at her. "You're an exception to the rule. The nightchildren work for the God, everyone knows that."

"Not this one."

Leon chewed on the inside of his cheek and looked at the steps attached to the platform. Yira was already halfway down, waving to a group of temporals and sahiit waiting at its base. "You're as good as your word. Thank you for helping us," he said and turned to Syron. "Viero will be waiting for us if you want to—"

"I'll catch up." She gave him a soft smile. He searched her eyes and nodded, taking the steps two at a time. He was probably anxious to put some distance between Adaline and himself.

Adaline must have thought the same, because as soon as he was far enough away, she let out a gust of air. "What a dolt."

Syron ignored her and took to the steps slowly, keeping her grip tight on the railing in case she lost her balance. She strained her eyes forward and waited until she could see Adaline's bluish-white glow in the corner of her eye.

"What did you mean when you said the Nightman was biding his time?"

Adaline hesitated next to her. Syron waited for her to take another step before continuing. "The last person I asked said he was a bedtime story for naughty children."

"For some people, that's all he is," Adaline whispered. Then, louder, "Leon was right, mostly. The nightchildren do work for the God. I'm the only one I know of that doesn't." Her hands knotted in the material of her dress. "The Nightman works for the God too. His existence is kept a secret. No one knows who he is or what he looks like, aside from the God, and any rumors about him are labeled as heresy. He created us to be his eyes and ears outside the city. Whatever he doesn't already know about, he will soon."

"How do you know he's real if you haven't seen him?" Ahead of them, Yira and Leon followed the group to a circle of light pressed low into the wall. Syron watched them push aside the sheet that acted as a door before turning her attention back to Adaline. The lights from the tree made disorienting patterns in her skin as she moved.

"I said no one knows what he looks like, not that we haven't seen him."

"Who's we?"

"The nightchildren. That's how we turn—he comes to us in dreams and just…watches us. Gets to know us." Adaline paused. "Just so we're clear, I'm only telling you this because I need your help. Yira's the only other person who knows, and I want it to stay that way, okay?"

Syron's shoulders tensed. Adaline waited until she gave a curt nod before continuing.

"The longer I stay like this, the more I forget what my life used to be like. I get glimpses sometimes, like I'm looking through fog. But the clearest memories I have are of the last couple of weeks before I turned, starting the night of my little brother's birthday party. I had fallen asleep thinking about how angry I was that everyone had ignored me, especially Mom. I know now how stupid it was to be jealous of Brantley. It was his party, after all, and it wasn't as if I was supposed to help him open presents. But it didn't change how furious I was.

"That was the first night I saw *him*, in my dream," she said. "I didn't think anything about it at first. He was just a dark spot on the edge of my peripheral vision. It wasn't until a few nights later that he moved, and I saw it was the shadow of a man. He didn't have a face, and I couldn't tell what clothes he wore, but I could feel him watching me.

"After that, I tried to stay awake. Any time I did fall asleep I would wake up screaming." She cleared her throat. "Mom would come in with a cold rag and keep it pressed to my forehead until I would calm down enough for her to go back to bed. But any time I closed my eyes, he always came back. He started whispering things to me, promising he would go away if I gave him control."

Adaline shook her head. "When someone is in your head like that, you can't hide your thoughts. He knew I missed how things were before Brantley was born. I was selfish enough to want him gone, but I knew how devastated my parents would be. I didn't want them to go through that kind of pain, even when the Nightman said I didn't have a choice. He whispered my darkest thoughts in my ear, Syron. Every night when I said no, he said I was already his."

"What happened?" Syron whispered.

"He left. I was ignorant enough that after a few nights of normal sleep, I had almost convinced myself he had been nothing but a bad dream. But he kept his promise. One morning at breakfast, the walls started moving. Lumps turned into elbows and stretched into hands. I could *see* faces inside the walls, screaming to be let out. I thought I heard Mom screaming too. I was trying to find her, and Brantley."

Adaline stopped moving. Syron did too.

"I thought one of them broke free. The wallpaper split, and all I saw was this mangled *thing* coming at me. I didn't think. I just grabbed the knife Mom left on the table." Adaline stared down at her shaking hands as if she didn't recognize them and sucked in a ragged breath. "When I realized what I had done, what *he made me do*, it was too late. Brantley was only two when I murdered him."

Syron's stomach knotted. She was staring down at her own hands, trying to stop herself from imagining them covered in blood that wasn't hers, slick and warm and so *red*.

Adaline touched her arm, and Syron resisted the urge to jerk away. She couldn't bring herself to look at her.

"I can still hear his voice if I get too close to the city. The Nightman is the realest thing I know. He's the reason temporals worship the God throughout Evangentine, not to mention why the sahiit speak araasi. Whatever the nightchildren hear gets reported back right away. The sahiit made the code to ensure that didn't happen. But the God wants angels, and the Nightman wants an army, and right now that's both of us."

Syron clenched her jaw. "Why are you telling me this?"

"The same reason the God denies the existence of the Nightman. With the threat of scavengers gone, he needed a reason to keep the worshippers inside the city. He needed something to make them afraid, so he could maintain his control over them. Syron," she said, letting go of her arm, "only an angel can take over someone's mind so completely. Children don't have their defenses up yet, so they're easy targets. Temporal adults are harder, and sahiit are harder still. Angels are impossible. You're the only person who stands a chance against him."

Syron's knees shook. She sat down on the wooden steps

and ran her hands down her face, clasping them at the back of her neck to relieve some of the pressure.

She didn't know how long she sat there, trying to calm her racing thoughts, when Yira emerged from the circle of light. She scanned the people on the ground before flicking her gaze to the stairs. What she saw must have been enough to leave them alone, because she only nodded once and ducked back through the doorway.

"I didn't want to scare you," Adaline said once she was gone, "or I would have found a way to tell you sooner. I know it sounds crazy to say it now, but you were safest with Idris. The God wouldn't come after you if he thought you were already his."

"I'm not scared," Syron said and looked over her shoulder. Adaline had sat down with her back against the dirt wall. With nothing but the solid color behind her, she almost looked tangible. But then Adaline raised her head, and the lights shifted in her skin. Syron couldn't help it; she thought back to how her own skin had looked when she was with the Watcher, caught somewhere above and below the worlds, and shivered.

"Whatever it was that helped you to find me, I can't change that it was my decision to follow you. I'm the one who said yes." She grabbed the railing and pulled herself to her feet. She made it two steps before turning back. "I want you to know I've been dreaming about Will. I know he's in the city."

Adaline didn't seem surprised. "So, you've decided, then? You're going?"

"I don't have a choice. He spent years trying to save me. If it comes down to it, I owe him my life." She watched as Adaline ran her thumb down the lace lining of her dress and nodded.

"A girl has many faces, Syron."

"Good thing for you I'm an open book," she murmured and took to the stairs. Her legs had stopped shaking, and she wasn't imagining her hands covered in blood, but she could still hear Adaline's voice in the back of her head. Whether it was from what she had been through or what the Nightman did to her, Adaline wasn't a child anymore. Not really.

Syron stopped at the edge of the doorway and ran her hands down the lengths of her hair, tucking it behind her ears. Whatever Yira's reasons for working with Adaline, it only proved their end goal was the same. Maybe it was luck that Syron's did too. She squared her shoulders and brushed aside the sheet with as much determination as she could muster.

Like in the tunnel, fairy lights lined the domed ceiling. It was a small room with a single wooden table. Leon and Yira each sat in one of the four chairs. The conversation died as Syron walked in, and Yira motioned to one of the two temporals standing on the far side.

"Syron, meet my father."

9

DRAGONFLY

The one who must have been Yira's dad smiled at her. He was severely middle aged with a freshly shaved face, close-cropped silver hair, and an air of importance Syron couldn't quite put her finger on. He rounded the table and held out his hand. His grip was firm but gentle.

"It's a pleasure to meet you, Syron. My name is Viero, but I'm sure you know that already. We were just discussing the…unfortunate situation that required you to come here sooner than expected. I hope the decisions Idris had taken upon herself won't stifle any relationship we can have moving forward."

Syron grimaced and let her hand drop. Across the room, the other man chuckled. He was dressed in the same loose black clothing as Viero, but his exposed face, neck, and arms were covered with deep gashes, long healed. They laced up his arms and thinned to white scars by the time they reached his face. "Girl nearly escaped with her life," he said. The lights danced in his cloudy eyes as he looked up, skipping past Viero to the space beside him.

"And you're asking her to trust the same people who condemned her?"

Viero grunted. "I suppose you have a point. Syron, this is Damien. For lack of a better word, I suppose you could call him my adviser. He's a bit of a smart-ass at times," he said, smiling, "but I'd say it's well deserved."

Damien nodded gravely and rounded the table. He kept one arm in front of him until he found Viero's shoulder. "I'll have their rooms made up."

When Viero nodded, Damien pulled away and took steady, deliberate steps to the door and swiped the sheet aside. Once he was gone, Viero took a seat at the far end of the table and motioned for Syron to do the same.

She couldn't help it: her eyes flicked between Yira and Viero for any proof they were related. It was obvious Yira's features weren't quite as sharp as the other sahiit, and her ears weren't as long, but that was true with Leon too. And Atlas.

The ones with mixed blood, Syron realized as she took her seat. But if there were any resemblance between Viero and Yira, she couldn't see it.

"So?" Yira asked. She was pushed far enough from the table Syron could see she was digging her nails into the material of the gear that covered her palm. "Have you told the others yet?"

Viero rubbed his dry hands together and folded them on the table. "As I said, the process has started. Sending a message to all the factions at once takes strategy. But yes, I have people working on it as we speak."

"But there are only seven factions."

"Which means there are seven ways it can go wrong," he said patiently. "If we do it right the first time, there won't be repercussions if one faction hears it sooner and decides, much as Idris has, that they would rather act on their own. It's smarter to set a date that everyone agrees on and discuss it as a collective." He gave her a look that said the discussion was closed and turned to Syron.

"Your initiation was splendid, by the way. The God must have a streak of jealousy to see us with an angel after all this time. Which leads me to my question. You are all welcome to stay for as long as you like, of course. But when they realize it's you three who are missing, this will be the first place Idris will look." Syron expected him to turn to Yira, but his gaze stayed fixed on her. "I should be able to buy you a couple of days at least, but what's your plan once you leave here?"

"We're going north," Leon said, cutting in. "It's the only way to make sure she's safe. If Adaline really is on our side, she can help."

Syron sat straighter in her seat, still looking at Viero. "No, this isn't something I can run from. I've seen the lengths the God will go to make sure he gets what he wants. Even with Adaline's help," she said, turning her attention to Leon, "there's no way I can make it out of Evangentine. I'd rather it be my decision to go to the city."

"But we can find a way to keep you hidden. The God isn't everywhere." When Syron didn't speak, Leon's cheeks flushed. "Then why did we bother leaving Idris's faction anyway? You would've ended up in the city regardless."

Next to her, Yira jerked upright. "Because," she answered, "Idris was going to hand her over like a piece of meat. Adaline knows how the city works. She can feel the minds of the other nightchildren even if she doesn't have access to their thoughts. At least this way, we can plan how to get in that doesn't involve handing Syron over."

The muscles in Leon's neck strained. "That isn't enough, and you know it."

"It will have to be," Yira answered just as seriously.

"You made the choice to come on your own. If it bothers you, you can always turn back. It would be safer anyway." She shifted to face Syron. "We're in agreement, then?"

Her eyes softened slightly as Syron nodded, and she lifted her chin higher.

"Then we'll leave as soon as we can. Once we figure out our next steps."

Leon jerked back from the table at the same time Viero placed a hand on his shoulder. Syron hadn't seen him get up.

"If my opinion holds any weight," Viero said, "I agree that may be the best course of action. If I learned anything from my time in the city, it's that doing what you're told when you know there's a better way never ends well for anyone. When the God saw Astrophe that day from the top of the spire, Yira, I swore to myself that if he touched you—"

"He didn't, though. Zariah was the one he punished. Her scars should have been mine."

Viero grimaced. "She always was a good friend to you, despite the circumstances. If there is some cosmic balance, Zariah will come out of this unscathed and the God will get what's coming to him." He paused. "But the right thing is often the hard thing. Just know that whenever you need it, you'll have my support. All you have to do is reach out."

Yira's mouth parted in surprise. The tension in her shoulders seemed to melt away, slowly. "Thank you," she said, and Syron could tell she was working to keep her voice even. She cleared her throat and dropped her eyes to Leon. "I think we need to talk."

Leon shrugged away Viero's hand and got to his feet. Syron looked away as he followed Yira from the room, not wanting to see whether his anger toward her had turned to resentment. But as soon as they were gone, Viero only rolled his eyes.

"I wouldn't worry about them too much. They're always bickering about something."

He retraced their steps to the doorway and motioned for Syron to follow. She ducked under the sheet he held up for her and looked around. Most of the people that had been out when they arrived were gone. She purposely did not look at Yira and Leon making their way back to the stairs, or Adaline, who still leaned against the wall where she had left her.

"It didn't seem that way," she said. "Any time Yira came up, he had only good things to say about her."

Viero started down one of the winding paths between the curling roots and clusters of flowers. Syron followed closely behind.

"He was so young when Astrophe died," Viero said. "I don't think he really knew how to handle it. I'm assuming he told you about his obsession with the flowers?"

"He did."

"Yira was the one who convinced him to stop. She did everything she could to make sure he grew up smart and strong. In a lot of ways, she's as much his mother as Astrophe was."

He didn't say anything else, and Syron didn't ask. It made sense, in a manner of speaking, at least enough to explain their familiarity. Leon's devotion to Yira hadn't been exceptionally clear, but she hadn't been around them enough to see it either.

From the platform, the canopy had blocked the network of roots that hugged the base of the giant tree. They formed a misshapen oval around a small pond. Viero stopped next to it and turned to her.

"Each faction specializes in something. Given the position of Idris's faction, though I doubt it will be hers for much longer, her focus is training. Ours is developing the sixth sense. The sahiit have extraordinary third-eye capabilities. For years, the God forced them to suppress it." He ran his hand along one of the higher roots. "This is proof of how much they can accomplish if that growth isn't hindered."

Syron moved closer to the pond and squatted down next to it. The lights reflected brilliantly on the surface as she ran her hand over it and waited for the ripples to reach the edge. "You keep saying sahiit. Back at…Idris's faction…there was stigma about mixed blood making it harder to use their third eye. Can temporals not…" She saw Viero's expression and backtracked. "I mean, I know that's not true. I've seen what Yira can do—"

"I know what you're getting at," Viero said, and smiled. "No, temporals can't do what the sahiit can. Some children show signs when they're very young, but it fades as they get older."

"Why?" Syron asked. "If there's anyone who should be able to, it should be you."

His smile turned wistful. "Yira's mom used to say the same. She believed that once our want for material comforts becomes a part of everyday life, our third eye closes. She called it 'transgressing against the self.' But then, you'd think it would be something you could come back from."

The smile slipped from his face for the briefest of seconds before he looked away from the water and composed himself.

He must have caught his reflection, Syron thought.

"So, is this tree the way it is because of the sahiit that live here?" She didn't ask for herself. His expression was one she saw in the mirror all the time. If she kept him talking, at least he wouldn't be lost in his thoughts.

He cleared his throat and glanced over his shoulder, back toward the stairs. "It is. But if you don't mind, there are a few matters that need my tending to. You're welcome to any room you like, but the three Damien prepared are there, on the second level." He pointed behind her, where three rooms covered in white sheets glowed with a warm light. "We're happy to have you here, Syron. Even if nothing comes of this, the best anyone can do is try."

Syron didn't pretend to smile when he did, but she did watch the crease of his shirt between his shoulder blades as he walked away. He was the type of man Syron had known fleetingly back home, who always tried to look on the positive side. But he's also the type, Syron thought, that had a piece of himself die a long time ago.

Soft music still played from somewhere out of sight. She switched her attention back to the pond and gripped the root around its edge. She peered inside the pond.

Sometimes, looking at her reflection was like trying to find a familiar face in a crowd of strangers. On the outside, nothing had changed. She still had the same long dark hair, except now it was mostly in tangles. Her pale skin accentuated the dark circles under her eyes as she planted her knees under the thick of the root and cupped her hands beneath the water's surface, scattering her reflection. Behind her, the world blazed with a million lights.

A drop trickled down her chin. She swiped it away as she looked up and caught Leon staring.

He looked away hastily. The muscles rolled in his shoulders as he followed Yira up the wooden steps and picked a room at random. Syron waited until they were both in their rooms to get to her feet, follow the curving path, and climb the steps herself.

She paused at the entrance to her room and looked out over the faction, but Adaline was nowhere to be seen.

Inside, a low table with a change of clothes folded on top stood at the foot of the bed. A circular wash basin was pushed against the left wall, along with a towel, a bar of soap, and a pitcher filled with water.

After everything, she wanted nothing more than to collapse on the bed, even though she knew her dreams wouldn't be her own. But she dumped the pitcher anyway and stripped down, keeping a close watch on the shadows of the leaves that pressed against the sheet in case she had to run for cover.

The thin, black cotton one-piece that had been set out for her cinched at the waist, but it was loose and comfortable as she wrung out her hair and brushed her fingers through. On the other side of the sheet, a shadow of a man started to walk past. He paused in front of her doorway and turned around, seemed to take a deep breath, and doubled back. He held something in one of his hands.

"Knock, knock."

Syron flung the sheet aside. Beads of water glistened in Leon's hair as he looked down at her. Pink colored his cheeks.

"I owe you an apology," he said, and raised the paper bag dramatically. "And before you tell me to get lost, I brought snacks."

Syron's stomach grumbled in response, but she crossed her arms instead.

"I thought you were mad at me."

His face fell. "Whatever your reasons for wanting to go there, it's not my place to change your mind. Even if I don't *agree*, I understand why it's important. And you're right. Getting out of Evangentine without the God's favor is close to impossible."

Syron's heart dropped to her stomach. "So, you're not coming with us."

"I never said that." He sat down so his back leaned on the raised entrance to the doorway. After a moment's hesitation, Syron sat beside him and peeked inside the bag.

"I couldn't remember the last time you'd eaten. Going through a big glamour takes a lot out of you, even for an angel."

Syron rolled her eyes when he nudged her and picked through the bag, pulling out loose strips of jerky, banana chips in a little cardboard container, and a couple of pale cookies. She piled them on her lap.

"Thank you for thinking of me," she said, letting out a breath. "I know it sounds crazy, but I keep thinking that we might be okay if he doesn't know we're coming toward him instead of away from him. After we get in, though…" Her voice trailed off. She didn't know the first thing that would happen, or how to go about what she wanted to do. That was where Yira came in, she supposed. "But Yira is right. It would be safer—"

"I meant what I said, Sy. I'm not leaving your side unless you turn me away."

Syron flushed and bit into a slice of jerky. It was a little oversalted, but it calmed the queasiness in her stomach.

"That will be a cold day in hell."

Fuck, I actually said it.

Leon's hair brushed his eyebrows as he smiled over at her. His hand twitched, and Syron imagined him reaching over to rest it on her knee, or maybe her thigh. Her heart beat faster in response.

"Do you mind if I ask you something personal?" she asked. "I'll understand if you don't want to talk about it."

"Not at all. What's on your mind?"

She flipped the cookie over in her hands. "The first time we talked, before we got to Idris's faction, I saw you slip something back into your pocket. I've noticed it a couple of times since. I guess I was wondering…" She let her voice fade, because Leon had already leaned back and was digging in his pocket.

The bag crinkled as he leaned closer and opened his hand. A golden dragonfly perched in his palm. Its body was as big as his pinkie, crisscrossed with delicate lines and broken only by the golden cog encapsulated in glass inside the center of its chest.

Leon's arm wrapped around her as the cog rotated and the wings unfurled. A thin edge of gold surrounded the watercolor blue-and-green glass. They fluttered.

"Here," he whispered, and wrapped his hand around hers. His breath fanned her neck as he positioned her finger and thumb at the end of the dragonfly, flicked her wrist, and kept her hand steady as the wings slid along the lines on the body and re-formed into a gold-and-glass blade. He pulled away.

"Mom never went anywhere without it. Yira found it in her ashes and gave it to me, around the same time everything happened with the flowers. I didn't know it was anything other than a trinket until years later."

Syron held it up to the light. Even through Astrophe's death, it didn't even have a scuff on it. Every detail was perfect, right down to the wisps of color in the glass. She pushed at the flat part of the blade, but it was locked in place.

"It's beautiful," she said.

"And deadly," Leon added. "I've only ever had to use it as an element of surprise, but I think that's what it was made for. A quick slice on the neck or ankle, that kind of thing. Don't worry, it was only watchmen."

Syron nodded and handed it back, careful to avoid the blade. She couldn't see the cog turning from the angle, but as soon as he touched it, the blade separated, shrank, and rounded out until it was the dragonfly with furled wings again. He tucked it back in his pocket at the same time Syron looked past him, out over the faction, and tensed. Near the pond at the base of the tree stood a solitary figure with a trowel in one hand and a pair of gloves in the other.

Rationally, she knew Damien couldn't see to look up at them, but he faced their direction, his head raised right to the spot where they sat. The light accentuated his milky eyes so they almost glowed. He didn't move. He didn't even blink.

Syron tore her eyes away, fighting the urge to run back into her room.

"It's late," she said instead. "And we have a big day tomorrow." She piled the snacks back in the bag and swiped at the crumbs on her clothes as Leon got to his feet. He caught her hand when she moved to push aside the sheet. Damien was still there in the background when she turned to face Leon, watching them with sightless eyes.

"You never said whether you accepted my apology."

Syron caught her breath. Being around Leon was like a drug. He made her forget everything that was good or bad or ugly until it was just…him. The way he looked at her when he thought she wasn't looking, how his eyes always seemed to get lighter when she said something that made him smile, all of it. It would be easy to invite him in. Easy to lose herself.

And it terrified her. There was too much at stake to put everything to the side, and besides, she had gotten lost before. And when the time came, because it would—it always did—she would be left with nothing but broken pieces to stitch back together.

No, she couldn't invite him in.

She squeezed his hand before letting it fall. "There's nothing to apologize for. Thank you for the snacks."

Leon nodded, but something in his face had changed. He closed the distance between them and hesitated. Syron breathed in the smell of him that was only *man*, only *Leon*, and thought perhaps she was already gone.

He kissed her on the forehead, warm and soft. "Goodnight," he murmured in her ear, and Syron shivered with pleasure before he pulled away. She didn't look back at the tree as she picked up the bag and went into her room. And she wasn't thinking about the man with scars as she slid under the blankets. All she felt were Leon's lips, and all she thought was that she wished he were with her.

"Goodnight," she whispered to the empty room, and shut her eyes.

10
NIGHTMARE

Will's scream echoed off the stone walls as the knife twisted deeper into his shoulder. The man dressed in black leather and a black mask leaned into it, digging the blade through to the other side, and ripped it free.

Will's screams turned feral. The chains that held him in place cackled like sadistic laughter as he thrashed against them, reopening day-old wounds that had just started to heal over. Sharp pain from old tortures blended with the new until he was nothing more than a mound of scarred flesh with a breaking resolve. But at least it wasn't the whip, or the fucking hammer.

Will's voice cracked and faded, but he did not whimper as the man cocked his head to survey his work. Instead, Will stared at where he knew his eyes would be and struggled to breathe in the sour air through the tremors that coursed through him.

"Fuck you," he managed to say, and spit. It flashed red in the weak light and landed squarely on the man's chest.

The mask twitched, almost as if he were smirking beneath it. He didn't wipe it away.

"You keep offering. One day, I'll be inclined to agree." His voice was deep and controlled, well educated. A sick fuck. He walked *around him slowly, trailing the flat of the knife along his abdomen and ribs. He stopped with the point against his back.*

"I'll ask one more time. Where's the other angel?"

"I already told you," Will said, seething. "There is no other angel. Tell the God—"

Fresh pain exploded in his lower back. Will gasped and tried to jerk away, but it only dug the manacles around his wrists and ankles deeper into his skin. The man laughed, hollow and lifeless, and tossed the blade aside. Black spots dotted Will's vision as the knife clattered to the floor.

Fingers wove through his hair, forcing his head back. "Syron?" the man whispered. "Syron? Syron!"

Someone was shaking her awake. Syron shot forward, sucking in a quick, desperate gulp of the clean air, and felt the ghost of scars all over her, the pressure in her chest, the trail of fresh blood down her back and shoulder. The covers were in a knot around her. She pushed them off and ran her hands down her arms, her legs. Touched her face. There were no scars there. No blood. It was another dream.

"Syron? Are you okay?"

She looked up at Yira long enough to see the knit of worry between her eyebrows and turned to press her forehead against the cool soil of the wall. She didn't want anyone to see her like this—not when fear coiled in a tight knot in her stomach. She felt it trying to grow, unfurling like a snake.

"I heard you screaming next door. Is everything okay?" Yira asked again, and the bed shifted when her weight settled on the side. She made a sound that was half laugh, half sigh. "That was a stupid question. Syron, I—I understand if you don't want to talk about it. But you said something yesterday that got me thinking. When Viero asked what your plan is after we leave, you said you saw the lengths the God will go to get what he wants. I guess what I'm asking is whether you meant literally, or whether you were going off what you've been told already?"

Syron pulled her knees tightly to her chest and looked back at her. The whisper of pain still hugged her wrists and ankles, but she ignored it, focusing instead on Yira's too-tight grip on the edge of the mattress. As soon as Yira saw her looking, she relaxed her hand.

"You've been working with Adaline since before I came here." Syron's voice cracked, and she cleared her throat. "Did she tell you I wasn't alone when she found me?"

Yira shook her head.

"My friend, Will, was in the water with me. He was reaching for the flower when I left, but I never knew whether he made the decision to come with me or not." Syron paused. She didn't know how much else, if anything else, she should tell Yira. She'd kept her dreams to herself so far because she hadn't known what they meant, not exactly. But now Will had a timer on his head, so that meant Syron did too.

"When my dreams started, I didn't know it was him. How could I when I never saw his face? But I've been in his head enough to recognize him. I was there when he was running from the watchmen, and when he gave up and decided to go back to the God's City. And then last night, I was there for what they did to him." Syron grabbed her shoulder where the knife had twisted and grimaced. It was always surreal waking back up without any evidence of the hurt.

"He doesn't have a lot of time, Yira. They chained him up, and there's a man in a black mask..." Syron's voice faltered, and she stopped. She drew in a ragged breath. "I don't know how much more he can handle."

"Does anyone else know about your dreams?"

Syron nodded. "Adaline and Leon know a little."

Yira shifted to rest her knee on the bed. "Astrophe had dreams like that too. She said it was like becoming someone else, and all their thoughts were hers too. But she saw discrepancies between what she witnessed in her sleep and when she was awake. A forest in her dream would be a city now, or a group of people that lived in one area would have migrated to another, things like that. The important thing to keep in mind is that in dreams, time is not linear. I've seen fallen who were captured by the God rambling about it before their deaths. It's a hard thing to manage, but the best way to start is not to let it affect your decisions in the real world. I guess what I'm trying to get at is there's really no way to know whether it's really Will."

There may have been a time Syron would have been relieved to hear her say it out loud. It gave voice to the illusion that her dependency and fear didn't hurt the people closest to her. But that's just what it was—an illusion. How could she explain the whisper of Will's memories brushing against hers, or the familiar way his thoughts jumped from one thing to another? And if there were any lingering doubts, the man in the mask had specifically asked about another angel.

It would be nice to imagine Will safe at home, but no matter what Yira thought she knew, there were no hard and fast truths. Not anymore.

Yira must have understood the look on her face. "We're going to the city anyway. If by some miracle you do find who the onocalcum linked you with, there's no way to know for sure without seeing their memories, and making someone relive trauma could damage their mind, or worse.

But *if* you're right," she added, her voice dropping, "and it is Will, then I have to ask. What are you going to do if he's already dead?"

The snake that had been idle coiled and struck, knocking over her haphazardly placed defenses. *This* was something she never allowed herself to think about, kept it wrapped up tight and just out of arm's reach. Of course, Syron had suspected Yira to be doubtful. Syron had stared at the passage about the onocalcum long enough to know it by heart. But she hadn't thought she'd say *this*—condemn her hopes in a single sentence, a single syllable, and turn her tilting world upside down.

No, she wasn't ready to hear it.

Her body wasn't either. She lurched away from Yira, off the bed, and ran the short distance to the basin. She splashed the cold, clear water on her face and considered submerging her head completely, just for a second, and thought better of it.

Her hands were shaking when she scrubbed her face with the towel and turned back to Yira, but she was gone.

There wasn't anything left to say anyway. There was no answer to a question like that, only a silence that would stretch out and consume her if she thought about it for too long. So she flicked each of her fingers in tandem to try to erase the conversation from her mind, and if not erase it, then store it away somewhere so compact she wouldn't be able to find it again. The sheet billowed around her, and she stepped out of her room, locking the thoughts away.

Outside, the faction had come to life. Past the railing and glimmering branches, a diverse mix of sahiit and temporals gathered around the tree. She stopped at the bottom of the stairs to let a group of children run past. A little girl near the back slowed to a crawl as the others squeezed between the people closest to the tree. Syron imagined them tucking themselves into the wildest parts of the roots.

The little girl tugged at the hem of her father's shirt. Her question was lost in the chatter, but he hoisted her onto his shoulders and pointed to one of the doors across the way, with the sheet pulled back. Almost immediately, smooth, calm music started playing.

Syron followed the soft notes of the melody with the same focused attention as she followed the path back to the other side of the faction. She nodded politely to the few people she passed and gave a silent thanks when they didn't try to talk to her. She had never been good at making small talk, and she didn't want to try now.

But when she peeked inside the room she had met Viero in before, it was empty. Even the chairs were pushed back in the same spots they had left them.

She stepped off the path to let a line of people pass and lifted to her tiptoes. Unless Viero was in the huddle of bodies by the tree, she didn't see him anywhere—or anyone else she recognized, for that matter.

"Careful doing that, miss. The flowers are as much a part of the ecosystem here as the tree."

"Sorry," Syron said, still scanning the crowd. "Have you seen Viero? I think I'm supposed to meet with him." She looked around, but it wasn't until the line of people broke and she stepped back onto the path that she saw the cluster of workers on the other side. Damien's gloved hands were deep in a wheelbarrow half-full of fertilizer. He smiled up at her, and Syron took a step back.

He didn't see it. "He finished the morning inspections. If you don't see him in the meeting room, I'd check his office." He swung his arm out, the scars curving gruesomely around his forearm, and nearly hit the man behind him. "It's on the ground level under the stairs."

"Damn, Damien," the man behind him swore. "Pay attention to what you're doing, will you?"

Damien smiled darkly to himself and nodded to her, dipping his face in shadow.

Syron didn't wait around to hear more. Tingles had started in the tips of her fingers, increasing almost painfully by the time she reached Viero's office and yanked aside the sheet.

This room was nothing like the last. It was wider and fuller, containing a large desk pushed to one side, a bookcase overflowing with thick, leather-bound volumes, and a large oak table sporting heaping portions of cabbage rolls, thick cuts of meat, mashed potatoes, and a wide bowl filled to the brim with what looked like orange pudding. But the seats were empty here too.

The sheet settled into place behind her as she took a few tentative steps forward.

"Hello?"

After a light shuffle of what sounded like papers being set aside, Viero emerged through another circular doorway half-hidden behind the bulk of the bookcase. He ran a hand through his silver hair.

"Ah, the angel has returned." He offered a tired smile. "Just in time. The food was starting to get cold."

"I told you she doesn't like to be called that." Leon shook his head as he trailed in behind, followed by Yira.

"And I told *you* the correct term is fallen," Yira said. "Angel was a given name by the God. It has no place here."

Syron looked away when Yira tried to meet her eye and slid into the empty chair beside Viero.

"I just don't understand one thing," Yira continued, as

if carrying on an earlier conversation. "If there's an underground level to the spire, why didn't anyone know about it? We were both in there almost every day."

"All I know is that it's beneath the Artist's Room." Viero reached for the potatoes, and Syron took the cue to load her plate with a little bit of everything. It didn't matter that the juices ran together—it had been days since she'd had a proper meal.

Viero twisted off a bite of pork and chewed slowly. He swallowed. "I was only in there long enough to grab Damien during the uprising. It's not my place to ask him what happened down there. If I were him, I doubt I'd ever say a word."

Yira leaned back in her seat and stared at him. "So, what I'm hearing is when our whole world turned upside down, not only did you go after Damien to save him instead of Mom, but you also know absolutely nothing about the room you rescued him from except that you had to go through a glamour to get there."

Viero paused with his fork in the air, dripping juices on the table. "If that's the conclusion you'd like to draw," he said icily, "then yes. Your mother was capable of saving herself."

"But she *didn't*."

The room lapsed into silence. Viero stared hard at his plate and continued eating, and after a while Syron and Leon did too. She caught his eye once across the table, and he gave her a look that said *welcome to the awkward family dinner*.

Syron wished she could lick the tension around the table like the end of the spoon and pull it out sparkling clean. The citrus danced on her tongue, and she cleared her throat.

"Does your faction always eat like this?" Syron asked,

pointedly not looking at Yira, who sat as still as a statue. She hadn't even touched the food.

"Not usually," Viero answered, and reached for seconds. "We have…certain connections outside the border. The portions were distributed between the households this morning, if that's what you're thinking."

"No, I was just curious."

She wanted to ask about Damien, or what they had been doing in the adjoining room, or whether Yira had told them about her dream. But Leon sat straighter in his seat. He hadn't bothered using the silverware, and spices from the chicken thigh he held stuck to his pale fingers.

"All right, I have a question. Why did the God walk into a bar?" His eyes flitted between everyone above his smile. "To check for any sin-dicates."

A beat passed before a bubble of laughter erupted from Syron, and she shielded her face with a napkin to hide her smile. Yira broke position enough to roll her eyes, but her lips turned up the same as Viero's, if only slightly.

"It's the Black Book we need anyway," she said, and leaned forward. "That's what he uses to keep the souls of the fallen in, right?"

Viero nodded but didn't look at his daughter. "The God craves knowledge. Short of the Nightman, it's the only thing that he—"

"Sir!"

Syron whirled to the voice. She recognized the temporal woman from the night before, who had been tending the flowers. She was covered in a sheen of sweat, her hand gripping tightly to the sheet over the doorway.

"Three sahiit just arrived. Idris is leading them."

The fork slipped through Syron's fingers and clattered against the plate.

Yira jumped into motion and drew the woman aside, demanding to know who was with Idris, what had been said, whether they had weapons. Syron watched as if she were far away, pulled suddenly and callously into a pocket of time that muted the world around her and forced everything into slow motion. When the woman answered, Syron was too deaf to hear and too far away to read her lips.

When a hand grabbed Syron's, the world came rushing back. "Tatia, I need you to stall them. The rest of you," Viero ordered, pulling Syron from the chair, "come with me."

His grip was firm as he led them through the door by the bookcase and into what must have been his bedroom. Half-opened books and hand-drawn maps lay scattered across the floor. Syron blinked, and then they were through another door, passing rooms that stretched out on each side before branching off, each one overflowing with fruits and vegetables in different stages of growth, rising up beneath thick clusters of fairy lights.

Yira and Leon sprinted ahead, leaving Syron to tighten her grip on Viero's hand for fear of being lost in the maze.

"How is Idris here? I thought you said we had a couple of days?"

Viero grunted, quickening his pace. "Not if they found Yira's glamour."

When they finally emerged under the light of the willow tree, they were on the other side of the faction. The music was louder here, and Syron fought the urge to look over her shoulder to see whether she could find Idris with her fancy clothes, or Briar with his arrogant stride, or Zariah with her fierce scowl. Viero angled them toward the room she had watched the father point to before, when the little girl had pulled at the hem of his shirt. Two temporals watched them with wide eyes through the door, one behind a battered piano and the other with a violin resting delicately under her chin. But the music didn't stop.

Leon had said something to her once about every faction having a back door. It made sense for it to be here, far enough away from the entrance and yet close enough in case of an emergency.

Yira and Leon had almost reached the corner of the room.

Syron craned her neck back even though there was no time, no seconds to spare, and let her hand go limp in Viero's. She felt his grip slip, even as she saw that her guess was right. Tatia had led Idris and the others to the entrance of the meeting room, making calming gestures even as Idris's head bobbed angrily. On either side of her, distinguishable even from the back, stood Briar and Zariah.

Syron started to turn back to Viero when a girl with flaming curls who had been hidden behind Briar took a step back. Her chin lifted to take in the massive tree, and Syron's breath caught.

Calais.

Calais's head dipped as if she heard her, and even so far away, Syron knew she was looking right at her.

But the stolen seconds slipped by and Viero had hold of her hand again, pulling her into the room filled with music meant to inspire, to calm, to grow, and all she could think was how disgustingly out of place it was, how each note hit her like a slap across the face. She could feel the sting of it behind her eyes just as she could feel Viero's hands wrapping like hot irons around her shoulders.

He looked her squarely in the eye. His were a watery green, and this close, the fairy lights on the ceiling made the wrinkles around his eyes and on his forehead stand out in stark relief.

"Let Yira know I'll send Adaline after you when it's safe!" he yelled through the music. "And be careful, Syron. There are more dangerous things than gods."

Then he pushed her through the wall.

II

WAYWARD SPIRITS WELCOME

Syron landed on her ass under a roiling sky thick with the promise of rain. Unlike the forest around Idris's faction, this land was barren except for awkward chunks of rock and long, thin twists of metal that broke off randomly before starting again farther away.

Yira and Leon were already down the way and looking off into the distance. Syron picked herself up off the hard ground and ran toward them, ignoring the bite of gravel against her bare feet.

"Guys! Idris will be here any second. We need to—"

"Fuck!" Yira screamed. It grated against Syron's ears, and she skidded to a stop next to Leon. Yira turned to look back in the direction they had come, her eyes half wild, and Syron followed her gaze to the invisible quiver of light that made up the glamour.

They waited. Syron vibrated with nervous energy, but she forced herself to stay still. When nothing happened, Leon shifted next to her.

"Where are we?"

Yira took a deep breath and glanced at the sky. "A

couple of miles past Viero's faction," she said in a forced voice. "I should have been more careful leaving Idris's. It's my fault they found us, but the good news is Viero isn't letting them through the glamour, or they would have been here already. If he had, trying to run would have been pointless, especially since Briar is with her." She paused. "I've been out here before. If we hurry, we should be able to get to shelter before nightfall."

"Calais is with them," Syron said. "I thought you should know. She saw me before I left."

Yira wasn't surprised. "Did you tell her anything before that would be useful to Idris? Any plans about where you wanted to go?"

Syron shook her head. "No, she doesn't know anything."

"Good, then it doesn't matter. Adaline left early this morning to scout the area. With any luck, she'll catch our trail and find us before Briar does."

Yira nodded to Leon before taking off at a jog, and Syron yelped in surprise as Leon hoisted her onto his back and followed. Her fingers dug into the feverish skin between his neck and shoulders. She was pressed tightly against him, all too aware of the rise and fall of her chest against his back, the way his arms contoured themselves to her thighs, and his hands, rough and warm, wrapped around the backs of her knees.

"Calais was there?" he asked quietly.

Syron looked down at him. From this angle she couldn't see his expression, just the sharp point of his nose and the hollow of his cheek. He raised his chin as if preparing for a blow.

Syron bit her lip. Instead of answering, she asked, "Did you ever think she'd do it?"

She didn't elaborate, but with Leon, she didn't need to.

He grimaced. "We've been friends for a long time. She changes her mind a lot about things that should be black-and-white, but until now she's always made the right call. I just…think she puts her faith in the wrong people sometimes."

"Well, the night I stayed in your room she put her faith in Atlas. She went to the party and told everyone I was staying with you to get his attention." She purposely glossed over the sleeping together part. "I came back to tell you about it after I confronted her. She said it was an accident, and I hated her for trying to make me feel bad when she's the one who messed up. But I thought that would be the worst of it, especially after we left."

His arms tightened against her thighs in response, but they had caught up with Yira and he stayed silent. Syron didn't mind it—despite the circumstances, she was glad for who she was with. Especially Leon, but even Yira. She may have spoken out of turn that morning, but at least she was up front about her worries, and more than that, had checked on Syron when she had heard her screams.

Unlike Calais, who had pretended to be her friend right up until Syron couldn't stand it anymore and called her out.

Syron fit her hands under Leon's arms and placed them against his chest. She rested her head on his back and listened to his even breathing, even if it were a little fast. His steps were smooth despite the rocky ground, as if he picked each one carefully.

She tried timing her breaths with Leon's to distract herself, but she couldn't keep from wondering when Calais's allegiances had switched. Maybe it was the same morning Syron had stood up for herself, or when she had told Calais and Leon about the conversation she had overheard between Briar and Zariah. Or could it be the night before that, when Calais had ditched her initiation to stay with Atlas?

Or had her mind been made up from the start? From the first night Syron had fallen, and she had patted the spot next to her on the grass, and offered her room when Idris said they would have to make one up?

The deceit hurt. The unknowing hurt worse.

She shook her head to clear her thoughts, and Leon readjusted her weight on his back.

"You don't have to carry me, you know," Syron murmured. "I do have feet."

"Not like a sahiit. Our skin is thicker, so it's rare we ever wear shoes unless we're in gear. Yira just likes to be ready in case of a fight."

At Yira's mention, Syron looked around and found her behind them. She walked slowly with her gaze locked on the horizon, trying to peer through the darkening shades of gray. She squinted at something in the distance, but when Syron turned to look, it was either lost or hidden away.

The wind was warm and sudden when it gusted behind them and flung Syron's hair forward. Leon sputtered when it landed on his face, and Syron swatted it back and held it in a tight knot at the base of her head. When the next gust came, she turned toward it, felt the wet inside of it, and waited for the rain.

She had no idea how long they had been walking. Breakfast from that morning was nothing more than a sour taste in her mouth, and even though the sky was darker, there was no way to tell whether it was nightfall or just the oppressive, low-hanging clouds.

Leon's loosened his grip on her, and she slid down his back, running her hands down her stiff legs as he stretched. At some point, the rock and gravel had given way to dirt and the occasional sparse grass. With the road behind them, there was nothing but empty land and the blurry start of the forest far to their left.

She wanted to ask how much longer it would be until they found shelter, but Yira pointed to a darker patch in the sky, and Syron's thoughts scattered. It was the wrong way: vertical instead of horizontal and hidden enough by the clouds to make the edges indistinct. It stretched from the ground up, so tall she couldn't see the top.

"The spire," Yira said with a mixture of awe and distaste, like eating something sweet on the outside before finding the rotten core. "We've made good time, and if that's there…" She walked to their left as the first drizzle of rain broke through the clouds, and Syron followed.

Yira paused mid-step and swung out her arm to block her from going any farther. Her arm dropped when Syron paused next to her, but it wasn't until Yira pointed that she saw they stood on the edge of a low, steep cliff. The drop-off was smooth and rounded, blending seamlessly in the low light with the ground below. Syron shuffled backward and, watching how Yira planted her feet to look over the edge, mirrored her stance.

Below them, a small town huddled against the base of the cliff.

She had seen the God's City in her dreams: bronze shops decorated in neon signs, wide streets and walkways evenly placed beneath the massive spire. This town was just the opposite. Rough wooden buildings clumped together awkwardly, each cockeyed to its neighbor. There was no sign to give the town a name, but next to each of the buildings was a perfect circle of black ash.

They watched, unseen, as a man with cracked emerald skin hauled the body of a deer from the back of a building and placed it, almost delicately, inside the circumference of one of the circles. The ash glowed red-hot, and he sank to his knees next to it, lifting his hands to the sky.

"Del-Amar," Yira said when Syron turned her face against the stink of burnt hair and flesh. "It's a pit stop for heretics. Besides the workers, it's rare anyone stays for more than a few days. That man," she said, jutting her chin at the stranger, "is one of the umbriels."

"What are umbriels?"

But Yira wasn't paying attention. A strike of lightning lit the sky, bright white against the trail of smoke, and she backed away from the edge.

"Is it safe?" Syron tried again. "Will they try to…I don't know. Rob us?"

She hadn't heard Leon come up next to her, and she jumped when he snorted. "Towns like these wouldn't last long if they didn't cater to visitors. So long as we don't cause any trouble, the worst thing they'll do is ask too many questions. This guy is a good example," he added and nodded to the umbriel. "He'll stay there for hours to prove his devotion to his chosen god, even in the rain. If we tried talking to him now, it would be an act of disrespect, and we'd probably be kicked out."

"That sounds…a little silly."

"Better than slaughtering the fallen," Yira said, and grimaced as a crack of thunder sounded behind them. Syron followed the sound to see the drizzle had grown to great sheets of rain in the distance, like a blanket laid over just half of the world. When she turned back, Yira and Leon had already taken off along the easternmost edge of the cliff. She ran after them, giving the edge a wide berth until the ground arched up to meet it, and she took a shortcut down.

They were faster than her by far, but not fast enough to beat the storm. The porch lights in Del-Amar flicked on at the same time the rain beat off Syron's shoulders, and she raced ahead. It slid down her clothes, warm at first, then chilling against the whip and thrash of the wind.

When she finally reached the shelter of a porch, she held her breath against the sordid stench of the deer and wiped the wet from her eyes, even as it slanted to reach her. Leon held the door half-open for her, and she paused only long enough to read the thin, gold script on the plaque above the frame before hurrying inside: *Wayward Spirits Welcome.*

Syron let the door slam shut behind them and hugged her arms tightly to her chest. They stood in an old, dim barroom lit by yellowed lampshades. Low tables lined the walls, framing a stained green-and-gold rug in the center of the floor. An open eye with lashes like rays of light embossed its center.

A young woman with skin the color of night perched behind the bar. Her white hair lay in perfect curls over her shoulders, fanning as she drew her attention away from the window and smiled. Her cheekbones were high and sharp, her white lashes thick and full. A rag dangled carelessly in one hand as she nodded to them.

"Wayward spirits welcome," she said, and Syron couldn't tell whether it was her way of saying hello, or the name of the bar, or both. "My name is Penny. I saw you all trying to beat the storm. Nearly looked like you were going to make it too."

"It's a shame we didn't," Yira answered. "We need room and board. Just one for the three of us."

Penny's eyebrows shot up. Her gaze swept over them,

lingering on Leon, and Syron resisted the urge to reach out and touch him. Barely.

"The charge is per person, not per room. Just so happens the upstairs is empty, if I could persuade you to change your mind?"

"One is fine…thank you," Yira added, almost as an afterthought.

Penny nodded thoughtfully and dipped beneath the bar, coming up a second later with a key. They followed her up a flight of stairs pressed tightly against the far wall and onto a small landing with three doors on either side.

She fit the key into the first door on the left and jiggled it open. "You have to pay before you leave, but as long as you mind your own, you can stay for as long as you like. Decency gets you a long way, as I'm sure you all know." She flipped on the light and moved to the side to let them in. "There are spare linens in the closet and a washboard in the bathroom for your things."

"Is there a shop here?"

"Across the way. Jaro is outside right now. You may have seen him on your way down, but he shouldn't be too much longer." Penny nodded to the window looking out on the waterlogged town and turned to Syron. "I don't mean to pry, but will you be expecting company? It's not often you see a temporal outside the God's City."

For the first time, Syron noticed her eyes. They were human except that the pupils set into the dark brown were shaped like slits. She wondered whether Penny was an umbriel too and, if so, whether that meant she and Jaro shared the same feature.

"No company," Syron answered. "But when was the last time you saw one? A temporal, I mean."

The edges of Penny's mouth perked up. "Looking for someone, are we? Sorry to say it's been years since the last one passed through. You wouldn't know him, but last I heard, he settled down with a pretty little thing and had a baby girl. Nineveh, I think her name was."

Yira glowered next to them, and Penny's smile widened before pressing the key into Syron's hand. "You all seem to prefer your privacy. I'll bring dinner up soon as it's done. The kitchen is behind the bar, so if you holler and I don't answer, you know where to find me."

She turned and shut the door behind her. Syron breathed in the sweet scent of her lingering perfume and turned her attention to the room. It was small, clean, and plain. All the wood had the same dark brown stain as the bar downstairs, only set off by the white sheets on the bed. Syron walked past the open door of the bathroom and leaned on one side of the window. Sheets of rain buffeted off the glass like nails, but through it she could just make out the indistinct shape of Jaro in the storm, still kneeling over his offering. Whoever his chosen god was, they must have turned a deaf ear.

"It's crazy, isn't it?" Leon asked behind her. "The lengths people will go to serve something they don't even know exists."

"It exists to him," Syron said, and looked back at Leon. He stood a hairbreadth away, close enough she could feel the heat rolling off him. She wanted to lean into him. Instead, he draped a towel over her shoulders.

"I'm running across the road to see what kinds of clothes they have. Hopefully that Jaro guy doesn't take too much longer."

Syron was about to object. It was raining, after all, but he winked at her. "Just don't eat my food if I'm not back in time."

Yira slid him coins from her pocket before he left, and then it was just them. Syron sighed and turned back to the window, holding the towel tightly around her with her free hand and running her thumb over the rough bit of the key with the other. The distant crack of thunder was dulled enough by the beat of rain against the roof that it could just as easily be the quick, ringing clamor of pots and pans in the kitchen below them.

"I'm sorry for what I said in your room earlier. I shouldn't have asked you that."

Syron stiffened before looking back. Yira's wet hair was pushed behind her ears, showing off the abstract markings across the side of her face and the one leaf tucked into the hollow of her cheek. She kicked the towel to the side that she must have used to wipe up the water on the floor and sat on the edge of the bed, running her fingers through her hair.

"I didn't think how it would sound until after I said it. If I hadn't needed to meet with Viero, I would've stuck around longer. I was on my way to him when I heard you."

Syron leaned her head back on the window frame and closed her eyes. She let a second pass. "You don't have to apologize. I know why you asked. I just can't accept that after all this he would be, well, you know."

"I understand. Astrophe used to say all fallen were sent here for another chance at life, and that fate must favor the ironic—to send them here just to die again."

Syron lowered her head. "Were you close with her, then?"

Yira's eyes danced. "She was my best friend. If the world were a better place and she were still here, I think you two would really like each other. She could read anyone like they were an open book—large print," Yira added and laughed to herself, as if it were an inside joke. "She was intelligent and passionate. She had this electricity about her, like everything she did was with her whole heart. It was effortless. Leon absolutely adored her. She was his whole world."

Syron smiled. Astrophe sounded like a poem—so real, so thrumming with life even after all the time she'd been gone, as if her pages were written in the wind and anyone who walked outside could breathe her in and feel the flash of her life as if it were their own.

And that's exactly what Yira had done, Syron realized. And then, only then, did she see the similarity between Yira and Viero. It wasn't in how they looked or acted, but how they thought. They kept the people they loved wrapped up close, even after they were gone, and breathed life back into them with their own. It was a romantic type of necromancy.

"You loved her," Syron whispered, tasting the words, knowing what they meant.

Yira let out a breath and looked up at the crease between the wall and ceiling, as if arranging her thoughts. It was a long moment before she spoke. "She was mourning the loss of Leon's dad when I met her. After the God found her and everything went to hell, I did the only thing I could think to—I broke her out.

"Viero had told me about an entrance to the underground tunnels he had found inside the spire. Some of them had collapsed, but there was still one that led outside the city. I took extra shifts to win the God's favor, so when the day of Astrophe's ceremony came and he needed a volunteer to guard her door, my request was approved.

"The only thing I didn't take into consideration was Leon. I tried explaining to her that in the God's eyes, he was the same as any other sahiit. He would be safe until the dust settled and I could come back for him," Yira said. "I know it sounds horrible to say out loud, but the days of the ceremonies were always organized chaos. No one stayed indoors, and with the merchants setting up shop, it wasn't as if I could grab Leon and take him with us without being seen.

"I begged her, Syron, but it was like she didn't even hear me." Her voice broke, and she continued in a whisper. "The last thing I saw was the hem of her auburn dress disappearing into the crowd."

Tears glistened in her eyes. She shut them tight and let out a shaky breath.

Syron was about to say she was sorry for her loss but held back. That was something people said to fill the empty space between themselves and the mourner. She didn't want to accidentally push Yira away or make her regret confiding in her; she wanted to help lift the weight from her shoulders.

"If this were a better world," Syron said instead, just as someone rapped on the door, "I would be honored to meet her."

Yira gave a ragged laugh and sat straighter as Leon bustled into the room. Two large brown paper bags were nuzzled into the crook of each arm. He turned and shut the door behind him, dripping water with each step.

"Penny said the food will be done soon. She should have it up in…" He gasped when he looked up and dropped the bags, but he wasn't looking at them.

His gaze was locked on the window behind Syron.

She whirled around the same time she heard the hollow, thin scraping sound through the storm, and a scream ripped from her throat. She jumped back as the nightchild raked her nails across the glass and grabbed hold of the window sash to force it open.

For a split second, Syron thought it was Adaline. But this child had smooth, flat hair, pearl buttons down her dress, and when she leveled her head and smiled, her eyes were pale and empty, with nothing but the storm raging through from the other side.

Leon pushed past Syron and she stumbled farther back, unwilling to look away. The child's head snapped to follow her, too quick to be natural, and the glass cracked. She pulled away, and Syron felt certain she would throw herself at the window to break in, but Leon raised his hand, gripping the hilt of Astrophe's knife. It glinted in the light, and the child rolled her head to him and bared her teeth. She was coming after Leon instead.

No, Syron thought. And lunged.

But the girl twisted instead and launched herself from the roof just as someone grabbed Syron from behind and yanked her back. The air whooshed from her lungs, and she fell, breathless, against Yira. She ripped herself away and ran to the window next to Leon.

Yira came up behind her, probably ready to yank her back at a moment's notice, but Syron gripped tightly to the edge of the sill and waited.

At first there was nothing but rain and the pounding of what could only be Penny's footsteps on the stairs leading up to their room, and then a blue glow took off like a streak of luminescence in the night, toward where they had seen the spire.

This time when the scream built in her chest, it took Leon's hand wrapping around hers for her to choke it down.

12

MIND, BODY, AND SPIRIT

The Watcher sat hovered over the stars, her uncombed hair curling like dark fingers around her temples and nape. With aged hands, she swirled her hair in a knot at the bottom of her head. The orange dress Syron remembered draped around her: the only color in the black-and-white space. If not for her dress, she would've blended almost seamlessly with the night itself.

Beneath her, shapes of stars like constellations with no names grouped together. She raised one hand, almost invisible against the backdrop, and pointed to each star in turn. It was peaceful and lulling, and for the first time in a long time, Syron knew she was dreaming. Each time she pointed, her lips formed to a name but made no sound. As Syron watched, she dipped her hand into a hidden pocket in her dress and drew out a star. It was just a little silver thing, cold and empty, and she arched her arm and threw.

It landed in the third grouping and blazed to life.

And Syron saw through her eyes a timeline of lives, half of them exploding in a great bright white, and more dropping like lead into the utter dark.

The star she threw faded to almost nothing. She swiped, and even so far away, the star flew and landed in the fifth group.

The voice that came from Syron's throat was husky and warm, but it was not hers.

"Stars burn the brightest just before they die. Yours, my dear, was blinding."

~

Syron woke to a tangerine-and-purple sky. The curtains were pulled back, and bits of dust floated on the sun's rays. At first, she thought only of her dream and imagined them as stars, drawing lines to connect the dots and find some pattern to link them together, but then she remembered where she was and sat up.

The room they were in was new. After Penny heard Syron's screams last night and ran upstairs, Yira explained what happened but glossed over the nightchild in favor of a crazed young woman to avoid suspicion. Horrified, Penny ushered them into a room across the hall. It looked out on the other side of town and was the same as the last, except the window was still intact and framed by white curtains.

Once Penny rushed downstairs to bring up dinner, Syron was the first to change clothes. The gear Leon found in the shop wasn't the same as what the sahiit wore—it was still black but thinner, with a zipper snug against the chest so it could be stepped into like a coverall—but it was comfortable enough to sleep in and even came with a pair of thin-soled shoes that were little more than slippers.

They devoured the meal in silence, Syron not daring to take her eyes off the window. Yira disappeared and came back a moment later, dragging a chair behind her. They took turns keeping watch in case the child came back, and it was only a little past Syron's turn starting when the rain finally stopped. She looked out over the static town in silence, tense and exhausted, and tried to lose her thoughts in the stretch of land past the buildings and the scattering of stars.

Leon woke before his turn and insisted, in a whisper, that she get some more rest and to take his spot on the bed. She had fallen asleep watching the white of Leon's hair turn silver against the backdrop of stars, unable to shake the feeling that she was being watched.

Now, Leon turned the dragonfly over in his hands, staring out the window. Syron climbed out of bed and padded over to him, placing a hand on the back of the chair.

He looked up at her and smiled. Despite his lack of sleep, he didn't look tired.

Syron started to nudge him when her stomach rumbled, and she put a hand on it as if to hide the noise.

Leon heard it, though, and chuckled. "You smell the bacon too? Penny must have bought it off one of the backpackers downstairs."

"You saw people come in?"

"Some. I found the key you set on the dresser a little before dawn and went into our old room. They were coming in from the other side of town."

"But there was no one else?"

Leon shook his head. "No, who else would there be?"

Syron bit her lip and looked past him out the window, hoping by some stroke of luck to see the blurry figure of Adaline running to meet up with them. She should have found them by now, especially if she hadn't gone very far away from Viero's faction in the first place. But if Adaline couldn't catch their trail, maybe that meant Briar couldn't either.

Still, having someone that knew the ins and outs of the

nightchildren, not to mention the God's City, would make her feel a lot better.

Leon caught her hand and wrapped it in his. "I know what you're thinking, but we should be safe for right now. That girl isn't coming back."

Syron shook her head, remembering what Adaline had told her before: that the other nightchildren were controlled by the Nightman, and the Nightman in turn by the God. If the girl were going to come back, she would have already. Which meant she'd either heard or seen enough to satisfy the Nightman, at least temporarily.

Syron felt stupid for not speaking araasi, especially when the language was meant to form a barrier between the speaker and the children. But then again, no one else had either.

Out loud, she said, "If the God didn't know where we were before, he does now."

When she looked back at Leon, the rest of his smile vanished. He squeezed her hand. "That's true, but I know the children don't usually come out during the day. Once Yira wakes up, we'll put some distance between us and this town. I think you were right when you said the God might not expect us to go to him. It could give us an advantage, at least."

"Maybe," Syron said, and shivered. "I just can't believe I had no idea she was right behind me. If you hadn't walked in when you did——"

"Then Yira would have made quick work of her," he said resolutely. "Yira has a hard shell, but she's fierce when it comes to protecting the people she cares about."

A thump came from behind them, and Syron pulled her hand from his and rounded the bed. Yira lay in a mess of blankets on the floor, with one arm out and her hand resting palm up against the dark wood.

"She's still asleep," Syron whispered, and caught sight of the dirty dishes they had left stacked on the dresser the night before. She picked them up and looked back at Leon as he turned the dragonfly over in his hands. The wings fluttered and went still. "I'll ask Penny to get us some food for the road. Any requests?"

"Extra bacon," Leon said, and Syron rolled her eyes playfully and made for the door. She didn't bother trying to shut it behind her, and she felt Leon's eyes on her as she crossed the landing and started down the stairs.

The voices turned from a murmur to a low roar as she emerged into the bustle of the barroom. She paused with her foot on the last step. People Syron had never seen before crowded around the full tables and filled the center of the room until there was barely enough space to walk. Some of them had the same hard, emerald skin as Jaro; others looked like temporals except for the splotches of vibrant scales over their elbows and shoulders. One of the men shifted toward his friend, and she spotted a patch on the side of his neck too.

Syron fit the plate that held the dishes to the divot of her waist and forced herself forward, scanning the crowd for Penny. She made it past the first table when something brushed against her calf and she stumbled back, turning in time to follow the swish of a tail to three blue-skinned women huddled over steaming plates. Each had the same charcoal black hair pulled into a high ponytail, sparkling gold jewelry, and small, narrow eyes. The tail wrapped like an accessory around the leg of one of the women and twitched.

She turned away hurriedly and squeezed between people to the bar, climbing to her tiptoes once she reached it. The people moved aside enough for her to spot Penny holding a tray of frothy, bright pink liquid and nodding earnestly to a group of men who seemed to be giving her their order, before turning on her heel to the next guest, and the next.

Syron debated calling out to her but decided against it. It was better not to draw attention to herself, and besides, she didn't want to be annoying. She slipped behind the bar instead and followed the hearty aroma of sizzling pork, freshly baked bread, and maple syrup to the cloth suspended next to the shelves of liquor. Penny had said the kitchen was behind the bar, and surely there would be something to write their order on for when Penny had the time.

But as she brushed aside the cloth, a hulking man with a barrel chest and scales the color of rust moved to block her way. Startled, Syron jumped back, and the dishes slipped from her grasp, landing in a crash of broken glass at her feet. The room fell silent as the man glared at the glass and then up at her. A strangled ticking sound came from his throat as he reached to grab her, but Syron scrambled backward and sprinted for the stairs.

This time, the crowd moved aside for her. She had just reached the foot of the stairs when a hand wrapped around her arm, trapping her in place. She whirled to find Penny with her mouth set in a firm line. Behind her, the man had followed to the edge of the bar. He still made the gurgling *tick-tick-tick* sound, but somehow it seemed angrier.

"I know," Penny seethed at him, and forced Syron in front of her. She just caught a glimpse of a hooded figure walking out the front door when Penny forced her up the stairs, over the landing, and back into the room.

Penny slammed the door shut behind them and let her go, shocking Yira awake and jerking Leon from his chair.

"I'm sorry," Syron said. "I was going to write down our order so I wouldn't bother you. I didn't mean to break—"

"I don't want to hear a word. Y'all need to leave. Now." Penny didn't even spare her a glance as she crossed the room next to Leon, unlocked the window, and pried it open. Syron flinched against the squeal of paint rubbing on wood. "I don't require names of my guests, and heaven knows I don't give away faces. But there's a woman downstairs who says she works for the city, and she described your group perfectly." A breeze caught the ends of her white hair and wisped it around her face. Despite her tone, Penny looked...scared.

Yira paled. She climbed to her feet as Penny motioned to the open window. "What did she look like? Did she give a name or...?"

Penny held up her hands in mock surrender. "She was wearing a hood, and I didn't ask. I told her my rooms were empty and that was that. But this girl," Penny added, pointing at Syron, "up and made a scene in front of good Mr. Henley, and now whoever it was knows you're here, and knows I lied for you. You can keep your coin," she added, dropping her hand. "I'd rather be out a payment than in the middle of whatever this is."

Penny looked at Leon expectantly, and with a nod from Yira, he ducked through the window. Syron kept her head down to hide the flush of embarrassment coloring her cheeks and followed Leon onto the roof before swinging her legs over the edge. The drop down wasn't far, and she saw bags stacked against the side of the bar that must belong to the people inside, but no one in a hooded cloak.

"Thank you," Yira said, and Syron turned around. Yira crouched outside the window, looking in at Penny. "You didn't have to help us."

Penny only nodded solemnly and gripped the sash to close the window back, but Yira put her hand on the frame. For a moment, Syron felt sure Penny would slam it shut whether her hand was there or not, but Yira said, "The wicked are around the corner," and Penny's face softened, if only for a second.

"So grab your bread and steel," she said quietly, and as soon as Yira moved her hand, she wrenched the window shut.

Syron used the sound to propel herself forward. She landed easily and took off in the direction the little girl had run in the night before. Yira and Leon were behind her in seconds, matching her stride as she rounded the bar and climbed the stretch of earth that rose to meet the side of the cliff. In the light of day, the spire shone like a distant beacon, and behind it rose the hill Will had been on in her dream, faded to soft shades of green like an old painting.

She tried to stifle the hope rising in her chest and failed. She laughed under her breath and shook her head when Leon looked at her questioningly, taking a deep gulp of the crisp air. The rain had been purifying somehow, and even after the morning they'd had, it felt like a new day. As if anything was possible.

Leon nudged her, and she leaned against him at the same time he wrapped an arm around her. She smiled again and glanced at the ground, felt the earth beneath her shoes, and decided she'd never felt quite so alive.

It was Yira who spoke first. "Did I smell bacon when I woke up?"

Leon's laughter rumbled against her, and she smiled over at Yira. "Trust me, I tried to get us some. But I wanted to ask…what was that between you and Penny? It sounded like a code."

Yira chuckled. "It's mostly used now to recognize other heretics, but it's not that serious. I wanted her to know we wouldn't forget her kindness, especially considering how easily she could have turned us in."

"I've heard it used only a few times," Leon said.

"It's definitely out of date," Yira agreed, and nodded in the distance. "Speaking of old things, you can't see them now, but we're heading toward some abandoned temporal houses. There should still be food and water stored there from the last time I was out this way. We'll stay there tonight, and as long as we don't run into any trouble, we should be in the city by tomorrow."

"And if we do run into trouble?" Leon asked.

"Then you let me handle it. According to Adaline, the Nightman doesn't control the children every night, and he never allows them inside the city itself. Viero sent scouts out last year who confirmed the tunnel leading out of the city was still intact, and there hadn't been any damage to the interior. If we can avoid the children until we reach the tunnel, we'll be fine. But once we're inside," she added, catching Leon's eye, "our first priority is the Black Book."

Syron slowed, letting her words sink in. Stealing some book might be their priority, but it sure as hell wasn't hers. "I'm not leaving without Will," she said firmly.

Leon tensed against her and dropped his arm.

"If Will is still there," he said in a pained voice, "then we have no choice but to bring him back with us too. Taking the book won't make a difference if the God has an angel at his disposal." He clenched his jaw and looked over her head at Yira, but Syron couldn't tell what he was thinking.

"But it's just a book, right? What makes it so important anyway?"

"It's a lot more than just a book." Yira stopped walking and turned to face her. "It's the whole reason the God is still alive. He was old when the uprising happened, and that was years ago. He should be long dead by now." She paused. "Do you remember the night you fell, when I took your hands and we both saw you lying beside the lake?"

She waited for Syron to nod before continuing. "The God does something similar, but instead of experiencing the memory with the fallen, he absorbs every memory they have—consuming them from the inside out until their souls aren't their own anymore. Whatever is leftover gets sucked into the Black Book for later, to use when the old one starts to fade."

"His addiction tricks his body and mind into a constant state of being," Leon murmured. "Like Yira said, he should have died a long time ago, but he learned how to cheat death."

Syron's eyes flitted between them for any sign they were lying or, at the very least, exaggerating. But their faces were open and honest, and she didn't doubt they were telling her the truth. Not for the first time, she thought back to what Naveen had told her in the field outside Idris's faction, about the hopelessness the sahiit had felt when the God touched the angels, but at least Naveen had spared her *this*—the knowledge that the God didn't just want her death, he wanted the entirety of her mind, body, and spirit.

"I don't understand," Syron finally whispered. "I thought the God was a temporal. I thought he couldn't harm angels like that."

Yira's eyes gleamed. She leaned in as if she were about to share a secret and didn't want anyone else to overhear. "That's where the fun part comes in. Nobody knows how he does it, and that's why the temporals here worship him as a god. It wasn't until after the uprising and I met Adaline that I started to suspect, but when she told me about her past, everything started to piece together. I had heard rumors about the Nightman, of course, but I thought it was all bullshit. The children could just as easily have been an experiment that went wrong. But when Adaline explained her dreams, her emotions, how in sync the Nightman was with her thoughts…You're absolutely right, a temporal can't harm the mind of a fallen. But if a fallen willingly *gave* a part of their soul to the God, however small, it would give the God the power he has now, and creating the Black Book would give him the ability to sustain it."

"And since the Nightman exists," Syron said slowly, "it means he kept the original angel whose soul he absorbed."

"Only a part of their soul," Yira corrected. "Otherwise, they wouldn't be alive. The only thing Adaline and I couldn't figure out is how the Nightman is so strong. He is only one fallen, after all, and even that has its limits." She shook her head and leaned back. "It doesn't matter now anyway. What's done is done. The important thing is that once we steal the book and get Will out if he is there, the God can't afford to take the rest of the Nightman's soul. He's manipulated his followers with the threat of the nightchildren, so if there is no sacrifice and the kids in the city don't turn, then they'll know the God has been lying to them. Either way, it works in our favor."

Syron's head buzzed. She turned to look back up at the spire, less like a beacon now than a looming threat, and froze. A group of coyotes wandered lazily to their right, their stomachs full and bulging beneath their patchy fur. Yira's hand was on Syron's shoulder in an instant, pushing her down. Syron obeyed, slinking into a crouch, and watched them pass until their bodies got hazy from the distance and it was safe to stand. But when they started walking, Leon hung back.

"Why didn't you tell me any of this before?" he demanded. Syron turned, but his gaze was fixed defiantly on Yira's back. "You never said a word about Adaline, or about the Nightman being real…being an angel." His voice caught on the last word, and the muscles in his neck tensed. "You never said any of it."

Yira paused mid-step. When she turned to face him, the gleam in her eyes was gone. "You were just a little boy." He bristled, but she continued in a soft, steady voice. "I know you don't like to remember what happened, but I was there too. I watched how everything you held tight got stripped away and you were given nothing in return. I saw your nightmares come to life, Leon. Can you blame me, then, knowing what I do, why I thought a man made of shadows wasn't your burden to bear?"

Leon's expression hardened. He held Yira's gaze, and Syron had the distinct impression she was watching a battle between light and dark—the sun and the moon holding equal sway over their own halves of the same world. But then Leon's lavender eyes darkened to amethyst, and he trudged forward. As he passed them, Syron couldn't tell whether it was the sun catching on his diamond markings, or a reluctant tear tracing its way down his cheek.

13

LULLABY

Syron forced herself to keep moving despite the sores she felt forming on her feet, and the ache that had started in her calves and spread to her shoulders and neck. Still, she was glad to be moving again. The last time they had stopped to catch their breath, she had lain with her back against the cool ground, staring up at the starless expanse of black. In the lackluster silence, she couldn't help thinking about how small they were, how infinitesimal, and she still couldn't tell whether it made her want to scream or disappear.

Even with her eyes adjusted to the dark, she had to squint to make out the dim shapes of Yira and Leon next to her. She knew they were there mostly because of their steady breathing and the soft scrape of their pant legs with each step.

"How do you know where we're g—"

"Shh," Yira interrupted, and stopped walking.

Syron paused next to her before she heard it: a trail of laughter, lilting and foreign, coming from somewhere in front of them. Yira's clammy hand found hers, and Syron was grateful, not for the first time, that Yira was with them. She always seemed to know what to do and when, so even though every instinct told Syron to run the other way, she let Yira steer her forward until a soft bluish-white light revealed the corner of a house. They crept forward cautiously, veering to the side, before they saw them.

"Are they…playing?" Leon whispered, unbelieving.

Until now, Syron had seen only two of the nightchildren, and never more than one at a time. There had to be at least twenty of them gathered here together, their light illuminating the playground and stretching to include the rows of houses with sunken-in roofs, chipped paint, and boarded-up windows. But the playground itself was small, and the nightchildren who couldn't find something to climb or spin or swing on gathered in the road, where a boy with spiked hair and pinched cheeks held up a ball and shouted rules.

Syron's heart leaped to her throat. Despite their glow, they were just normal children. Nothing like the crazed girl who had shown up outside the window in Del-Amar, trying to break in. And nothing like Adaline.

"These are the old houses I told you guys about," Yira whispered, releasing Syron's hand. "Stay close to me. As long as they don't know we're here, it's safe."

"Safe?" Leon strained. "You saw what they're like the same as I did! It won't hurt us to walk a mile or two more and sleep out here."

"There's no food or water out here," Yira reminded him steadily. "And even if we do come across some, which we won't, it's not safe to eat or drink it. You know that as well as I do."

"But—"

"Trust me," Yira interrupted and put a hand on his shoulder. She pointed at the playground. "The Nightman was possessing the girl who found us in Del-Amar. Whatever control he has over these kids, he's not using it now. So would you rather eat and rest under cover, or starve miles away from shelter with nothing to hide behind when he decides to control them again?"

Leon clenched his jaw. It was the first time they'd spoken more than a few words to each other since their argument, and Syron could tell he had more to say. But when Yira raised her eyebrows at him, her face tinted with the glow of the children, he only nodded once. "Stay close, then, and stay quiet," she whispered, and pulled away.

A cold sweat started on Syron's lower back as Yira led them to the outskirts of the abandoned town. The shouts and laughter were louder here, so innocent and playful that it would have seemed almost normal if not for the watery blue glow spilling through the thin gaps between the houses. Syron held her breath each time they sprinted past one of the gaps, and strained her ears for any indication the nightchildren might be getting closer. But Yira was right. They were only playing, and there was no reason for them to be peering through the dark looking for a lost angel.

Yira's dim outline led them deeper along the edge of town, and the farther away they got, the more Syron couldn't help trying to pin down what made the nightchildren so terrifying. It couldn't just be because the Nightman controlled them, because he wasn't controlling them right now. Maybe it was what they looked like, or how they acted. Or maybe it was the idea of taking a child so young and alive and stripping them of what made them human in the first place.

A high, sweet voice cut through Syron's reverie, and she peeked through the gap between the houses to look out. A little girl sat on the porch across the road, singing softly to the mound of blankets in her arms.

"…Swirling, curling, wisping shadow, close your eyes now, it'll last forever,

Forever and a day.

By numbing touch my darling slept

As forgotten memories brush away, stolen promises, unkept beds,

Hands of Fortune fade away, leaves you numb, my baby love,

Open your eyes now and you'll see forever,

Forever and a day."

Her voice fell like lead over the other children, and Syron realized it was a lullaby. For a moment, the world seemed to take a collective deep breath. Even the air tasted stale. But the girl shifted her weight, releasing the hold, and a child Syron couldn't see shouted that the ball was stolen, they had lost their turn, and calls of injustice rose to a fever pitch as a hand settled on Syron's shoulder. It was warm and strong, and she didn't have to look to know it was Leon. She turned to him, dazed, and let him lead her away as the girl's song picked up again, lower this time.

They hugged the backs of the houses without speaking, moving deeper into the dark until a light appeared in one of the windows a few houses down. They slowed to a crawl with Yira in front, and the light disappeared and re-formed on the back porch, beckoning to them.

"Adaline," Syron whispered. She quickened her pace, keeping close at Yira's heels until they climbed the steps of the porch and followed Adaline inside.

"Where have you been?" Adaline demanded in a whisper, shutting the door firmly behind them. "I've been here over a day. I was starting to think Briar caught up with you."

"We stopped at Del-Amar," Yira said, and brushed past her to get to the kitchen. "The rain couldn't have come at a better time, really. Our trail from Viero's should be long gone by now, and I doubt even Briar could track us in weather that bad."

Adaline grunted. Her glow wasn't as strong as the other children, but it was enough to see the barren living room with boarded-up windows, exposed beams where parts of the ceiling had fallen in, and the corner of the fridge that Yira held open. Glasses clinked together as she riffled inside, finally pulling out a lumpy, folded stack of clothes.

"She thought rats would get into it anywhere else," Adaline said at Syron's quizzical expression. "Or people, if someone happened in and found food sitting here waiting for them." She glanced at the window shrouded in darkness above the sink, where her light had shown through before, and grimaced. "The children don't know I'm here. As long as we don't give them a reason to be suspicious, they'll leave this place alone." With a subtle nod toward the other end of the room, Adaline beckoned them to follow. She led them into a narrow hallway with a warped floor and into the first room on the left.

Syron scrunched her nose against the earthy, sour smell of mold and old wood. It was worse this deep into the house, but it was worth it to be off her feet. She collapsed on the floor and stretched her aching muscles as Adaline sifted through the nightstand. It was the only piece of furniture save for the bed, and when she found a lighter and lit the candles on top, Syron saw the sheets on the bed were moth eaten and threadbare, and a black blanket had been draped over the curtain rod to keep the children from looking in, or the light from getting out.

She glanced behind her, but there were only specks of black along the walls and the moving, inhuman shadows cast by the lucid flames.

Leon and Yira sat on opposite sides of her in an open circle, with the gap facing Adaline. Yira shook out each of the shirts in turn, and a collection of freeze-dried and dehydrated food in sealed bags tumbled out into a pile. From the sweatshirt came a little cardboard container Syron recognized from Viero's faction, but this time instead of banana chips, it was overflowing with maang.

Syron reached out instinctively and bit into the doughy ball. The water that flooded her mouth wasn't cold, but it was fresh and invigorating. She grabbed another, relishing the life it brought back into her, before picking a package at random and working at the seal.

"You said you were worried about Briar catching up with us," Syron said to Adaline as she ripped it open. "Does that mean you got back to Viero's in time to see everyone Idris brought with her?"

"I did. Idris is fond of causing a scene, so it didn't take long to figure out what happened. But while she and Briar were throwing their weight around, Calais and Zariah were arguing about whether you would try to leave Evangentine or not. Apparently, Calais saw you looking pretty hard at the wrong spot on a map and thought you'd be more likely to take off to the city. Guess she put two and two together about your friend Will."

Syron's eyes widened in astonishment, and the bite of the dehydrated fruit landed like acid in her stomach.

"What did she say?" Leon asked in a hard voice.

"I left before they did, so I don't know how it played out, but Calais was adamant that if you showed up at the city without the sahiit bringing you, any promise of peace from the God would be forfeited since you escaped and came of your own volition."

"I never thought..." Leon said under his breath, but Yira rolled her eyes.

"She's always been as loyal as a temporal. That morning when you were scouting, did you see any children besides the ones here in town?"

Adaline crossed her arms and leaned with her hip against the nightstand. "Six or seven of them were headed to the border. Idris may be prideful, but she wouldn't keep the loss of an angel to herself." She looked at Syron. "She needs the God's resources to have any certainty of finding you, and the children are the best resource the God can give. They're here temporarily until the God can get more information about where you're heading, but they're confident the watchmen won't be sent out, at least for the time being."

"How do you know all this?" Leon asked. "You're too far from them to eavesdrop. I thought you couldn't read their thoughts."

Adaline cocked her head at Leon. Her gaze was unwavering, and only when he shifted uncomfortably next to Syron did a sad smile tug at her lips.

"I can't blame you for not understanding what I am, but you forget that I'm trapped somewhere between what the Nightman made me and the temporal I was before. I may be one of the nightchildren, Leon, but that doesn't mean I am the same as them. My consciousness is my own —theirs is shared between themselves and the Nightman. I can't read their thoughts, but if I focus enough, I can feel the emotion behind what they're thinking. At first it was like remembering parts of an old book, but it got clearer with time. And since their minds are as static as their bodies, I learned the intricacies of their feelings better than I can recognize my own. Whether the Nightman anticipated this for an outsider like me or not, I have no idea. It's not something the children have thought about. But what I do know for sure is that nothing is as black-and-white as it seems. We're a patchwork quilt with more gaps than the Nightman would like to admit."

Syron tried to imagine it: living as a collective without the rest of the pieces, an outsider to her own kind. She remembered the first time Adeline had come to her in the library, the whispered words *"I didn't look like this before. With your help, I won't have to anymore,"* before running back through the glamour.

She's still human, Syron thought, even if she didn't look the part.

But when she said as much out loud, Adaline's face fell. "I hope so," she said, glancing down at herself. "Thirty years is a long time to be a ten-year-old girl."

Syron raised her eyebrows and was about to ask more when something slammed against the side of the house and three things happened all at once.

Adaline turned and bolted down the hall, Yira sprang into a crouch, and Leon grabbed Syron's hand and raced to the window. He paused only long enough to blow out the candles, sinking the room into darkness. Syron breathed in the scent of smoke and wick as he wrapped an arm around her and held her tightly against him. She felt the hard lines of his chest through the gear and the tickle of his breath on her neck as he lifted the side of the blanket and peered outside.

A cluster of the nightchildren had broken off from the rest and gathered in the road, their eyes locked on the front door as Adaline stepped through. The pinch-faced boy stood in front, raising his chin defiantly as Adaline descended the porch steps and stooped to pick up the ball. Behind them and off to the side, a girl with a wave of silk hair held a blanket in her arms tight to her chest.

"It must have hit the house when they kicked it too hard," Leon whispered in her ear, but Syron wasn't paying attention. She hadn't been able to see the girl's face when she was singing earlier, but now a pang of recognition coursed through her. It was the nightchild from Del-Amar.

She had none of her earlier hostility. If anything, she looked uncomfortable this close to the house. She readjusted the blanket in her arms and a little bluish-white leg popped out, the foot wrinkled and kicking, before she tucked it back inside the haphazard swaddle.

The front door slammed shut and Syron jumped involuntarily. Outside, the children turned and ran back up the road, the girl with the baby trailing along behind. Syron almost wished she would hug the baby to her shoulder so she could see its face, but Yira sucked in a breath and Leon let the blanket over the window fall.

When she turned around, Adaline stood in the doorway.

"Is everything okay?" Yira asked, standing straighter.

Adaline rolled her eyes. "If I had known it was just the stupid ball, I would've stayed inside." She leaned against the frame and looked from the candles to Leon. "You were watching, weren't you? Did you notice how they wouldn't even set foot in the yard? They think the house is cursed."

"Why would they think that?" Leon asked, but Yira took a step forward.

"Are we still safe here? Should we…"

"If you try to leave now, you'll be caught for sure," Adaline said. "By now, they would've already told the Nightman I'm here, but he doesn't know I'm with you. Just—"

Adaline's face twisted in pain. She sucked in a sharp breath and brought her hands to her temples, stumbling forward. Syron ripped herself from Leon's arms and ran to her, but Yira was already by her side, catching Adaline before she could crumple to the ground.

"What's happening?" Syron asked, panicked. Her hands flitted over Adaline's convulsing body, worry mixing with horror and fear, but Yira only held her tighter.

"It'll pass," Yira whispered. Then, louder, "His presence is stronger with the other children here. He's trying to get in her head."

"Who?" Leon demanded behind them.

Yira clenched her jaw. A strand of hair fell in her face, but she didn't seem to notice. "The Nightman. He thinks it's a game."

Syron locked her hands together and watched, helpless, as the convulsions turned to tremors. Adaline's neck snapped up, and for a moment her eyes were a full haze of opaque inside her translucence, and then they rolled back, her head fell, and she went still.

Syron's heartbeat thudded in her ears.

Yira said something, but Syron couldn't hear over the pulse. She reached out tentatively and took Adaline's still, cool hand in hers.

It was a strange thing to touch one of the nightchildren. It felt like flesh and bone, but she could see her own hand through Adaline's, and there was no pulse when she touched her wrist.

"She'll be fine," Yira said in a stern voice, as if she were repeating herself.

Syron set Adaline's hand back down gently and sucked in a breath. "How do you know?"

"If she weren't," Yira said simply, "she'd be dragging you outside to the others. Hopefully it never comes to that, but you do whatever you have to do in that situation. Do you understand?"

After a moment, her voice softened. "I'll stay in here with her. There are two more rooms in the hall. Grab a couple of candles and the lighter and get some rest. We're leaving as soon as the sun comes up."

Syron heard Leon riffle through the drawer behind her and walk down the hallway, but she took her time lingering in the doorway, watching the flutter of Adaline's closed eyes and the protective way Yira held her. *It won't come to that,* Syron thought. *Adaline is stronger than Yira's giving her credit for.* When she finally turned away, warm light flickered through one of the open doors in the hall and seeped beneath the bottom of another.

Leon must have lit candles in her room too. She debated knocking on his door but thought better of it. They both needed time to process the events of the last few days, and if she were being honest, she craved privacy more than company.

She closed the door behind her and glanced around. This room had the same two pieces of furniture and dark blanket over the window, except planks of wood stuck out from beneath it, nailed to the wall from the inside instead of out. The only difference was a closet to her left.

She started toward it and paused, listening to the creaks of the old house. *It's abandoned,* she thought. *There's probably nothing but old clothes inside anyway. Nothing that hasn't already been left behind…but it can't hurt to look.*

The door pulled open soundlessly. The closet was wide and deep enough to step into. Old, tattered dresses flecked with mold hung along the bar at the top, and a pile of dry-rotted shoes and toys littered the floor. She poked her head inside, holding her breath against the smell, but it was only more of the same.

She started to pull back when the candlelight glinted off something gold tucked into the corner, half buried under the mess. She nudged a boot, ready to jump back if a spider crawled out, and used it to shift the toys aside. A baby book crinkled under her weight as she stepped inside, eyeing the newly exposed chest, and grabbed the handle.

The candlelight flickered off the glossy brown wood when she finally pulled it free. The gold turned out to be an embossed inverted triangle surrounded by flowers. She ran her fingers over it, lingering on the lotus petals, and flipped the latch.

She didn't know what she had expected to find, but it wasn't baby clothes. She took them out carefully, separating the girl's clothes from the boys into two piles on the floor. Most had animal patches sewn on, and each was spotted with little brown stains that looked curiously like fingerprints. At the bottom, a gold frame peeked from the edge of a swaddling blanket.

Syron unraveled it carefully until she held a smiling family of four. A little boy and girl were locked in the embrace of their parents, looking up at the camera. She kept her eyes on them as she got to her feet and moved to perch on the edge of the bed beside the candlelight. The children both had the same ringleted hair of the mother and the father's wide, innocent eyes. But the boy's hair was shorter, and his skin wasn't as deep. Despite the years between them, they looked nearly identical. And familiar.

Her eyes shot to the door to make sure it was still closed before brushing her thumb against Adaline's face. Her curls were a frizzy halo now, and Syron had never seen her real smile, but there was no doubting it was her. Adaline and her family, memorialized inside a chest in the bottom of a closet, tucked away in an abandoned house, but Adaline had kept it. A memory in a frame, glowing amber now against the candlelight.

Syron's heart ached deep in her chest. She wondered whether this had been Adaline's house when she was alive —really alive—and whether the other children knew that, whether that's why they thought it was cursed. She flipped the frame to the back. In the lower right-hand corner, "Verlice Family" was written in an elegant script. The date had been smudged out.

Carefully, quietly, she went back to the keepsake chest and wrapped the photo back up and placed it inside. She was careful not to touch any of the brown spots on the clothes as she stacked them inside, and she did her best to put the chest back exactly as she had found it in the closet before shutting the door behind her.

The bed squeaked beneath her as she climbed up and fit the pillow to the hollow of her neck. Her thoughts raced, but she forced herself not to think about the children outside, or the picture in the closet. Instead, she thought only of what the day would bring, and tried to imagine seeing the massive gate of the God's City in person as she had in her dreams. When exhaustion finally weighed on her eyelids, she slipped them closed, and let herself drift into that place of muted calm before sleep takes hold. She was still there when she heard the door opening.

"Adaline? Adaline, is that you?" she murmured through the fog. "I'm sorry I looked in the closet. I didn't know…"

She must have fallen asleep. Her eyes fluttered open when a weight settled on the bed behind her, goading the creak of the springs. Syron shifted uncomfortably and moved to sit up when an arm reached around from behind and pressed a rag against her nose and mouth.

I'm dreaming, she thought. *Will must have escaped. They must have found him in a room like mine.* But the acrid stench of chemicals was real. It was everywhere, fogging her brain worse than sleep.

She tried to twist away, to jab her elbow back and break free, but the rag was gone. Her mind cleared. She sprang unsteadily to her feet and tried to run for the door, but her legs and arms were numb. The room swirled in chaotic circles as her knees buckled. She landed hard against the floor, dazed and nauseated, and craned her neck up. Shadows of candlelight danced along the walls. The fog came rushing back, violent this time, and she just had time to glimpse a hooded figure in the corner of the room before her eyes welded shut.

Somewhere above her head, she could swear she heard the crashing of waves.

14
THE CONTACT

A voice came from far away. The words were jumbled and confused, pushing up against the darkness. Syron strained against it and felt herself falling. There was a sharp noise, like the thwack of wood against stone, and pain blossomed in her temple, sparking light where there was none before.

The voice was closer this time. A woman, cursing. Then Syron was moving, the cold pressure against her head and arm gone. She opened her eyes groggily. The room that swam into focus was all dark wood and black metal that arched along the ceiling and walls. A cabinet spanned the wall on her left, fitted with heavy wooden doors and a sink. Shelves with preserved food were suspended above it. Opposite sat a low dark couch and coffee table, both supported by curving metal legs. She shook her head to clear it and squinted against the light pouring in through the giant window across from her. Metal bars crisscrossed the textured glass, meeting in the middle to form an inverted triangle. Inside was a bust portrait of a man.

His long silver hair lay over one shoulder. Startling blue eyes looked out from a purely masculine face—all hard edges and sharp corners. Tucked against his chest, only half visible in the point of the frame, rested a book of inky leather.

The whisper of someone moving drew her eyes away. She swallowed against the tightness in her throat, tried to turn toward the noise, and gasped at the sudden flare of pain. She looked down at herself instead and winced, pulling against the thin wire that bound her to the chair, but it only bit into her exposed flesh.

"I wouldn't bother if I were you," said a familiar voice behind her. "The contact will be here soon, and I doubt Julian will appreciate you getting bloodied up before meeting the God."

Syron stopped moving and listened to the tap of footsteps drawing nearer. A shiver raced down her spine, forcing her chest tighter against the wire as the hooded figure came into view.

"I know you," Syron said, thinking back to when she had first glimpsed the figure in the bar, and then again in the corner of her bedroom. "You followed us from Del-Amar." Her voice came out stronger than expected. She bit her tongue to keep her resolve from faltering.

The figure chuckled and moved closer. "I wasn't the only one, but yes. Briar and Zariah came too."

Syron struggled to keep her face impassive as realization dawned on her. The figure drew back her hood, revealing a face washed in freckles and framed by scarlet hair. In the late afternoon light from the window, the bruise along her jaw looked mottled and swollen.

"Let me guess," Syron quipped, "Idris didn't want to ruin her good shoes."

Amusement sparked behind Calais's eyes, but she only

regarded her thoughtfully and reached into the folds of her cloak. A glint of gold caught Syron's eye before Calais held Leon's dragonfly to the light.

The anger dispersed as quickly as it had come, and Syron sucked in a ragged breath. She remembered sitting with Leon under the lights of the willow tree, looking up through the wisps of color and committing the delicate lines on the body to memory. She waited for the clockwork heart to spring to life, for the glass wings to unfurl and flutter in Calais's open palm, but it stayed motionless. Leon's voice came to her then, as clear as if he said the words aloud. *"And deadly. I've only ever had to use it as an element of surprise, but I think that's what it was made for. A quick slice on the neck or ankle, that kind of thing."*

Luckily, Calais didn't see it for what it was. She placed it on the edge of the table and turned back to Syron.

"If you had listened when I told you to go north, all this would have been over already. Idris went back to our faction to deal with the mess you caused at Viero's, but she told the rest of us to follow your trail. I have to say, you didn't make it easy. Zariah was certain you'd be too scared to go to the city, even if you thought Will would be there. I guess she was wrong."

"I guess so," Syron clipped.

Calais gave a fleeting smile. "I suppose you want to know where Leon is?"

Anxiety coiled in her stomach. Of course, she wanted to know—how could she not? Not only about Leon, but also Yira and Adaline. But Calais had shown the dragonfly to goad her, and she couldn't be sure Calais would tell the truth anyway. She had no reason to.

"After I saw you in Viero's faction," Syron said instead, "I couldn't stop thinking about what I could have done that made you hate me so much. I went over every conversation we had, from that first night I fell up until the day I left. But then I realized it all boiled down to one person. It was Atlas, wasn't it?" Her eyes flicked back to Calais's jaw. "He decided he wouldn't give me a chance, so he thought you shouldn't either. You disagreed with him."

But Calais was already shaking her head. "No. You can make up whatever story you want to, but the truth is that Atlas is right. Damn it, Syron, why can't you just get it through your head that you don't belong here? No angel does. The God may be a giant prick, but what he does is necessary even if we don't agree with how he does it. It's really that simple."

"Do you hear yourself? What happened to the Calais I knew that said it was all superstitious bullshit?"

"She grew up," Calais snapped. "Maybe you should too."

Heat flooded Syron's cheeks. Her eyes darted to the dragonfly on the table. Maybe if she rushed at it…but even if her hands were free, she doubted the blade would be able to cut the wire.

Calais didn't see her look. Her hands were in fists by her sides, and she kept glancing behind Syron. "The Faces of Fortune proved your life affects multitudes. You were pissed at me for spilling where you were at the party, but I was pissed that's all anyone wanted to talk about. Each person that woman changed into was a life you'll impact, whether by meeting that person or not. There would've been a lot more if she could've shown the men too, but they're locked into their own gender."

Calais sucked in a breath and met Syron's eyes. "Giving you to the God is the only way to make sure you don't hurt those people. I know you won't mean to," she added when Syron tried to interrupt, "but you can't help that you will. Atlas knows that, and now I do too."

She sat on the edge of the table closest to the window and twisted a curl around her finger. "It's for the best," she said, but the words were strained, almost as if she were trying to convince herself.

Syron squeezed her eyes shut and flung her head against the back of the chair. It helped to clear her muddled thoughts, if only a little. She knew Calais was only a mouthpiece, but her words carried the weight of thousands of people. Yira and Leon believed Syron was good, and Adaline had, if nothing else, proved that the God's manipulation spread throughout Evangentine. But could it really be as black-and-white as they said? Wasn't there at least a little truth in any given lie?

Could I really hurt those people without meaning to?

"You don't know what it's like," Calais whispered, almost to herself, "to give someone else the other half of your soul, and it's bleeding because they're bleeding."

Syron's head lolled to the side. The light coming in through the window had dimmed, but she could still see the exhaustion that hunched Calais's shoulders and the bruise, blended by shadow, along her jaw. Calais had avoided her question, but that was answer enough.

"How long ago did it happen?" Syron whispered.

Calais looked up. Her eyes flashed, and for a moment, Syron thought she would rush to his defense again, but she only lifted her hand, brushing her fingers gingerly across the swollen skin.

"When Idris found out you were missing. He thought I had something to do with it."

The anger Syron felt toward her shifted and warped, whittling down to something close to familiarity. Calais dropped her eyes and turned almost completely to the window, watching the distant snaps of blue light through the panes. Her back was straight, her shoulders curved forward almost as if she could protect the wound inside her chest. But Calais wore her heart on her sleeve, and she was right. It was bleeding.

Syron's was bleeding too, but the pain wasn't as fresh. Evyn had poked holes in her heart until the time came when it would collapse entirely, too weak to stand on its own. She'd lost count of the nights she had woken up with strange bruises on her arms and between her thighs, the ridiculous fights, the endless guilt after she gathered the courage to confront him. And she had only leaned on him more.

But she was better without him. She was *alive* without him when she wouldn't be if she had stayed. If being in Evangentine had taught her one thing, it was that she was stronger than she had ever given herself credit for.

"It isn't love if they hurt you, Calais. No matter how much of yourself you pour into them."

Calais made a sound somewhere between a laugh and a sob. It was bitter and abrupt, almost blocking out the groan that came from the other side of the room. Syron stiffened and tried to look behind her, but the razor-sharp wire sliced past the gear over her chest and wedged into her skin. She let out a cry and pressed her back tight to the chair, trying to hear over her own erratic breathing.

"I know it doesn't change anything," Calais said in a tight voice, "but for what it's worth, I am sorry. I never wanted it to go this far."

Syron looked down at her chest. The gear was sliced where the wire had eaten through, and the edges were wet.

"Then why let it?" Syron asked through gritted teeth.

"Do you remember the night of your initiation? After we got in that fight, I went to find Zariah. I couldn't just sit back and let Atlas leave, so I decided to do something about it. I told Zariah he might be a liability and asked if she could deny his transfer request. She agreed, but only if I gave you the map. She started asking all these questions, and I was so mad and confused…" Calais sucked in a worried breath. "She said that if you were going to run, then it was my responsibility to make sure you would go somewhere they could easily find you."

"That's why…wait, you told Zariah about my dream? About Yira helping us?"

"No, I only told her you overheard the conversation between her and Briar. I kept Leon's name out of it too because I didn't want him involved if I could help it…I just never thought he'd actually leave with you. Or Yira, for that matter."

Saliva pooled in Syron's mouth. She must have looked as disgusted as she felt, because Calais sneered and stood up, all traces of remorse gone.

"It's not like it matters what you think of me now," she said, walking past Syron. "Everything will be over soon anyway."

The tap of her footsteps slowed and stopped. The seconds stretched, and it wasn't until Syron had almost convinced herself that she had pushed Calais too far too fast, and now she would murder her here in cold blood, when Syron heard something heavy being dragged across the floor. The motion was halting, as if Calais had to pause to gather her strength. When it came closer, Syron turned her head toward it, careful not to move her body. The edge of Calais's cloak came into view, then her back, and another tug revealed her hands, gripping the ankles of someone in gear.

Syron couldn't bring herself to look away. If she were being honest, she didn't want to. She clenched her fists, letting the bite of the wire distract her enough to keep her expression in check. She didn't so much as twitch as the next tug brought Leon's unconscious body next to her. He lay facing the door, his white hair dingy with dirt and sweat, and his arms splayed above his head. Syron's eyes dropped to the slow, steady rise and fall of his chest.

Calais let go of his legs. They thumped against the floor, but he didn't seem to notice.

"I didn't know how long the toxin would stay in an angel's system," she explained. "If you woke up before getting here, I needed something to guarantee you wouldn't try to run."

Syron kept her fists clenched. Warmth trickled down her fingers and fell in steady drops to the floor.

She ripped her eyes away as a shadow passed over Calais's face. "It isn't my fault," she said to no one in particular. "Whatever happens next, it isn't my fault." She took a step back, right in front of Syron.

Syron didn't think. She just lunged.

Or more like *fell*.

She jerked the weight of herself forward in the chair, trying to lift off her tiptoes. The wires seared into her like knives as she crashed into Calais.

Syron dared to hope she would be able to knock her head against the table, but Calais only called out in surprise and tried rolling out from beneath her, using the corner of the chair as leverage. Syron twisted, biting into her hand hard enough to draw blood, and Calais screamed. The chair shuddered with what could only be the force of Calais kicking it and launched Syron across the room.

She couldn't feel her toes, or at least she didn't think so. Her lips tingled. Her head swam. She tried to look up, but the shelves above the sink turned to blurry spots of color before the wire mercifully went slack, and she was pulled to her feet.

She swayed, and a hand steadied her. Dizzily, she looked up into the face of a boy about her age with sage-green eyes, milky skin, and short-cropped, shaggy black hair.

It would've been shocking to see someone who looked so much like her—human—had it not been for the monster of a man next to him. Syron backed up and slipped. She grasped the edge of the counter with numb fingers before she could fall and glanced down. Her blood puddled on the floor, vibrant red except for the smear from her shoe, and then back up at the watchman. He was half naked, broad-chested, and weaponless. Black ink covered his chest and arms, with the point of an inverted triangle resting on the swollen skin between his eyebrows.

Her breath caught, but he wasn't paying attention to her. He mumbled something under his breath, and the boy sighed.

"Go outside, then. Wait for me."

The watchman turned and ducked through the door, closing it firmly behind him.

The boy said something else, but his voice was muffled and far away. Syron felt herself drifting, sliding, falling, and then something was being forced past her numb lips. A wave of cold broke across her tongue. She swallowed out of instinct and her eyes fluttered open, suddenly aware. The boy held her in his arms. Somehow, he'd had the time to take off his jacket and wrap it across her arms and chest.

"She wasn't supposed to—"

"Don't," the boy said, glaring at Calais with a wild ferocity.

Syron tried to lean up and gasped. The boy shushed her, pressing the cloth gently to her wounds. It was thick, but not thick enough to keep the blood from seeping through. His hand came away red.

"You must be Julian," Calais tried again. "Idris had to—"

"Do I look like I care about *Idris*?" Julian sneered the name. "A mutilated angel and unconscious sahiit were hardly the terms of the deal. Here," he said, careful not to jostle Syron as he dug in his pocket and flung a key at her. "Belle keeps a stock of healing tonics at her house. She isn't there now, but you'll know it by the sign in the window."

"You want me to get her medicine?" Calais asked, casting a disgusted look at Syron. "In case you missed it, she's the one who attacked me. Besides, she's more resilient than you'd think."

"*She* may be, but are you?" His voice was like daggers. "The watchman will accompany you in case you decide to run off."

Calais went pale. She stooped to pick up the key and paused.

"Hurry!" Julian shouted.

The door slammed behind her, but Syron didn't watch her leave. She was too far away to see whether Leon's chest was moving, and she didn't want to be held by a stranger regardless of what condition she was in. She gritted her teeth and scooted off him, using the cabinet handle to pull herself into a sitting position. She felt normal when she wasn't moving…almost.

"I wouldn't try to stand if I were you," Julian said, as if he knew what she was thinking. "What I gave you is temporary. It's strong enough to dull the pain and keep you conscious, but it's Belle's tonics that will hurry the healing process along."

Syron nodded, but it wasn't herself that she was worried about.

"Is he still breathing?"

"She used a stronger dose on him. He should be awake soon."

When she didn't answer, Julian got to his feet. She must have been too distracted before to notice the smell of incense and night air, but it clung to him as he walked past. He crouched next to Leon and cocked his head.

"This boy…what's his name?"

Syron jutted out her chin. "Why?"

If she were concerned about Julian losing his temper, it disappeared when he laughed. It was a soft, amused sound, little more than a chuckle. He looked…happy.

"It's crazy how small the world is, sometimes. Other times, it's so vast we can hardly take a step without getting lost. I'm sorry for Calais's actions. I take full responsibility."

It wasn't just Calais. But Syron didn't say that. He was the God's contact with the sahiit, after all, the one who had tipped Idris off about an angel falling. He was also the one who had met with her after Syron's initiation and planned to steal her away, to let the God murder her in front of his whole city.

"Just because you're pretending to be nice doesn't mean I don't know what you are."

His smile faltered. "And what is that?"

"You're the contact for the God. It's your actions that led to my being here, bleeding all over your floor." She started to knit her hands together and thought better of it, pulling the cloth tighter around them instead. She watched Leon's face as she talked, trying to discern the white of his eyelashes against his pale skin. She imagined those eyes opening, disoriented and terrified, and landing on her. Would he blame her for their being here? It was because she was an angel, after all. She supposed she couldn't fault him if she tried.

"You knew Idris would be willing to do anything to bring me to the God. I wasn't even with her for a month before she tried getting rid of me, but I had already made up my mind to come. Me and the people I was with. You can ask Calais, they tracked us for long enough."

She pursed her lips, unsure whether she had said too much, but Julian's green eyes washed over her with a look that said he wanted to say something but stopped himself.

After a moment, he said, "I don't trust you not to come to him, and the more strain you put on yourself, the faster the draught will wear off. I can't lift him, but I can drag him to you, if you'd like?"

Syron fought against the sudden urge to cry. She shook her head, slowly, and raised her knees to her chest, even though it ached to move, and buried her face between them. A part of her hoped Leon would hate her when he woke up. At least then he wouldn't be hurt again because of her.

She heard Julian walk back to her, the whisper of cloth sliding down the cabinet as he sat back down, just before something started buzzing. She wiped her eyes on her pants and looked over. It came from the dragonfly, probably the whirl and tick of the clockwork heart in tandem with the wings. Syron straightened her back. Surely, he would be surprised that it moved, maybe even consider keeping it, but his sage eyes sparkled as he offered it to her, and Syron accepted. She glanced at the table.

"Why are you giving it back?"

"Because I'm curious," Julian said, "and I have something to prove. Which is one of the things I'd wager we have in common." His voice was clear and concise, almost scholarly. A hint of an accent played at the edges of his words that she hadn't noticed when he was angry.

Syron wanted to ask what he meant but was interrupted by arguing outside. A moment later the door banged open, and the pinks and yellows of sunset flared to life around a black silhouette. Calais slammed the door shut behind her and flicked on the light.

"The children followed me from Belle's," she explained, hurrying across the room. She dropped a basket overflowing with medical supplies at Julian's feet. "There are more coming out of the forest. They tried talking to me, and when I didn't answer, they started pulling at my clothes until I shouted at them to go away. I think they're still outside."

Worry flashed across Julian's face so fast that Syron thought she must have imagined it. "Are you surprised? Their purpose is to gather information, after all." His gaze flicked over Calais before pulling the basket closer to him and digging through. When he seemed satisfied everything was there, he pulled out the painted jars and set them to the side, careful to avoid the blood on the floor. Next came the cloth wraps, white tape, and a thick pair of fabric scissors.

"I need to cut your clothes where the lacerations are so I can treat them properly. Normally I would have you lie down, but I don't want to risk moving you around too much. Is this okay?" he asked, waving his hand at the position she was in against the cabinet.

Syron nodded and, knowing what would come next, started peeling off the jacket. Her stomach soured when it stuck to her wounds, fastened by dried blood, and she was tempted to rip it off all at once. But she forced herself to go slowly, to minimize the bleeding, and pointedly did not look down. She went by touch only, ignoring the wet where her sore hands brushed the skin and worked her way down.

By the time she finished, there were tears in her eyes.

Julian already had the scissors and told her to take a deep breath, and then to keep her breathing even. She tried, but the gear was worse. It tugged against her where he pulled it off, but he was careful and quick, and Syron didn't feel any fresh blood, or maybe her chest had gone numb like the rest of her.

When he laid the cloth wraps on his knee and picked up a jar, Syron let herself look down. She didn't know what she ought to feel, but surely it should be something other than fascination. Lacerations like a spiral wound their way down her chest and arms, breaking off at the dip of her armpits. They were an angry red, livid against her pale skin, and puckered. She pressed the fabric she held closer to her breasts and lifted her arm. Only the inside was unmarked.

He started with her hands, still against the cloth. "This will hurt," he warned, "but it'll heal faster than anything else I can give you, so it'll be worth it."

Syron let her head fall back and stared at the ceiling where the metal supports reached up and looped to form a perfect circle. She nodded, grinding her jaw against the growing burn that started in her hands and spread. By the time he reached her shoulders, it was a thousand angry bees, a million granules of glass shoved beneath her skin. Her resolve faltered and she choked, breathing in the sour, chemical stench of the liquid on the cloth, but just when she decided she couldn't take it anymore, Julian moved away and popped the lid off a different jar.

She flinched, but he whispered something she couldn't hear and poured out a handful of thick white cream and lathered it between his palms. "It'll take away the pain," he said. "I promise." And it did.

After the wraps were taped off and Syron had sufficient cause to feel like a mummy, Julian beamed at her.

"See, was that so hard?"

Syron wanted to slap him.

Calais looked as if she were about to. "Can I leave now? I've delivered the angel. You've made sure she won't die of infection. There are people waiting for me."

"Yes," Julian said, cleaning off his hands with a spare cloth and placing everything back in the basket. "They are waiting, aren't they? I almost forgot." He turned to face her, not bothering to stand up. He didn't need to. Calais paused midstride and looked back at him, then at her, lips pursed.

"I can bring Leon back with me too. He doesn't belong in the city."

"Leon," Julian said, tasting his name. "Yes, I suppose you could. The same way you brought them here, then? Oh, don't look so flustered," he added when Calais gawked. "I saw your friends out there, waiting in the shadows. You'd think Idris would have trained them better. Briar and Zariah, am I right?"

Calais's expression turned guarded. "Idris assigned them to help."

"And how did they help the others that were with the angel?"

"I wouldn't know. Zariah didn't want a part in it, whatever it was. She's the one who helped me move them here. Briar said he would catch up with us later."

Julian clucked his tongue. "The deal is done, but the way I see it, Leon is the one who decides whether he stays or goes. I'm assuming Idris has a glamour ready for you?"

When Calais didn't answer, Julian nodded. "Tell the sahiit they don't have to worry anymore. The water will take a while to purify, but everything else will return to normal." He waved at the door. "Grab your friends and leave quickly. The children are out of sorts tonight, and it's hard to tell what they'll be inclined to do with guests who wear out their welcome."

Syron watched Calais cross to the door with lidded eyes. For all the plans Yira had made, all the knowledge Adaline had shared, and all the strength Leon had lent her, they had failed. *Hell, besides Leon, I don't even know whether they're still alive.* It was her own fault, of course, for letting anyone try to help her in the first place. They had attempted to carve their own path, but the God had his ways of pulling people into line. It was enough to make her sick.

Past the open door, the sunset had morphed into the deep onyx of night. Calais froze in the doorway, still gripping the handle. Syron's whole body tensed. Warm light spilled out onto the watchman lying unnaturally on the ground outside, surrounded by a pool of glistening black. Something shifted above him, and Syron's eyes snapped higher. Briar was looking straight at her, a thin smile curving his lips. A flash of blue darted next to him before a woman's scream cut the night, and the thud of someone falling.

Then it erupted into chaos.

15

ARMY OF LOST SOULS

Briar jerked his head toward the scream the same time Julian rushed at him. Syron hadn't even seen him get to his feet before he pushed Calais out of the way. She landed hard against the wall with a sickening thud as Julian launched over the watchman's body and straight into Briar's chest. The force sent them deeper into the darkness until it swallowed them whole.

Syron willed herself to move. She had already lost too much blood, and even with the creams Julian had applied to her chest and arms, everything still ached. She ignored it and used the cabinet at her back to inch her way to her feet and push forward, hardly sparing a glance at Calais, who had fallen in a heap on the floor.

She avoided the dead watchman and stepped out of the filter of light from the door and into another world. Silver moonlight cracked across the sky, tracing the edge of the black clouds against an even blacker night. An intense, bluish-white glow shone in the darkest shadows between the scattered houses, like individual shocks of lightning. It

197

took a moment too long for Syron to realize the glow came from the unmoving, inhuman children, and a moment longer for the thuds and grunts of fighting to reach her.

Syron turned just as Briar shoved Julian off him. His fiery eyes reflected the glow of the house as he wrenched himself to his knees, feeling wildly at the ground for something Syron couldn't see. Her heart leaped to her throat, and she stumbled back. Her wrapped hands fumbled with the pocket of her gear where she had slipped the dragonfly before, but Julian was already on his feet. Already standing over Briar. Already kicking him brutally in the side and grabbing a fistful of his hair.

He just jerked Briar's head back when an angry cry sounded from behind her. She whirled around, the dragonfly slipping deeper into her pocket, and flinched. The nightchild looked up at her with wide, curious eyes. Syron's hands shot to her mouth to stifle a scream as the boy smiled politely and stiffened, as if hearing something too low for anyone else to hear, and beckoned to her.

Syron wanted to run, but her legs wouldn't listen. The boy took a step closer, his expression falling slack, just when a metal staff twirled through the air between them. A pale face appeared out of the darkness at their side, half-beautiful and half-scarred, but Syron wasn't paying attention because then the boy was laughing. His voice was dim and layered, echoing as if from a great distance, when in truth he couldn't have been more than a few odd feet in front of her.

Chills crept down her spine and kept her rooted in place even as the boy's gaze slid over her shoulder. Milky white broke across his eyes like fog and he slipped into silence, oblivious to everything except Briar and Julian locked together on the other side of the house.

"Heretic!" Briar shouted, and the spell broke. Syron looked around frantically. She'd heard a woman's scream, had seen...*no, no one else is here.*

She backed away from the child and snapped her attention to the fight. Briar had managed to get to his feet. Silver glinted in his hand as he slashed, but Julian was lithe and quick. He ducked away and came up close, grabbing both of Briar's arms and twisting them beneath his. Briar snarled and tried pulling away, but he was locked in place, the knife still grasped in his fist.

"Why did you murder my watchman, Briar? All you needed to do was deliver the angel and go home. He was a newborn, as far as they're concerned. The poor thing didn't even have a weapon."

Briar jerked, and this time Julian gave a breathy laugh and let him go. He stumbled back as Julian took a step closer. The children did too. Like an army of ghosts, or prisoners, or lost souls, they moved in perfect synchronicity. Fear blossomed in Syron's chest, but neither of them seemed to notice.

She risked a glance at the little boy. He was still frozen in place, but the fog whirled in his eyes.

"That hunk of meat died the moment you turned him into a monster. He'd thank me if he could." Briar flashed a wicked smile and wiggled the knife. "I coated it in lotus extract. Not that it matters for the watchman, but it works wonders on the children. Idris has been under the impression you speak on behalf of the God, but that's not true, is it? Adaline had plenty to say about your little plan, and I've wasted too much of my time hunting down this *hiiyah*," he said, slipping into araasi, "just for the sahiit to lose her for a false promise."

"I don't know what you're talking about."

Briar barked a laugh, his black eyes laced with venom as he caught sight of Syron, then of the little boy next to her. The humor vanished as quickly as it had come, replaced with a sheen of sweat on his upper brow as he looked around wildly.

The children looked back at him with sightless eyes.

Briar panicked and thrashed savagely at Julian, who jumped just out of arm's reach.

"I'm not leaving here without the angel," Briar snarled, but it sounded more like a prayer than a promise.

Next to Syron, the little boy moved. She whipped her head to him as the last wisps of fog cleared and he darted forward. She blinked once, and the boy leaped through the air. She blinked twice and Briar screamed, high and piercing, as the child landed on his back.

It happened fast. The children rushed at Briar like a wave as Julian scrambled back. They forced Briar to his knees, ripping at his gear and punching, clawing, kicking, *pulling*. Syron heard wet snaps beneath the layer of bodies, and she *felt* inside her bones, at the base of her skull, running like ice through her veins the moment when the little boy nuzzled into his neck. The screams turned to garbled cries, and when the little boy pulled away, his mouth and teeth and cheeks were stained red, impossibly vivid against his translucence.

A hand grabbed hers. Syron jumped and looked over, a scream building in her chest, but the hand was warm and gentle. Leon's pale skin and hair shone brilliantly in the children's glow. His violet eyes mirrored the threat of tears in her own as he pulled her, whispering warnings she couldn't hear over the thrash of bodies behind them. She stumbled and let him lead her away, glancing over her shoulder every few seconds to make sure they weren't being followed.

Their shoes squeaked on the floorboards when Leon finally pulled her inside and snapped the lock into place. Instinctively, her eyes darted to the window. Surely the children would break the glass and swarm them, but there was nowhere else to go. The nearest house was too far away to make it without being seen, and there was no guarantee anyone inside would help them. These were people of God.

Leon pulled her against him. One arm wrapped around her waist, and the other fisted itself into her hair. His chin rested on top of her head. She breathed him in, held the seams of his gear through her bandaged hands so tightly it hurt, and squeezed her eyes shut. It didn't help. The little boy was a portrait painted on the backs of her eyelids.

"It was Calais, wasn't it?" he asked tightly, pulling away and running his hands gently down the bandages on her arms.

Syron nodded, avoiding his gaze. "Zariah helped her." She sucked in a breath to steady herself. "Briar stayed behind with Yira and Adaline. I don't know what he did… but he said Adaline got away."

"And Yira?"

Syron stared at the floor. They had tracked in the blood from the watchman, leaving the tread of their shoes visible. "I'm sorry. If I had said no when you guys offered to help me, none of this would have happened. He hurt Adaline, and I have no idea whether Yira is s still…" The words lodged in her throat.

Leon lifted her chin, so she had no choice but to look up at him. "None of this is your fault," he said forcefully. "Do you hear me? None of it." His shoulders fell, and his eyes dropped to her lips. He brushed his thumb against them and shut his eyes, pressing his forehead against hers.

"I should have come outside sooner. I woke up when Calais hit the wall, but she started moving as soon as you left, so I pretended to be asleep. I tried to follow her, but she must have taken off and I saw…well, you know. I believed what you said about her of course, I just—"

"She was your friend. You needed to see it for yourself."

"Of course he did," said a woman's voice from across the room. "They've been friends for as long as I can remember."

Syron twisted, but Leon was faster. He moved in the direction of the voice to shield her with his body, but Syron peered around him. A woman in black detached herself from the shadowed corner of the room. Her gear was speckled with grime and pockmarked with tiny bite marks. She limped forward, keeping one hand firmly on her hip. Her eyes skipped past Leon to Syron. When she smirked, the scar pulled one side of her lip down.

"Calais was lucky the children were distracted, or it would have been her instead of Briar getting ripped apart out there. If I had to bet, I'd say she's already safe and sound at home."

When no one spoke, Zariah rolled her eyes. "You can relax any time now. Briar got it in his head that Julian wasn't who he made himself out to be. If it turns out he was right, and Julian is a heretic, then I don't see how it's any of my business either way."

"You don't care if what Briar said is true?" Syron asked. Her head whirled. She didn't have time to consider whether he was being honest, or what it would mean if he was. For all she knew, he had made the whole thing up.

Zariah snorted. "The only thing I care about is that the son of a bitch is finally dead. I would've killed to stay out of the angel business, but he's the one who insisted Idris pull me into it. She won't be happy about all this, but she's reasonable enough to put her maternal feelings for Briar aside, if there ever were any."

"How do we know you didn't sneak in here to finish what Briar started?" Leon asked.

"Because I wouldn't waste my time talking when I had the perfect opportunity to knock you both out," Zariah snapped. "Twice, actually. I could've let the little demon out there do it for me, but I distracted him when he started ogling Syron."

It was *her! I knew I wasn't seeing things.* But Syron kept her mouth shut.

Leon must have recognized the look on her face. He turned back to Zariah and whispered, "You never had a grudge against Syron, then. You were mad at Idris and Briar for putting you in the middle of it."

She nodded. "I don't know whether you remember, but I took the fall for Yira after she got caught trying to get Astrophe out of the city. I went right up to the God and told him it was my idea." She tucked her hair behind her ear to show off the scars, as if to prove her point. "I never wanted a thing to do with angels after that. And being ordered to chase down Yira? The years haven't been kind to us, but I can't stand the thought of hurting her. Briar knew that, so he sent me to help Calais while he stayed behind with Yira and the child. I could've stopped him. I wanted to stop him." She rocked back on her heels, her expression souring.

"Why didn't you?" Syron asked, just as someone banged on the door. She jumped, Leon squared his stance, but Zariah only scoffed.

"So he could run back to precious Mommy and tell her

I went back on my word? No, an old crush wasn't worth getting kicked out of the faction over. And Yira is resourceful. Whatever Briar did to her," she said, limping to the door, "as long as she's still breathing, I know she can figure a way out of it." She unlocked it and stepped back.

Syron braced herself for the nightchildren to rush through, but it was only Julian. He paused in the doorway, eyeing Zariah.

"Are you going to try to kill me too?"

"She's safe," Leon said, the same time Zariah said, "I don't have a death wish."

Julian straightened his gore-splattered shirt and ran a hand through his shaggy hair. His eyes found Syron's, and she gave a slight nod.

"What are you going to tell Idris?" Julian asked Zariah.

"Exactly what happened. Briar got a hair up his ass and killed the watchman, and your children took care of him."

"They're not *my* children," he said with more force than necessary. "I sent them away for now. Are you...?" He motioned at Zariah's hand still on her hip.

"I'll live."

"Then I'd say you're free to go." He moved aside, but Zariah glanced back.

"For what it's worth, I'll tell Idris you guys gave her a run for her money. Viero is having the meeting with the factions tomorrow night to discuss what's going on. Just a heads-up." She paused next to Julian and whispered something in his ear. Julian's eyes widened, and he nodded once before she was swallowed by the dark.

He started to follow her but turned back. "I have to clean up the mess the children left behind. I dismissed them, but they like to stay around the outskirts of the city.

If you try to leave and they see you by yourselves, well, you saw what happened to Briar."

It wasn't meant to be a threat, but it certainly felt that way. The latch slid into place, leaving her alone with Leon and her spiraling thoughts. She hated how easily Calais had managed to capture her, and how much of a target it had put on everyone's back. If she could go back and change everything, she would. If only…

She hadn't realized she'd spoken out loud until Leon stopped pacing. He flinched as if she had slapped him, surprise and pain flashing across his face.

"You want me to what?"

"I—I want you to leave," she repeated, steeling herself. "Julian said before you woke up that it's your decision whether you stay or go. As soon as he comes back and we can be sure the children won't attack you, I think it's best if you go home."

She looked over his shoulder to keep her resolve from slipping but kept the rest of her body perfectly still.

"Why are you just telling me this now?"

"Because you said to tell you if I didn't want you near me." She'd been replaying the words over and over in her head. She knew what came next. "This is me telling you."

Leon didn't move for a long time. Neither did she. After what felt like hours but really could've been only a couple of minutes, he turned away and stalked to the far side of the couch. She could see in the hard line of his mouth and tense set of his shoulders that he was mad, but maybe that was good. Maybe that would get him to listen.

"I don't want you getting hurt," she whispered.

He looked away at that, toward the window. Syron followed his gaze. The portrait of the God looked down at them with hard, mocking eyes. Suddenly, she wanted nothing more than to break the glass.

She sat on the opposite side of the couch instead, drawing her knees tightly to her chest. It hurt, but it wasn't the kind of pain that mattered.

"Leon, I—I know you don't understand me, or what it is I'm trying to do. I just wanted you and Yira to be safe, but everything I do puts a bigger target on us." Her cheeks flushed, and she tried blinking away the threat of tears that burned the back of her eyes. "I'm not worth losing people over. It's because of me that we don't know where Yira and Adaline are, or whether they're even okay. And you're here, and I don't know what it is I'm supposed to be doing." She couldn't help the way her voice came out strangled and thin, but she forced herself to keep going. "All I know is that Will is in the city. I can *feel* it. Back home, he tried saving my life more times than I can count. If I can just find him and get him out somehow, then even if I die, it will be worth it. I owe it to him to try, and if you come with me, I—I can't have the person I love dying too."

She sucked in a breath and looked away, back toward the door. The words had spilled out of their own volition, too quick to hold back.

She expected him to yell, to say she was selfish and wrong, and that he would be better off without her. But he stayed silent. Then, slowly, a hand slid to her knee. It burned through her gear straight to her skin.

"You're right. I don't understand you—but I do understand parts of you." He took a deep, shaky breath. It fanned against her when he let it out, making the hairs on the back of her neck tickle her skin, but she couldn't bear to look at him. Not yet.

"I understand that you push away the people you care about so they don't get hurt, and that the more you feel for them, the harder you push. I understand that you are selfless, and you'll do anything to make sure the ones you care for are safe even if it means sacrificing yourself to do it. You made up your mind to come to the city on your own, so that makes you independent, and brave, and fierce. You love strongly or not at all." He paused. "And I understand that you just said you love me, so you're pushing me away the hardest of all."

She looked over at that, forgetting for a moment to hide her tears.

Leon's mouth parted slightly when he saw her. Then his hand was against her cheek, gently wiping them away. Heat tumbled off him in waves. "Yira told me what my mom thought about the angels—how she believed they were all sent here for another chance at life. I don't know what your past life was like, Syron. And I'm not asking you to tell me. All I'm asking is that you let me help preserve the piece of it you have left. Will deserves a chance as much as you do, and I'm willing to do anything to make sure that happens."

He pulled his hand away, and his glistening eyes searched hers. "I'm not trying to change your mind. If you really want me gone, I'll leave. But I don't think you want that, and I'd rather take my chances with the children than watch you go into the city alone. Because I—"

Syron's lips crashed against his. It wasn't because of the affirmation or his promise to help her. It was the simplest and most profound thing he could have done, and it was understanding and accepting her need not to talk about her past, for choosing to help her cross the miles of terrain that separated her from who she wanted to be and who he believed she already was.

Her pent-up fears and hopes and dreams spilled into the kiss, onto his soft mouth that opened hers with a flick of his tongue. His strong arms wrapped around her, and she pulled him closer, dropping her knees and curving her body to his.

He was on top of her, his lips burning a trail along her tear-streaked cheek, her ear, down the curve of her neck. She ran her fingers through his hair, and he let out a soft moan as the door whooshed open. They just had time to break apart before Julian swung the door shut behind him.

"We have a lot to discuss in a little amount of time," he said, walking to the chair Syron had been tied to and shaking off the wire. He dragged it to the other side of the table across from them and plopped down before looking up. He did a double take, and Syron had the distinct impression he was fighting back a smile. "My apologies. Have I come at a bad time?"

Syron's cheeks flamed. She cleared her throat. "No, ah, what were you saying?"

Julian coughed suspiciously and shook his head. "Well, I was going to say that I don't know how much of the city Leon remembers, but a lot has changed in recent years. Besides the expansion, the most noticeable difference will be the God. He doesn't come out of the spire anymore, so I doubt you'll meet him until the time comes for the cere-mony…if it comes."

Leon leaned forward and rested his elbows on his knees. "If?"

Julian nodded and looked up through his lashes at Syron. "I know you heard what Briar called me. He was right that I know Adaline, but he drew some pretty hasty conclusions. I'm advising you both to keep that knowledge close to your chest. I may very well be your only friend inside the gates. As for Yira," he added, leaning back, "I want to let you know I'll be asking around to see what I can find out. I have just as many contacts outside the gates as I do within. We'll find her, I'm certain of it."

"It sounds like you're just telling us what we want to hear," Leon said matter-of-factly.

Leon was right. Unless…

"Wait, do you know Yira?" Syron asked.

Julian smiled wistfully. "*Knew* her, yes. I did some work for her father before the uprising."

"But you're so young." She hadn't meant to say it out loud, but he only chuckled.

"Working with the God has its perks, I suppose. There's a wealth of knowledge on how to make people appear younger."

Syron raised her eyebrows, but Leon scoffed and said, "What a temporal thing to say."

"I suppose it is." Again, Syron noticed his enunciation. She wondered idly whether it was just the way he spoke or whether it was how all temporals were taught. "If our positions were reversed, Leon, I would have the same reservations about you. As of right now, the only trustworthy thing I've done is give you back your weapon."

Leon's eyebrows knitted together. He reached for his pocket, but Syron was already pulling the dragonfly from hers. She held it cupped between her bandaged hands.

"Calais took it when you were still unconscious. Julian gave it to me after he let me out of the chair."

Leon looked from the dragonfly to Julian. "How did you know what it was?"

"I was there when it was commissioned. When your father found out Astrophe was pregnant with you, he wanted to make sure she had the means to protect herself when he wasn't there."

The air whooshed out of Leon as if he'd been punched in the stomach. Syron almost didn't notice Julian reaching over until he plucked it from her hands. He sat back on the edge of his chair, holding the dragonfly at eye level, when the wings unfurled. It flapped twice before hovering above his open palm, showing off the beautiful mottle of green and blue inside the edge of gold.

Syron stared in awe. She had seen it move before, of course, but she hadn't known it could *fly*.

"It's the only one of its kind. Your father was very secretive about the whole matter, but tinkerers don't get a reputation for being the best by hiding their achievements. Frankly, I'm surprised it found its way to her after word got out. I always assumed it had been destroyed."

"I—" Leon started to say, but the dragonfly buzzed louder and zipped in a tight circle before flying to Syron. She felt it land on her head, and a giggle broke through her lips.

Leon smiled. "I never knew. Mom never said."

Hesitantly, he held out his hand. It hummed above her, almost lovingly, before landing in his open palm. The cog in its chest slowed to a creep, the wings folded under its belly, and it came to rest.

"It's a curious little thing," Julian said, "but beautiful and deadly. A weapon that knows who it can trust."

"That's why it didn't move for Calais," Syron realized.

Julian nodded somberly, while Leon tucked it safely back into his pocket. He raised his eyes to meet Julian's.

"So, you really are a heretic?"

Syron pinched the thin, loose fabric over her elbow. Despite the wraps, her chest and arms were bare, and the night air bit into her as if she were submerged in icy water. There was no moon or stars, nothing to light their way except for the looming spire in front of them. The light was dim at the top, pressed tightly against the sky like the moon itself.

She glanced over her shoulder. They hadn't thought to turn off the lamp in the house, and it glowed dull and weak in comparison.

"When we get to the gate, just let me do the talking," Julian said. "Once we're past the watchman, you'll be escorted to the assimilation chamber. I'll have your rooms made up while you're there." The artificial moon reflected wickedly in one eye as he looked over at them and slowed his pace to match theirs.

A clawing suspicion nagged at her, but she forced the thought away before it could fester, and stared forward. She shivered, and Leon, thinking it was from the cold, drew her in close.

"What does the chamber do?" he asked.

"It's, um…rather hard to explain. On paper, the goal is for you to get a rudimentary understanding of the God's City, but in reality, it's a hoop to jump through before you get to explore the city itself. Neither of you will be in any danger, if that's what you're thinking."

Leon said something smart, but Syron stopped paying attention. In her dream, the gate connected to a massive wall that spanned the circumference of the city, but now she could make out only the slight gleam of something high in front of her. The light from the spire disappeared gradually with each step until it was blocked out entirely.

Syron waved her hand in front of her face, but the only telltale sign that she moved at all was the whisper of wind against her nose and cheeks. She looked up at Leon, thinking maybe she could spot a hint of white in the blackness, when a sudden, brilliant light erupted around them. Syron flinched away and, heart hammering, squinted through splayed fingers at the giant man sauntering toward them.

"Who's there?" a deep, gruff voice demanded.

"It's Julian! I have the angel."

Syron's determination faltered. If she ran now, maybe she could get away before the watchman caught up to her. She could go back to…where? The safest place was Viero's, but Idris had gotten there easily enough. There was nowhere else for her to go except ahead.

She wanted to sink into the ground at her feet, but instead she schooled her expression into impassivity, straightened her back, and dropped her hand. The watchman didn't stop until he stood directly in front of Syron. This close, she could see he wore a suit of dark chain mail with buckles down the front, but his features were lost in shadow.

"She doesn't look like much," he said, reaching out a gloved hand to tip up her chin.

Syron jerked away, ripping herself from Leon's arm and clenching her hands into fists so no one could see that she was shaking.

"You've been listening to the rumors again, haven't you?" Julian said a little too lightly. "I know it's been years since the last angel fell, but you know as well as I that they don't have wings. It's an old wives' tale."

The watchman grunted and let his hand fall. "You may bring the angel, but I can't allow entry to one of *them*," he said, nodding to Leon. "His kind are worse than even the umbriels. They have no place here anymore."

"His mother was an angel. An exception has to be made, if only to study—"

"Only under the God's direct orders would it be permissible. Feel free to go in yourself and goad him from his spire if you like, but the boy will remain here."

"I will do no such thing. He either enters with her, or she does not enter at all. I'm sure the God would come at a second's notice if he knew you refused entry to an angel."

The watchman turned his head, and the light caught his eyes lingering on the wraps over Syron's chest. He wet his mouth. "If you refuse to leave the boy, then that may be the best course of action on your part, Julian, though it's doubtful the God would come himself. I'll escort them personally to the barracks until something gets decided." He smiled, huge and ugly. "I'm sure they'll feel right at home."

Syron tasted bile. Out of the corner of her eye, she saw Leon's hand inch toward his pocket.

"If you so much as touch me—" Syron started, but Julian held up his hand.

"Not to worry, this watchman seemed to forget his place is all." Julian eyed him up and down. "But I think it may be for the best. When it's been too long since their last visit to the Artist's Room, a little of the old mind starts to bleed into the new, doesn't it, Cornelius? But it's nothing another session can't fix."

Cornelius's nostrils flared. "I have strict orders to—"

"To what? To turn away the God's angel after all the time and resources we've exhausted to get her here? You're either acting out of stupidity or heresy, and unfortunately for you, both options lead to the same place. Unless," Julian added in a voice that was cool, quiet, and commanding, "I tell Raoul that it's time you were expired. Maybe the Artist's Room is too good for you."

Cornelius puffed out his chest and glared at Julian, seeming to gauge the truth in his words, while Syron dug her nails into the wraps over her palms and waited. Finally, when she didn't think she could stand the tense silence any longer, Cornelius sneered and turned on his heels. She hadn't noticed his hand holding the hilt of his sword until he let it go. Each clink against the chain mail was like a timer counting down the seconds until the light dimmed and faded.

Green dotted Syron's vision. There was a whirl of ticks and clicks as the gate cracked open and neon light spilled through. Syron sucked in a breath that tasted a little like victory and a little more like luck and squared her shoulders.

Next to her, Leon fit his hand into hers and squeezed.

16

ASSIMILATION

If Syron were being honest with herself, the God's City never felt real until she stepped through the gate. She stood in a wide half circle that ended abruptly in small, dark houses with steep-sloped roofs. The light from the top of the spire tower stood sentry above the city, dwarfing even the tallest buildings. Lampposts glowing vibrant shades of pink, purple, and blue spilled neon light onto the wet cobblestones at her feet, illuminating the watchman who stepped out of the shadows and the woman who followed behind him.

Her pin-straight hair was pulled over her shoulder, and she clapped her hands together as she caught sight of Syron. "You did it! Thank the God."

"Tia," Julian said, surprised. "I thought you would already be inside."

She shrugged. "I came outside when I heard the gate. I suppose it's a good thing I did, considering you brought a sahiit with you." Her eyes darted to Leon, drinking him in, before flitting back to Julian. "Raoul won't be pleased, you know."

Julian grimaced, and for the first time Syron noticed the frown lines around his mouth. "If anything, he'll be excited. Leon's mother was an angel, years ago."

Syron sneaked a glance at Leon, but his face was unreadable.

"Interesting," Tia said. "Well, I'll have the watchman escort them back to you as soon as we're finished. Is your house appropriate, or have you made other arrangements?"

Julian hesitated for a fraction of a second. "Around the back of the spire, if you would. The God wants her close."

Tia's eyes widened the same time Syron stiffened. If Julian really were a heretic, wouldn't he want her as far from the God as she could get? But when Julian caught her eye, it was with a soft smile.

"You'll both be in good hands," he said, just loud enough for Tia to hear, and turned on his heels. He disappeared into the maze of houses as Tia cleared her throat.

"Follow me, then. It's just right here." She headed toward the gate with Syron and Leon close behind. The watchman trailed along after them, and Syron had the crazy notion Tia would lead them right back outside until she made a sharp right and walked straight up to a door recessed into the wall around the city.

A black cat with eyes the color of citrine stretched its thin body against the door, tail raised as Tia bent to both pet it and push it out of the way. The watchman moved to stand along the wall, the inverted triangle on his forehead standing out even in the shadow. Syron just had time to think how eerily similar he looked to the one outside the gate before Tia pushed the door open and blinding white light spilled out. She smiled politely, almost obligatorily as they filed inside. Syron's hand was slick with sweat from where she held Leon's, but he squeezed it tighter as her eyes adjusted and the room swam into focus.

Everything was perfectly, uniformly, spotlessly white. Both the ceiling and floors seemed to give off the bleached light, so she didn't notice the desk until Tia dipped behind it to grab a pale yellow folder, or the door until she placed her hand on the handle. Syron's leg hit against something hard. She looked down and could only just make out the white pew pushed against the wall.

"This is the assimilation chamber?" she asked, running her hand along the arm of the pew.

Tia nodded. "It is. For your first time, it can feel a bit unnerving. All of this," she said, starting to wave her hand holding the file but then seeming to think better of it, "is to make sure there isn't anything that can obstruct how the assimilation works. It's the only place in the city so plain, I can assure you." She forced a laugh. "If it helps, just think of it as a safe environment to have a little conversation before you're escorted to your rooms."

"How does the assimilation work?" Leon asked skeptically.

Tia raised her chin and opened the door to more white. "You'll see for yourself soon enough, son of an angel. But since this room is personalized for the individual, you'll both have to decide who will go first."

Syron and Leon exchanged looks. He let go of her hand and stepped forward, but she caught the material of his gear to hold him in place. She shook her head at him, and Tia moved aside as Syron walked past her into the next room. When she glanced back, Leon was leaning, displaced and nervous, on the pew.

As soon as the door closed, everything changed. The air wavered slightly, like looking above an open fire, before stretching outward. Syron whirled around, panicked, as wisps of *something* curled and molded itself to the edges of the room. She blinked, and suddenly they were standing in the library at Idris's faction. Tables stretched on either side of her, flanked by rows of bookcases against the walls.

She held her breath. Surely she was sleep deprived, or under too much stress, or maybe there were drugs in the air. She flitted through the list of possibilities and waited for the white room to reappear, but Tia walked past her calmly and settled into a seat in the middle.

"For the purpose of the assimilation, can you state your full name, please?"

"Syron Theodora Lennox," she whispered, reaching out tentatively to touch the table. Somehow, it was solid. She trailed a finger along its length and walked to the bookcases, pulling a book out at random and riffling through. All the pages were blank.

"This chamber is constructed by you, Syron. It shows an environment you're familiar with to help calm any anxiety you may have about being somewhere new. Your memory fills in where things are supposed to be, but it won't add details you did not already know. If you had never read that book before, there wouldn't be anything for your mind to fill in."

Syron flipped the book over, running her thumb along the ribbed cover before sliding it back on the shelf. "Why bother trying to make me comfortable? It's not like your God wants to keep me around for long anyway."

Tia motioned to the seat across from her, and Syron sat.

"This is, admittedly, the first time the God has chosen to acclimate an angel. I am in no position to guess at his logic," Tia said, "but I have faith he is doing what is beneficial for his people and his city, despite the concerns."

"By concerns, you mean the nightchildren?"

Tia's lips tightened. "We will not speak of such matters in this chamber, except to say that our city grieves the loss of the children who have suffered because of the angels. It is a wrong that must be righted. But if the God sees fit to wait, I am certain it is because he is saving us from a worse fate. His is the guiding light, and if a pebble slipped beneath his arm while protecting us, it is undoubtedly because he is being pummeled with boulders.

"Now," Tia added, opening the folder to reveal a collection of old photos, "my purpose is to provide you with some knowledge of the city's origins so you can better understand our way of life. These are all very old, so I ask that you don't touch them. I've advocated for a museum so they don't get shuffled around so much, but, in the meantime, I've preserved them as best I can."

She laid out the photos one by one, describing in detail how the God cultivated his following and started building the city. After laying down the sixth photo, she said, "It's worth noting that before the God came to power, everyone did what they thought necessary to survive. The God is the one who secured Evangentine's future, even if the name of the land wasn't decided until later."

She laid down the seventh photo, and Syron blanched. A giant pit had been dug in the middle of a level plain, stacked high with piles of dirty, naked temporals and sahiit alike. Black-and-white flames obscured the edge of the frame, catching and spreading mercilessly. Syron's hand shot to her mouth, but Tia was already on to the next, and the next.

By the time she finished, the images covered the table like a scrapbook of time showing the city in various stages of development. Tia leaned back, observing her work. "The God asked me to show you the ugly as well as the beautiful. Defending something precious in the middle of chaos meant he couldn't spare the heretics who came against him, but each life taken only added to his sorrow. It was necessary, in the face of evil, to protect what was righteous."

Syron resisted the urge to argue that a true God wouldn't murder hundreds of people, hunt down angels for the sake of preserving himself, or manipulate thousands of people into following him blindly. Instead, she nodded to the photo of the bodies.

"And if someone comes to the city and doesn't convert, what then? Does the God have them thrown into a pit and burned like the rest?"

Tia leveled her gaze. "Of course not. No one has tried attacking the city since I've been alive. There are merchants, of course, who pass by and decide to set up shop for a day or two, but as long as they don't intend on staying, conversion isn't necessary. There will always be people who don't accept his teaching. The God understands this, but he also understands that word of our religion is spreading. New temporals who come wishing to worship are given homes outside the gate, since our capacity is full."

"What about the ones who believed in your religion and changed their mind?"

"Easy," Tia said, and shrugged. "They're reacclimated as watchmen."

Syron gaped at her. She knew the watchmen all looked the same, but she'd never really considered *why* or *how*. She recalled her dream about Will, remembering how he had compared the two watchmen outside the gate, but his reflection hadn't gone deeper than their appearance. He likely hadn't thought about it any more than she had.

Questions lodged in her throat as Tia stood and

rounded the table. She started to lift herself to follow when a shaking hand settled on her shoulder.

"You haven't practiced with your third eye before, have you?"

What? "No, why?"

Tia shrank into the seat next to her, taking her hand back and clasping them tightly in her lap. "That's what I thought. According to Julian, Idris was careful to avoid mentioning anything that would make you curious about your own third-eye potential. I don't think she wanted you getting any ideas."

"I thought the third eye was just a way of thinking."

Tia looked at the ceiling and laughed under her breath. It almost sounded as if she were choking. "It is, in a manner of speaking…but Raoul asked me to make sure you take a personal interest in your assimilation. You're an angel, Syron. Once you touch my hands, you'll have access to my memories. You don't have to believe in our God to leave this room, but I do need you to understand him a little better than you did before, and to question any heresy you were exposed to while living with the sahiit."

Syron shook her head. "I'm sorry, Tia, but I can't see into people's minds. That's not…I've never…" A pang shot through her chest thinking of Yira, but it was she who had read Syron's thoughts before, not the other way around.

"I know you've never done it before," Tia said, and this time her voice wavered. "But angels can do twice as much as the most advanced sahiit. You're more than capable. Just be careful and only focus on what I show you. Minds are fragile things, and they'll break if you push too hard."

I don't believe you. I can't do what a sahiit can do. I don't even know how Yira did it.

But Tia couldn't hear her thoughts, and she lifted her hands to Syron, palms up.

Syron wanted to refuse, but what would it mean if she did? She had to finish the assimilation to leave, and afterward she would be one step closer to finding Will. If she had to attempt the impossible, surely there were worse things than seeing Tia's memories.

She unwrapped the bandages on her scarred hands and stretched them to Tia, whose hands were cold, and her pulse thrummed where Syron's fingers rested on her wrist. But nothing happened.

Just when Syron was about to give up, she thought of Yira sitting across from her on the floor, hands linked, and asking whether it hurt.

"No," Syron whispered.

"Good, I did it right this time," she said, and laughed. "But it's easier if your eyes are closed."

Syron shut her eyes and focused on Tia's heartbeat, following it up her arm and into her chest. Slowly, tingles started in Syron's hands and worked their way up, coiling almost painfully at the base of her neck before spreading over her scalp.

Tia must have felt it too. A shock went through her, and Syron saw a flash of purple. She leaned into it, felt it unfold around her, and suddenly she was standing inside an elaborately decorated cathedral with a high ceiling and rows of plush pews. A man stood in front of her. His brown hair had been knotted into a bun, and stubble grazed his cheeks.

Syron found his name in Tia's thoughts: *Raoul.*

When he took her hand, his eyes were wide and dark, almost black.

"Tia," he said, drawing out her name, "do you believe the God would trust you with this if you weren't ready?"

"I didn't mean any offense," she replied hastily, looking down. "I'm worried the assimilation won't work for some-one…like her. What if she's not what we think? We don't know what she can do."

"Angel or no angel, that girl is flesh and bone. Look around," Raoul said, gently lifting her chin with the hand not holding hers. "This spire is testament to the God's knowledge. If he didn't think you could acclimate her, he would have chosen someone else he deemed worthy."

Tia's eyes widened. "He believes me worthy?"

"He has faith in his followers too, dove." He let her hand drop and bowed slightly. "Let us know when the assimilation is finished. The girl is all that matters now."

The memory wrinkled and re-formed. Tia stood inside a one-room house identical to the one Syron had been in before except for a fireplace against the far wall. An old woman she knew instinctively to be Tia's grandmother lay on a pull-out bed behind her, next to a tray of untouched food. Father and Avery, her little sister, were huddled together by the window to watch the revolt.

They had been holed up in the house for hours. Tia still held on to the wild hope that Mother would make it back to them, but the one time she had asked, Father only looked at her long and sad, and held Avery tighter.

Outside, the shouts were getting louder. Blurry, frantic shapes darted back and forth on the other side of the textured glass. Tia gripped the iron poker tighter as a bang came from the front door. She jumped back, hating the wash of adrenaline that surged through her, and raised the poker as if to swing.

"Go away!" Tia screamed, but her voice came out hoarse and weak instead of the roar she had imagined.

The banging intensified, shaking the door on its hinges. Father shushed Avery while Grandmother started rambling, low and gravelly, under her breath. The bedsheets tangled around her thick waist as she rocked side to side. It was the first time in days Tia had seen her move.

And it was the first time she ever saw her father scared. He turned and raced past Tia to the small kitchen, half pulling, half dragging Avery, who held her mottled-green blanket like a lifeline. Sweat beaded on his forehead and upper lip as he thrust the table on its side. It crashed against the floor as he grabbed Tia's arm and pushed both girls in behind it.

Avery's face was slick with tears, wetting her shirt as Tia wrapped an arm around her.

"Don't move," he commanded, and snatched the poker from Tia's hand. Avery let out a devasted wail as he turned away and Tia squeezed her closer, covering her mouth to hide her cries as the door burst open. It smacked violently off the wall as two disfigured sahiit barged in.

Tia's scream lodged in her throat. Boils covered their light gray skin in thick, oozing clumps, and patches of hair were missing from their scalps. The male in front had wild eyes that took in the room in one fell swoop before landing viciously on Father. The female behind him crouched low and bared her teeth, staring at Tia with one bright blue eye. But all sahiit looked the same; Tia didn't recognize them.

"Please," Father begged. His knuckles turned white where he gripped the poker, and he raised it to ward them off. "This is my family. Have mercy."

"Mercy?" the male spit back. "You think you deserve mercy after what you've done to us?"

Tia's face and chest felt hot. She wanted to jump to her feet and scream that they were wrong. Father and Mother were both scientists. They would never hurt anyone. But before she knew what was happening, Father rushed forward.

Tia just had time to shout his name before the male grabbed the hooked end and twisted it up and out of Father's hand. The female rushed at him too, and Tia bolted to her feet. She heard Avery's screams, and Grandmother's coughing, heard too the shouts of the watchmen outside and the savage, animalistic cries of the sahiit. But when the female stiffened and backed away, and the male straightened his back, then she saw the blood.

Bright vermilion colored the back of Father's shirt, spreading from the sharp, hooked end of the iron poker she had held moments ago, before he had snatched it away to protect them.

The male must have still been holding the handle, because he grabbed Father by the shoulder and pushed him back.

Tia didn't realize she was moving until she hovered over Father where he had fallen on the floor, her hands flitting uselessly over his ruined chest. Then he coughed, and vermilion was on his lips too, dribbling down the sides of his face. She had never seen so much blood.

"Father," Tia whispered, but he didn't seem to hear her. She blinked away tears and leaped to her feet, clenching her hands into fists by her sides.

"You're monsters! You're all just fucking monsters!"

She was too young to curse. If Father heard her…he couldn't, though. Not anymore.

Avery's screams were getting louder. She looked over and Avery's face was beet red, her blanket fisted in one dimpled hand, dragging on the floor behind her. Tia ran over and scooped her up, holding her so that her chin rested on the ball of Tia's shoulder, and faced the sahiit.

The female stepped forward, but the male held out his

hand and she froze. This close, Tia could see the thin white scar that ran down the length of her throat.

"Leave them be," he said, his vicious eyes contemplating Tia. "Gods and monsters aren't so different, after all."

The poker clattered against the floor as he turned his back to her. The female's lips twitched, and she glanced back twice before following him through the door.

Tia waited until she was sure they were gone to look down at the poker slick with Father's blood. "It'll be okay," she whispered to Avery, and she felt something inside of her break. She sank to her knees and buried her face in the crook of Avery's neck.

She didn't cry.

~

The memory faded as Syron pulled her hands away. The library was still warm and familiar around her, but it felt wrong—as if she were looking through the wrong lens. She rubbed her temples and leaned back, letting the table dig into her side.

"That was…"

"That was brilliant!" Tia exclaimed. "I was doubtful when Raoul said I shouldn't worry, but you did amazing. Truly, Syron."

"I was going to say that was horrible. Tia, I can't…I don't know what to say. Are you okay? Is your sister okay?"

She waved her off. "The revolt was a long time ago. I don't know how much Avery remembers, but I think we've both made peace with our loss. Besides, Father oversaw most of the experiments then, and without him we wouldn't have half the medical knowledge we do today."

She stood up and ran her hands down her plain dress.

Syron looked back at the way they had come in, but the wall was smooth just like in the real library.

"Come," Tia said. "The watchman is waiting for you outside. He'll escort you to your room."

"But Leon—"

"Will be along as soon as he's assimilated. It shouldn't take too long." She smiled politely and led Syron to the front of the room and through the shadowed doorway that should have opened to the stretch of hallway and the cafeteria. Instead, it led outside.

The cool night air wafted against her, carrying the faint scent of incense. She perked up and looked around for Julian. They were standing in the same cobblestone area, just a little farther down the wall that spanned the city. But it was the watchman who stepped from the shadows instead, and Syron's spirits sank.

Tia placed a hand on her shoulder. "The God works in mysterious ways. Even if you don't believe as we do, try to have faith that there is a grander plan at work than you or I could ever comprehend." To the watchman, she said, "Take her around the back of the spire. Julian will be waiting." She turned on her heels and disappeared back into the wall, leaving Syron alone in the giant city with only the watchman for company.

She'd rather be back in the assimilation.

The watchman didn't even look at her. He turned and sauntered off into the maze of houses, his chain mail clinking with each step. Syron hesitated before following him into the shadows, guided more by sound than sight. The narrow street twisted, turned, and branched off until she wasn't sure which way she had come from or which direction she was heading, and still he led her deeper in.

The farther they walked, the more nervous Syron became. In a big city like this, shouldn't there be more people out? Back home, even in the middle of the night, there were college students and drunks loitering on the sidewalks, waiting for cabs or spilling out of flashing doorways in search of food. Here, the whole city felt… empty.

The watchman took a sharp left, and the narrow street widened to a large, curving cobblestone road lined with tall buildings. Neon signs advertised things like personalized jewelry, carpentry, and cosmetics. One building with purple lights beneath the display window showed off a large deck of tarot cards, the word "psychic" displayed proudly on the glass.

She was so distracted she almost ran straight into the watchman, who had stopped at the entrance to a low, dark pavilion. She stumbled back as he glanced over his shoulder.

"Wait here," he muttered, and passed underneath. A moment later, a light clicking and whirling sound came, followed by the grinding of gears.

Syron hadn't noticed the cables above her head until an intricately detailed metal cage that served as a lift emerged from the shadow of the pavilion, held to the cables by a C-shaped bar. The watchman leaned out and offered his hand. It swallowed her own as he pulled her inside and shifted the lever on the floor.

She gripped the bars as the lift started forward. It was wide enough to hold at least a dozen people, and a bench made of the same thin, curling metal spanned three of the four walls. She picked her way to the back and sat, trying to calm her racing thoughts as they were pulled, quite literally, to the spire.

The steady drone of the lift was the only noise in the silent city. Syron watched for movement in the alleys between the shops or through the windows, but there wasn't a soul anywhere. The empty streets only made her unease grow, and her stomach knotted.

"The God prepared a communion service for your arrival," the watchman said, as if reading her thoughts. "It started hours ago, but most of the more pious citizens are probably still in the cathedral."

"What about the rest of them?"

"It's past curfew." He shrugged and shifted the lever again. The lift slowed to a crawl as they came up on another pavilion, but Syron's eyes shifted back to the spire. It sprouted from the earth like a bronze giant reaching for the sky, and as the lift came to a stop and the watchman helped her down, she couldn't help thinking of the Bible stories she had learned as a child and wonder whether, perhaps, this God had built his own tower of Babel.

The shops had given way to more houses, arranged in a wide circle around the spire. She wanted to ask whether these were the oldest buildings in the city, but kept her lips pressed tightly together as they reached the large opening.

The spire itself was wider than she had expected, and windowless. The door marking the entrance was thrown wide open, spilling honeyed light into the darkness to her right. Syron could hear the muffled voices inside, and this close, the aroma of bread was mouthwatering. She ignored the ache in her stomach and followed the watchman around the circumference of the spire to the back. Her shoes tapped on the cobblestone streets in tandem with the jingling of his chain mail, stopping only when they reached a smaller, plain metal door.

Syron squinted. It was set into the spire so perfectly that without the light beneath it, she never would have known it was there. The watchman pounded on the door and stepped back. She counted to thirty, and just as he raised his fist to pound again, the door swung open.

Julian had bathed. His damp hair curled wildly around his temples, and the gore-splattered clothes had been replaced with a black silk robe tied in a knot at his waist.

"Thank you, Boris," he said, and the light behind him changed from blue to red.

Boris straightened and cast an uneasy glance behind Julian before nodding and turning away, following the path they had taken back to the lift.

"Well," Julian said after a moment, "you're here in one piece."

Syron started. "Was there a chance I wouldn't be?"

Julian cracked a smile and ushered her inside, shutting the door behind her as she walked down a flight of steps and into a lab lit with blue light. A large counter lined the wall on her left, below three tiers of shelves stacked with beakers, scales, and a myriad of other equipment Syron didn't have a name for. Glass refrigerators filled with purple vials were pushed against the right wall. She moved aside as Julian came down the stairs, and past the racks of shriveling lotus flowers in the center, she spotted a single white door set into the opposite wall.

"How did your assimilation go?" Julian asked.

Syron ripped her eyes away and turned back to him. A wrought iron elevator nearly the same as the lift she had ridden in with the watchman was pressed into the wall behind him, next to the stairs. The doors were already open.

"Tia showed you her memories, didn't she?"

When Syron didn't answer right away, he sat on the bottom step and patted the space beside him. Hesitantly, Syron sat. The heat in the lab pressed against her, making her arms itch beneath their wrappings. She stretched them out on her raised knees and watched the crease of her knuckles with newfound fascination.

Until the assimilation, she had only ever believed that being an angel meant the God wanted her dead. Now that she knew her third eye allowed her to do *things*, whether or not it was limited to seeing memories, she couldn't shake what Yira had told her after leaving Del-Amar: that without part of an angel's soul, the God wouldn't have the power he has now.

I should have put two and two together. I should have—

"I wouldn't worry about what she showed you. I doubt anyone's bothered to tell Tia what her parents did in the name of the God, though I'm sure she would find a way to justify it if they had."

Syron linked her hands and looked over at him as the lights switched to purple. His expression was kind, but she couldn't begin to guess what he was really thinking.

"She said Raoul wanted me to take a personal interest in my assimilation. What if he asks me to use my third eye again and I hurt someone?"

Julian chuckled under his breath and nudged her. "You would have to either force someone to show you a memory they want to keep private or dig one up they've buried in their subconscious to do any permanent damage. But you don't seem like you want to deep dive into anyone's psyche, and besides," he said, standing up and offering his hand, "I doubt even Raoul would want to risk you getting more familiar with your third eye."

Syron grimaced and let him pull her up, then lead her into the elevator. He shifted a lever on the floor, and it hummed to life.

"Are you taking me to my room?"

Julian nodded. "Like I told Tia, the God wants you close."

They lapsed into silence as the elevator lurched upward. Syron suppressed a shudder and gripped the handle, watching the light shift to red beneath the thin, curving metal at their feet.

When the red light couldn't have been bigger than a pinprick below them, the elevator slowed to a crawl and stopped. She followed Julian through the open doors and into a wide hallway with bronze walls and a dark floor. They passed rows of doors on either side, separated by simple, abstract paintings in black frames.

When they reached the end of the hall, Julian turned to the last door on the right and pulled out a key.

"Leon's room will be across from yours," he said, sliding the key into the lock. "I imagine he's on his way to the spire now."

Syron nodded. "You know, you never did tell me what's really going on."

The hum of an elevator answered her. Syron followed the noise to another intricate bronze door on the wall closest to them, opposite the elevator they had used. The humming slowed, and beneath it she could hear the murmuring voices of two men on the other side.

Julian's hand was on Syron's lower back in an instant, gently but firmly pushing her into the room.

"What are you—"

"Just trust me," Julian said in a whisper. "We'll talk more tomorrow."

Syron turned just as the door swung shut. She heard the scrape of metal as the key fumbled in the lock, and then she was alone.

17

SCENT OF SAGE AND SMOKE

he first early rays of morning filtered through the damp treetops as they barreled through the forest. Syron's cheeks ached from smiling so much, but she couldn't help it. It had been so long since she'd felt weightless.

"Keep up!" she yelled over her shoulder, and Leon laughed from somewhere behind her.

"Where are we going?"

"I'm not sure," she admitted, jumping over a moss-covered log and relishing the feel of the cool, crisp air against her skin. She ran farther, dodging thickets of brambles and low-hanging branches until the trees thinned to reveal a small clearing.

She skidded to a stop. A pond dotted with purple and white lotus flowers sat in its center, the roots winding like knots beneath the smooth surface. Carefully, she knelt on the muddy bank and cupped a purple lotus in her hands.

"What are you doing?" Leon asked breathlessly. He collapsed next to her as she lifted it out and leaned back.

"Isn't it beautiful?" she asked, glancing up at him. His eyes, half-hidden beneath his tousled white hair, matched the lavender shade

of the petals. Shadow accentuated the sharp curve of his jaw as he wrapped an arm around her. "I'm not sure how I knew it was here. I just had this feeling…"

"You're right," he said. "It is beautiful. Do you like it here?"

"I think so." She smiled. "But you don't have to stay if you don't want to."

"And here I thought sirens were famous for luring sailors to their deaths."

Syron gasped. "Are you making fun of my name, sir?"

Leon laughed. It was warm and hiccupy and shook her from where she was pressed against him. "Forgive me, ma'am, I meant no offense."

Syron started to elbow him as the petals unfurled in her palms, revealing the whole of the yellow center. She stared down in awe as Leon stiffened.

"Do you think it's true that when the flower opens, your third eye does too?" she asked, but Leon was staring across the clearing, where a cracked branch hung limply against a trunk.

"Something feels off about this place," he murmured. Syron started to look back at him before doing a double take.

Something was moving.

The brown roots shifted closer to them, too quick to be the gentle sway of the water. Syron jerked back. The lotus fell from her hands and sent ripples across the surface as she tried climbing to her feet, but the mud had seeped in through her pant legs, numbing her skin and locking her in place.

The steady pressure of Leon's arm was gone. Vaguely, she knew he was still beside her trying in vain to wrench himself free, but her eyes were strained on the tangled mass rising from the surface of the pond. The sides stretched and came back together, pulling the roots from its face.

But it wasn't a monster at all. The air whooshed from her lungs the same time a strange calm settled over her. He was handsome in a rugged sort of way, terrifying because he was so different, startling because he was so familiar.

Will crossed the pond slowly, the roots unraveling around him until he stood before her in a soaked T-shirt and jeans. Syron shivered but stayed deathly still as he leaned in, spilling droplets of water across her shoulder and chest.

His voice was warm and husky in her ear.

"Have you found me yet?"

Syron woke with a start. Her arms were caught, and for a split second she thought Will had grabbed her to drag her into the pond, but then she looked around and remembered she was in the spire. It was only a dream.

Slowly, she untangled the sweaty sheets from her limbs and sat up. The room Julian had pushed her into was huge and decorative, with thick black metal beams overlapping the corners and cresting to reach the middle of the ceiling. Where they met, a giant chandelier shaped like the wicked edges of a treetop sprouted, with each of the tips holding a glowing bulb.

Syron ran the palms of her hands over her eyes and stood up. She hadn't thought about the white sheets when she had climbed into bed, and now they were stained with stripes of dirt. A chest lay at the foot of the bed, perfectly matching the vanity table, desk, and wardrobe. A wide dressing screen hugged the corner of the wall closest to her, its panels arching to form a single point.

She started toward it and paused, walking in a slow circle. The room was breathtaking. Under different circumstances, she would be content to curl up with a book and stay here forever, but there were too many things to do. She needed to make sure Leon had gotten back from his assimilation and find a way to speak with Julian alone. He had promised to try to find out what happened to Yira, and even though she didn't trust him completely, he was her best bet. Not to mention she needed to start poking around about Will, but short of shouting his name from the rooftops, she wasn't sure how to do that either.

But she was close. She could feel it.

A smile crept up her face, and she laughed. It started small and built, erupting into peals of laughter until she had to bend over to catch her breath. It may have gone horribly wrong, but somehow, impossibly, they had done it. She was *alive*. She was *inside the spire*. And she wasn't alone. Leon was with her.

When she looked up, her reflection stared back at her. Her gear was stretched, stained, and torn, and her hair frizzed wildly around her face. She tucked it behind her ears and went in search of a bathroom. It didn't take long —the dressing screen obscured the claw-footed bronze tub, and she stripped down eagerly, climbing in while the water still ran scalding hot before turning the handle to cool it down. A tiered bath cart stacked with towels and loaded with sprays, oils, and multicolored glass bottles sat next to her. Steam rose in thick tendrils around her as she got to work scrubbing off the grime of traveling. She had taken the wraps off her arms and chest the night before, and she went over these spots more carefully, gently pressing the sponge against her bare skin before moving on.

She reached for another of the bottles when the sound of the door opening drew her up short. She scrambled for a towel as the heeled footsteps came closer and just managed to wrap it around her as a woman with cold eyes peeked around the screen.

"Oh, good. I was worried about your personal hygiene."

Syron's fingers fisted in the towel. The woman's gray hair was pinned up in curls, with a few loose pieces framing her too-pink cheeks. Thick golden hoops dangled from her ears as she folded the screen back, revealing a cluster of three woman on the other side. Two of them held silver cases, and the third nodded politely over a silver tray stacked with what looked to be cantaloupe, rice cakes, and a single glass of water.

"What are you waiting for?" the older woman asked. "The angel needs a robe, does she not?" The others dispersed, one heading to the wardrobe and the other two to the vanity, as the older woman looked Syron up and down.

"You've been asleep for over a day," she said simply. Condescension flavored her tone, making the back of Syron's neck prickle. "It's by the God's good graces he didn't allow us to wake you until now, but I see you were already up."

"I guess being chased by the God took its toll on my sleeping schedule," Syron said. "I'll have to remember not to make it inconvenient for you if it happens again."

The woman's eyes narrowed before darting to the floor and clucking her tongue. She stooped to pick up the pile of gear, careful not to let it touch her clothes, and swiveled.

"Girls, do try to make her look presentable. Raoul will be expecting her shortly."

Without another word, she turned and marched from the room. Syron pursed her lips as she watched her leave, looking away only when a girl with dark skin and short, curly hair handed her a robe. Syron accepted it, and the black silk was thin and cool as she shrugged it on before letting the towel fall.

"Thank you," she murmured under her breath.

The girl waved it away. "No, thank you. Ambrosia treats everyone terribly. Her manners are as ancient as she is."

Syron smiled despite herself, and the girl held out a hand. "My name is Maggie, but you can call me Mags. Cleo is the one setting up the makeup, and Avery brought your food. Please," she added, taking back her hand and motioning to the vanity, "take a seat. You must be starving."

She *was* starving. Her stomach twisted painfully as she took the seat at the vanity and Avery placed the tray on her lap. Syron nodded in thanks and considered asking Avery whether she was related to Tia, or whether she only shared the sister's name, but thought better of it. She didn't want to explain how she would know that, and besides, she had Tia's same pale green eyes and long blond hair.

She settled for pickling up a slice of cantaloupe instead, letting the cool, sweet liquid calm the ache in her stomach. When she reached for the glass, the water fizzed on her tongue and tasted faintly of lavender.

"What do you think of the city so far?" Mags asked, switching out her silver case for a brush and working the tangles from Syron's hair.

Syron swallowed and fingered one of the rice cakes. "It's…a lot. I mean, I only saw it at night, but there's so much here. It reminded me of where I came from but, different, if that makes sense?"

Mags nodded. "There's a lot to take in. The city is beautiful in the daylight, though. You'll get to see it as soon as we head down."

Cleo snapped open the silver cases and selected a variety of sprays and creams from one and an assortment of makeup from the other.

"Why doesn't Raoul live in the spire?" Syron asked. "I haven't been here long, but I've heard his name more than anyone's. I thought anyone that would be important to the God would live here."

"We're all important to the God," Mags corrected. "But you're not wrong. His most trusted followers are allowed rooms in the spire, of course, but Raoul declined."

"Why would he do that?"

"Because he's not just the God's adviser," Cleo said, lining up the bottles. "He's also a Keeper. They value knowledge more than anything. Usually, it gets added to the library inside their Citadel, but he's using it to help our city instead. My guess is that the closer he is to the public, the more he's able to learn."

"Or he just wanted his own space," Mags said, and shrugged. She reached over Syron's shoulder and handing Cleo a styling tool.

Syron ate thoughtfully as they flitted about her, rubbing creams along her face and neck, and holding different shades of makeup against the soft underside of her left arm.

"How long ago did the last angel fall?" Syron asked finally. The question burned like a fire in the pit of her stomach. If she were going to start anywhere, it might as well be here.

For once, neither of the girls answered right away. Avery had taken over curling Syron's hair while Mags moved to help Cleo with the brushes, and Syron caught Avery's reflection as her eyes shifted to Syron's back, as if she wanted to pull back the robe to see beneath it.

"I think all of us were too young to remember the last ceremony. There have been a few angels since then, but when the God sent the watchman out to collect them, they didn't survive the fall."

"You mean they…"

"Yeah."

"But how? I mean, I kind of just, I don't know, woke up."

Mags dabbed the brush along Syron's forehead. "No one knows how it all really works, Syron, except for maybe the God. Those poor women, though, deserved to be redeemed before leaving our world."

Women. So there wasn't a ceremony for Will. Maybe he's still in the stone room from my dream.

Syron let her eyes flutter closed as Mags ran the brush along her lids and the soft skin underneath before opening them again. Avery swiveled her around and moved aside for Cleo to take her place. Her brown hair was pulled on top of her head in a sleek bun, her lips full and glossy as she tilted Syron's head to the side and ran a brush along her cheeks, chin, and temples. With a final flick of her hand, she tilted Syron's face to the light, examining, and grabbed a silver powder from the vanity and dotted her collarbones.

"I wonder where—" Cleo started to say but was interrupted by a knock at the door. She shifted toward it, but Mags waved her off.

"You two finish up," Mags said, already heading to the door. "You only have a moment longer."

Cleo nodded and spritzed Syron's hair with a fine mist. Behind Syron, she heard what must have been the wardrobe opening and closing, and then Avery walking toward them. She started to turn around when Cleo placed her hand gently on Syron's chin.

"Oh, none of that. You wouldn't want to spoil the surprise, would you?" Then she pulled the belt at Syron's waist and the robe slipped from her shoulders. She caught the quick glance Avery cast at the mirror behind Syron, the fleeting expression of shock and confusion, until Cleo moved to block her view and something soft and smooth was pulled over her head. The dress hugged her chest and waist, and the thick straps tickled her arms just beneath her shoulders as Avery applied a thick oil to her lips.

Syron waited until she set it aside to catch her eye. "You thought I had wings," Syron said simply, and Avery flushed.

"I, um, I didn't mean to be rude. I heard that angel's backs need to be sewn up after the wings fall off. I assumed there would still be scars."

"No, I never had wings. I doubt any angel has."

Avery's eyes widened as Cleo reached over and swatted her arm. "See? I told you it was just a parable or some-thing." Cleo dropped a pair of black flats on the floor and Syron slipped them on, then Cleo placed her hands on Syron's shoulders and spun her to face the mirror. "Okay," she said, moving out of the way. "You're ready."

Syron gasped. The person looking back at her was a beautiful stranger. Her black hair fell down her back and draped across her exposed shoulders in soft waves. Her lips were full and soft, eyes wide and framed by thick lashes. A dusting of rose colored her cheeks, and when Syron turned to get a better look at the black dress, the stranger did too.

She had the sudden desire to rub her scarred hands down her face to see how much of the *real* her, the flawed her, would show through. Instead, she hid them in the folds of her dress.

"Ambrosia said there may still be scars from your journey here, but you can't really tell unless you look closely. Your hands, though," Cleo said shyly, "will take the longest to heal because you use them more. I could've covered them too, but I didn't want it to interfere with their healing."

"No, it's perfect. Thank you," Syron murmured, and took a deep breath to steady herself. Next to her, Avery looped an arm through hers and together they followed Cleo out into the hall, where a tall temporal with golden brown skin, a sleek beard, and thick eyebrows ending in sharp points glanced from Mags to her. His smile was dazzling.

"This must be our angel," he said in a sultry voice, and took Syron's hand. "You girls had it easy." He laughed. "I nearly had to beg to give this man a haircut."

As if on cue, Leon appeared in the open doorway across the hall. Syron forgot all about the man in front of her or the girls' gaggle of answering voices. She remembered her surprise at seeing Leon dressed up the night of her initiation into the factions, and how she had been careful not to stare at him for very long. But now she couldn't look away.

Leon's hands were tucked deeply in his pockets. His black silk shirt was tucked into his dress pants, with silver buttons scrawled with intricate designs. His hair had been trimmed on the sides and textured on the top, with swirling patterns shaved into the sides. The diamond markings on his skin danced in the light, highlighting his cheekbone as he looked up through his lashes at her. His lips quirked up on one side, and Syron's heart skipped a beat.

They stared at each other, Syron's stomach winding itself into knots, until the elevator opened across the hall. A handful of temporals filed out, stopping short when they saw their little group.

"Come on," Avery whispered. Syron flushed and stared at the floor as they walked the length of the hall to the elevator. The temporals inside backed as far away as they could in the tight space, leaving Syron grasping the handle and sneaking glances at them as the elevator hummed and started its descent. Every time the gears slid into place and opened at a new floor, she would look up at the people leaving or coming in, and every time their eyes glossed past her and fixed on Leon.

She focused instead on the cool, calm expressions of Mags and the others who had gotten them ready, and realized with a start that they must have been instructed not to let Leon and her feel out of place—to treat them as if they belonged. The other temporals had probably never seen a sahiit before, or at least weren't familiar with them, and were acting the only way they knew how.

Finally, when sweat beaded on the back of her neck and the crook of her elbows, the doors opened to a wide, curving staircase. Mags led them down the steps with the other temporals talking in hushed tones behind them, too low for Syron to hear, and into a grand cathedral.

Just like in Tia's memory, rows of lavish pews sat on either side of the aisle. More temporals filed down another curved staircase opposite them. In place of windows, the bronze walls were separated into large rectangles and sculpted in relief, the scenes rising out of the wall with an artist's eye for detail. Syron craned her neck up, and found the ceiling was crisscrossed in dark metal beams wrapped in black wire and dangling with large, circular bulbs.

She followed Mags through a row of pews and down the center aisle. The temporals in line moved aside for them as they passed, stopping at the edge of the platform where a large decorative bowl of water sat. Past it, the pulpit stood tall and proud in front of a wrought iron elevator shaft that ran from the ceiling to the floor.

"Bow your head," Mags whispered, dipping her fingers in the water. Syron did, and watched as Mags tapped her wet fingers against her forehead and murmured a short prayer. Syron mirrored her, though barely touching the water and keeping her lips tight. The back of her neck prickled as she turned away and followed Mags back down the aisle toward the arched cathedral doors.

"One thing hasn't changed," Leon whispered, falling into step beside her. "That elevator goes all the way to the top of the spire. I'd bet it lets out on any floor too, so the God can go wherever he wants."

Syron shivered at the thought and glanced up at him. She wanted to ask what it was like for him being back inside the city, but as soon as she started to speak, a piercing scream rang out behind them. It pounded off the walls and Syron clapped her hands to her ears, twisting around the same time as someone grabbed her from behind. She just had time to see a woman sprinting toward them, her wet mascara tracing lines down her face like fractured stone, as someone moved to block her way.

The man who had gotten Leon ready stood sentry in front of her. She jerked to see around him and found the temporals in line had caught the woman and forced her to her knees.

"What are they doing?" Syron asked. The woman pulled desperately against them, throwing her body weight forward as hard as she could. "What are they doing?" Syron asked again, louder this time. She could hear the hysteria rising in her voice. "Get off her!" she shouted at the crowd. "You'll hurt her!"

Syron tried running to her, but the grip on her arms was like iron locking her in place.

"Let the angel come, Joseph! It's for my baby," the woman said, and her voice cracked. "It'll help my—"

"No," Joseph said, striding forward, "it won't. Nothing can bring your little boy back, Nora."

Her cracked face was disfigured in rage as he jerked

her arm up and reached inside the billowed sleeve, drawing out a small dagger.

Syron's hand shook as she brought it to her lips. Her stomach lurched as someone twisted her away, and then Avery was beside her instead of behind her, rushing her to the cathedral doors.

"Her little boy turned a couple of weeks ago," Avery whispered in her ear. "The poor thing wasn't even a month old." Her fingers dug into Syron's arm, but she didn't seem to notice. "It's the youngest anyone's ever changed. She thinks—"

"That if she kills me, her child will be saved," Syron finished for her, remembering the nightchild holding the swaddle outside Adaline's house. "But I'm not the one who's hurting them."

Avery looked at her strangely as Mags pushed open the cathedral doors, and Syron's thoughts scattered. What had before been small, dark houses and looming neon shops were now all beautiful, polished, and gleaming bronze. The same sunlight that warmed her shoulders reflected off the city so completely that for a moment, she forgot all about how dangerous it was for her to be here and thought only of the city as a living body, and the mass of people in brightly woven silk were the soul.

Avery detached herself from Syron's arm and formed a triad with Mags and Cleo. Syron and Leon stayed close behind, following them past the houses that circled the spire before taking a sharp left at another lift, opposite the direction Syron had come with the watchman before. The city opened and then folded around them as they turned off the larger, busier streets to weave between the smaller shops and stands. The temporals outside seemed too busy to give them much notice, and the few who stopped to stare were quick to look busy when Syron met their eyes.

"It's so weird," Leon whispered to her. She looked over and found his hand buried deep in his pocket, and she knew without having to ask that he was holding tight to his mother's dragonfly.

"You mean the woman in the spire?" Syron whispered back. "What do you think they'll do to her?"

"Alert the watchmen, definitely. After that, though…" He let the sentence hang. "The city has changed so much. I keep trying to piece together things I remember with what we're seeing, but the whole atmosphere feels different. If Yira were here, she would know—"

"We're here," Mags said, calling over her shoulder, and Syron snapped her attention forward. Mags angled them toward a rich-looking house the same bronze shade as the others, but with thick columns holding up the porch roof, and a single stained glass window set into the front door.

Syron followed them up the porch steps cautiously, unsure what to expect. Mags knocked twice and turned to Cleo and Avery. "Wait outside for me. I'll only be a moment." When they nodded and stepped aside, she beckoned to Syron and Leon and twisted the handle, holding the door open for them.

Syron's first thought was that the house was empty. The entryway was dim and sparse, with only a small table holding a measly stack of books on the wall across from them. A wrought iron spiral staircase hovered in the shadow to their left, almost invisible when Mags clicked the door shut behind them.

"This way," she whispered, leading them past the staircase, through a dark, narrow hallway, and into what Syron assumed to be a living room. Enough muted light filtered in through the curtained window to tell that the room was large and wide, and littered with stacks of newspapers high enough to reach her knees.

"Raoul?" Mags asked.

Something shuffled in front of them. Syron stumbled back as Mags flipped on the light, revealing a tall, lean man wearing a blindfold. He stood in the center of the stacks and held up a finger at them, took three more steps, and knocked over a pile of newspapers. He hummed as if it amused him and turned another direction.

"Excuse me, Raoul, but—"

"Haven't I already asked not to be disturbed?" he interrupted. "The vendors can set up wherever they like, for all I care. I'm not their policeman."

Mags pursed her lips. "I brought the angel. Ambrosia said you were expecting us."

With that, the humming stopped. He swiveled toward them and felt at the air in front of him. Syron just had time to think that Raoul was either very dull or very strange, but then he pulled down the blindfold, and the thoughts vanished. The purple bags under his eyes stood out like a bruise, and the lower half of his face had the same wild stubble Syron had seen in Tia's memory. Despite that, he held himself with poise, his dark eyes landing on Syron with an unnerving confidence.

"Syron, is it?" Raoul asked. His lips turned up in a wolfish smile as she nodded and clasped her hands nervously behind her back. "It's so nice to finally meet you. I see you brought a friend."

"This is Leon," Mags said, cutting in. "His mother was—"

"Yes, yes, Julian told me all about it. Thank you for bringing them, Maggie. It'll be nice to sit down and have a civilized chat."

Mags dipped her head and turned to Syron and Leon, clasping them both on the shoulders before rushing out of the room.

"Now then," Raoul said, cheating his way out of the maze, "if you wouldn't mind coming with me. I'll get us some refreshments upstairs and—"

"What were you doing in the dark?" Syron interrupted.

Raoul clucked his tongue. His musky scent of sage and smoke seemed to fill the room. "I have a theory that our minds have an innate pattern they follow. I wanted to test it on myself before sending word to the Keepers."

"That's…" she tried to say, and Raoul chuckled.

"It's a difficult thing to determine. From an outsider's perspective, I imagine I look quite mad."

"I doubt you care very much what we think," she murmured, and Raoul's eyes narrowed.

"On the contrary, I care what you think very much. You and Leon both." Coming back to himself, he strode past them and into the shadow of the hall. Syron and Leon exchanged a wary glance and followed him back to the entryway and up the spiral staircase. Their shoes tapped on the thin metal as they wound their way up, and then on the smooth wooden floor as they reached the top. Black curtains were pushed back to let the sunlight stream in. The room was large but comfortable, dominated by a U-shaped leather couch and lined with bookshelves tall enough to reach the ceiling. An arched doorway was centered on the left wall.

"Please, make yourselves comfortable. I'll be back in a moment."

As soon as he left the room, Syron let out a breath she hadn't known she'd been holding. She tried to go through everything she knew about Raoul, but it wasn't much: Mags had said he was the God's assistant as well as a Keeper, Tia had shown her that he wanted Syron to change her mind about the God's City, and Julian had said he doubted Raoul would want her to practice more with her third eye. Not to mention that outside the gate, Julian had threatened Raoul to the watchman. All things considered, she didn't want to be anywhere near him. She could run back down the steps and out the door, but if Raoul were half as powerful as he seemed, she would just end up right back here. But…

"If anyone in the city knows about Will, it would be him," Syron whispered, but no one heard her. Leon had walked over to the window and sat on the edge, seemingly lost in thought.

Syron felt suddenly guilty. This was the city that had abused his people and murdered his mother. They had no idea what had happened to Yira, or how to get the Black Book. Adaline was gone too, and she had been the key to finding out who the Nightman was. Grief welled within her like a silent storm threatening to spill out, and the guilt grew around it. Leon had history with this city, its people. He had lost first Calais as a friend, and then Yira, who was like a mother. He was alone.

She started to go to him when Raoul walked back into the room, holding a tray with three steaming mugs. The aroma of coffee and caramel filled the room as he set the tray on the table and took a seat, indicating that they join him.

Leon positioned himself close to Syron, but she restrained the urge to reach out to him with Raoul's eyes on them. She reached for the mug instead, blowing gently on the top as Raoul stretched an arm along the back of the couch across from them.

"It took a long time to get you here, Syron. I was angry with you at first, but I would be lying if I said I didn't hold respect for you as well. Avoiding the watchmen I sent out the first night you fell, freeing the sahiit they captured, *and* forcing the God to broker a deal with the sahiit?" He whis-tled. "You're a fighter."

"She's more than a fighter," Leon said. He hadn't touched his coffee. "She's a person. She deserves to make a life for herself just like the rest of us."

Raoul chuckled. "Leon. The little birds told me a lot about you. You were in the group she rescued, and one of the two she ran off with. It's funny how the mind works, isn't it? Even if it's destined to fail, it's in our nature to draw us to what feels familiar. Tell me, does she remind you of your mother?"

Syron's neck grew hot as Leon shot to his feet. She reached up and grabbed his sleeve to hold him in place, glaring daggers at Raoul. Warmth seeped through her dress to her thigh, but she didn't look down at her spilled coffee.

Little birds, Syron thought. He must mean the nightchil-dren. "Leave Leon out of this. Did you ask us here for any other reason than to gloat? If you really cared what I thought, you'd let me talk instead of making assumptions and pressing buttons to see what makes us tick."

Raoul's eyes lit up. He leaned forward and clasped his hands together.

"I think you're scared of what my third eye can do if I practice with it," Syron said, pouring her grief, guilt, and anger into her words. "I think you want to needle us to see what makes us scared or sad or angry. I think you're playing a game that isn't yours to play, and moving pieces around just to see what happens. I think you're worried the God hasn't murdered me yet, and you and I both know it has something to do with the Black Book."

She didn't know—she had no way of knowing—but Raoul's expression darkened, and she knew she had guessed right. Why else would the God keep her close by, if not to have her within easy reach? And despite the claims everyone made, the God had no reason to keep her alive when every other angel, except for Will, had been murdered right away. And the book was the only thing standing between her life and her death.

"And I think you know I'm right, and that scares you too," she finished.

There was a sick satisfaction in watching the cracks in his carefully orchestrated appearance seal back up. Maybe it was because she had surprised the man who seemed to know everything about everyone, or simply because she had stepped outside the box he had placed her in.

I'm an angel, Syron thought, *and I wasn't sent here to die.*

Raoul cleared his throat. "I admire your display, but the Black Book has nothing to——"

"Excuse me," someone said behind them, and Syron turned.

Julian stood at the top of the spiral staircase with his hand on the railing. He shifted uncomfortably. "I'm sorry to interrupt, but the God requested you in the spire, Raoul."

Raoul stood and dusted himself off. "So it's that time again, is it?" He nodded to each of them in turn and gripped the lapels of his jacket. "Feel free to explore the city at your leisure, accompanied by a watchman, of course."

As soon as he turned his back, Syron tried and failed to catch Julian's eye. His only focus was on Raoul.

"Oh," Raoul added, looking back at Syron and winking, "do try to stay on your best behavior, dove. We wouldn't want that mouth of yours getting you into trouble."

Syron flushed but stood her ground as he turned and walked down the steps. Julian followed close behind, dipping his hand in his pants pocket. A scrap of paper fell out a second later, so quickly Syron almost missed it.

She crept forward and strained her ears for the sound of the front door. As soon as she was sure they were gone, she stooped to pick it up.

The handwriting was messy and slanted.

Wait for me in the attic. I need your help.

18

SKELETONS IN THE ATTIC

Leon led the way up the narrow stairs in silence. He hadn't said a word after Raoul had left, even when he'd looked over Syron's shoulder to read the note. He had turned instead to search for the attic, and Syron had trailed along behind him, eventually finding it past a thin door in the upstairs hallway.

"What do you think he needs our help with?" Syron asked. Her voice was little more than a whisper as they crested the stairs.

"Whatever it is, I'm willing to bet it's the reason why he's helping us in the first place."

Syron nodded pensively and looked around. The attic spread the length of the house, with diagonal beams that sank the corners into darkness. The only light came from the circular window on the wall closest to her, but it wasn't until Leon pulled the cord dangling from the ceiling that the single bulb flickered on, and she blanched.

Raoul had a skeleton in his attic.

It stood on a low pedestal between a set of the beams, held up by wire. She hugged her arms to her chest and walked closer, inspecting the loops, swirls, and flicks of what must have been black paint or ink that covered the bones. The skull was mostly untouched except for the inverted triangle painted on its forehead.

She gripped Julian's note tighter and turned to Leon, but he was hovering over a set of boxes. He reached inside and pulled out a piece of burnished bronze armor, turned it in his hands, and dropped it back into the box with a dull clang.

"It's from an old watchman," he said absently, and rubbed his neck. "This city gives me the creeps."

"It's fucked up," Syron agreed. "Just like what Raoul said to you. You didn't deserve that."

Leon shrugged. "You were right. He's trying to see what he can do to get under our skin. I just hate that he figured me out so easily."

"He's good at that," someone said behind them.

Syron startled and turned to the voice. Julian had come up the stairs silently, standing misplaced at the top. "I heard what happened in the spire. Are you two all right?"

"We, um, we're fine," Syron said, sparing a glance at Leon. "How did you know?"

"Everyone is talking about it. News travels fast around here." He rolled his eyes in an attempt at nonchalance, but he couldn't shake the crease between his eyebrows. "I'm sure it'll be one of the first things Raoul will discuss with the God…but that doesn't matter now. We don't have a lot of time before he gets back."

"Does he meet with the God often?" Leon asked.

"Every day." Julian's voice had a bite to it as he moved closer and plopped down on the floor, motioning for them to join him. Syron fussed with the folds of her dress before giving up and sitting with her legs bent to one side. Leon joined them to form a loose circle.

"That note I left needs to be destroyed. I haven't said a word about what I'm about to tell you to anyone. If Raoul finds out…" He shook his head once and clasped his hands in his lap, his knuckles bone white against the black of his clothes. "Syron, when we were in the house outside the gate and you asked me why I gave the dragonfly back to you, do you remember what I said?"

"You said you were curious and had something to prove," she replied automatically. It had been the first time she had started to think of him as anything other than a vessel for the God.

Julian nodded. His sage-green eyes flitted between her and Leon. "I wanted to make sure I could trust you and find a way to earn your trust in return, despite the circumstances. That being said, I know I have a lot to explain. Hopefully by the end of it, you'll understand why I was so vague. I had to make sure I made the right decision."

Leon glowered at him. "There's a lot of little things that aren't adding up. If you want us to trust you, why don't you start with how you know Adaline? Briar made it sound as if you two have history, and he didn't have a reason to lie."

"You heard that, did you?" Julian asked. "I met Adaline by accident, years ago. She was alone and still grieving the loss of her family. If the God were to condemn me, I suppose he would call her my accomplice, or maybe it's the other way around. We keep correspondence like how I do with your factions, Leon, except she informs me when something interesting happens outside the city too. That included monitoring you, Syron. I'm assuming she explained the Nightman to you?"

"Yeah," Syron said, clearing her throat. "She told me how the Nightman turned her, and that he's here in the city somewhere, working for the God and building an army."

"Yira told us he's an angel," Leon added, "and that the God uses the threat of the nightchildren to keep the city worshipping him."

Julian's eyes widened. "Those are bits I don't have to explain, then, though I'm surprised Yira managed to piece that much together on her own." He drew his knees to his chest and looked behind him, as if expecting Raoul to be standing at the stairs listening. "This is my house too, you know. Raoul took me in when I was a child…young enough that my third eye was still open. He said he was leaving the Keepers to come to the God's City, and that he needed an assistant. I didn't know enough to think it was suspicious at the time, but it hasn't been until recently I've had to think back to it at all."

"Julian," Syron said softly, "what is it you need our help with?"

"Nothing yet," he said, sighing. "I have to find a way to get more information before we can do anything."

"Information about what?" Leon asked.

Julian took a deep breath and let his knees fall. "When the God learned an angel would be falling, there was a session that ran late in the Artist's Room. I came home after curfew, but the house was empty. I was almost asleep when I heard Raoul walk in the door, but he wasn't alone. He was talking with another man and a little girl, but I couldn't make out what they were saying, and they were coming closer to my room.

"I don't know what came over me, but I pretended to be asleep. I had this," he scrunched his face, "feeling, I guess, that I wasn't supposed to overhear them. I was trying so hard to keep my breathing slow and even that I thought for sure I would suffocate, but then the footsteps stopped, and the little girl's voice said, '*I know him.*'

"'*Do you know his name?*' Raoul asked.

"'*No,*' she said simply. '*We call him the Nightman.*'

"But I never…no, it doesn't matter. The point is, I didn't open my eyes until I heard them walking away. She was wearing a cloak, probably since she wasn't technically allowed inside the city, but just the back of her head lit up the room like a light."

Julian looked around the attic, lingering on the watchman's skeleton displayed between the rafters. His eyes glistened. "Her hair was up in those plastic beaded hair ties that kids use. I had never seen her in my life, so it didn't make sense how I knew the beads were supposed to be yellow, or how her mom used to pull her hair back so tight it hurt.

"I didn't sleep at all that night, even after they left. I was scared of what she had said, and it made it worse that neither of the men had corrected her, or acted surprised, or anything. It was like they *already knew*. And the next day Raoul acted like everything was normal."

"But you're not an angel," Syron said in a rush. "Why would she think—"

Leon gasped as if in understanding, and Julian nodded. He tapped his temple. "Raoul didn't offer to bring me to the city until he asked about my third eye. Most temporal children aren't even aware of it, but mine was active. I couldn't use it intentionally like an angel, or even like a sahiit, but every night when I dreamed, it would show me pieces of different lives that weren't mine. They felt like memories, and sometimes I would see faces I recognized walking down the street or through shop windows.

"But the dreams stopped a few weeks after we came here. When I asked Raoul about it, he said that even the strongest third eye will fade when we lose the innocence of childhood. I never had a reason not to believe him, until now."

"So you're saying…what? Raoul brought you here to let someone steal your third eye?" Syron asked. She wanted desperately to understand, but how was that even possible?

"We already know the Nightman controls the children through their third eyes since he comes to them in dreams," Leon said, his eyebrows knitting together. "Maybe he just did it differently with Julian. We just don't know why."

Syron sucked in a sharp breath, and their heads snapped in her direction. She was surprised she hadn't realized it sooner. "We do, though. Yira said it didn't make sense how one angel could be so strong. If the Nightman found a way to lock Julian's third eye away, he could draw on it whenever he needed to. It might even make him strong enough to create the nightchildren."

"If that's true, maybe it means he's using Julian's third eye to hide behind, so none of the children will recognize who the Nightman really is," Leon added, lifting himself to his knees. "Julian, you said your dreams stopped when you came to the city with Raoul. Was that around when the children started turning?"

"I can't remember exactly, but it was around the same time, yes. Raoul can't be the Nightman, though, if that's what you're thinking. He isn't an angel."

"Are you sure?" Leon asked. "If Raoul were hiding something this big from you, he probably lied about his past too."

Syron caught Leon's eye and nodded. "I don't think Raoul would think twice about turning a child, especially since the God has the city convinced their kids will turn if the angels aren't sacrificed."

"Maybe," Julian said, pursing his lips, "but I still think the best place to start is to find out who the man was with Raoul and the nightchild."

"And we can help," Syron said. "Just tell us what to do and we'll—"

Downstairs, someone banged on the front door. It was harsh and loud even in the attic, followed by a muffled voice. Syron tensed and fisted her hands in the folds of her dress, unsure of what to do.

"It's probably the watchman who was supposed to escort you," Julian said, climbing to his feet. They mirrored him. "Raoul must have locked the door when he left. Listen, before you ask, I've already reached out to my contacts about Yira. I haven't heard anything back yet, but I'll let you know as soon as I do."

"What are we supposed to do in the meantime?" Syron demanded. "I'm not going to waltz around the city like everything is fine when we can help find out who the Nightman is."

"That's exactly what you're going to do," Julian said, moving to the stairs. "It'll be less suspicious if you're in the public eye. The city really isn't all that bad if you can ignore the…intricacies of how it runs."

"With a watchman hovering over us, though?" Leon asked, grimacing, and then they were following Julian down the stairs, past dark doorways, and through the room covered in bookcases. They paused at the top of the spiral staircase, and Syron scanned the room. The sunlight glinted off the silver tray Raoul had carried their coffee in on, and she could just make out the stain from where hers had spilled trying to keep Leon from confronting Raoul.

"I'll distract him so you can sneak out without him tagging along. After what happened to the woman who tried attacking you this morning, I'm sure if you keep your heads down, you'll be fine."

"Wait, what happened to her?" Syron asked, but Julian was already halfway down the stairs. She rushed to catch up, with Leon close behind. The watchman's banging literally shook the door as they reached the bottom.

"Here," Syron said, almost as an afterthought, and thrust the small, crumpled note at him. "I don't want to risk losing it."

Julian tucked it into his pocket. "Hide in the hall in case the watchman comes into the foyer. Oh, and Leon, if you want a recommendation, check out Belle's shop. It's just past the lift on the west side. She's a firecracker, and I think she can give you some insight about that trinket in your pocket."

The watchman shouted again, angry and threatening, but Julian only rolled his eyes, winked at Leon, and shooed them to the hall.

"Coming!" Julian shouted back.

19

SUNLIGHT AND SIN

As soon as the voices faded and it was clear the watchman wasn't coming inside the house, Syron grabbed Leon's arm and together they darted out the door. Leon passed her quickly, his black dress shirt and pants contrasting sharply with the oranges, blues, and yellows of the few scattered temporals. He glanced back at her with a mischievous grin, and Syron's stomach did somersaults as she rushed to catch up.

They wound through back roads, their shoes tapping loudly against the cobblestones and slowing only when they reached a street lined with large shops. The lift cables hung suspended above the center of the road, stretching from the wall around the city to the spire in the center. Syron leaned on the wall of the closest shop to catch her breath and looked around. There were no watchmen in sight, and the groups of temporals were too busy talking among themselves to notice two more people slipping onto the strip.

Leon fell into step beside her as she pushed off the wall, worrying at her bottom lip. She looked over her shoulder, unsure whether they were going the right way, but Leon snaked an arm around her waist and guided them forward.

She flushed. The last time he had touched her waist… no, this wasn't the time or the place to let her thoughts wander. She leaned into him instead, trying to lose herself in the present. The bronze shops glistened in the sunlight, their front doors recessed beneath black awnings and the windows covered in advertisements for creams and nail enhancers, and closest to them, a huge display of a ginger-haired man regrowing a bald spot.

The doorbell chimed as a man rushed out, his hair parted too far to one side and brushed over the top of his head, gripping a brown paper bag. Syron paused, unsure whether she should say something, but his eyes widened and he ducked his head, barreling past them.

Leon's laughter rumbled against her. She felt a smile stretch across her face and wrapped both arms around him, effectively knitting them together.

"What has you in such a good mood?" she asked, looking up at him. His diamond markings sparkled brilliantly as he shook his head, still smiling.

"I just realized how little I actually know about you, Syron Lennox."

Syron gaped at him. "Excuse me, but I could say the same for you. I don't even know your last name."

He chuckled. "That's because I don't have one. I only know yours because I was eavesdropping on you and Tia in the assimilation chamber."

"Hold on. You don't…have a last name?"

The steady drone of the lift sounded behind them as he shook his head. "Usually, a sahiit will inherit one of the parents' last names after they die, but since my mom was an angel and I never knew my dad…" He shrugged. "So technically I do have one, but I don't know what it is."

She wasn't sure what she was supposed to say to that. The lift passed them then, coming to a stop inside the low pavilion at the end of the road. Past it, Syron saw a long, squat building with no windows and a faded sign out front.

"Do you think that's Belle's?" Syron asked, dropping her arms from around his waist. It looked older than the other buildings, or maybe it just wasn't well kept. The bronze didn't have the same gleaming finish, and the walls were patchy with a color somewhere between aquamarine and teal where they met the cobblestone road.

"Only one way to find out," Leon said, rushing ahead.

Syron jogged after him, avoiding the curious looks the temporals threw their way as she climbed the steps and Leon held the door open for her.

A bell chimed above her head as she walked inside and paused, taking in the cluttered shop. Machines lined the walls between stacks of wood and piles of random metal. Chipped wooden shelves had been hung above them, over-flowing with a random assortment of glass jars, cloth, and vellum.

A woman peered up at them from where she sat cross-legged on the floor, riffling through a trunk. "I'm a little busy," she said brusquely. "Can I help you?"

Syron stepped forward awkwardly. "Are you Belle? Julian recommended that we stop by to see the shop."

The woman snorted as she pulled out a white tube and a paintbrush from the trunk and climbed to her feet. Unlike the other temporals, she seemed to avoid bright colors, having opted instead for baggy, ripped jeans and a black tank top that showed the base of her stomach. When she moved to set the items next to the hunk of metal on the workbench in front of her, Syron saw that a tattoo covered one shoulder, but it was too faded to make out.

"Julian sent you here? Well, there isn't much to see. Most of what's in here was my dad's, but I can make anything so long as there are no moving parts. That was his expertise, not mine."

"We're not looking to buy anything," Leon said, and his hand found the small of Syron's back as he moved to stand beside her. The other he slipped into his pocket. "Where is your dad now?"

"Dead," Belle said casually, swiping her arm across the workbench and sending wood shavings spiraling to the floor. "Why do you ask?"

Leon hesitated before taking the dragonfly out of his pocket. "Because I have something I think he made, years ago. Julian seemed to think you could tell us more about it."

"Dad made a lot of things," Belle said, but waved them over. Up close, the wings of her eyeliner were smudged from work and heat. She tucked a loose strand of hair behind her ear and reached for the dragonfly, her eyebrows knitting together.

Syron half expected it to spring to life as it had with Julian, but it stayed motionless even as Belle ran her thumb down the lines etched into its golden body.

"I kept some of his notes on the later projects he worked on. I recognize this one." She held it up to the light, studying the golden cog encapsulated inside the center of its chest before looking suspiciously at Leon. "The dragonfly was his last entry. How did you get this?"

"From my mother. Julian recognized it too. He said my dad had it commissioned."

Belle's face tightened almost imperceptibly. "So it's true, then. You're Astrophe's son."

If Leon were shocked at hearing his mother's name, he didn't show it. He nodded stiffly and plucked the dragonfly out of her hand. It was back in his pocket a second later.

"Did you know her?" Syron asked.

Belle shook her head. "I knew of her. I had heard rumors about an angel hiding somewhere in Evangentine, but it wasn't until the ceremony that I ever saw her in person. How Julian got the idea I'd know anything about the dragonfly is beyond me."

"So there's nothing you can tell us about it?"

"Nothing you wouldn't already know." Belle's eyes skipped to the hunk of metal on the table. She wet her lips. "My father disappeared after the God found out what he had made. Leon, yours wasn't long after that. I'll show you the notes I kept, but first I want you both to answer one question."

"Wait, how did you know his name?" Syron asked, but Belle only rolled her eyes dramatically.

"Everyone in the city knows your names by now. It's deliberate if they choose not to use them." She leaned almost casually on the workbench and turned the hunk of metal to face them. Three miniature statues had been carved into it, the bronze rearing up in a half circle around them like a craggy backdrop.

Syron forgot what she was going to say next. The man in the center had collapsed to his knees, elbows digging into the metallic dirt, and his hands fisted in his hair so Syron couldn't see his face. Standing on his left was a confusing-looking creature with too many wings and way too many eyes. It perched on hoofed feet and had four faces on either side of its head, only one of them human. The angel on his right was tall and muscular, with curly hair that reached the collarbone of his exposed chest. Two giant, gorgeous wings jutted proudly from his back. Both the creature and the angel rested a hand on one of the man's shoulders.

Belle nodded at the broken man, her eyes flicking from Syron to Leon and back again.

"If this were you, which would you choose to listen to?"

It felt like a test, but the answer was obvious. Syron pointed to the angel, with his soft, feathered wings and peaceful smile. "He has an angel and a demon on his shoulders. I know the choice wouldn't be black-and-white to him, but why give us the option if we can see which is which?"

Belle smiled sadly and looked to Leon, who pointed to the angel too. She hummed under her breath and tapped the bronze dirt next to the demon. She paused, and Syron felt sure she was thinking about what to say next. "There's supposed to be a ring right here," she said finally, wistfully, "the color of sparkling beryl. The buyers like it the way it is, but my old man used to talk about a scripture from outside Evangentine regarding angels. It boiled down to our perceptions being flawed—angels aren't the ones who need to hide their true faces. Evil knows what we perceive good to look like and can replicate it perfectly, maybe even making us question the reality of what we're seeing."

She pulled away and strode to a doorway in the back, pausing with her hand on the handle. "Well? Do you guys want to see the notes or not?"

Syron hesitated, tempted to touch the second set of folded wings over the strange creature's chest, but Leon was already halfway to the door. She rushed after him, passing smaller stands crowded with welding supplies and others filled with rocks that had been split open to reveal their opal and cerulean centers.

The back of the shop opened to a small living area. A

large chalkboard stood where Syron had expected the textured glass wall to be, covered entirely in a hand-drawn map of the city. The spire dominated the center, and as Belle crouched opposite a filing cabinet pushed against the wall and riffled through the drawers, Syron peered closer. Thin, interconnected lines had been drawn all over the map, with most of them ending in an *X*. Inside each building were scrawled things like "bs dome," "dickhead's house," and "funny guy."

She understood why Julian had called her a firecracker.

Belle pulled out a manila folder and bounced to her feet. "This is everything I have on your dragonfly. It isn't much, but I hope it helps."

"Thank you," Leon murmured, accepting the folder and taking a seat on the worn couch. Syron settled in beside him, watching as his body curved protectively over the papers in his lap. Belle's father had handwriting like most of the men Syron had known: small and cramped, with each letter capitalized. She thought about reading it aloud when Leon squinted but didn't want to distract him while he was trying to focus. She clasped her hands in her lap instead.

"I wanted to say thank you," Syron said, shifting her attention to Belle. "I knew I recognized your name. It was your house outside the gate that had the first aid supplies, right? If it wasn't for Julian treating my wounds, I don't know what would have happened."

Belle had moved to the aged leather armchair across from them. She leaned forward as Syron spoke, her eyes shifting to her scarred hands.

"You don't have to thank me. Angels aren't high on my priority list of people to help, but everything I keep out there is for those who need it. You just happened to be one of them.

"Julian did do a good job, though," she added grudgingly when Syron didn't speak. "I'd offer more of the balm for your hands, but I don't keep any of that stuff inside the city."

Syron looked up from the formulas on the page. "I appreciate the thought, but they'll heal."

"They'll probably scar."

Syron shrugged, and Belle looked taken back. It must be weird, Syron thought, to speak with someone in the city who didn't try to look perfect all the time. Besides Belle, Julian, and Raoul, everyone else they had either spoken with, been in the same room with, or seen on the street looked immaculate. The idea of visible scars must be horrendous to them.

"I can tell you haven't been in the city long," Belle said. "The standards for beauty here are very high."

Syron fought back a smile. "Higher than sanctimony? I guess I'll have to get my priorities straight."

Belle surprised her by laughing. It was high pitched and short lived, but it seemed to melt away the tension and erase the delicate line between her brows.

"I have to say, you're not at all what I expected. I'm glad Julian sent you two over, if only for an excuse to take a break. All this stuff," Belle said, waving at the door, "was my dad's passion. I keep it up and running to honor his memory, but at the end of the day, I'd rather be in my house taking care of the people who actually need it."

"What do you mean?"

Belle rocked back in the chair and shifted so her feet were tucked between the cushions. "This city has so much we could share. No one here needs to worry about how to disinfect a cut or, I don't know," she paused, contemplating, "how to cultivate new skin cells after a burn. I know I can't help most of the people who need it, but there are days where the line from my front door stretches clear to the forest. The God couldn't care less about any one of those people, but I think it's our responsibility to try to help them too. No one should be refused treatment because of their faith."

Next to her, Leon stiffened. He looked up from the papers, his eyes blazing. "Do you help the sahiit too, and the umbriels? Or is it just the people who look like you?"

Belle matched his gaze. "If you're asking whether I'm a bigot, the answer is no. I'm helping you right now, aren't I?"

"Point taken," he said, "but it's strange the God is letting you treat people in the first place. Unless he doesn't know about it?"

"Oh, I'm sure he does, but there are bigger things he has to worry about now."

"Like an angel showing up?" Syron asked.

"An angel who managed to evade him. Twice. I'd wager you're different than he expected, too. In fact, I wouldn't be surprised if he asked some of the temporals to keep watch on you while you're here, to make sure you don't do anything that would compromise the ceremony."

Syron frowned. The way she said it… "Wait, are you saying the God is having people watch me?"

She put a finger to her lips and stood up quickly, glancing back into the shop. "At communion, before you came," she said quietly, "he asked us to report to the watchmen if we suspected anything."

"But Julian said to—"

"Julian wasn't there when the God announced it. Spending too much time in one place is a red flag. Assuming you're finished with the papers, Leon, I'd suggest taking the lift back to the spire to let the people get a good look at both of you. It'll be less suspicious than taking a back way and will attract more attention than just walking."

Leon snapped the folder closed and stood up. "I don't suppose you'd have any ideas on how to get us out of this mess?" he asked, handing the folder back to her.

Belle's eyes darkened before turning to stuff it back in the drawer. She slammed it shut. "I have a few, but things take time, and Julian likes to plan for the worst-case scenario. Now come on, before someone comes in pretending to buy something."

Before Syron really knew what was happening, Belle was leading them back into the shop, navigating expertly around the clutter and holding the door open for them.

Syron swallowed thickly. The street was busier than it had been before, and it left no doubt it was because of what Belle had told them. She grabbed Belle's arm without thinking and pulled her aside, behind the open door and out of hearing distance of the temporals.

"Have you…I mean…You must have been young when the dragonfly was made. Have you lived in the city your whole life?"

Belle's eyes flashed. "What does that have to do with anything? You need to leave—"

But Syron stopped listening. The question burned on the tip of her tongue, and she was painfully aware that if she didn't ask now, she might never have the chance to again. "I'm asking because there's a room somewhere in this city with stone walls covered in chains. I'm assuming it's underground, since the streets are cobblestone. Would you have any idea where that is?"

Leon sucked in a breath, and Syron startled. She hadn't noticed him move to stand beside her, but he was leaning forward in expectation, his expression caught somewhere between interest and worry.

Belle, on the other hand, looked as if she'd seen a ghost. "You're talking about the cells. They're rumored to be beneath the spire, but they were supposed to be shut down after the uprising. How do you know about them?"

Yes! If the cells were under the spire, Syron could work with that. Julian had already shown her the lab, and whatever was past the white door might lead to where she needed to go. It was worth a shot, at least.

To Belle, she simply smiled. "I heard things about the city I doubt anyone wants me to know. I just want to see for myself what's true."

It came out smoother than she had expected, but lies were always easier with bits of truth mixed in. She rounded Belle and passed through the door with Leon, out into the crowded street. The line for the lift was long and curved, and snatches of conversation wafted up to them. Syron heard "angel," "announcement," and "celebration" among them.

She turned to say goodbye, but Belle was already right behind them. She pulled them both close, shocking Syron, and then her breath fanned Syron's neck as she tucked her head between them.

"The wicked are around the corner," she whispered.

A pang shot through Syron's chest at the thought of Yira, saying those exact words on the roof at Del-Amar. She started to speak, the ghost of six words shaping themselves to her lips, but Belle had already pulled away, shutting the door firmly behind her.

They stepped off the lift beneath a low pavilion. They hadn't ridden it alone—each seat had been taken when they climbed up, and it was only when a thin-boned man with a long nose and drawn eyes had dropped to his knees, begging Syron to take his seat, that she relented. Afterward, the ride had been spent in awkward silence between all the passengers, with Leon standing uncomfortably in the center.

Syron started to wipe the sweat from her brow before remembering the layers of makeup Mags, Cleo, and Avery had applied, and let her hand drop. For all the ways the God had advanced his city, transportation still seemed to be lacking.

She paused before leaving the shade of the pavilion and waited for two ample women to shuffle past. Leon was already at its edge, looking up at the spire past the rows of houses. Syron wondered how he could stand the heat in pants and long sleeves; she hardly could in a dress.

"So Belle is a…" she whispered when she was sure no one could overhear.

"It makes sense. After her dad disappeared, it would be enough to change anyone's mind." He stuffed his hands in his pockets. "The papers she showed me were all technical writing, right down to the amount of each material used to craft it. I checked twice, but there was nothing about how the dragonfly can move on its own."

"Do you think her dad left it out for a reason?"

"I'm not sure," he said, and stepped forward. "But I think we have company."

Syron followed his gaze to two watchmen striding toward them. Their black chain mail shone in the sunlight, and sweat glistened on their bald heads.

"You two are to come with us," the one on the left said. His voice was the same baritone as the other watchmen she had heard speak. Syron glanced around nervously, but the stream of people outside the pavilion ignored them completely. Only a child tugging at his mother's hand paid them any mind, but the mother only scooped him up and walked quickly away.

"Now," the watchman barked. Syron pursed her lips and walked forward as if to follow, but as soon as Leon fell into step beside her, the second watchman came up in the rear. She steeled herself, allowing them to lead her along the thin path between the houses and into the wide gap of open space before the cathedral doors.

Except that it was crowded with people.

Syron's breath caught in her throat. Surely, the God wouldn't do the ceremony now. He was holding off, wasn't he? Or had Raoul told him about the accusation she had made about the Black Book? Would he figure out a way to do it sooner, to spite her for thinking she could predict why a god did the things he did?

Her hands fisted around the silky folds of her dress. She'd run out of time, and she didn't know any more now than when she had started. *I—I have to run.*

"Syron! Leon!" It was Julian's voice, shouting over the crowd. She looked around wildly, relief washing through her as he broke through the mass of people, smiling as if everything were fine. And maybe it was. Maybe she was overthinking.

Julian looked up at the watchmen, completely relaxed. "I appreciate you both for finding them, but I'll take it from here."

The watchman in the back stepped forward. The chain mail jingled right next to Syron, but she schooled herself to stay still. "Raoul said to bring her inside for the announcement."

"That he did. As I said, I have it from here."

She felt the watchman tense beside her, but before they could say anything, Julian threaded an arm through Syron's and Leon's and pulled them away, inside the throng of densely packed bodies. A flash of irritation shot through her—she deserved to know what was going on, especially because it most definitely revolved around her, and Julian seemed to be leading them directly to the spire. She tried to whisper to him to ask what was going on, but her voice was lost even to her own ears.

Right before they reached the doors, Julian ducked down, pulling Syron and Leon with him, and dodged to the left. A man gave a yelp of surprise and jerked back, giving them just enough room to slip by. They pressed ahead, arms still linked, fighting against the jab of shoulders and elbows, and sliding against the cool silk of ruffled blouses, deep-cut dresses, and tailored pants.

They came out, panting, on the other side of the spire. The temporals next to them turned to stare, and Julian nodded politely. "May the God watch over you."

"And you," they murmured back, confused, but Julian was already pulling them around the back of the spire, slipping a key into the lock, and ushering them hurriedly inside.

Syron raced down the steps and into the purple luminosity of the lab. It was exactly the same as before, right down to the racks of shriveling lotus flowers in the center. And past that, the single white door.

"What's going on out there?" Leon's voice was strained as he descended the stairs. "Why did they want us in the spire?"

"Because of the God," Syron answered for Julian, ripping her eyes away from the door and meeting Leon's. "I heard some of the temporals talking when we left Belle's. I think he's going to announce the date for my ceremony."

Leon tensed as he made his way to her. "But we've only been here for a day. I thought he was waiting."

"I thought so too," Julian said, joining them. Even in the purple light, he looked ashen. "Raoul told me when he came back from the spire. I wanted to be the first to tell you, Syron, but word spreads fast."

"No surprise there," Leon said bitterly. "When is it?"

Julian looked worriedly between them but didn't speak. Above them, the faint whisper of footsteps brushed across the ceiling, and Syron knew without having to ask that it was the people above them in the cathedral.

"It's tomorrow," Julian said finally. "But if we can——"

"Tomorrow!" Leon nearly shouted, rocking back as if he'd been struck. "That's not enough time!"

"Shh! Nobody knows we're down here!"

"As if that matters when Syron's *murder* is being celebrated as we speak," Leon hissed back, and whipped his head to her, as if expecting her to either boil over with rage or break down in tears.

And maybe she should. *It would be normal, wouldn't it? Under the circumstances?* But in truth, all she really felt was a burning curiosity. She needed to get to that white door and find the cells. Everything else was just background noise—because even if there wasn't time for anything else, there *had* to be time to find Will.

"…need to go up to your rooms," Julian was saying. "You saw the map on Belle's wall? She made it to have a visual of the tunnels that run beneath the city. We'll leave through them tonight."

"We?" Leon asked, snapping his attention back to Julian, who nodded.

"I couldn't find anything about who the other man in my room could have been, and I'm not willing to ignore the part that I'm playing, however small, in the children being turned. It sucks, but I think leaving is my only option."

"In that case," Leon said, "what do you think about helping us steal the Black Book?"

Julian stared at him for a long moment before clearing his throat. "You're serious?"

"Deadly."

"That's not…" Julian shook his head. "The Black Book never leaves the God's side. He comes down from the spire only for services, and he leaves before fellowship. You'd have to be suicidal to even try."

"But maybe if we—"

"No," Syron interrupted, jutting out her chin. "Julian's right. I know it's what Yira would have wanted, but we don't have her and Adaline to help us. It isn't worth killing ourselves over."

Leon's face contorted. "You make it sound like she's gone."

"Not gone," Syron said, correcting him, "just not here to help us. We might not be able to take the book by ourselves, but we can stop the God from being able to use it. Right now, there are only two angels in the city, right?"

Julian cocked his head at her, but she wasn't looking at him. Leon's eyes were striking in the purple light. She willed him to understand. Out loud, she said, "As long as the God doesn't have an angel to use it on, he can't sustain his body anymore, right? So…"

"So his only choice would be to consume more of the Nightman's soul," Leon finished. "The temporals would know the God has been lying to them because the children would stop turning. But what if there are souls left in the Black Book?"

"If we can't get it away from him, then it's a risk we have to be willing to take." She shrugged, trying to appear nonchalant. "You saw Raoul's face when I brought up the

Black Book, though. Something is going on that he doesn't want us to know about."

"Hold on, what was that about another angel?" Julian asked.

"You asked us to trust you," Syron said, turning her attention to him. "Now I'm asking that you do the same for me. I need the key to that door." She jutted her head to the side and held out her hand, palm up.

Julian gaped at her. "I don't, I mean…" He shifted uncomfortably. "What does the Artist's Room have to do with anything?"

Fuck. She tried to hide her disappointment under a mask of confidence and set her jaw. Maybe it wouldn't be as easy to find the cells as she had thought, but it was still worth checking. There had to be an entrance somewhere, and if it wasn't in the Artist's Room, she would just have to look somewhere else.

"Why don't you tell me what you're looking for? Maybe I can help."

Because I don't know whether you would try to stop me.

"Because," Leon said, rushing to her defense, "she's asking you to have faith. Give her the key, and after we're finished, we'll wait in our rooms like you asked."

"No," Syron nearly shouted, and made a conscious effort to speak lower. "Leon, I'm going alone. I *need* to do this alone."

She waited for the flash of anger or sadness, but it didn't come. Instead, he met her eye and gave a quick, barely there nod.

Julian cursed under his breath and reached into his pocket, drawing out the key. It was larger than she had expected, with geometric lines etched into the bow to look like layered petals. He placed it in Syron's palm with a severe expression.

"Don't. Touch. Anything. There aren't any watchmen scheduled for today, but the others who have a key to this area of the spire are dangerous. Normally I would insist on coming with you, but I've been away from the cathedral for too long as it is. As soon as you're finished, go straight to your room and wait until dark, then head over to Belle's. It'll be after curfew, but if you stick to the back streets, you should be able to avoid the watchmen without any problems."

"I'll be quick," Syron promised.

"I'll come with you," Leon said to Julian. "It'll look less suspicious than if she and I were both gone, and if anyone asks, I'll just say Syron isn't used to the heat or something."

Julian looked almost gratefully at Leon before turning away. As soon as his back was to them, Leon grabbed Syron's hand and pulled her against him. She gasped in surprise as his arms folded around her, one holding her tightly against him and the other cupping the back of her head. He smelled like soap and sweat, like sunlight and sin, and she buried her face in his chest, unspeaking.

"Be careful," he murmured into her hair, and she rolled her eyes in mock annoyance as he pulled away.

"I'll be fine," she promised. His lips twitched into a sideways smile as Julian coughed under his breath. He had already pushed the call button for the elevator, and he stood half inside, holding his hand against the door.

The lights shifted to blue as Syron's fingers brushed against Leon's, and then she was walking between the racks of dried lotus flowers with their long, twisting roots on her left and the glass refrigerators on her right. The hum of the elevator started behind her as she fit the key into the lock and pushed it open.

She paused in the doorway, confused. The Artist's Room was roughly the same size as the lab, filled with rows of evenly spaced, sparsely padded black leather chairs. They were reclined almost all the way back and supported by a single pedestal. Straps dangled down their sides, almost touching the floor. A stand was next to each chair, gleaming silver-blue in the light.

Syron shut the door behind her and wandered forward. The walls were covered in framed symbols that crested and fell randomly: harsh slashes looping into softer wavelike lines, a pattern of interconnected circles, a set of inverted *C*s linked by thick blobs of ink. She walked in a slow circle, scanning the room. Each symbol was different from the one before, and they covered each of the four walls. The door she had come through was the only reprieve. Which meant, Syron thought fiercely, that there wasn't a way to the cells from inside this room. Will wasn't here.

She gripped the key tighter and started to leave before remembering the skeleton in Raoul's attic. She walked to the closest stand instead and tugged at the top drawer. It opened soundlessly, revealing an ink tray filled with circles of black and a watery purple color she suspected was the same as the vials in the lab. Next to it was a neatly bound cluster of cords, attached to the end of a black-and-gold tattoo gun.

Tentatively, she picked it up. It was cold against her skin, with faint wear marks around the handle. If she was right and the symbols on the walls were tattoo designs, she couldn't help wondering whether all the watchmen were as illustrated as the skeleton had been, whether the act of inscribing their bodies had somehow changed them from the heretics they used to be into the watchmen they were today. If so…

She shook her head to clear it. *I need to focus on what's happening now. The only thing that matters is finding Will and getting the hell out of here.* The tattoo gun scraped against the drawer as she set it back inside, and froze. A man's voice came from everywhere and nowhere, muffled but close. Syron cursed under her breath and slammed the drawer shut, flinching at the harsh noise, and looked around wildly. Sweat that had already beaded on her hairline trickled down to her temple. She wiped it away in haste and sprinted to the back before dropping to her hands and knees.

Impossibly, the voices were louder this far back, but still muffled, like trying to hear while submerged underwater. She ducked beneath a chair, the cool metal of the pedestal pressing against the divot in her waist, fingers splayed against the floor, when a memory came suddenly and sharply into focus. She was sitting around a table piled with food. Viero and Yira were locked in an argument. Viero looked displeased. Yira was furious. *So, what I'm hearing is… you know absolutely nothing about the room you rescued him from except that you had to go through a glamour to get there.*

The air was humid and suffocating. Her heart pounded frantically in her chest and she took deep breaths, counting her inhales and exhales as the voices grew louder, closer, clearer. She leaned forward, about to run, just as someone stepped out of thin air.

20

ADRENALINE

She recognized him immediately. A shiver like a blade of ice shot down her spine as the man in black took a couple of steps, paused, and looked over his shoulder. Just like in Syron's dream, the leather was reflective and formfitting. The black mask fit seamlessly at his neck, hiding everything but the angles of his face.

"...waste of time. It might be worth moving on," he said.

"No." The answering voice was low and muffled until Raoul stepped out of the glamour. He tugged at the hem of his jacket to straighten it and looked around pensively. "At least until tomorrow. After the ceremony, I don't care what you do with them."

"I won't be here after the ceremony. We agreed—"

"I'm familiar with our agreement. The God has already taken care of the specifics, but the cells must be cleared first."

When the man in black hesitated, Raoul slapped him on the back and smiled perversely. "What's wrong,

Nightman?" he asked, sneering the name. "Is the taste of freedom taking away your edge?"

"Fuck off," he spit back, jerking away from Raoul and striding toward the front of the room.

Syron resisted the urge to sink lower beneath the chair and focused on trying to keep her breathing even. One movement, however small, and they might notice her. The only silver lining was the glamour. It sounded as if they had come from the cells, and from this angle she could see the sliver of opal light suspended in the corner.

Three rows down, Raoul chuckled to himself and followed behind the Nightman. When she was sure they couldn't see her, she slunk lower, laying her face against the cool linoleum, and watched the backs of their legs through the gaps between the chairs. They hesitated near the front of the room, but only for a moment, before Raoul passed the Nightman and held the door open for him.

As soon as it swung shut behind them, Syron crawled out from beneath the chair and fisted the length of her dress in both hands. The lights shifted from blue to red, staining the Artist's Room a bright crimson as she launched herself at the glamour.

She clenched her eyes shut at the last second, half expecting to run belligerently into the wall, and opened them to blackness. The heat from the Artist's Room was gone, replaced by a stale blanket of cold that was dwarfed only by the smell of earth and rot. She scrunched her nose against it as her eyes adjusted.

She stood at one end of a stone corridor lined with cells on either side. Old, dented sconces hung between them, giving off enough pallid light to see the other end had collapsed into chunks of rock and dirt. She started forward cautiously, peering into the closest cells. They matched the one she had seen in her dream: small and confined, with metal cuffs attached to chains on the ceiling and floor. Only one thing was missing.

"Will?" she called out in a whisper. She heard the urgency in her own voice and glanced over her shoulder. Hopefully, the God's announcement would keep Raoul busy. She tried not to think about the Nightman—how the shadow in Adaline's dreams was the same masked man that had tortured Will in her own. She could still feel the spike of pain in her lower back, followed by the sickening tug as the Nightman pulled the blade free, how the terror and hatred had welled within her and Will both in equal measure, threatening to consume them.

"Will?" she called again, louder this time, pleading.

There was nothing, and then chains rattled.

She raced down the corridor, tripping over a chunk of debris and catching herself on the rough wall before skidding to a stop in front of the cell. Past the bars, she could see the dim shape of someone hanging, suspended, in the center. They jerked and the chains clanked together again, twisting the torso back and forth. Syron had the sudden notion she was looking at a battered marionette, and her heart squeezed in response.

"Will, is that you?" She gripped the bars with both hands, the metal clanging as she strained against them, before remembering the key. "Fuck," she whispered, pulling away and running her hands down the folds of her dress, willing it to appear. She dropped to her knees and felt hastily at the cool, grimy stone at her feet, but it was nowhere to be found. She must have dropped it in the Artist's Room.

She brought her shaking hands back up to the bars and peered closer. Whoever was inside faced away from her, the black clothes filthy and pockmarked with holes and slashes that glistened around the edges. They let out a soft groan and rolled their head to the side, facing Syron.

The tips of her ears were downturned and pointed, sticking out from beneath a greasy mess of black hair. Abstract leaves decorated her temple, tinged with red.

"Yira?" Syron choked, but the only response was Yira's ragged breathing and the rapid pounding of her own heart. Syron strained against the bars again, kicked at the lock because it was old and might break, and finally slammed herself against the cell door, a sob escaping her lips.

When she finally looked up, Yira was watching her. She was pale, making the dirt and blood stand out more on her face and neck. They weren't feeding her either; her eyes were sunken in, and when she spoke, it was through cracked lips.

"It's really you?" Yira's voice was raw and hoarse.

"It's really me," Syron said, a hitch in her voice. "Yira, I'm sorry. I'm so sorry. I'll find a way to get you out, just— I'll be right back, okay? I'll find the key."

She started to back away when Yira coughed. Her whole body shook with the force of it, making the chains rattle. Syron wished more than anything she could go to her. She felt worthless, forced to watch when she wanted to help.

"Don't come back," Yira said finally, and took a tiny breath to steady herself. "He was talking about you. The man in the mask. He was the one from your dreams, I think."

"What did he say?"

But Yira only shook her head. "Where's Leon?"

"He's in the cathedral with Julian. He's safe, I think."

A bead of red formed on Yira's lips when she smiled, but she didn't seem to notice.

"Good, you can trust Julian. He'll do what he can to help. What about Adaline?"

"We thought she was with you."

Yira made a scathing sound that was half laugh, half cough. She spit out a glob of red. "Adaline got away. Right before Briar dumped me with the watchman outside the gate."

So Adaline got free. That's good news, at least. "Yira, I need to get you out of here. There's an elevator past the glamour. If we can get you to my room without anyone seeing, you'll be safe until I can get Belle. She has medical supplies. She can help, and then you'll be okay." She hoped it was true, but once Yira's gear was off and they could see the extent of her injuries, Syron suspected they would need more than just balm and cream.

"No," Yira said quietly. "I heard what they said, Syron. Your ceremony is tomorrow. Don't go worrying about me. I know," she rasped when Syron started to speak, "there's no way you could have known I was here. Go look for Will. See for yourself that he isn't here and," she paused, her voice turning gravelly, "do whatever the hell you have to do to get out of this damned city."

"What about the book? You wanted—"

"I know what I wanted," Yira said, eyes gleaming. Even in the dimness, Yira was able to cut daggers through Syron with one look, as if she were seeing down into the deepest parts of her. "What matters is you and Leon getting out safely. You *found* me, Syron, now let me rest. Go look for Will."

Syron hesitated, but only for a second. No matter what Yira said, leaving her here wasn't an option. She would find the key and come back, and if she was wrong and it didn't fit the lock, she would just have to find the key that did.

"*When* I find him," Syron said, "I'm coming back. For both of you." She turned her back before Yira could argue and jogged down the corridor, more careful this time. The closer she got to the collapsed wall, the more stone that littered the floor. She avoided a slab in the center of the aisle, peering into the cells on either side, but it was only when she was nearing the end that her spirits sank. Surely if Will were down here, he would have heard the clamor and yelled for help.

Unless he couldn't. Unless something was very, very wrong.

Something moved in the cell to her right. She whirled toward it, hope rising in her chest, and then plummeting as she caught sight of something small huddled in the corner. A set of glowing eyes looked up at her. It scuttled forward and Syron flinched back before a little boy climbed to his feet. As far as she could tell, there wasn't a mark on him.

"Miss? Is my observation done?"

Syron gaped at him, speechless. He reached out gingerly, almost as if he were afraid, and his hand turned translucent where the light touched it.

"It's really scary in here. Mom doesn't like me gone for too long. Are you—"

He jerked back suddenly, wrapping his arms tightly around his chest. "It hurts. Right here," he said, clutching at his heart. "What's happening to me? There's something —it's in the shadows."

Syron snapped her mouth shut and came closer, leaning down so their eyes were level.

"What's your name?" she whispered.

"Tomlin. But my friends call me Tommy."

She fumbled for the right words, trying to keep her expression calm. There were so many things she could say, but how many of them were true?

"Is it okay if I call you Tommy?"

His eyes widened as he nodded, slinking farther back into the cell.

"I know a little girl around your age. She's braver than anyone I've ever met, and she's smarter than anyone gives her credit for. You remind me of her, Tommy. You're becoming something…different. But it doesn't have to be a bad thing." *Doesn't it, though? Did I just lie to him?*

But Tommy started mumbling. She leaned closer to hear him better.

"It's behind you, miss. The shadow. Please just make it go away."

Goose bumps rose on her arms. She gripped the bars, wishing she could melt them with her bare hands. "You're so brave, Tommy," she said, and her voice cracked. *He's hallucinating about the man from his dreams. This is why Julian is leaving the city, to make sure this never happens again.* "I'm going to get you out, okay? I have to find the key, and I'll be right back."

She spun around, meaning to check on Yira before heading back through the glamour, and gasped. A shadow, barely darker than the gloom itself, was sliding down the wall toward her. She stumbled back, stealing a glance at the boy to make sure she wasn't going crazy, but his skin had turned a radiant bluish-white. He was crouched in the corner, and Syron saw in his eyes the same mirrored terror that must have been in her own.

The shadow shot to the floor and rose upward, wispy black tendrils shaping themselves into black-clad feet and legs, a torso and arms, sculpting out the form of a man.

Syron screamed.

A deafening chorus ricocheted against the stone walls. Cold adrenaline thrummed through her veins, numbing her senses as she raced past before it could fully form. She imagined it reaching out…

Something hit her, hard, in the side. She didn't realize she was in the air until her head cracked against stone, her shoulder twisting painfully as she landed. Pockets of light danced in her vision, her stomach churned, but she forced herself to her feet. She'd been in worse pain than this. She felt her shoulder, her head. Nothing was broken. There was only a little blood.

Her vision cleared enough to tell she was standing inside one of the cells. The doorway was swathed in shadow. She took an involuntary step back, blinked, and then the shadow was gone. In its place stood the man in the black mask.

"Why are you doing this?" she demanded. Her voice came out stronger than she thought possible, but it didn't give her courage. Yira was shackled in the other cell, and from the looks of it, she wasn't far behind.

The mask twitched, almost as if he were smiling beneath it.

He took an exaggerated step forward. Syron ripped her eyes away to scan the room, but it was barren; there was nothing to use for protection, and he blocked the only exit. Time seemed to swell and stretch as he closed the distance between them and raised his hand, slowly, to caress her jaw.

With the same hand that had mutilated her friends. For the first time in years, maybe even her whole life, she didn't flinch away. His gloved hand left a trail of cold along her skin, but all she could do was stare defiantly at the black void of his mask and tell herself she wasn't afraid.

She flexed her jaw. "My friends know where I am," she lied. "You can't keep me here."

"I know," he said, and his voice was steady and strong, reverberating through her. It was a whisper and a curse.

And then he dissolved. Like something out of a nightmare, the solidity of him seemed to crack and crumble into blackness that pooled on the floor before disappearing entirely.

Syron ran. She didn't look back.

The night air hit her like a slap to the face as she barreled out of the spire and into the neon lights that stained the city hot pink, purple, and electric blue. Somewhere between the cells and the lab, she had lost her shoes; her bare feet kicked off the freezing stone, stride after stride, numbing them as she raced to the circle of houses and navigated through them.

She would need to find the key when she came back with Leon, Julian, and Belle. She hadn't risked stopping to look for it in the Artist's Room, not when the Nightman could have appeared behind her and dragged her back through the glamour.

Not that he would have, Syron thought. It seemed as if he had wanted her to run. As if he were waiting for something.

She slowed her pace as she came to the edge of the houses and peered out, leaning her bad arm against the frigid wall of a house to ease some of the ache. A group of watchmen were circled together close to the lift, their throaty laughter a mixture of snarls and rasps. To her right, two more were walking silently along the road, facing away from her.

Julian had said to take the back streets to get to Belle's shop, but she had to cross the main street to get to them.

Hopefully, they were still waiting for her. She hadn't realized how late it was, and she wasn't sure how much time Yira had left. She would need their help to get Yira and the boy out of the cells, especially if the Nightman was still there.

Tomlin, she reminded herself, but he goes by Tommy. How long had he been locked up down there, forced away from his family and friends? It was enough to make her sick.

The watchmen were moving now, rounding the other side of the lift. Syron saw her opportunity and darted forward. The towering neon signs shone brightly above the smaller buildings, and she knew she had to follow them west to get back to Belle's, knew she was getting closer.

She tried not to think about Will as she ducked into an alley. She had been prepared for him to be the one who was hurting, not Yira. She had been prepared to see him strung up, broken and beaten, and she would have been the one to save him. Because that's what she owed him. Because it was her fault that he was there in the first place.

But she had been too late.

"What are you going to do," Yira had asked, sitting on Syron's bed in the earthen underground faction, "if he's already dead?"

Loss trickled down Syron's face, just a drop, but she didn't wipe it away. The alley opened to a narrow, winding street lined by houses. The lights were off in each, and it was so silent that, if she hadn't known about the curfew, she would have thought they were vacant. She lifted her chin to the sudden gust of air and looked around. It was darker without the streetlamps, but the moon was full, and her eyes were used to the dark after the cells. There were no watchmen in sight.

She took off at a run, letting the cool, clean night air eat away her thoughts. Adrenaline urged her faster, pushed her farther until her knees shook and her ribs ached, but she didn't let herself slow down. Moonlight pooled like liquid silver on the roof of Raoul's house as she passed it. She was almost there.

Chain mail jingled somewhere behind her. She turned sharply into the gap between two houses, looking over her shoulder to make sure she hadn't been seen, and slammed against something solid. The air whooshed from her lungs, and she staggered backward as a hand reached out to steady her. For a wild moment she thought it was the darkness reshaping itself as it had in the cells, but then the watchman stepped forward. Neon light from the single lamppost illuminated the inverted triangle on his forehead and sank his eyes into shadow.

Syron tried jerking away, but his grip on her bad shoulder tightened. She clenched her jaw to keep from crying out.

"Boys!" he shouted, his deep voice lashing through the silence like a whip. Syron could hear the clamor of chain mail from all directions as he dragged her farther into the open and yanked her into place beside him.

"It's about damn time you showed up," he growled. "It's not polite to keep the God waiting."

<h1 style="text-align:center">21</h1>

ROILING DARKNESS

Syron's shoulder throbbed by the time they reached the arched cathedral doors. The watchman hadn't bothered to move his hand, and his gloved fingers dug painfully into the soft spot under the bone as two others strode past them and positioned themselves on either side of the door. In her peripheral vision, she could still see the ones who formed a tight half circle around her, and that wasn't counting the other watchmen who had filed along behind them. She suspected there were at least twenty altogether, more than enough to stop her even if she could manage to twist free.

They yanked at the doors and yellow light spilled through, landing on the watchman beside her. She glanced over at him, spotting the curve of ink in the gap between his glove and chain mail. The clamor of their synchronized footsteps still rang in her ears as he pushed her and she stumbled forward inside the cathedral, squinting against the light.

The doors slammed shut behind her. Empty pews lined the aisle, leading up to the platform, pulpit, and the wrought iron elevator shaft beyond them. The cathedral was empty.

She shivered involuntarily and clutched her arms to her chest, grimacing at the spike of pain in her shoulder. Logically, she knew something must have happened for the watchmen to be searching for her, but the optimistic part of her believed that maybe it was all a misunderstanding. For all she knew, Leon could be up in his room. She started toward the curving staircase she had come down with Mags and the others that morning, hugging the wall, when someone coughed across the room.

"I see you've decided to join us."

Syron stopped breathing. The voice didn't say anything more. She steeled herself and turned around slowly, half-terrified and half-curious, and squeezed her arms to keep her fingers from shaking.

Every scenario she could think of played itself on a loop in the time it took her to see him. To see *them*. It was Leon whose eyes she found first. He was sitting on a pew in the back corner. He looked calm, but she knew him well enough now to tell there was a storm raging behind the façade. Next to him, less than a foot away, sat the God.

"The curfew is very strict, I'm afraid," the God said, and smiled amiably. It was striking how similar he looked to the portrait, right down to the length of his white hair where it draped across his shoulder. His face was angular and sharp, the curve of his neck disappearing beneath a deep purple robe. He gestured her closer, and when he lifted his arm, she saw he wore a sash that came down both sides of his chest. A single design had been woven into each side, its familiar point facing down, and inside was the creamy color of skin or bone.

Syron didn't budge. She was never supposed to meet the God; she didn't want to be anywhere near him. She didn't want *Leon* to be anywhere near him. Her eyes found his, beseeching, and for a moment he did nothing, said nothing, and then his head bobbed in a slight nod.

But her feet felt rooted in place. "You can let him go," she said instead. Her voice rang out in the cathedral and rebounded like a shrill plea. "I'm the angel. He doesn't have anything to do with this."

The God's smile faded as the lights grew brighter. Syron craned her neck up so that she faced the high ceiling, and past the metal beams and the dangling bulbs, she could swear something was moving. She watched in gross fascination as the well of shadows stretched above her, like a wire pulled taut, and broke apart. They pooled around the circumference of the ceiling before spilling over, distorting the sculptures along the walls. Here, a fallen angel with a serene face and chiseled body lost his wings. There, a group of children with messy hair and blank eyes stared out from a forest rich with darkening cypress trees. Next to her, a sculpture of the God cupped a blooming, wilted, and then withered lotus flower in his outstretched hands.

Syron cringed away from the wall just as the shadows beneath the pews lurched forward.

Someone screamed, and it wasn't until she was running, the cold tendrils lapping at her heels, that she realized it had been her.

"Enough!" the God shouted, and suddenly the cold was gone. She risked a glance behind her, half expecting to find an ocean of roiling darkness like smoke, but there was nothing.

Nothing except for the man in the black mask, standing exactly where she had been moments before.

"I think it goes without saying you are not in a position to make demands. That being said, I'm sure you were just on your way. Please," he added, tapping the wooden beam of the pew in front of him and settling back into his seat.

Syron obliged, more from fear of what the Nightman would do if she refused than from a want to be near the God, and slid into the gap between the pews. She sat opposite Leon, who gripped his knee in a clawed hand. She felt the weight of Leon's gaze as she stared at the God, then back to the Nightman, her mouth set in a firm line.

"I'm sorry to say I have made a number of assumptions about you, Syron, and I'm afraid most of them seem to be true. I'm willing to wager you feel the same toward me, though, so I won't burden you with hearsay." He looked at the rip in her dress with stark disapproval, and she raised her chin defiantly.

"I found the cells," she said, so suddenly it surprised even her. Her gaze slipped to Leon. "Yira's down there. I tried to help, but I didn't have the key to get inside with her and—"

"And nothing." The God leaned forward, close enough she could see the faint lines on his forehead and around his mouth.

"You're an angel, Syron. You saw the heart of the universe, and you're worried about one small soul, when your own will fade in such short a time? There will be no more talk about superstitions, however vividly you imagined it. I am proud of Belle for coming forward, though," he added, his lips quirking up in a sly grin. "If it wasn't for her telling us where you would be meeting this evening, I doubt the watchmen would have known where to station themselves."

Syron gaped at him. Belle had promised to help. Julian had trusted her. If anyone were to blame, she would have expected the Nightman to be the one who had alerted the watchmen. Her gaze darted back to him, but he only watched silently, standing so incredibly still she doubted whether he was human at all beneath the mask, or just a man-shaped void.

"Leon, what was it you said to me? You were just a child at the time, mind you, but it's hard to forget wisdom spoken from one so young."

Leon looked lost. His chest deflated, his eyes so dark they almost looked black. He was thinking about Yira, Syron could tell, losing himself in the thought of her trapped somewhere out of reach. His lip curled. "I don't remember."

The God chuckled. "Memory is fickle, isn't it? Allow me to remind you. It was right after your mother's ceremony. Her ashes had grown cold by the time I finished reading, but you had pushed your way to the front of the crowd. The congregation—"

"Stop." Leon clenched his jaw, the vein in his neck throbbing. Syron wanted to reach out to him, to cover his clawed fist with her hand and find a way to steal the layers of pain that clothed him like rusted armor, but his hard eyes met the God's with a look of hatred so intense she shrank back.

"I told you that I hated you. That I didn't know how fiercely I could love until you taught me how deeply I could hate."

"There he is!" The God clapped and leaned back, a sordid smile twisting his face. "I knew that little boy was in there somewhere. We never really change, do we? If there's anything I've learned from the angels, it's that history has a way of repeating itself. I'm sure you've wondered, Syron, why there's so much here in the city, but so little development in terms of technology. That always seems to be where it falls apart, and I have to make sure my city stays standing."

He tapped his temple, oblivious to Leon's pain. Syron's heart broke for him the same time a bead of desire sparked inside her. Leon looked up at her quickly, almost as if he had heard her thoughts, and his mouth parted slightly, eyes blazing, before the God laughed.

"But enough of my rambling. My point, Syron, is that the memories locked away in your mind may benefit the city, but they will not show me what I want to know. When you fell, I decided I would ask you face-to-face in hopes you could satisfy some of my curiosity." The God leaned forward, his cracked amethyst eyes drinking her in. "What did you see when you were between worlds, Syron? When you stood on the precipice of creation and turned your back on your home, what was it like?"

Syron blinked. She hadn't thought about the Watcher for a long time. She didn't really know how to think about her, much less how to voice her. She was a force of the universe, as real and intangible as a thought or a dream.

"Why do you want to know?"

"Why do we want to know anything? But I think the real question you're dying to ask is where the man is who you believed would be locked in the cells. Answer my questions, little angel, and I'll answer yours."

Her hands fisted in the silky, tattered material of her dress. So the Nightman *had* told. "You mean Will? Is he—"

The God held up a hand, and across the room, the Nightman moved. He walked the length of the cathedral and sat on the far side of the pew behind Leon and the God.

The God didn't seem to notice.

Syron took a deep breath. No one seemed to know anything about Will being in the city, and this could be her only chance to figure out what had happened.

"She said her name was the Watcher," Syron began

slowly. She spoke quietly and paused often, because how could she describe color that flashed like cosmic lightning in a place that didn't really have a name, with a person she wasn't even sure was human? She skipped over the more personal parts with Adaline and Evyn, elaborating instead on how her own skin had changed to a light, reflective silver. She told them how it had felt to be offered the choice between life and death, and how, when she had made up her mind, the Watcher had already known her answer. How her last thought was that at least Will would be okay because he would be home, and safe.

Her face was flushed by the time she finished, and she stared at her bare feet hanging over the side of the pew, stained black now with dirt from the street. She wondered where the Watcher was right now, whether she was listening, whether it was okay that she had told. Warmth spread through her chest, and it wasn't until she looked back up at the two sets of amethyst eyes that she saw the God was looking at her greedily, and Leon's eyes sparkled as if she were a miracle.

She realized then that in the time between when the God's portrait had been taken and now, the angel's souls must have changed the God's appearance in the same way the flowers had changed Leon's. It was strange, Syron thought, how two people could have features so similar and look completely different.

"I recognized her somehow," Syron added, talking about the Watcher, "but I still don't know where I remembered her from."

The God ran a hand down his face. "It is minute, but the Keepers have knowledge of the Watcher. It is my understanding that she is with us when we are born, meant to keep things in order. Past that, I cannot say." He nodded to himself and stood up.

"Wait, you promised—"

"I promised?" His eyebrows shot up.

Syron ground her teeth together. "You said you'd answer my question. Where is Will now? I know he was in the cells before. I saw him. I saw what the Nightman did to him."

The God's face went blank. Then he laughed, suddenly and forcefully, and gripped the edge of the pew to steady himself. "Your friend wasn't the person you think he was. He came here, what was it, thirty years ago now?" He looked over his shoulder at the Nightman, who stayed silent. "Time works differently in real life than in dreams, Syron Lennox, and just because you left your world together doesn't mean you fell here together. By the time we found him, he was already outside of Evangentine. We bargained with him—he would come to the city for a time, and in return we would leave his wife and child alone."

"That doesn't make sense," Syron said. She shook her head, fumbling for the right words, and gasped. "I never told you he was in the water with me. I never said—"

The God waved a hand dismissively. "I haven't heard Will's name in longer than I care to remember. If he were still around, I doubt you would even recognize him."

He started to turn away, and for the briefest of seconds his shoulders seemed to sag, and his face twisted as if a sudden flash of pain had lanced through him. He tucked a hand into a hidden pocket in his robe, and the look was gone as quickly as it had come. "In the morning, Mags and the others will get you ready for the ceremony. As for Leon, after the ceremony I will allow you to return home as a sign of good faith. So long as the sahiit capture and bring the angels who fall to the city from now on, we will no longer be a threat to you."

He looked as if he were about to say more but turned his back to them instead, walking away.

No, Syron thought. She launched herself forward and grabbed hold of the God's wrist just as he reached the end of the pew. It jerked from his pocket, and she thought she saw something black and rectangular fly from his hand before pins and needles shot up her arm, numbing her shoulder and chest, and spreading rapidly to the base of her skull.

Distorted images flickered behind her eyelids, covered in static too thick to make out. She pushed harder, trying to conjure up his memories of Will. The static turned to a haze, and she just made out a mop of blond curls before the God shook himself free, and a searing pain raced up her arm and wrapped like nettles around her skull.

The back of the pew dug into her spine as she jerked back, blind with pain. Flashes of light colored her vision and she landed, hard, on the floor. Somewhere far away, she thought she heard shouting. The floor shook as someone landed beside her, and she glimpsed a lock of long white hair that must have been the God's snaking across the floor, as if he were being dragged away.

"Leon," Syron choked. Her head buzzed, her back and shoulder screamed, but she used the pew to force herself to her feet. She breathed in the scent of aged spirits and sour wine and looked around, but shadows swirled around her like black smoke, obscuring her vision.

"Silly girl," the darkness whispered in her ear, and its voice, if it could be called a voice, was violent and sensual and sad. "That could have killed you."

Syron shivered and pushed against the blackness, stumbling forward, but it wasn't just around her. It was everywhere, wisping in thick clouds of black and charcoal gray.

"Syron!" Leon's voice shouted, and she ran for it

blindly, smacking her knee off a pew and skirting around it.

"Leon!" she shouted back desperately, and a voice that was not hers echoed back. Her heart slammed against its cage as she spotted a lick of light and raced ahead. Vaguely, she knew she must have been in the aisle because she ran freely, barreling into a circle of whitewash gray. Something was glowing inside it, but all she saw was Leon. He stood with his back to her, his black satin sleeves rolled up to the elbows, the shirt cinching at the line in the center of his back.

"Leon?" she asked, hesitant this time.

He didn't turn around. "Syron. She—she came back for me."

Syron walked forward warily, shielding her eyes against the glow.

Leon was crying. Beads of tears trickled down his cheeks and followed the curve of his jaw, wetting his neck. His pale skin matched the gray light so closely that she reached out to him, scared he would evaporate like mist and disappear entirely. But he was still warm, still real under her hand.

She squinted into the light. At first there was nothing, and then the light shifted, and her eyes adjusted.

"Leon," it said, and laughed. The voice was soft and musical. "My handsome boy. You're everything I dreamed you would be."

The woman sat cross-legged on the floor, looking up at him with loving eyes. Her brown hair was long and wavy. Freckles dotted her nose and cheeks, with a single speck in the center of her chin. It was the woman from his drawing.

Syron stared at her in shock.

"I tried to take you away from here," Astrophe said,

her eyebrows creasing. "This city…it's dangerous. I wanted you to be safe."

"No, it's not your fault," Leon said, and his voice cracked. "I should have been there with Yira. I should have figured out what was happening, and I would've left with you. We could have stayed together."

Astrophe shook her head and stood up, impossibly alive. She reached out to him. "We're together now. Come with me, Leon. I've been waiting for you."

Syron held his arm tightly. "This can't be…no, this isn't real," Syron whispered to herself, and looked up at Leon. "Astrophe died, remember? You watched it happen. Whatever this is, it isn't your mom."

But Syron could see the need written clearly on his face. Astrophe could too. She smiled sweetly and beckoned to him.

"Please," Syron begged, but he was already prying her fingers from his arm and slipping out of her grip. His lavender eyes stared straight ahead as he brushed her aside, walking forward.

Syron watched him go, helpless. She was going to lose him too. She looked around, but there was nothing and no one to help. They were trapped, and Astrophe was the bait.

The muscles in his back shifted as he reached out to Astrophe. Syron's legs were moving before she told them to, carrying her forward, and then she was crashing into Leon's side and they were rolling together, coming to a stop at the edge of the gray circle. She clambered on top of him before he could get his bearings, but his hands were already on her shoulders trying to push her off.

She slapped him. Her palm stung as he finally looked at her, *really* looked at her, and his cheek blossomed pink. "That's not your mom!" Syron hissed, risking a glance over her shoulder to make sure Astrophe hadn't moved. "I can prove it. No one knew her like you did. Ask her something no one besides her would know."

Leon gaped at her, but the dazed look was gone. His mouth closed slowly, and his hands slid down to her arms. Where before he was pushing her away, now he was gripping her tighter. He swallowed and nodded, and when he moved out from beneath her and Syron glanced down, the ghost of his fingers left imprints on her arms.

"Mom?" he asked quietly, getting to his feet.

Syron stood up next to him. Astrophe's arms were wrapped around herself. Her face was red and splotchy.

"Please, Leon. The doors are closing. If you run, you can make it."

Leon glanced at Syron, who nodded, and he took a breath to steady himself.

"When the watchmen came to take you away, do you remember what you said to me?"

"There's no time—"

"What did you say?" Leon asked in a hard voice.

Astrophe looked taken back. "I said I loved you, of course. I still do."

Leon's chest deflated. His head sagged, and Syron wasn't sure whether it was a laugh or a sob that broke through his lips.

"No," Leon said, as if to himself. "No, that wasn't it at all."

Syron watched Astrophe look him up and down. Her eyes dried up instantly, and her head cocked to the side.

"How inconvenient. Tell me, then, what was it your precious mother said? I'm waiting." Her voice changed midsentence, deepening into the sophisticated tenor of a male. The outline of her was blurry and indistinct as she got to her feet, the illusion evaporating like mist until the man in the black mask stood before them.

"She would have been with you up until the end," he said. "You would have died happy."

"You're sick," Leon spat, but the Nightman only laughed under his breath and walked toward them, his hands curling and unfurling at his sides.

Syron stumbled backward as Leon grabbed her hand, and together, they ran into the darkness.

22

OCEAN EYES

The darkness was all-consuming. Syron bit back the wild fear of suffocating inside it—that each breath would fill her lungs with black poison until she couldn't move, or think, or speak, and focused instead on the pounding of their footsteps against the cathedral floor and the strong, steady pressure of Leon's hand in hers. She knew when they reached the arched front doors because Leon jarred to a halt, deftly rearranging their entwined fingers and tugging her forward. The door was smooth and cold as they fumbled for the handles and pushed.

It wouldn't budge.

"Fuck!" Leon yelled, straining against it, but Syron was already pulling him away. She *felt* something in the darkness behind them, and the not knowing only made it worse. Her free hand skimmed along the wall, over the raised sections that she knew were statues, until it smoothed out and her foot bumped against something solid. She tripped and caught herself, pulling Leon up the steps that led to the elevator.

Her frantic breathing mingled with his as she flung herself forward, colliding with a solid wall. She gasped, pulling away from Leon and running her hands over it, pushing against it.

"This can't be real," Leon choked from beside her, and she heard his fist strike the wall at the same time footsteps pounded on the cathedral floor behind them.

Leon's breath caught. She reached out to him and felt the back of his shirt, cold and damp with sweat, from where he had turned to face the steps. His shoulder rolled, and Syron imagined him reaching into his pocket for the dragonfly before the air whooshed from his lungs and he was jerked away from her.

"Leon!" Syron cried, startled. The blackness pressed against her, sucking up her voice like a void. She stumbled down the steps after him, arms outstretched, when the cathedral brightened. Tentacles of smoke twisted their way to the high ceiling, fading rapidly. She whirled in a tight circle, but Leon was gone. The God was gone.

"You're just another angel, you know," the darkness said from across the room. The Nightman had crouched next to one of the pews; he stood up now clutching a book of inky leather. "If our roles were reversed, it would be you standing here instead of me."

Syron's nails dug into the soft skin of her palms as she planted her feet. Her body screamed at her to run, but there was nowhere left to go. The Nightman had made sure of that.

"What did you do with Leon?" she demanded. "I know you can make people see things. He's in the room with us now, isn't he?"

The Nightman shook his head, less like he was answering and more like he was amazed.

"What made you so sure Will was still alive?" he asked,

avoiding her question. "Were you really so desperate to save him that you put your friend's lives in danger? Your own life? You escaped the sahiit, Syron. You could have gone anywhere."

She clenched her jaw. "Why do you care? Just let me go. Leon—"

"To hell with Leon!" he shouted, dissolving into whirling smoke that raced toward her, stopping only a few feet away. His arms fell to his sides, spilling open the Black Book from where he only gripped the back cover. The binding was weak and sagging, and this close she could see the decorative metal points along the corners. The pages were blank.

"I heard you and Raoul in the Artist's Room. After I'm dead, you can leave the city," she said. "Is that what you're doing? You want to kill me now, so you don't have to wait?"

A feral, pained noise ripped from his throat and his hand swung back. Syron recoiled before he could slap her, but he reached for the back of his mask instead and tugged it up and over his head.

An older man with short silver hair, hollowed cheeks, and piercing ocean-blue eyes stared down at her. "The God is dying. He used up all the souls he had left in the book—otherwise, I wouldn't have been able to touch him. He doesn't think I know he has to drain what little of me is left to steal your soul too. But if we both leave, he could only survive for a couple more days. A week, at most." Shadows seeped from his black suit and puddled on the floor at his feet, coiling around Syron's ankles. "Will you?" he asked, reaching out to stroke her face.

Syron jerked away from his touch. "Will I what?"

"Come away with me," he murmured. "Somewhere safe."

"Safe?" Syron gaped at him. She wanted to laugh at the incredulity of it. Here stood a liar, a manipulator, and a *murderer*—it was because of him that so many children were lost, and that so many parents were grieving. It was his fault that Adaline was trapped inside a body she didn't recognize, and without him at the God's side, Yira never would have been chained up inside the cells, struggling just to stay alive. A million accusations sprang to her lips, but she held them back. Sometimes, there was strength in simplicity.

"I don't even know who you are," she said finally.

His brow furrowed. Syron tried to back away, but the shadows tightened around her ankles, locking her in place as his expression hardened.

"What?" he asked, ocean eyes glinting. "You don't recognize me?"

The Black Book thudded against the floor as he lunged forward and wrapped his hands around her throat. Syron choked and flung herself to the side, but his grip was like iron as he slammed her against the wall. She clawed the fabric over his wrists, kicking savagely, the bitter taste of fear blossoming in the back of her throat. A blow landed against his knee, and he grunted, banging her head against the wall and dragging her to the floor with him.

Blood pounded in her ears, her cheeks, her forehead. Her vision speckled with black as her foot touched something solid. Lungs screaming, she looped her ankle around it and kicked it closer, fumbling with numb fingers to find it.

The Nightman watched her face with a morbid, almost self-loathing fascination as she snatched up the Black Book and forced it between them, digging the metal corner into his chest. It snagged against his leather suit, and she pushed harder, raking it across to the other side. The

Nightman yelled and jerked away, clutching at his ruined chest.

Syron fell to the side, shaking, sucking in sandpaper air that tore at her throbbing throat. The cathedral was too bright, her vision too blurry, but she scrambled to her feet and ran unsteadily to the door, hoping it would open for her now that the Nightman was distracted. Every step sent a spike of pain lancing through her skull until she reached the doors and pushed.

They opened soundlessly. Clean, chilly night air wafted against her as she rushed outside and skidded to a halt. An army of watchmen stood guard like black-clad sentinels, lined up in rows. She glanced behind her, but the Nightman was already striding toward her. He grinned maniacally as two of the watchmen grabbed her arms and lifted her off her feet. Her shoulder rolled painfully, her head spun, but she kept her gaze locked on him as he passed through the arched doors and stood in front of her.

His blue eyes shone silver in the moonlight, almost the same shade as his hair. The gash she had made was deep and oozing red, exposing his chest where the material dangled, dripping with blood. She could see the swirl of ink on his chest through it, and at first glance she thought it was the strange tattoos of the watchmen before the blood drizzled lower and she recognized the crest of a wave, the point of a sword. The tattoo that had once been so vivid had blurred and warped with time, but the angels and demons were still there. Still fighting. She looked for the demon with the forked tongue, but it was swallowed by a gush of bright crimson.

"What made up your mind?" Syron had asked.

Will had shrugged, a smile playing at the edges of his lips. "I didn't want it to just be the angels winning, you know? They're fighting over a man who doesn't want either of them. It makes more sense that they destroy each other."

"No," Syron whispered. Her body shuddered involuntarily, and the watchmen on either side of her tightened their grip. She thought back to how the Nightman had thrown her into the cell after she had run from him, and moments ago, when he had tried to kill her after she had refused his offer. Both times, it had been her dismissal that sparked him to violence. But it had been him both times. All this time.

"Will?" Her voice sounded far away even to her own ears, as if she were speaking down a very long, very deep tunnel.

"Guess you found me," he said, smirking, and she could see the resemblance now: the way his mouth always quirked up when he was being sarcastic, the set of his eyes, the once-soft curve of his cheekbones. She had thought everyone in the God's city looked younger than they were, but he hadn't bothered to hide his age. His ocean-blue eyes that had once been kind and protective were now hard and flat, like a closed door he had bolted up tight.

The God was right; she didn't recognize him. The Will she knew was gone.

"I heard what you said in the cathedral," he said, "about your dreams. The onocalcum can link you with anyone so long as you share the same emotional trauma. Whatever you were thinking before you went to sleep would have caused it, and afterward it would only have gotten stronger. Whoever it linked you with, I do think it's ironic you caught a glimpse of me too—but I was never the one in chains."

Syron shook her head. The darkness she had pushed down for so long reached up with chapped fingers and grabbed the cracked thing inside of her chest. She blew out an unsteady gust of air, blinking back hate-filled tears.

"How could you hurt all those people? All those kids?" Her throat ached, and her voice came out raspy. "Will, I—I loved you."

His smile faded. "I know," he said, and glanced down at himself. Fear flashed across his face, as if he were suddenly aware of who he had become, but it was gone so quickly she must have imagined it. "If there is a God, he'll forgive us," he murmured, barely louder than a whisper. Syron doubted anyone else heard him.

He turned his back to her and disappeared inside the cathedral, returning a moment later with Leon in his arms. His body was limp as he handed him over to a watchman with a high black collar beneath his chain mail. "He's not dead, so make sure he stays that way. The God wants them both taken to the Artist's Room. If Raoul isn't there already, find him."

"What are you going to do?" the watchman holding Leon asked.

"The God retired to his study," he lied smoothly. "He asked that I join him."

Syron jerked beneath the straps that bound her to the chair, but the watchmen had cinched them as tight as they could go. The coarse fabric dug into the exposed skin of her arms and chest. They had lifted her dress to her knees and bound her there too, probably to make sure she couldn't slip out.

Not that it would matter.

She looked over at Leon in the chair next to hers. They had restrained him too, even though he was still unconscious. He was facing her, eyes closed, his face innocent and relaxed. It would have been easy to think he was asleep if not for the discolored welt on the side of his forehead, barely visible beneath the soft wisp of his pale hair, stained blue in the light from the Artist's Room.

"Leon," she whispered hoarsely, and grimaced. Her body felt like one giant bruise, her head pounded, and her throat burned as if she were swallowing a constant stream of fire. She gritted her teeth and called out again, but he didn't budge. Instead, a whisper of noise came from the other room, past the open door. She whipped her head to it and leaned forward as much as she could, straining to hear.

The humming grew closer, clearer. She didn't recognize the tune so much as the voice before Raoul shouldered open the door, hands in his pockets, an amused glint in his otherwise black eyes. He strode up to her casually and opened the top drawer of the metal cabinet, still humming, and pulled out the black-and-gold tattoo gun. It glinted in the light.

"Did you know?" Syron asked quietly. She worked to keep the accusation out of her voice—placing blame wouldn't do her any good when she couldn't even lift a finger to defend herself.

The humming broke off, and Raoul chuckled under his breath. Syron laid her head back, watching warily as he opened the bottom drawer too, and plugged the wire into the black box and the tattoo gun.

"It's not like anything you tell me will make a difference," she continued when he didn't speak. "The God is already punishing Leon and me for trying to escape. Even if we could manage to get out of the spire, there's no way we could leave the city without the watchmen finding us."

Raoul shook his head and turned to face her, wearing a

sly smile. "You think it's the God who's punishing you? It wasn't the God who ordered you in here, dove, despite what the watchmen were led to believe. A smart man would have seen this coming, but I suppose everyone underestimates the people closest to us now and again."

"What do you mean?"

Raoul turned the tattoo gun in his hand, seeming to decide how much to say, and grimaced. "You're right, you know, as much as I hate to admit it. And for all the years I've kept the God's secrets, the Nightman has proved to be the most bothersome."

"Then tell me," Syron begged. "In the cathedral, the God said that Will had a family. That he agreed to come to the city to protect them. Is that true?" She could hear the desperation in her voice, but if Raoul noticed, he didn't show it. Instead, he looked surprised.

"Will? You mean the Nightman? He hasn't gone by that name in decades."

"Is it true?" Syron asked again, flinching against the fire in her throat. Realizing that Will had been the Nightman...it was more terrible than she could put into words. But she couldn't understand *why* he had done all those terrible things, short of this one vital piece of information. If it were even true.

Slowly, Raoul nodded. The light shifted to red, hiding his eyes as he leaned against the metal cabinet, the tattoo gun forgotten. It hung limply in one hand.

"We didn't find Will until years after he fell. My best guess is that somewhere along the line he had told someone he came from another world, and eventually word got back to the God. That's when the God reached out to me. We were friends, before he left the Keepers' Citadel to build this city, and he was looking for a way to harness the abilities of the angels. With his help, I managed to create what others would call the Black Book, but it's really just a backward version of the tomes in the Citadel's library.

"But to better answer your question, Will had already established a life for himself. He had a family, yes, a beautiful wife and a curious little girl," Raoul said. "But for the God's plan to work, Will had to come to the city *willingly*. The only way I could think was to go through his child. At that time, the God already had a wealth of applications for the lotus flowers; it didn't take long to find a way to manipulate the child's dreams. Its effects were only temporary, of course, but it was convincing enough that when we offered him a chance to save her, he jumped at the opportunity."

Raoul, coming back to himself, flipped a switch on the black box, and the tattoo gun buzzed to life. Syron tensed as he dipped it into the tray of ink inside the drawer, alternating between purple and black, before hovering the needle over her wrist.

"There's no use fighting it," he said, when she tried to twist her hand free. "The more relaxed you are, the less it will hurt."

"Why even bother?" Syron rasped. "If Will wants to kill me, he can do it himself."

Raoul tsked, and Syron winced as the needle burrowed into her skin. Spikes of heat shot up her arm as he moved his hand and she gasped, clenching her eyes shut.

"I think," Raoul said over the drone of the machine, ignoring Syron's struggles, "that being forced to create the nightchildren is what gave him his edge. He did everything we asked, so long as his own child remained safe. Hell," Raoul added, tracing the needle up her arm, "if the God hadn't taken half his soul, I'm willing to bet the guilt would have eaten him alive."

Syron focused on his voice to distract her from the

pain. Parts of her arm had gone numb, and when she looked down, lines of ink wisped beneath her skin, inching away from the needle before Raoul even moved his hand.

She looked up at him in horror, envisioning herself transforming into one of the watchmen, when something small and glowing darted through the door and out of sight. She whipped her head to follow it, but it was gone.

Is this how it starts? Do the symbols drive me mad before I turn into one of the God's monsters?

"Yes and no," Raoul answered, and Syron gaped. She hadn't realized she had spoken aloud. "This is the first time an angel has been inscribed with the symbols. Or a sahiit," he added, glancing over at Leon. "If I had to guess, Will might be hoping it will share a similar effect so he won't be so alone."

"He's the one who did all this," Syron said. "He chose to be alone."

Raoul shook his head. "He chose to save his family. When you get down to the bones of it, it's really just a sad story."

Syron saw it again: a wisp of blue light in the background, the size of a child. Her pulse sped, but she wasn't sure whether it was from hope, or horror at what Raoul had said.

I'm not crazy. I need to keep him talking.

"Why not create a new Nightman and let Will go? From what the God told me in the cathedral, it sounded as if it would only be temporary."

"Originally," Raoul said, curving the needle in a tight loop, "that's what we had intended. But after Astrophe, none of the angels survived their fall. The God was forced to use only enough of the Black Book to keep him alive. The Nightman…Will, as you call him, was smarter than we gave him credit for. Using Julian's third eye keeps him strong, much stronger than the God. When we didn't have your ceremony right away, the Nightman must have realized the Black Book was empty. I suspect he knew even before I did, biding his time.

"After the God's announcement, the Nightman asked me to bring Julian to the God's study. I suspected then, but I'm not stupid enough to ignore his requests—not when the God is hardly able to walk, let alone protect me."

Raoul jerked the strap down from over Syron's elbow. Fresh pain exploded through her arm, like a searing brand had been pressed against the raw, sensitive skin. She flung her head back, biting her lip to keep from screaming.

Raoul swiveled and dipped the needle back into the tray of ink before hovering over her upper arm, tracing lines of fire. This close, she could smell the harsh scent of burned sage that clung to him.

"You're doing well," he murmured. "Much better than the watchmen. Most of them would have passed out by now."

Syron's finger twitched. She scanned the room, but the blue light was gone.

"Why?" she asked, more to stifle her rising panic than to sate her curiosity.

"Why what, dove?"

"You said he wanted Julian brought to the God's study," she said, trying to twist her other arm out from beneath the strap, but it was stuck tight.

Raoul looked up at her, smirked, and dipped his head back down. "Julian drank nearly half the decanter before he finally passed out. He didn't want to, of course, but he didn't have a choice. When he's asleep, it's easier for the Nightman to manipulate what people see. Shadow and all that, but it can work with solid objects too."

"So if Julian were awake…"

"The Nightman would be significantly less terrifying, yes. It's an art, really. One he's grown into through years of practice."

Raoul leaned back, surveying his work. Syron followed his gaze and barely stifled a scream. The ink was moving more freely now, blossoming under the surface like watercolor paint, stopping along the ball of her shoulder.

"We're just about finished with this side," he said, leaning forward. "Hopefully Leon stays asleep long enough to—"

The blue light darted behind Raoul. Syron glimpsed something large and heavy clasped between both hands before it slammed against Raoul's head. His body crumpled to the ground, sending the tattoo gun skidding across the floor. Mercifully, the buzzing stopped.

Adaline stood above her, still holding the microscope, but now it was flecked with gore.

Syron smiled up at her. She knew she probably looked crazy. Hell, she felt a little crazy, but Adaline smiled back at her kindly. Her blue glow contrasted sharply in the red light, and the Artist's Room through her translucent body was distorted and magnified as she set the microscope on the cabinet and reached to undo the straps. She did Syron's arms last, and as soon as Syron was free, she jolted upright and threw her arms around her.

The relief at seeing Adaline again was shocking. She hadn't realized how violently she had missed her until she was in her arms, impossibly solid despite her appearance. Adaline reached up tentatively to return the hug, and her hair where it tickled Syron's nose smelled like crisp midnight air.

"Are you okay?" Syron asked hoarsely, pulling away. "Briar said—"

"Briar is an arrogant, flashy asshole," she interrupted harshly. "If he were here——"

"He's dead," Syron said, and Adaline's mouth snapped shut.

"Well," she said after a moment, "if he weren't already, I would have killed him myself." She glanced worriedly at the tattoos on Syron's arm. Syron looked too; the ink had already settled into her skin, winding around even to the side that had been pressed against the chair. She recognized some of the symbols from the frames along the walls, but there were others too that were foreign, blurring when she looked at them too hard, as if they were shifting under the weight of her gaze.

"Angels have a higher tolerance to the flowers," Adaline said, rounding Syron's chair and undoing the straps around Leon. "You should be fine, I think. I would have knocked him out sooner, but I doubt we would have gotten that information any other way."

Syron nodded, sliding off the chair and standing dizzily. She went to Leon's side and checked his pulse, then pulled the hair back from his face. The welt on his forehead was purple-black, but there was no blood.

"How did you get into the city?" Syron asked, turning to Adaline. "The watchman who guards the gate barely let Leon inside."

Adaline rolled her eyes. "Our plan was to get in through the tunnels, remember? But enough about me—I heard what he said to you. It sounds like we have bigger problems than the God. Is that true?"

Syron nodded. "I think the Nightman knocked him out, but I couldn't make out much of anything at the time." She couldn't bring herself to call him Will when speaking with Adaline. It felt wrong, somehow.

Adaline must have understood the look on her face. "I'm sorry, you know. I didn't have any idea he was…"

"It doesn't matter," Syron said, shaking her head. She didn't know who she was trying to convince more, Adaline or herself. "He hurt Yira. She's—"

"No, please. I don't want to know…not yet, at least. If we can get to Julian and wake him up, it'll make the Nightman weaker. This is our chance to finally end the cycle. Everything else comes after."

Syron bit her lip and glanced at the invisible glamour in the corner of the room. She nodded. "Here, help me get Leon. We can't leave him behind in case the watchmen come back."

Together, they pulled Leon into a sitting position. Syron looped his arm across her shoulders and moved to stand when a small, wounded cry escaped Adaline's lips. Syron looked over in alarm, but she was already hunched over, hugging her hands to her stomach.

Syron fumbled, trying to lay Leon back down to help her, when Adaline sucked in a sharp breath. She leaned up slowly, her expression pained.

"Do you remember the last time we saw each other?" she asked quietly. "We were in my house, right after I came inside from speaking with the nightchildren."

Syron nodded. It would've been hard to forget. "You collapsed and started shaking. I tried to help, but there wasn't anything I could do."

"It happened because the presence of the Nightman was stronger with all the children in one place. It's worse here. I can feel him everywhere, like a wave threatening to pull me under." She paused, and Syron saw her jaw flex. "I practiced fighting it. That's why it took me so long to come…I had to make sure I wouldn't hurt anyone. But it's not something I can withstand indefinitely." She looked over then, eyes pleading. "You can recognize the signs, right? If I change, you'll know right away?"

Syron tensed. "You're controlling it now. Can't you just—"

"Aren't you listening to me? I *can't*. If something distracts me, even for a second, that's all it will take. The Nightman doesn't need a door, Syron. Shadows only need a crack to slip through. If he gets in my head, I need you to kill me."

"What?" Syron gasped. Leon's weight suddenly felt heavy where she propped him up. The room spun. "Adaline, you know I would never hurt you."

"It wouldn't be me you were killing, and Leon's life would be in danger too. You have to promise me."

Syron shook her head, adamantly at first, and then slowly as she realized what side of Leon she was on. She slipped her hand into his pocket and, holding back a wave of guilt for taking it without his permission, drew out the dragonfly. It caught the light beautifully: a kaleidoscope of blue and green mixing with pink and gold, twisting in swirling patterns as she flicked her wrist.

"Here," Adaline said, and Syron looked away from the glittering blade to find her holding out an ink tray from the drawer. "Lotus extract is the only thing that can hurt me. Coat the blade in this. It'll dry quickly."

Syron did so. When she finished, it felt like a lead weight in her hand, and much colder.

"If you try to hurt Leon, then…I promise."

Adaline studied Syron through eyes sharpened by pain and determination. They weren't a child's eyes, but Syron had always known she was anything but.

"Good. Now help me carry Leon to the elevator."

23

HEART ON FIRE

Raoul's crumpled body was the last thing Syron saw as the elevator kicked into gear. It lurched upward, and she gripped the handle with her free hand, her other arm wrapped securely around Leon. Adaline stood on his other side, illuminating the metal latticework with a bluish-white glow. Syron spared a glance in her direction and, seeing the careful control of Adaline's expression, tried to mirror it with her own.

If Julian was still in the God's study, she told herself, then all they had to do was wake him up. She didn't want to think about the rest.

The elevator slid to a halt. Syron pushed off the metal bar and, together with Adaline helping support Leon's weight, they shuffled their way down the long hall. Syron suspected every floor in the spire must look identical, right down to the intricately carved bronze door on the opposite end.

Adaline pressed the call button. Syron looked nervously over her shoulder, half expecting the sleeping temporals to burst from their rooms with cries of outrage for using an elevator reserved for the God, but the hall stayed silent as the humming drew closer. The doors opened to reveal a smaller metal lift, with arched doorways on two of the four sides.

They crammed inside. Adaline shifted the lever. Syron closed her eyes and took a deep breath, listening to the steady drone as they were pulled to the top of the spire. She couldn't help thinking about her dream, when who she had thought to be Will stood on a hill overlooking the wall around the city. She remembered how the wind had beat against him as he looked up and saw the God's silhouette, black against the bright interior, and shivered.

This time when the doors slid open, Syron saw the sky. It was a slate of smooth graphite, untouched except for the hint of pale yellow on the horizon, and the ashen face of the moon. The city stretched out below in pinpoints of neon, and past the wall glowed distant spots of light, a body of shimmering water, and miles upon miles of forest.

Syron and Adaline exchanged a glance and stepped into the God's study. It was larger than she had expected, spanning the circumference of the spire, and mostly empty. In front of them, the carpet stretched to a wide mahogany desk covered in neat stacks of papers. A decanter and glasses sat on a metal tray, and on the opposite side, the bust of an opal owl perched with its talons wrapped around the edge. Slouched in the chair behind the desk sat the gray afterimage of the God, his skin stretched tight over bone, leaden eyes open and sunken in.

Syron looked away quickly and found the sofa, out of place in the otherwise barren room. A boy with a swath of jet-black hair covering his forehead snored softly, with one arm slung across his chest. Together with Leon between them, they rushed to Julian's side. Syron placed her hands on Julian's chest as Adaline lowered Leon gently to the floor. The thin satin of Julian's shirt did nothing to hide his feverish skin as she shook him, hard, and let out an exasperated sigh when he didn't so much as twitch. She grabbed his arm, meaning to pull him off the couch, when Adaline placed her hand on Syron's shoulder.

"He's different when he's sleeping," Adaline murmured, almost to herself. "Something about him changes, I think. Raoul wasn't lying about his third eye. If I had known sooner…"

"It wouldn't have changed anything," said a voice behind them.

Syron whirled. Will leaned casually against the side of the elevator. He hadn't bothered to put his mask back on, and he wore a crooked smile.

"He won't wake up," he said. "Not for a couple more hours, at least."

Syron's hands clenched into fists, but he wasn't looking at her. He flashed Adaline a smile. "How long has it been? I must admit you've become a favorite pastime of mine. A stupid thing to do, coming here."

"Probably," Adaline agreed, rounding the back of the couch and yanking Julian into a sitting position. "But at least I don't hide behind people to do my dirty work." Her voice was sharp enough to cut glass as she slapped Julian. Syron jumped as an audible crack split the room, but Julian didn't wake up, and Will only smirked.

"Who's hiding?" he asked, and his shadow against the elevator shaft moved, clinging to his leather suit like smoke as he strode forward. The gash on his chest had been bandaged, Syron noted, but it didn't seem to be bothering him. "I don't pretend to understand how it works: that somehow you managed to find Syron and me in our past lives, before I turned you in this life, but I recognized you afterward. You were such a small, jealous thing. Funny how circumstances change us, isn't it?"

Will paused, his head cocked to the side as if he were listening. "I can hear your heartbeat, Adaline," he said, and Syron felt a shiver run up her spine. "All you have to do is let go. It'll be so easy."

Adaline's gaze locked onto Will's. "Stay out of my head," she snapped, and her small fingers skimmed over Julian's jaw before grabbing his neck. "Don't think I won't do it. Not if it means you can't hurt me anymore."

"Adaline——" Syron warned, and a sudden, wild idea gripped her.

Neither of them was watching her. She felt the waistband of her dress—checking to make sure the handle of the dragonfly was easily accessible from where she had tucked it carefully between the layers of fabric—and then darted between Will and Adaline. If Will got too close, at least she would have a weapon. And if she stayed where she was, all she would have to do is reach back…

"Leave Adaline alone. You killed the God, Will. You can go wherever you want."

"No," he said, staring past her. "This is her fault. If she hadn't found us—"

"Then you wouldn't have met your wife or had your daughter. If they could see you now, what would they think?"

She heard Adaline suck in a sharp breath and glanced behind her. She was relieved to find Adaline's hands were off Julian now, but she was gripping her temples instead, leaning against the back of the couch for support.

"Raoul told me about them," Syron continued, whipping her head back to Will, who had moved a few steps closer. "I can't change that I asked you to come into the forest with me that night, or anything that's happened since. I know how much you must hate me, but it's over now. You ended it. You can go home."

"Keep them out of your mouth." His eyes were wild when they found hers. "When the city finds out the God is dead, they'll know it was me. But he was going to kill me, and I didn't have a choice. *This* was the only choice. I thought maybe if you…" He shook his head, eyeing the tattoos marring Syron's arm. She thought she saw the shadows swell around him, but she couldn't be sure because then something solid slammed against her back.

The air whooshed from her lungs, and she doubled over, sending something crashing to the floor in front of her. She just had time to glimpse the fog whirl and settle in Adaline's eyes before she shot to her feet and lunged.

Adaline's body collided with hers—all hard knees, sharp elbows, and nails like razor blades that burrowed into her back as she latched on. Syron felt hot breath on her neck, and suddenly all she saw was an army of nightchildren with Briar in the center. She heard his strangled cries and the wet, sinewy snaps of bone and muscle being torn apart.

She didn't have time to think. There was no heartbeat in Adaline's chest to mimic her own, and so there was no hesitation when she wrenched the dragonfly free.

The soft skin of her throat gave easily.

Adaline's teeth skimmed Syron's neck before her body went slack. It thumped against the floor, taking the dragonfly with it.

Syron choked back a sob. She wanted to collapse with her and shrink under the weight of what she had done, but Will was hovering over her, wisps of gray smoke reaching out from his suit like long fingers.

She had been trying to appeal to the half of his soul he still had, but it was already gone.

"They were right," she whispered in a cracked voice. "All of them. You are a monster."

He reached out to her, and she saw his surprise when she grabbed his hand and held it, then reached behind her and clumsily grabbed Julian's too.

Pins and needles raced up her arm, but she wasn't scared because she knew what she was looking for—if it would even work. She gripped their hands tighter and focused on Julian, imagining a back door opening inside his mind that would lead her straight into Will's.

The tingling reached the crown of her head as Will seemed to realize what she was doing. She saw his face as if from a great distance: the medley of confusion and disbelief transforming irrevocably into an aching throb of raw fury. Syron couldn't help thinking there must be a piece of his soul left after all—for him to feel so strongly that his heart was on fire—before the darkness closed in around her.

Soft streaks of silver light filtered through the lapping waves far above her head. The water itself was cold and heavy, and she felt its weight pressing against her as she stood and squinted into the darkness. The light didn't reach this depth; she picked her way blindly over broken seashells and sand that tickled the bottoms of her feet, pulling her hands through the water to propel herself forward, when a light flicked on somewhere in the distance.

She wasn't sure how long it took her to reach the crooked mailbox, but the pathway next to it led up to a house overgrown with coral. It wrapped tightly around it like a cocoon, gapping only where the cracked front door glowed with a soft yellow light.

The front-porch steps shifted under her weight, but if they made any noise, the water sucked it all up. She pushed the door open gently and stepped into a small living room. The light came from a lamp floating high over an end table, held into place by a cord in the wall. Water-damaged photos hung on the walls in thick frames, and in the corner, huddled over a stuffed doll, stood a little girl.

Her long ebony hair was sectioned and pulled back at the top of her head, and her bright yellow sundress had a fresh stain on the chest. She raised her eyes from the doll as a woman carrying a suitcase bustled into the room. She had the same ebony hair, cut close and shaggy around her face. She glanced despairingly at the little girl as she set it next to the armchair.

Neither of them had seen Syron.

The mom turned and rushed back to the hall when Will stepped out. He was older than when Syron had known him and younger than when she had last seen him, and he smiled a sad smile at the woman, who folded herself into his arms. She carried a strong dignity, and all the while she was watching the little girl.

"Daddy?" she said from the corner.

"Yeah, baby?" Will asked, pulling away and going to her. The woman held a hand up to her mouth while the other rested possessively on the slight bulge of her stomach. Will wrapped his hand around the back of his daughter's neck, holding her head to his.

"Do you really have to go?" she whispered.

"Yes," he said softly, "but I'll be back as soon as I can. Take care of your baby brother for me, okay?"

Her eyes darted back to her mom, and she nodded. "Promise me you'll come back?"

"Cross my heart."

He leaned in and picked her up quickly, holding her close as he turned back to the woman. The daughter faced Syron now, still standing immobile by the door, but her eyes filled with a wealth of terror so intense that Syron blanched.

"Have I come at a bad time?"

The voice came from behind her. Syron whirled around in slow motion, the water obstructing her movement, just as someone passed through her. He smelled of sage and smoke and wore a long black overcoat, perfectly tailored.

"I believe I was expected."

Will's shoulders tensed as Raoul crossed the space between them. "Of course," he said in a forced voice. "Raoul, this is Thera. You've heard a great deal about Nineveh, I'm sure."

Raoul nodded to Nineveh, who shrank back, and extended his hand to Thera. An awkward moment passed while she stared at him. It seemed to Syron she was measuring what would happen if she refused and what would be gained if she didn't, but then the scales tipped and she placed her hand in his.

He smiled, amused, and kissed the back of her hand before letting it drop.

"An honor. I assume all is ready?"

"It is. We just need a moment to say our goodbyes."

Raoul inclined his head and turned away. Syron moved aside as he walked out the door and disappeared into the dark.

As soon as he was out of sight, Will's chest sank. Thera's hand wound through his, still watching the door.

"I don't trust him," she whispered, "but I do trust you. I know you'll do whatever it takes to keep them both safe." Her glistening eyes shot to Nineveh, wet with unshed tears, then down to her stomach. "They are the only ones who matter."

A sob escaped Nineveh's lips. She was very pale, and unlike Thera, her cheeks were slick with tears. Will held her tighter, pressing his forehead against hers and squeezing his eyes shut.

"That's him," Nineveh said. Her voice was small and fragile. "The man from my dreams."

Will pulled away, his eyes flashing. "I know, baby. I'll make him go away."

· · ·

Syron sat up groggily and found herself on the floor next to Leon. Julian still snored softly on the couch, oblivious, his hand dangling over the edge where she must have let go of him. She blinked and stood up, unsteady on her feet, and shook her head to clear it.

Outside, the sky had blazed to life in streaks of pink and yellow, splotched with clouds. She looked away and found the dragonfly on the floor, its blade sharp and clean, and lying in a fine gray powder that shifted and shone like wet lake rocks. She stooped to pick it up and hesitated, not wanting to touch the powder, and closed her hand on empty air instead.

She couldn't think straight; her mind felt sluggish, still not completely her own, and all around her she imagined the weight of the black, black water pushing down on her, felt again the surprise when she had breathed through it, and the terror of walking straight into the unknown. But sometimes, knowing was worse. Sometimes, it wasn't the water that crushed you, but the truth of what was hidden beneath.

That's when she spotted Will. At some point, he had crawled over to the side of the elevator shaft opposite the sunrise, where the barest hint of shadow still clung. She walked toward him slowly, uncertainly. She knew forcing someone to relive their trauma was a bad thing, but she hadn't had a choice, and now she didn't know what to expect.

The leather suit stretched tightly over Will's back and thighs where he had curled himself into a ball, facing away from her. She stopped inches from his feet, eyeing the shadow warily, and peered down. Will's eyes were wide open, their ocean blue clear and framed by thin, gray lashes. His lips were moving quickly and without sound.

"Will?" she asked.

Blood gushed from his mouth. His unseeing eyes stared straight ahead as his body slackened, arms and legs shifting slightly where he no longer held them tight.

For a second, Syron couldn't move. Then her knees shook under her weight, and she gripped the gaps in the curling metal of the elevator shaft to hold her upright. The only mark on him was covered by the bandage on his chest, but it was perfectly white, and he had been fine before she had touched him—before she had forced him to share a memory he had buried.

Suddenly the light streaming in through the massive glass walls wasn't beautiful, it was mocking. Shouldn't there be storm clouds broiling outside, or rain beating against the glass like angry fists? Fury and grief welled inside her in equal measure, and walking the thin line between them were memories. Before Will had been manipulated into working for the God, before he had lost his family and stolen the minds of children, tortured Yira, and made her kill Adaline, he had been gentle.

She saw it now, like a timeline leading back to her childhood: Will taking her hand when he knew something was wrong, his laughter when she got bored on their trip to Centralia and shouted out the window at passersby, and when they were younger too. They had made a fort of couch cushions and blankets, lining the inside with white Christmas lights to mimic starlight. They had talked, planned, and schemed for hours, believing without question that they held the secret to the universe in the palms of their hands, and all they had to do was what no one else could guess.

She saw everything, and she didn't hate him. Worse, she understood him.

Her hand slid from the elevator shaft. She turned her back on Will, walking past Leon and Julian and the dead

God. The glass was warm where she leaned against it, staring out at the sky painted with vibrant pinks, yellows, and oranges, woven together by feathery white clouds. She slid down the glass as the city inside the wall came to life, and outside the wall was the shocking green of treetops and the brilliant blue of the lakes—and all of it was only half her own, if she could lay claim to it at all.

For once when she closed her eyes, it was dreamless.

Someone was shaking her. She looked up through the fog of sleep and saw Leon. He crouched in front of her, his violet eyes bright and worried. Except for the purple and green welt on his forehead, his face looked as if it were chiseled from perfectly hewn stone.

"You're awake," Syron said, and flinched against the stab of pain in her throat.

"I could say the same for you." He smiled half-heartedly and offered his hand. She accepted, letting him pull her to her feet, and tensed as something moved in her peripheral vision.

She turned toward it, hearing Leon's gasp when he must have noticed her tattoos, hidden before against the glass.

"Sy," Leon started to say, but she wasn't listening because Belle was standing next to the couch with Julian. Her hair was down, but she still wore the same baggy jeans and black tank top from when Syron had last seen her. Either she hadn't bothered to change, or she hadn't slept.

Not that Syron cared either way.

"What the hell are you doing here?" Syron demanded.

"It's okay," Leon said quickly. "She's not—"

"Not what? A liar? She ratted us out to the God, Leon.

It's her fault we're in this mess." She looked past Belle, out the window. The sun had risen higher in the sky. It was nearly midday—the day of her ceremony. Her gaze flitted to the God, still very much dead, and the sight of him brought everything that had happened rushing back. She wheeled around before she could look at the barely there remains of Adaline's body, or the very real remains of Will's, and found herself in Leon's arms.

Suddenly everything was too much. Her breaths came in short, shallow rasps. Her chest felt tight, like a band had been wrapped around her and someone was pulling from the other side. She was drowning, the walls she had built inside her mind splintering like tinder, but Leon was there to catch her. His hands were warm and calloused where they gripped her arms before sliding to her back. She remembered the first time she had touched those hands, knew the callouses were from training and drawing for hours on end. She knotted her own hands into his shirt, holding him desperately against her as if they were both lost in the sea of the sky, and he was the only thing keeping them both afloat.

And that terrified her too, relying on someone else for strength.

She didn't know when her gasps turned to sobs, but just when she felt the ground beneath her again, a hand settled on her shoulder.

She looked up and, seeing Belle, jerked away.

"I know what you must think of me," Belle said, "but I'm not sorry. I didn't have a choice."

Syron scoffed, pulling away from Leon to face her directly. "That's a lie, and you know it. If you hadn't told the God we were leaving, none of this would have happened. I wouldn't have had to—" *Murder my best friend.*

It had been right on the tip of her tongue. She swallowed down the lump in her throat. "This is all your fault."

Belle's gaze raked across the bruises on Syron's neck and the tattoos on her arm. Her expression softened.

"The temporals reported me to the watchmen, Syron. After you left, they came in my shop to question me. I couldn't just turn them away. They're quick to label even the most pious of us as heretics, and I've learned how to cover my ass. I only told them you had asked to meet at my shop after curfew, but you wouldn't tell me why. They made their own assumptions, and I put on a show about how I was on my way to tell them before they barged in."

"But if you didn't know what would happen, how did you find us?"

"When Julian never showed, I got worried. I checked his house first, but there was no sign of him or Raoul, and the spire was the only other place he would be. He told me which rooms you two were in before," she added, glancing at Julian, "but when both were empty, this was the next logical place to look.

"For what it's worth, I *am* sorry for what you went through." She looked at the God with a mixture of awe and dread, and then behind her at Will. "I just—I'm not sure how you managed this, is all."

"How *did* you manage this?" Julian asked. "I didn't think the God could be killed."

Syron tensed, and Leon's hand found hers. "Belle said before that we didn't have a lot of time, right? That's why she had me wake up Syron," he said. "We should focus on getting out of here first, and circle back to the details later."

"Adaline said she got in through the tunnels," Syron said, eager for the distraction. She swiped away a stray tear. "Belle, you know where they are. Can we get to them without being seen?"

She looked up at Belle expectantly, realizing too late that they wouldn't have known Adaline had been here, or what she had sacrificed to save them. She shifted uneasily at their surprised expressions, but then Belle glanced at Leon, as if taking what he had said to heart, and sucked in a sharp breath.

"The closest entrance to the tunnels is inside the cathedral. We can get out that way."

"What about the temporals?" Leon asked. "Won't they see us if we try to leave?"

Belle rolled her eyes, but it was Julian who answered. "The God made this city famous for its ceremonies. The temporals won't want to miss a second of it, especially the vendors. They come from all over to sell their wares, both inside Evangentine and without. The God would have sent word before you even left the sahiit, Syron, to make sure they got here in time." He nodded to the glass wall, in the direction of the gate.

Syron moved toward it to see better. Below and to their right, the gates of the city stood wide open. Brightly colored tents littered the semicircle inside the entrance, spilling out past the houses and lining the main streets with streaks of color. Throngs of onlookers gawked at the wares while men and women unloaded large crates and set up displays, their glass cases gleaming in the sunlight. Julian was right—the whole city was buzzing with excitement.

Syron felt suddenly nauseated. She turned away to find Julian standing closer to the elevator, gazing down at Will's lifeless body.

"It was his voice I heard in my room that night," Julian said softly. "I've seen him around, but only a couple of times. I never knew his name."

Syron couldn't remember ever wanting to leave a place more in her life, except for maybe the Artist's Room. "His name is…was Will."

Leon startled next to her, his hand nearly slipping from hers, but she held it tighter.

"Come on," Syron said. "Belle, if you're serious about wanting to help, you can lead the way. There's just one stop we need to make first."

24

EMBERS

As soon as they reached the lab, Syron bolted from the elevator. Leon's, Belle's, and Julian's footsteps pounded behind her as she passed the rows of dried lotus flowers on her right and the counters and shelves on her left. She had given a vague explanation of the glamour in the tense intermission between floors, but only Leon knew about Yira's being there, and none of them knew about the nightchild.

The door to the Artist's Room was still open, revealing a row of leather chairs and the stretch of floor, stained red from the overhead lights. She stopped halfway to the door, a sense of unease creeping up on her, and stared.

Raoul's body was gone.

"What's wrong?" Leon asked, breathless.

"It's nothing," Syron said, almost to herself. Of course his body would be gone. Adaline had knocked him out hours ago—if anything, it meant she should be rushing to make sure they could get Yira before he came back.

"Syron," Belle said with a sigh, pushing past, "we don't have *time* to just stand here. Your ceremony—"

Belle's voice cut off in a startled cry as she passed through the door and jerked back, at the same time a watchman stepped into the frame. He lunged at them, and Syron scrambled out of his reach, looking up to find Leon raising the wicked edge of the dragonfly. She just had time to think that he must have found it before leaving the God's study, when another watchman shot through the door and knocked it from his hand.

It flew through the air, but she couldn't tell where it landed because now a small army was flooding through the door, bearing down on them, and Syron lost track of everyone through the clamor of chain mail and the tight press of bodies.

Someone grabbed her—a set of large, gloved hands. She wrenched herself free, a scream building in her chest, when her feet went out from under her. A spike of pain lanced through her elbow as she landed, but the watchman had already grabbed the back of her dress and was forcing her to her feet. She thrashed against him, but he only held her tighter, his chain mail digging into her spine.

"Shh," he murmured into her ear. Even speaking low, his voice was gruff and deep. "Look here." He turned so they faced the door to the Artist's Room, and Syron's heart leaped to her throat. A fine sheen of sweat covered Leon's skin where he was pinned against the floor. Belle's hands were locked behind her back, and Julian's neck was wedged between a watchman's side and the crook of his elbow.

Syron went still. Even if they could somehow manage to get free, they wouldn't all make it out of the spire, and she had no delusions the temporals would just let them walk through the gate. Fear blossomed in the pit of her stomach like acid, eating away any hope she had of finding Yira or the nightchild, or escaping with Leon and Julian. They were trapped.

Apparently, Julian had reached the same conclusion. "John," he murmured under his breath, and the watchman who held him looked down in surprise.

"The God is dead, John. You don't have to do this anymore. You can let—"

"I expected better from you." It was Raoul, leaning against the doorframe. His face was drawn and ashen as he looked at Julian. "I spent too much of my time shaping you for you to turn out a heretic. As it stands, it looks as if the only thing you learned from me was how to keep your true intentions a secret."

Julian flinched as if he had been struck, but Raoul was taking in the scene before him. It seemed to replenish his energy, and he stood a little straighter, his gaze landing on Syron last.

"I should have learned by now that angels don't fit neatly into one box. It was my fault to try and catalog you, Syron. But the temporals out there, and the parents especially, they just can't wait to watch you burn."

"The God is dead," Leon spat. "He can't hurt anyone anymore."

"Oh? But dead gods make great legacies, and his people are wholesome in their faith. They already know that you murdered the God, Syron. What I couldn't figure out is how you managed to free the sahiit girl from her cell." His dark eyes shot to Julian. "Until a moment ago, that is. He gave you his key, didn't he? Oh, who am I kidding," he said, sneering, "the heretic probably freed her himself."

Syron gaped at Raoul. "What are you talking about? You know Will killed the God. But Yira, she's...you mean—"

Raoul nodded at the watchman, who pressed his hand flat against her mouth, cutting her off.

"Yira's not in the cells?" Leon asked from the floor.

Raoul made a noise that was half laugh, half cough. "Loyal until the end. The watchmen will find her, though, wherever you hid her. Of that you can be sure."

Syron caught Leon's eye. He was still pressed against the floor, arms locked behind his back, so he had to crane his neck up to look at her. Wonder and apprehension glimmered there, turning to dark ovals in his face when the light switched to purple and the watchman holding him jerked him to his feet.

The watchman holding Syron dropped his hand from her mouth and moved to the side. Raoul's demeanor changed instantly. The wolfish smile was back in place, his eyes crinkling as Tia walked into the center of the circle, followed closely by Avery.

"The stake is set up," Tia said calmly. "The temporals are having fellowship, but tensions are high, and many are asking about the angel."

"They will have more than just their angel today, Tia, but thank you."

Tia inclined her head and moved to the side. Avery took her place, keeping her head down. "This was found in the cathedral this morning," she said quietly, and pulled a rectangle draped in cream-colored silk from her bag. She pinched the fabric and pulled it free, revealing the tattered remains of the Black Book. The pages were warped and falling out, the surface scuffed and scratched, and the metallic corners dull and flecked with dried blood.

Muffled protests rose from Belle, Julian, and Leon, but everyone else remained silent. Raoul's eyebrows shot up, his smile slipping into a frown.

"There's nothing special about it anymore—it's nothing but aged leather and yellow paper. Keep it or destroy it, I don't care." He waved his hand, and Avery clutched the remains of the Black Book tightly to her chest and turned, her pale green eyes meeting Syron's briefly before walking past.

Tia went next, followed closely by Raoul. Syron took a shaky breath and looked back at Belle, Julian, and Leon. She wanted to say something, anything, but then the watchman behind her grabbed her wrists in one of his large hands, his other settling firmly on her shoulder, and twisted her into line behind Raoul.

This isn't how it was supposed to happen. Syron's head swam. Her knees shook as the watchman forced her forward. There was nothing she could do but walk, her bare feet silent against the linoleum. The inverted triangle repeated over and over on the watchmen like a dark omen in the purple light, and she looked away only when they reached the steps that led out of the spire.

Someone must have opened the door. A sliver of sunlight landed on the sloped ceiling above her, the dull roar of the crowd transforming into a tumult of cheers and shouts as the watchman forced her up the steps and into the light.

Syron blinked away sunlight and stared. More watchmen blocked the crowd from getting too close, but the temporals were everywhere. They had packed themselves into whatever space they could, filling the gap around the spire and overflowing onto the roofs of houses and pavilions. Their fists were in the air, red-faced, excitement and hatred rolling off them in waves.

Raoul was right. They were excited to watch her burn.

Syron felt suddenly dizzy. Hundreds of faces swam across her vision as the watchman shoved her forward, catching her back up to Raoul and rounding the side of the spire. There, erected in front of the arched cathedral doors and flooded at its base with wood and tinder, stood the stake.

Her heartbeat pounded in her ears, dulling even the thunderous shouts of the crowd. She gritted her teeth and threw herself to the side, twisting and yanking even as the watchman's fingers dug into her wrists and hauled her, screaming, onto the stacks of wood and tinder.

Gasoline, or something like it, filled her nostrils. Watchmen holding fistfuls of rope rushed forward and forced her back against the stake, knotting her wrists and ankles as she strained against them.

They moved away, and suddenly the chanting was all-encompassing, deafening.

Burn!

Her nerves rattled with fear and pain as she looked out at the congregation: their mouths twisting into sneers, their eyes dissecting her cuts and bruises, her ripped dress, her matted hair. She wasn't one of them, their eyes seemed to say. She was a wrong that needed to be righted.

But there were other people in the crowd too, weaving closer to the front line. Their faces were pale and solemn, as if they hadn't seen the sun in a long time. A woman with a determined set to her jaw looked directly at Syron and nodded, but she wasn't familiar, and before Syron could guess who she was or what she was doing, the crowd parted.

With a shock, Syron recognized Joseph, the man who had gotten Leon ready in the spire. He walked up to Tia and handed her something small; it wasn't until a flame licked to life that she realized it was a pack of matches.

The ropes dug into her already raw wrists as she pulled against them, her gaze jumping over Tia to the trio behind her, still clutched in the grasps of the watchmen. Belle was trying vainly to twist herself free, and Julian stood resolutely still, arms locked behind his back, and watching the congregation with a mixture of awe and dread. Leon was the stark opposite of Julian. Even though he stood deathly still, his forehead was slick with sweat, and she saw the absolute terror when their eyes met, as if he were watching something over again that tore open an old wound—one that had never fully healed in the first place.

Something in his face changed, and suddenly he was thrashing against the watchman and cursing, but his voice was lost in the uproar as Tia walked closer. Syron realized belatedly that Raoul had disappeared, and that the pale-faced temporals were even closer now, pressing against the watchmen who were supposed to be keeping the crowd at bay.

Fire flickered in Tia's eyes. Syron pulled anew against the rope, heat rushing to her face and blossoming around her wrists as Avery rushed to stand beside Tia, throwing the remains of the Black Book at the same time Tia threw the match.

Syron screamed. It ripped from her throat with serrated edges until she tasted the metallic tang of blood and the salt of tears. The tinder was catching and crackling around her, flames shooting up in a perfect circle and reaching like sanguine fingers to the sky.

Burn!

Syron's scream choked off. She gasped, sucking in air thick with smoke and embers and wheezed, her chest squeezing, her body dripping with sweat and prickling with unbridled fear. She doubled over, feeling the scorching bite of the flames against her bare feet…

When suddenly the rope gave. Someone was with her in the blaze, catching her as she fell. She leaned into them, clutching her throat with shaking hands, before darkness rushed in from the edges of her vision and swallowed her whole.

She glimpsed what looked to be the high ceiling of the cathedral, and then a quick flash of pews before she was jarred; someone must have jumped with her, down and down into something dark. She smelled stale air. She heard voices as if from far away: low, astonished voices, all clearly worried. There was a quick flash of milky white eyes, a face covered in thin white scars, and then everything went black.

25

ASHES

A faint throbbing pulsed through her temples, matching the steady rhythm of her heartbeat. For a moment Syron didn't move, or think, or speak. She just lay silently, breathing in air that smelled of dust and mold. A draft picked up, and she turned her face toward it, her eyes fluttering open.

"You're finally awake?"

Syron startled and looked around. The room was dim —through the window it was almost nightfall—and sparsely furnished, with only the bed she lay in and an old wooden chair, occupied now by Damien. His eyes were downcast as he leaned forward, offering her a vial.

"Here," he murmured. "This will help with the pain."

Syron accepted, wincing at the stab of pain in her side, and drank it quickly. It was cold and sweet; she leaned her head back and felt her muscles relax, the tension melting away, and pushed herself up slowly into a sitting position.

"What happened?" she croaked and cleared her throat. "How am I here? Is Leon—"

"Leon's fine," Damien said, leaning back. "He should be returning shortly."

Syron nodded, watching him. His hands were folded in his lap, his bare arms strong and pitted with old gashes. From this angle, she could see the disfigurement beneath his shoulder blade; it looked as if a chunk of skin had been taken out, and what remained had been stitched back together, leaving a sunken-in, misshapen oval where there should have been muscle.

She remembered the sharp, searing pain clearly in her own shoulder, and her eyes widened.

"Thank you," Syron said, finding her voice. "For saving me."

Damien smiled shyly, still not looking at her. "I thought I felt you stir when I jumped in the tunnel, but I couldn't tell for sure. You don't have to worry, by the way," he added quickly. "It was mostly the smoke that hurt you, and Belle already treated your burns."

"Belle?" Syron shook her head, half in amazement and half in disbelief. "How did you…?"

"It wasn't just me. Viero got the factions together and told them what Idris was doing."

"And they believed him?"

"No, not until Zariah showed up. She testified against Idris, giving her account of everything she had been asked to do, and listing everyone involved." He grimaced and waved his hand, as if he didn't want to talk about the details. "Idris and Calais are going to stand trial, but my point is that Viero petitioned to intervene in your ceremony. You had your initiation into the factions, Syron. You're one of us, so you should have been protected by us regardless. The others agreed, and more than that, they offered to help."

Syron gasped. "You mean that woman's face I saw in the crowd was a faction member."

"I can't say for sure, but most likely, yes. The temporals in the factions pretended to be new worshippers and came through the city gates. When the fire started," he said, and Syron flinched, "they had incited a mob to distract everyone, screaming that the nightchildren had broken into the city. It gave me enough time to run in and grab you, and for Leon, Julian, and Belle to break free. After that, it was only a matter of barring the cathedral doors. There's an entrance to the tunnels beneath the pulpit, where the others were already waiting."

Syron twisted the empty vial in her hands. Her thoughts were muddled and confused, but she couldn't tell whether it was from the medicine, or her brain working too hard to catch up. She supposed it was a little of both.

"Viero found Yira, if that's what you're wondering."

Syron looked up. She hadn't heard the door open, and Julian stood in the doorway. He still wore the same black silk clothes, stretched and tattered around his thin frame, and his hands were buried deep in his pockets. He looked, Syron thought, as if his whole world had been turned upside down.

"Leon told me she was the reason you brought us to the Artist's Room," he said, shifting uncomfortably. His gaze kept darting to Damien. "There was a little boy in there too. A nightchild. He's outside with the others now."

Syron sat straighter. "Yira's here? I—I need to see her. I need to make sure she's—"

"She'll be okay," Damien said. "Viero is in the other room with her now, but some of the sahiit are making a glamour. She needs time to rest and reorient herself before we take her through."

"Is it dangerous for her to go through a glamour in her condition?"

"What's dangerous is if we stay here for too long," Julian said. He pursed his lips. "The city should be distracted, but there's no telling what they will or will not do. There's no one to guide them, not unless Raoul steps up, but he disappeared before we left. The sooner we get to the factions, the better."

Syron bit her lip. She hadn't considered what would happen to the city, or what it would mean for the sahiit. Thankfully, it wasn't something she had to worry about now.

"I just wanted to see how you were doing," he said, offering a small smile. "But considering Leon has hardly left your side since we got here, I think I should let him know you're awake."

"I'll come with you," Damien said, standing.

"Wait!" Syron said. They both hesitated, and Syron blew out an unsteady gust of air, looking sideways at Damien as he placed his hand on the back of the chair, waiting.

"You knew, didn't you? That the onocalcum linked us?" It was just a guess, but it made more sense than anything else. She remembered Yira and Viero arguing in the faction before, about how he had saved Damien from a place beneath the Artist's Room. She touched the spot beneath her own shoulder where the Nightman…where Will…had forced the blade through. It had been the first and only dream she'd had of him being tortured.

"It must be weird for you," she hedged, "saving another angel and all."

Damien's head snapped up, the milky white of his eyes seeming to glow in the dimness, and Syron wondered whether that was caused from his time in the cells too—eye trauma, or maybe malnutrition.

"I was wondering whether you knew. I caught glimpses of you in my dreams too. Not your physical appearance, of course, but the sound of your voice, the feel of the world around you. I didn't realize until I heard you talking with Leon the first night you got to our faction."

"I didn't know for sure," she admitted. "Not until now."

By the door, Julian swayed on his feet. He grasped the door handle, and it jiggled under his weight.

"You're...but no one reported a male angel falling," Julian said. "Astrophe was the last one who survived the fall, besides Syron."

Damien grimaced, looking sightlessly in Julian's direction. "I escaped the city before the God made the announcement that he had captured me. I didn't find out until later that Astrophe had fallen too—not until I was brought to the cells and...questioned. They had tracked me near the lake, you see, around the same time they thought she fell. Apparently, that was all they needed to assume I had helped her go into hiding. Years later when they finally found her and realized I had nothing to do with her getting away, I was worthless to them."

Damien looked back at Syron, frowning. "Whatever the onocalcum showed you, Syron, I can promise it was only a little piece of the hell they put me through. After what they did, the God didn't want someone who looked like me standing in front of the congregation. I was flawed —but the only real difference was they could hide their scars, and I wore mine on my skin. I was sure I was going to die down there, but then the uprising happened, and Viero saved me, just as he saved Yira."

Syron raised her eyebrows, and Julian seemed to come

back to himself. "So it makes sense how Viero knew where to look for her."

Damien nodded. "And it helped that he found a key. He said it was lying on the floor outside the glamour, beneath one of the chairs."

Heat flooded Syron's cheeks. She avoided the look Julian cast in her direction and focused on Damien instead, who was smiling to himself, lifting his face to the breeze coming in through the window.

Syron's heart went out to him. The fact that he had survived the cells for so long was incredible, and that the onocalcum had linked them was even more so. Everyone involved in rescuing first Damien, and then Yira and Syron, had contributed so much, and there were so many small things that had to happen for it to work out the way it had, that it was almost overwhelming.

Farther in the house, the sound of a screen door banging open drew her out of her reverie. Julian and Damien turned toward it, and Julian disappeared down the hall, returning a moment later with Leon.

There were dark circles under his eyes, and his clothes, like Julian's, were torn and stained, but when he looked up at her, it was with a mixture of wonder and amazement. He smiled, and even in the dimness she could swear his eyes brightened to lavender, her new favorite color.

"How are you feeling?" he asked from the doorway. The vein in his neck pulsed, as if he wanted to run to her but was holding himself back.

Syron kept silent as Julian scooted past him, beckoning for Damien to follow. He seemed to realize too late that Damien couldn't see him and hissed under his breath instead.

As soon as they were gone, Leon rushed to the side of the bed.

"I'm not asking to be polite. I'm asking because I care whether you're okay. You look like hell."

"Excuse me?" Syron gasped. She snatched up a pillow and swatted at him. He ducked it easily, laughter rumbling in his chest. "If you really want to know," she said playfully, "whatever was in the vial Damien gave me is working wonders. I almost feel normal."

"Good…because there's something I want to show you."

He flung the sheet aside and offered his hand. "Belle said you'd be fine to move around after you woke up, as long as you're careful. I already asked. Or if you'd like, I could carry you?"

Syron glanced at her feet, wrapped in a thick layer of gauze to look like socks. She pressed them against the ground tentatively before reaching for him. His fingers laced through hers, warm and strong, and she let him pull her gently off the bed, through the dilapidated hallway and living room, and out the front door.

The sun had dipped below the horizon, painting the houses across and to the right in muted shades of gray and white. To their left, a sporadic outcropping of trees marked the start of the forest, pressed tightly against the abandoned town.

"Where is everyone?" Syron asked, just as a hoot of laughter sounded somewhere behind them.

"Out back," Leon whispered, tugging her down the cracked concrete steps and over to the edge of the house. "Some of the temporals found bottles of old wine stashed away in one of the houses."

His breath fanned her neck as she peeked around the edge of the house. A handful of sahiit and a couple dozen temporals were scattered around the backyard, laughing and talking. She didn't recognize anyone, save for Belle and

Julian sitting off to the side, watching everyone with amusement. Damien must have gone in the other room with Viero and Yira.

Leon's arm extended past her, pointing, and Syron shifted to the side to see better. Past a woman with a high brow and sharp collarbones, a nightchild sat silently with his back to them, looking out at the fireflies blinking neon green against the great boughs of the forest. Tomlin.

Syron's heart stuttered. "I thought…"

"That he would become a regular child? We passed a couple more of them after we got out of the tunnel. They're just…wandering, like they're lost."

Syron pursed her lips, thinking back to the first time she had seen Adaline in the library. She had been foreign, strange, and terrifying, but also certain that if the Nightman were gone, then the nightchildren would be saved. She looked up at Leon, but his lips had slipped to a frown. It was clear he didn't know any more than she did.

"What were you going to show me?"

Leon squeezed her hand, still not looking at her, and led her silently past the pocket of trees and into the forest. They picked their way carefully across roots and shrubs tangled in shadow, her footsteps clumsy and loud compared to Leon's, before the ground gave way to thick, soft grass and the trees parted to reveal a small pond.

"I thought it would help take your mind off things."

The water was dark and still, reflecting the flashing glow of fireflies. She let Leon go, enjoying the wash of cold as her feet sank into the mud, and took a seat on a moss-covered log that was only partially sunken in.

She would need fresh bandages, she knew, and would likely get a scolding from Belle. The thought made her smile, though, that Belle and Julian had managed to leave the city with them. She had thought the sahiit were as much her enemy as the city, but if what Damien had said were true—and she didn't doubt him—it meant they were on the same side. The factions were her sworn family, as much as they were Leon's or Yira's.

"Did you know?" Syron asked suddenly, staring out at the water. "About what I could do as an angel?"

"No," Leon said quietly, and took a seat beside her. "I had heard things, sure, but nothing I could be sure of. Mom never told me anything about it. I didn't even know she was an angel until Yira found us."

"Really?" she asked, looking over, and he nodded.

"When the watchmen came to take her away, she touched my hand. She showed me a memory of her holding me when I was born, of how she felt. That's how I knew the Nightman was lying when I asked him what my mom said to me, because she hadn't said anything at all.

"You know," Leon said after a moment, "I never did say thank you for saving me from him. And for keeping me with you when I was passed out. I'm sure it was hard."

Syron shook her head. "You would have done the same for me."

He wrapped his arm around her and pulled her in close, resting his chin on top of her head so hers lay against his chest; she felt his heartbeat speed up.

"Do you regret coming here?" he asked into her hair. "If the…Watcher, I think you had said, came back right now and gave you the choice, would you leave?"

Would you stay? He had picked his words carefully, she could tell, as if he were giving her an easy out and all she had to do was say yes, but she heard the silent question in the gruffness of his voice, the speed of his pulse, the way his body anchored itself to hers.

All she had to do was say yes. Because why, after everything, would she stay?

She held him tighter against her, entwining her fingers over the ruined satin of his shirt, and let her mind wander. The Watcher saw them now, she was sure. Looking down on them from her cauldron in the sky, maybe, or standing invisible just across the pond. Just to say it out loud would have sounded crazy, but that, if nothing else, she was sure of.

"Why," she asked, "after everything, would I leave?"

Leon relaxed around her. His fingers traced the tattoos on her arm, and she shivered involuntarily.

"I know there are things you're not ready to talk about. Things that happened while I was passed out." He paused, as if he were waiting for her to speak, and took a deep breath when she didn't. "But I want you to know that if you ever do want to talk about it, I'm here. I don't understand how you did it…but I know there's no one besides you that could have."

"I didn't kill the God, Leon."

"No, I know. That's not what I mean."

Syron looked up at him. His face was very close to hers.

"You're the bravest person I've met, Sy. I would've given anything to be the one on the stake instead of you. I wished for it, a thousand times over. I owe Damien more than my life for saving you. For doing what I couldn't."

Syron blinked back tears and looked away, out at the calm, dark water in front of them. He was avoiding talking about Will and Adaline, and for that she was grateful. But there were some things that cut too deep, things she couldn't bring herself to talk about, not yet, at least. And if she really thought about it, it was as if some fundamentally good part of Will was still alive through her.

She looked back at him. His eyes burned into hers, flashing with the lights of fireflies. She tried to imagine what he had looked like before—with brown hair and freckles—but this was the Leon she knew, and some changes weren't all bad.

"Sy," he whispered, his hand sliding to her waist, and then she saw her own reflection: wide, dark eyes staring up at him curiously, thoughtfully, and she could swear she saw change there too.

Surely, they could build on top of the ashes. Make something new.

Leon leaned forward, and she just felt the brush of his lips against hers when a voice called out behind them. She startled and looked over her shoulder, squinting into the dark.

"Here!" Leon called.

There was scuffling, and then a man ducked beneath a low-hanging branch and stood up. His hair had been shaved down, and he wore a tired smile. Viero.

"The glamour is almost ready," he said, "if you two want to start heading this way."

"We're coming," Syron said quickly, and he nodded before disappearing back through the trees. She looked one more time at the pond, remembering another night long ago and a world away, when Leon's breath caught.

He grabbed her hand, turning it to the light filtering in through the crooked branches, and stared.

At first, Syron didn't see anything. She looked down at her arm in confusion, the ink like stains of black on her alabaster skin, and gasped.

"Does it hurt?" Leon asked. His voice was low and tense.

"No," she whispered back. "I don't feel anything." She bit her lip, wishing that if she just focused hard enough, it would be only a passing illusion. The shadows from the branches maybe, or just her vision adjusting.

She could hear drunken laughter coming from the direction of the house, the faint rustle of the forest around them, and the frantic patter of her own heart as she lifted her arm and twisted it around to the other side.

"The symbols," she whispered. "They're moving."

Thank you so much for reading! If you enjoyed this book, please consider leaving a review—it's like a piece of chocolate cake after a long day. To be updated on new releases and receive exclusive updates from the author, visit prezzleybuckhannon.com and subscribe to her newsletter!

Prezzley Buckhannon writes books about ghosts, tattoos, and alternate worlds. She is the author of *From Angels to Ashes*, the first novel in The Onocalcum Series. She's a fan of anything supernatural and paranormal, and grew up surrounded by horror novels from the likes of Stephen King and Dean Koontz.

When she's not staying up way too late writing, you can find her biking through tunnels with her partner, strategizing in *Magic: The Gathering*, or playing in the backyard with her vivacious little girl.

For exciting updates, release dates, and cover reveals, visit her at prezzleybuckhannon.com.

www.ingramcontent.com/pod-product-compliance
Lightning Source LLC
Chambersburg PA
CBHW022002310726
48972CB00006B/1474